D1403116

# THE SWORD

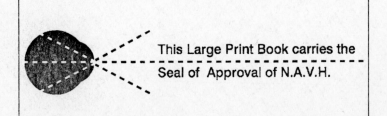

This Large Print Book carries the
Seal of Approval of N.A.V.H.

THE LAST CAVALIERS, BOOK 2

# THE SWORD

# GILBERT MORRIS

**THORNDIKE PRESS**
*A part of Gale, Cengage Learning*

GALE
CENGAGE Learning·

Detroit • New York • San Francisco • New Haven, Conn • Waterville, Maine • London

# GALE
## CENGAGE Learning®

Thorndike Press, a part of Gale, Cengage Learning.

Thorndike Press® Large Print Christian Historical Fiction.
The text of this Large Print edition is unabridged.
Other aspects of the book may vary from the original edition.
Set in 16 pt. Plantin.

LIBRARY OF CONGRESS CATALOGING-IN-PUBLICATION DATA

Morris, Gilbert
  The sword / by Gilbert Morris. — Large print ed.
    p. cm. — (Thorndike Press large print Christian historical fiction) (The Last Cavaliers; 2)
  ISBN-13: 978-1-4104-4176-8(hardcover)
  ISBN-10: 1-4104-4176-8(hardcover)
    1. Large type books. 2. United States—History—Civil War, 1861–1865—Fiction. 3. Soldiers—Fiction. 4. Large type books.
PS3563.O8742S96 2011
813'.54—dc22                                          2011032332

Published in 2011 by arrangement with Barbour Publishing, Inc.

Printed in Mexico
1 2 3 4 5 6 7 15 14 13 12 11

■ ■ ■ ■

# PART ONE:
# FLORA & JEB
# 1855–1861

■ ■ ■ ■

# CHAPTER ONE

Flora Cooke glared at her full-length reflection in the cheval mirror. So far, in the endless preparations for a young lady of good family to ready herself for a ball, she had put on her chemise, knickers, and stockings and then had pulled on the great bell-shaped crinoline. She pushed it to one side, and it swung airily back and forth, never touching her legs. "Ding, dong," she said whimsically.

The nineteen-year-old girl in the mirror was plain, Flora knew very well. But she was so lively, so quick and intelligent, and of such willing wit that she was well known as a "charmer." She did have some good physical attributes, too; her chestnut-brown hair was shiny and thick and took a curl very well, and she had that very unusual combination, for brunettes, of having royal-blue eyes. Her brows were perfect arches, and her long, thick lashes were the envy of many women. Her complexion was like the most delicate magnolia blossom. Though she was not conventionally pretty, Flora had always had her share of male admirers.

And another reason for that, Flora knew, was because of her figure. From a skinny, awkward thirteen-year-old with blemishes covering her face, she had bloomed into a delicate, small woman with a tiny waist and hands and feet, sweetly rounded shoulders, a long graceful neck, and a perfect bosom. She had the classic hourglass figure, while being as dainty as a porcelain figurine.

She was still contemplating her reflection with some satisfaction when her maid, Ruby, came in holding her new ball dress, a peach-colored taffeta confection. The neckline was low, the sleeves off the shoulder, as was fashionable for evening wear, and Ruby had just finished starching and ironing the eight cotton, lace-trimmed ruffles in the wide skirt. Carefully she laid the dress out on Flora's bed then turned to her, hands on hips. "Miss Flora Cooke, am I standin' here looking at you with no corset on?" Ruby snapped, her eyes flashing. She was a shapely girl, an ebony black with wide, liquid, dark eyes, only two years older than Flora herself.

"You are," Flora answered absently. "Mm,

the dress looks heavenly, Ruby!" She picked up a ruffle and rubbed it between her fingers, savoring the crisp feel of the thick taffeta and the still-warm stiffness of the cotton ruffle underneath.

"Don't you be gettin' around no subject with me," Ruby sniffed. "Why am I standin' here looking at you with no corset on? You know you ain't going to no ball without no corset on like a Christian woman."

"I am a Christian woman, and I am going to the ball with no corset, and you know I don't need one, so help me get my dress on," Flora said. "We need to hurry and do my flowers and my hair. You know it just won't do for me to be late. Father would probably order a squad up here to drag me downstairs."

Ruby proceeded to help Flora put on the dress, which was quite a process. The skirt itself was fifteen yards of taffeta and six yards of cotton ruffle. It was heavy, it was stiff, and putting it over Flora's head practically amounted to throwing a canvas tent over her.

As Flora struggled to find the neck opening and the sleeves, through the crackling of the fabric she could hear Ruby muttering, "They is Christian women with corsets, and they is Christian women with no corsets. . . .

Leastenways she got bloomers on. Mebbe they go next . . . liken as if Colonel Cooke would allow a dragoon . . . ten-foot pole near you. . . ."

Finally the dress was in place, and Ruby buttoned up the twenty-three buttons in the back. Though of course Ruby would never admit it, Flora did not need a corset to pull in her waist. A man's hands could span it easily.

Flora carefully spread her skirts so she could sit at the dressing table for Ruby to do her hair. Sitting while wearing a crinoline was tricky. They were cages, in effect, wide cotton petticoats with whalebone or sometimes even very light steel sewn into slowly widening circles. The sewn-in ribs were stiff to hold out the circular shape of the very wide skirts but still thin enough to bend so the wearer could sit down, and they had enough tensile strength to regain their shape when standing. However, when sitting down, if a lady did not learn how to spread her heavy overskirts out — in a graceful manner, of course — to distribute the weight correctly, the entire hoop could simply balloon in a great circle up over her head. At boarding school, Flora and her friends had often played this game, laughing like pure fools at the sight but still fervently learning how to do it correctly so that this abomination would never happen to them, especially, heaven forbid, in public.

Early that morning, Ruby had rolled the ends of Flora's hair tightly around little rags. Now she began to carefully remove them, leaving little ringlets. Then she parted her hair in the middle, pulled it back, and began to secure it at the base of her neck, with the springy curls falling down her back. On the grounds of Fort Leavenworth, Kansas, many of the officers' little houses had gardens, and Flora had found a friend who had a camellia bush with peach-colored flowers. She had gathered enough that morning to arrange in her hair and have a small bouquet at her breast. With their shiny, dark-green leaves, they adorned Flora's hair and complexion perfectly.

As Ruby began to arrange them in her hair, Flora watched her carefully in the tri-mirror mounted on the dressing table. Her eyes narrowed. "Don't just poke them in there any old way, Ruby. Arrange them elegantly," she chided her. "I want to look just perfect tonight."

"Mm-hmm," Ruby said knowingly. "Just gonna aggravate them soldiers, ain't you? Knowing that Colonel Cooke —"

"I know, I know," Flora interrupted her,

"wouldn't let 'em get a ten-foot pole near me. You're wrong, you know, Ruby. Father is perfectly fine with me socializing with soldiers. After all, he's been one his whole life, and I've been around them my whole life. And besides, I don't want to aggravate them, whatever that means."

"You'm knows right well what it means, Miss Flora. Don't I see you right here right now in that there mirror, smiling and practicin' taking 'em with your eyelashes?"

Ruby had a habit of quoting Scripture, usually incorrectly, and Flora was fairly certain that this reference had something to do with a proverb about women and their eyelids, but already Ruby had moved on. She was now more carefully arranging the flowers in Flora's hair, and she talked constantly. "Miz Lieutenant Blanton's flowers sure are pretty with your dress, Miss Flora, if I do say so, and I was talking to her girl Lizzie, and you know what? Lizzie says that she heard Miz Blanton talkin' about her brother Leslie Spengler marryin' their cousin! Their own cousin! And him from a good family, as good as yourn is!"

"It's only his fourth cousin, Ruby. It's hardly —"

"I don't keer. It ain't right. What about that handsome Finch boy, prancin' around in his showy uniform? Is he gonna marry up wif Miss Leona? That man what always wears those big tall hats — stovepipes, they call 'em, and don't they look just like that and silly besides. What's been chasin' after her ain't as good-looking, but he's got money, Miss Leona's maid, Perla, says. I think Miss Leona Pruitt better look ahead, 'cause without no money, the mare don't go. Leastenways you ain't gonna have to worry about that, Miss Flora. Some rich man in Phillydelphia is gonna snatch you right up soon as you go to capturvatin' them —"

"I think you mean 'captivating' them, and I do no such thing," Flora said haughtily.

"— captivatin' 'em, and you do do such a thing, begging your pardon, miss," Ruby said sassily.

Flora's brow lowered, and she started to argue with Ruby, but something stopped her.

Flora had been brought up in a world of men. She had been born in Jefferson Barracks, in Fort St. Louis, and had lived in one army fort or barracks or encampment since then. Her father, a career army officer, had been at posts all over the United States, including Indian fighting in the far West. Now he was colonel of the Second

13

U.S. Dragoons, the commanding officer of Fort Leavenworth, Kansas.

Her mother had died when she was young, and her father had brought her up as a young lady, sending her to a prestigious boarding school in Detroit. Flora had graduated that spring of 1855, an accomplished and elegant young lady, and had come to visit her father for a couple of months before going to stay with her St. George relatives in Philadelphia to make her social debut.

Still, for most of her life, she had been surrounded by men, and she knew they liked her. They were attracted to her, but it was none of her doing. She didn't encourage them or flirt with them.

Or did she?

"Well," she now said good-humoredly to Ruby, "maybe I do."

When she was finished dressing, Flora went downstairs to the parlor.

Her father sat in a straight-back rocking chair by the window, reading the *U.S. Army Ordnance Manual.* All he ever read were the Bible and military manuals. He looked up and smiled, a mere quick softening of his thin lips. "You look very lovely, my dear."

"Thank you, Papa," Flora said, pleased.

She seated herself on the sofa. "Thank you for the new dress. Thank you for all of them. And especially for the riding habits." Flora was an avid horsewoman.

"You're welcome, my dear, and seeing you tonight makes all that money that I've spent on those fripperies worthwhile." Although the words were light, he had reverted to his stern manner.

Colonel Philip St. George Cooke was every inch a soldier, a cavalryman. A handsome man, he had thick silver hair, intense, dark eyes, and a dashing, neatly trimmed mustache and short beard. He had a military bearing, always holding himself erect and always precise in his movements and speech. He was a rather humorless man, though not ill-tempered. He was simply austere.

Now he said in his somber manner, "Flora, there is something I must tell you before we go to the ball. This morning Gerald Small came to see me."

Surprised, Flora asked, "Mr. Small was here this morning?"

"No. He came to my office. He said he had to see the quartermaster, so he thought he would just stop by on his way. Rather unorthodox, I think . . . considering the topic."

Flora rolled her eyes. "Please don't tell me I was the topic. Oh Papa . . . I was? Oh, how like him! To just 'stop by on his way' to a business meeting to make a romantic gesture!"

"Flora, perhaps he is not the most romantic of men, as you say, but he does come from a good family, and he is a fine, upstanding young man. The Smalls are very good people of business, and he is going to be a very wealthy man."

With exasperation Flora said, "Papa, we are not talking about investing money with him. Please do not tell me that he asked for my hand. Even though he's been calling for the last month, he's never made any sort of overture such as that. He's usually too busy talking about his silly sawmill."

"No, Flora, it was not that he was asking my permission before he even asked you," Colonel Cooke replied. "He was just, in the most gentleman-like manner, inquiring if his attentions toward you were viewed favorably by me."

She stared at him. "I was wrong. This is a business deal. What did he do next, suggest that you discuss prices?"

Cooke frowned, and that was a stern thing indeed. "Flora, I'm surprised at you. That is crude, not at all something that I would expect a daughter of mine to say."

She was defiant for a moment, but then she dropped her head. "I'm sorry, Papa," she said quietly. "You're right, of course. I beg your pardon, and I will attempt never to be crude again. It's just that Mr. Small is so — so businesslike. He is not romantic at all. He rarely does speak of anything but business matters. And besides, you do want me to go to Philadelphia, don't you? To enter society? I thought you didn't want me to be stuck here with a penniless soldier or some *nouveau riche* merchant settler."

Cooke's eyes softened slightly. "I don't know why we're arguing about him anyway. I knew you wouldn't have him. And Flora, believe me when I tell you that I want what's best for you. And I want you to have the kind of life and man and marriage that you want, whether it is here or in Philadelphia society. But Flora, do you know exactly what it is that you want?"

"Maybe." Flora shrugged. "But Father, I don't — I want — that is —" She stopped awkwardly. Her father had been a good parent, in his way. He loved her dearly, Flora knew that. But there were some things that she could never explain to him, could never make him understand.

Flora, in her secret heart, wanted a man

to love her with a heat and a passion that would match her own. Though she was still an innocent, she knew that she could have deep and intense love — emotional, spiritual, and physical — for the man of her dreams. He would be dashing and careless and courageous, and she would start falling in love with him as soon as she met him. She had no face in her mind. Truth to tell, she didn't care what he looked like. She just had a vague sense of a man with a commanding presence, with spirit and daring. But how could she tell her father — the stolid, unimaginative soldier — of her dreams?

Suddenly she smiled affectionately at him. "Papa, I will tell you what I don't want. I don't want to spend the rest of my life talking about sawmills. Now, sir, you look very smart and officer-like in your uniform. Will you consent to escort me to the Independence Ball?"

Fort Leavenworth, Kansas, Flora reflected on the way to the ball, was not nearly so bleak as many of the army outposts were. It was finely situated on the gentle bluffs overlooking the Missouri River, in the easternmost part of the territory. The endless plains and prairies were only a few miles away, but Fort Leavenworth was still in fertile country, with the Missouri River to the east, the Little Platte River just to the south, and countless streams and tributaries crossing the green unsettled lands in between.

A small town had sprung up, mainly because Fort Leavenworth was the eastern terminus for the Santa Fe Trail and the Oregon Trail, and so the fort had assumed great importance. The town — appropriately called Leavenworth — had been born to support the settlers moving west and the fort itself. Although it had only formally incorporated in 1854, it was already thriving and growing quickly.

Accordingly, the fort had more and better accommodations and appointments than most. One of these was the Rookery, a fine two-story home with a wide veranda where the commanding officer lived. Another was the meetinghouse, a large hall where town meetings were held, where the troops assembled for instructions or visiting lecturers, and where festivals were held. One of these was the July 4th Independence Ball; this was the second annual one, she had learned, and the entire army post and most of the town's citizens were expected to attend.

Escorted by her father, Flora entered the ballroom and hungrily ran her eyes over the floor, delighted as always with the kaleidoscope of color created by the women's dresses. Scarlet, emerald green, pink, and purple, all shades and hues, blended wonderfully as the couples danced a waltz. It was exactly the sort of thing that Flora delighted in, for she loved color, excitement, crowds, dancing, and music.

As soon as they came in, Gerald Small rushed to Flora's side. With a stiff smile, she offered him her gloved hand and he bent over it, a sort of deep dip as if he were bobbing for apples. As the thought occurred to Flora, her smile widened and her eyes sparkled. Gerald Small obviously mistook this for gladness to see him, and with some surprise, he returned her smile. It was an automatic, spare sort of smile, as if it was practiced. Flora suspected that it might be.

Formal greetings were exchanged, then Colonel Cooke went to speak to a group of the older officers in a corner of the room, while Gerald began to shepherd Flora to the chairs lining the walls. With an inner sigh, she allowed him to lead her.

Gerald Small was, like his name, a short, compact man, with ash-blond hair and mild blue eyes. His features, too, were small, with a thin, straight nose and short lips in a rather sharp-boned face. He always dressed stylishly, and tonight he wore a fawn-colored pair of trousers and a dark brown coat with a bowtie drooping fashionably down from around his neck.

They reached the chairs and sat down. Gerald pulled his chair close to Flora, looked deep into her eyes, and said in a low voice, "I thought I was going to be late, for I have been literally in despair trying to find a skilled saw filer. I had heard that a man coming in the latest wagon train from Chicago was such a man. I questioned the wagon master and several of the trail hands and thought that perhaps this might have been one of the settlers named Odom, but when I finally located Mr. Odom, what do you think I found?"

Already Flora was having trouble concentrating on this deadly boring conversation, but she managed to reply, "I don't know, Mr. Small. What did you find?"

"He was nothing but a common cutler," Gerald groaned dramatically. "A knife sharpener, for goodness' sake! And so I have yet to find a saw filer, and it's possible I may have to hire one from Kansas City! Can you imagine the cost of paying a skilled saw filer to move out here and begin work in a brand-new sawmill?"

"No, I can hardly imagine it," Flora said wearily. "Mr. Small, I know this is very forward of me, but they are beginning the polka, and I should love to dance. It is one of my particular favorites."

He looked bemused at Flora's peculiar request — women simply did not ask men to dance — but gamely he took her arm. "Of course. I declare, I have been so worried about my saw filer that I quite forgot my manners. May I have this dance, Miss Cooke?"

He was not a bad dancer, but he was mechanical, and his conversation during the dance was very much like his previous one — indeed, much like all his previous ones, Flora reflected. He led her around the floor, the oddly automatic movements seeming peculiar in the spirited dance, still lamenting about his saw filer and, also, if Flora was hearing him correctly, about something called a "pitman arm."

When the polka ended, he led her back to her chair, holding her arm. As they reached their seats, he said in her ear, "I shall fetch you some punch, as it is rather warm in here and I should like you to be refreshed. There is a matter of some importance I want to discuss with you when I return."

She took her seat, suddenly wishing she was going to hear more about the saw filer and Mr. Pitman's arm.

However, as usual, Flora was not alone for long. She had made three particular friends, two girls whose families were at the fort and one girl from town. They crowded around her, bringing their gentleman escorts at hand, and some other of the troops from the fort joined them. Flora found herself at the center of a crowd, and as always, she was entertaining them. Someone had complimented her on her hair, and she was telling the story of Ruby poking the flowers into it. "It was like she was sticking them into a vase, all every which way. I think if I hadn't made her do it all over, I'd be looking like I was wearing an urn on my head," she said drolly.

Miss Leona Pruitt — who would have incurred Ruby's wrath had she known it — had the "handsome Finch boy" on her arm and said warmly to Flora, "Oh, that's nonsense, Flora. You always look so lovely, especially with all of your new clothes for your debut! And that new dress . . . Please, stand up and turn around. Let us see it!"

Choruses of agreements followed, so Flora stood, held her skirts gracefully, and turned slowly.

"Oh, it's just beautiful," Leona Pruitt sighed, a little enviously. She had six sisters, she was the fourth one, and she very rarely got a new ball dress.

Flora had completed her turn and started to reply, but suddenly a man standing in a group rather far down the room caught her attention. He was tall with reddish hair and a fierce mustache and thick, long beard. He was barrel-chested and strong-looking, and Flora could have sworn that even at this distance she could sense an immense physical strength.

Abruptly, midlaugh, he turned to look directly at her, and their eyes met. The smile faded from his face, and Flora's eyes widened. To Flora, it seemed as if they stared at each other for a long time, but she knew it must only have been seconds.

When she collected herself to turn back to the group, they were still saying admiring things about her new dress. She felt odd, answering them automatically, still sensing some sort of vague physical connection to the man. It was as if he were standing too close to her, and she felt uncomfortable. But of course he was not; she stole another quick glance, and he, too, had turned back to his acquaintances and was laughing again.

Now she noticed Gerald at the fringe of the group, holding two cups of punch, and saying rather ineffectually to two dragoons who were crowded close, "Mm, excuse me? That is . . . if you would excuse me, please, um, sir? Private?"

Admittedly the group was rather loud and merry, and for an instant, Flora felt sorry for Gerald. He never seemed to actually have any fun. She started to say something, to beckon him to her side.

"Good evening, ladies, gentlemen," a booming voice said. He was looking directly at Flora, and she froze. He was not quite six feet, but his sheer physical size made him seem like a big man. His dark blue dress uniform was of a 2nd lieutenant of the 1st U.S. Cavalry and was immaculate and pressed to perfection, his thigh-high cavalry boots shined to dark mirrors.

She looked into his eyes and suddenly felt much too warm and knew her cheeks were flushing. He had blue eyes, hot blue like the July noon sky, and he looked at her as if he already knew her, all about her — too much about her.

He stepped into the circle around her — people automatically moved aside for him — and stood looking down at her. He smiled at her, and the smile was gentle, but

25

his eyes danced with devilment. "Hello, ma'am. I'm very new here, so I don't know many people yet. But I would like to dance with you. The very next dance."

With a supreme effort, Flora collected herself. What was wrong with her anyway? She'd met at least a hundred soldiers in her life, many of them strong, handsome, dashing men. Here was another. And a very forward one at that.

"Sir, I hope you feel welcome here at Fort Leavenworth, but I'm afraid we have not been properly introduced," she said, much more stiffly than she intended. She sounded like her father, she reflected with exasperation.

He turned around and looked at the people around Flora. They all stood close, waiting eagerly for the progression of the interesting scene. Except Gerald, who looked utterly taken aback.

Finally the man pointed to a soldier, a private in a 1st Cavalry uniform. "You! You're Eccleston, aren't you? Private Eccleston? Jerry Eccleston, is it?"

"Sir, no sir," he said, stepping forward and standing at painful attention. "I'm Private George Cary Eggleston, sir."

"Do you know this lady, Private Eggleston?" he demanded, gesturing to Flora.

"Yes, sir. No, sir. I've been introduced to her, sir," he answered, his boyish face turning deep crimson.

"Then introduce us," the lieutenant ordered.

"Yes, sir," Eggleston said and then, still at attention, stepped to stand by the lieutenant's and Flora's side. "Lieutenant Stuart, I have the pleasure of introducing you to Miss Flora Cooke, the daughter of our commanding officer, Colonel Philip St. George Cooke. Miss Cooke, it is my honor to present to you Second Lieutenant James Ewell Brown Stuart of the 1st Cavalry. He has just arrived here from a posting at Jefferson Barracks, near St. Louis."

Lieutenant Stuart took Flora's hand, and even through her glove she could feel the heat from his lips as he pressed a kiss to her hand.

Private Eggleston, with ill-disguised relief, stepped back, quickly grabbed a girl's arm, and rushed off to the punch table.

James Ewell Brown Stuart took Flora in his arms and swept her off right in the middle of a waltz. Already Flora could tell he was a wonderful dancer, both powerful and graceful. "My friends call me Jeb," he said.

Flora still felt a little breathless, but she

was a resourceful woman, and the little charade of the introductions had given her time to calm down. "Do they, sir?" she replied lightly. "What do first acquaintances call you when they've only known you for about thirty seconds?"

"Lieutenant Stuart. But I want you to call me Jeb."

"I will not, sir. We may have been properly introduced — of a sort — but I would never take such a liberty with a man I've just met."

"Hm. And so I suppose I may not call you Miss Flora?"

"Certainly not."

"Guess I'd better behave" — he sighed theatrically — "since you, Miss Cooke, are the daughter of my commanding officer. But you can still call me Jeb whenever you want to."

"I'm afraid at this time I don't want to, Lieutenant," Flora said, teasing him. She sensed the high spirits of her dancing partner and was quite sure he sensed hers as well.

"You will," he said airily. "Won't be long, either. You will."

Flora rolled her eyes. "You're very sure of yourself, aren't you?"

"Pretty much," he answered airily. "Aren't you?"

She was taken aback at his words.

The dance ended, and Lieutenant Stuart took her back to her seat.

Gerald, who was sitting alone waiting for her, rose, his finely modeled face rather sulky. "There you are, Flora. I thought you were supposed to wait for me to bring you some punch."

"I'm sorry, Gerald, but the waltz is my favorite, you know," she said carelessly.

"Thought it was the polka," he muttered darkly.

"No, not at all. The waltz," she said brightly. Then she introduced the two men.

Gerald looked up at the powerful bulk of Jeb Stuart and his penetrating eyes and fierce beard. To Flora, his face registered something close to contempt, as if he were a nobleman being introduced to a commoner. "How do you do, Lieutenant?" Gerald asked frigidly.

"Much better, now that I've been introduced to Miss Cooke and have had the great pleasure of dancing with her." He turned back to Flora, bowed slightly, and said, "Since you love to waltz, Miss Cooke, I'd like to claim the next one. Until then . . ." He moved to return to his group of friends, and Flora couldn't help but watch him walk away. He knew it. When he

29

reached them, he turned and winked at her.

"Arrogant," she breathed to herself, turning quickly back to Gerald.

"I thought that I was to get you some punch, and then we were going to talk," he said accusingly as they sat down. "The punch grew warm."

"I didn't realize that we were on a time-table," she said, a little sharply. "I understand those were your plans, but this is a *dance,* Mr. Small. People *dance* here."

"Yes, yes, dancing. But I have something very important I want to speak to you about, Miss Cooke."

"But — but surely we don't have to have such a serious discussion right now, do we?" she pleaded. In spite of herself, her eyes kept searching out Lieutenant Stuart.

"It is, as I said, very important," Gerald insisted. He reached over and took her hands, and Flora was so startled she didn't draw them back. "Miss Cooke — that is, may I call you Flora?"

"No," she said absently. The musicians were playing an allemande now, and Lieutenant Stuart, Flora saw, was dancing with her friend Leona Pruitt. Leona had a brilliant smile that lit up her face, and she was definitely bestowing that smile on the lieutenant. It distracted Flora much more than it should have.

"What?" Gerald said, shocked. "But — why ever not? I've been calling on you for almost a month now."

With an effort, Flora turned her attention back to him. "Yes, I know, Mr. Small. You've been very attentive, and I enjoy your company. But just think, we have only known each other for less than a month. In fact, we hardly know each other at all, do we?"

He blinked several times. "I thought we knew each other. We do know each other."

She sighed. "What is my favorite color?"

He looked utterly blank.

"Do I play any musical instruments?"

Still the same uncomprehending stare.

"And where, Mr. Small," she continued, now gravely, "am I moving to, in just a little over one month, to make my social debut?"

"I know this one," he said desperately. "Philadelphia. You're — oh, I see. You are leaving in a month, then."

"Yes."

He shook his head and took her hand again, though this time Flora resisted slightly. She didn't want to vulgarly yank it away, however, so he held it and looked at her, his mild blue eyes suddenly filled with determination. Flora thought that it must be how he looked when he was about to close a business deal. "No, Fl— Miss Cooke. I think — I know that before then you will find that you want to stay here, with me."

"Please, Mr. Small, you are mistaken. I do appreciate your attentions, but I'm afraid you may have misunderstood mine." Flora went on as reasonably as she could to try to convey that she was not at all interested in him, but the look on his face merely grew more closed and stubborn. "And so, you see that I am trying to make certain that you make no mistake concerning our — our —"

"Miss Cooke," Lieutenant Stuart said jovially, "finally! It is our waltz." He held out his hand. Flora pulled away from Gerald, but he stood with her, looking up at Jeb Stuart.

"I think you should know, Lieutenant," he said with a definite snobbish timbre to his voice, "that I have spoken to Colonel Cooke."

"Me, too," Jeb said mildly. "He's my commanding officer."

"No, I mean — what I mean is, I've spoken to him about Fl— Miss Cooke," Gerald insisted.

"Have you?" Jeb asked with interest. "I don't blame you. I'd like to talk to people about Miss Cooke, too. But mostly I'd like to talk to her. So if you'll excuse us, Mr. Small . . ."

Again they left Gerald standing helplessly alone, confused and irritated.

Jeb grinned down at her. His grin, and his laugh, were completely infectious. "Is he a lawyer or something?"

Flora found herself smiling like a girlish idiot the entire time she talked with him. "No, he's a businessman. Right now he's opening a sawmill. He and his family already own a hotel and a flour mill."

"Is he rich?" Jeb asked.

"I don't know," Flora answered carelessly. "It's really no business of mine."

"That's good," Jeb said beaming. "So you're not going to marry him then?"

"What! Marry him? No, no, no. No, that's just not possible," Flora fumed.

"No, it's not," Jeb agreed. "It's not meant to be. That much is obvious."

"What are you talking about? You don't know him. What am I saying? You don't know me, either."

"But you just told me you're not going to marry him."

"But that doesn't mean it's not meant to be," Flora shot back.

Jeb threw back his head and laughed. All

33

around them people watched him, and they couldn't help it; they grinned.

Finally Flora saw the absurdity of the conversation and giggled a little in spite of herself. "I think — no, I know that was the silliest argument I've ever had with a person."

"Let's hope all our arguments turn out to be silly, and then we'll laugh at them afterward," Jeb said. He squeezed her hand the tiniest bit. Men, of course, did not wear gloves during dancing or dining. She was very aware of the heat of his hand, of how it swallowed hers, of the way he very gently touched her back, but she could still sense the power, the vitality of him.

"All of them?" she asked. "So we are to have arguments, then?"

"It was meant to be," he said, now quietly. "All of it. You, me, this night, this dance was meant to be."

She searched his face and found none of the usual frivolity there. He looked thoughtful. "What do you mean, Lieutenant?" she asked softly. "How can that be?"

He searched her face for long moments. "I have always believed that God prepares a man for one certain woman. And He prepares that woman for him."

"That is a very deep theological concept,

Lieutenant Stuart," she said, trying to restore some lightness to the curious turn the conversation had taken. "So how would this woman know which man was fated to be her husband?"

Sensing her slight withdrawal, Jeb answered, "All you have to do is take a look at Eve. There she was. There he was. She knew right away that God had made them to be together."

"Your logic is flawed, sir. She had no other choice to make."

He made a slight shrug, although it didn't affect the grace of his dancing. "You're probably right, ma'am. Logic isn't my strong point. Dancing, however, is. And may I say that you are one of the finest dancers of any lady I've ever seen."

"Thank you, Lieutenant. You are a very skilled dancer yourself."

"Thank you, ma'am! I love music, and I love dancing," he said enthusiastically. "I'm afraid I have no skill in music, except for a keen enjoyment of it. Do you play an instrument or perhaps sing, Miss Cooke?"

"I play the piano, and even some guitar, and I enjoy both very much. I do sing, although not as well as some. But like you, sir, I do enjoy all good music."

"And waltzing," he added. "By any

chance, may I claim the rest of your waltzes tonight, Miss Cooke?"

"It would be considered very impolite for us to monopolize each other, you a newly arrived single gentleman, and an officer, and me, the daughter of the commander of the post," she considered. "But I don't think either of us shall be ostracized too much. Yes, Lieutenant Stuart, you may have the waltz for the rest of the night."

"How about all of the dances for the rest of the night?" he asked impishly.

"That would be entirely too scandalous. The waltzes are enough. And you, sir, do not tell me how 'it is meant to be.' I've already pointed out the flaw in that theorem."

There were several more waltzes during the ball. In general, Flora felt neither Lieutenant Stuart nor she was considered to be acting in a rude manner — except by Gerald Small, who continued to try to monopolize her — but the fact that she and the lieutenant danced together so much was certainly noted. She was certain Jeb Stuart commanded attention wherever he went and with whatever he did. And of course, as Flora was the commanding officer's daughter, her actions were of interest to the entire fort and the little town.

Toward the end of the evening, Gerald Small began dancing with a pretty blond girl whom Flora did not know, and he kept casting triumphant, slightly mean glances at Flora. She barely noticed and was sure she missed some.

As it happened, the last dance of the night was a waltz. At the end, Lieutenant Stuart escorted Flora back to her father. They exchanged greetings, and Jeb said, "Sir, I have found out that Miss Cooke has quite a reputation as an expert equestrian, so I have asked her to go for a ride with me tomorrow afternoon. She has agreed. Will that be acceptable to you, sir?"

"Of course, if Flora wants to go," Colonel Cooke said.

Jeb said in a most courtly manner, "I count it a great privilege, and I will be very careful to see that your daughter is safe. Thank you, sir." He turned to Flora. "Miss Cooke, I cannot adequately express my appreciation for your company tonight. It has been a delightful evening, and I owe my enjoyment of it expressly to you. Thank you, and until tomorrow, Miss Cooke." He bowed gallantly.

"Until tomorrow, Lieutenant," she replied as she curtsied prettily.

Colonel Cooke studied his daughter's

glowing face. "You just met him tonight, and you've already agreed to go riding with him, Flora?"

"Yes, Father. Surely you have no qualms? Already I have ascertained that he is a Southern gentleman of the first quality, from a noted Virginia family, and a Christian man. I'm sure no one would think ill of me or of him."

"No, of course not. That's not what I meant," Cooke said as they walked slowly toward the door, arm in arm. "He's a fine man and a truly excellent soldier. It's just that I suppose I've never seen you take to anyone quite so quickly."

She laughed, just a little, and squeezed his arm. "Papa," she said lightly, "perhaps it was just meant to be."

# CHAPTER TWO

Laughing with delight, Flora looked over her shoulder and called, "Is the 1st Cavalry always so slow?" Easily her mare jumped a broken-down snake fence and reached the border of the pecan orchard half a minute before Jeb Stuart caught up to her, his big white stallion easily clearing the fence.

He jumped down, grinning as always, his blue eyes dazzling in the blinding summer sun.

"Begging your pardon, ma'am, it's not that the 1st Cav is so slow. It's that you're fast. You beat me fair and square, Miss Cooke." He reached up to hold her hand as she dismounted. "I thought I would let you win, you know. Turns out I should have asked you to spare my manly feelings and let me win."

Affectionately Flora patted her mare's heaving sides. She was a pretty gray palfrey, a gift from her father upon her graduation.

"Her name is Juliet, a noble and delicate name, but she runs like a hardworking quarter horse."

"This is Ace," Jeb said, slapping the big horse's haunch. "And we always won until we met you two. Let's walk them out, shall we?"

"Yes, let's walk back to that little creek where we started. It's very warm, and I think that the water may be much cooler than what we have in our canteens."

Jeb had shown up at exactly two o'clock, as promised, resplendent in his cavalry uniform with the dark blue coat and sky-blue trousers, both with golden trim and insignia. He wore a wide-brimmed black hat with a golden band.

Flora had been so excited about seeing him again that she could barely get dressed, alternately berating Ruby for being so slow and urging her to hurry up. Finally, however, she had dressed in her very best new riding habit, emerald green of heavy cotton with a snappy jacket with a tight waist and peplum. The skirt was ground-length and had a small train, as it must for women to be able to cover their legs and feet appropriately while riding. She wore a dashing brimmed hat, pinned up on one side with a gold brooch that had belonged to her mother.

Jeb had made appropriate greetings to her father, but Flora was so anxious to ride that she had almost immediately demanded that they go. They had cantered outside the fort and come to one of the countless streams that crisscrossed the rolling hills above the river. On the other side was a wide field filled with black-eyed Susans growing riot-ously and the graceful lines of a pecan orchard on the far side. Flora had im-mediately challenged Jeb to a race.

Now they walked slowly back across the field. Jeb looked at Flora's sidesaddle, mysti-fied. "I've never understood how ladies can even sit on a horse on those contraptions. And especially I've never thought a lady could beat me in a race riding one. What I've heard is certainly true, Miss Cooke. You are one fine rider."

"I've been riding since I was four years old," Flora said. "And I do love to ride. I even like to shoot." She glanced up at him slyly.

With his dress uniform, he wore his cav-alry saber and his pistol in a black leather holster. "No, no, ma'am!" he blustered. "You've already beaten me soundly at riding. I'm not going to let you shame me

41

right down to the ground by outshooting me."

"Maybe some other time," she said.

"I hope there are many other times," he said quietly. Then, as he was wont to do after a sober moment with her, he reverted back to jollity. "Now I know you can ride and sing and play the guitar and piano. I know you can dance better than any lady I've ever seen. Tell me everything else about you."

"Everything?"

"Everything. I want to know it all."

"Oh, but no lady would ever tell all about herself. We must remain mysterious, so as to keep men intrigued," Flora teased. "Besides, you already know a lot about me, and I know very little about you, Lieutenant. Tell me about your home and family."

Jeb told her about his family in Virginia, about his father, Archibald Stuart, who had long represented Patrick County in the Virginia Assembly and then was a congressman. He mentioned some of their connections to other prominent Virginia families, such as the Prices and the Pannills and the Letchers. "But it was through one of my father's political connections that I got my commission to West Point," he said with some pride.

"A fine institution," Flora said. "My father says West Point cadets make the very best soldiers in the world."

"I'm a better soldier than I was a West Point cadet," Jeb told her, eyes dancing merrily. "I graduated with 129 demerits. I think they just graduated me because I was so rowdy and raucous they didn't want me to corrupt any more cadets. I had a nickname there, you know."

"What was it?"

"They called me Beauty. It was because I was so homely, I guess. Like you call a tall man 'Shorty.' "

"I don't think you're homely, Lieutenant," Flora said casually. "Not at all."

He looked pleased, like a young boy. "Really? Anyway, that's why I grew the beard . . . to cover up my homely aspects."

As they walked, Jeb bent and picked about six of the black-eyed Susans, then presented them to her with a bow. "Now you, Miss Cooke, have nothing at all homely about you. You're like these flowers, bright and glowing in the sunshine. And I must say that your riding outfit there is about the prettiest concoction I've ever seen. You truly are a 'beauty' in it."

"Thank you, kind sir," she said, accepting the wild bouquet with a queenly gesture.

Flora was rather accustomed to compliments from men, but deep down she knew that Jeb Stuart's admiration pleased her more than any other.

They reached the cool deep shade of the cottonwoods that bordered the little singing stream, and Jeb filled their canteens with the cold, fresh water.

Flora watched him, bemused. In truth he was just a little above average height, but he was a big man, with broad shoulders, giant hands, and long legs. For being so brawny, he was curiously graceful, with a rolling stride, but on horseback he had a power and grace that she had never seen before.

*And whoever in the world could say he was homely? He's one of the most handsome men I've ever met! Men are blind to male beauty, I suppose . . . but women certainly are not. They crowd around him like honeybees to the comb! He's just so imposing, so . . . commanding . . . so . . .*

The end of the thought made her blush, and at that moment he stood and turned back to her. A knowing, amused look crossed his face as he stepped up to hand her the canteen. She dropped her eyes and took a long drink of the refreshing water.

Jeb drank then led the horses up to the stream so they could drink. "Would your mare wander, do you think?" he asked her.

"I don't think so, but even if she does, she always comes to me easily," Flora answered.

"I've got a trick to get Ace to come to me if he's off foraging," Jeb said, looping the horses' reins around the pommels. "Let's take a little walk along this stream."

They walked in the shade of the trees along the grassy bank. The stream was really just a little bubbling trace only a couple of feet across at its widest part, but in places it was waist-deep.

"I love this little stream. I ride here often," Flora said. "I don't even think it has a name."

"Then let's name it," Jeb said. "How about Beauty's Stream? Meaning you, of course, Miss Cooke."

"And you, Lieutenant Stuart. After all, if West Point says it, then it must be so."

They came to a great fallen hickory tree just at the edge of the water. Flora sat down on it. Still holding her little bouquet, she threw one of the bright yellow flowers into the stream, and they watched it bob merrily away.

Jeb cocked one booted foot up on the log and leaned over her, not too close but near enough for her to again feel the sense of his physical presence so strongly that he might have been touching her. "I hear, ma'am, that you are planning to go to Philadelphia soon, to make your social debut."

Her face still averted, watching the peaceful stream wander by, she answered quietly, "That is true, Lieutenant. That has been my plan. I mean, it is my plan."

"I see." He was quiet for a moment, his piercing blue eyes gazing into the distance. "How soon?"

"Next month. Around the fifteenth."

He roused a little. "Oh? Oh well, that gives me plenty of time." He was teasing her again.

She looked up at him and made a prim face. "Plenty of time for what, sir?"

"Plenty of time for my plan."

"And what, exactly, is this plan?"

"Just because you told me your plan," he said jauntily, "doesn't mean I'm going to tell you mine. Not yet, anyway."

"Not yet? Then when?"

"Maybe . . . mm . . . maybe when you start calling me Jeb."

She sniffed and tossed another flower into the water. "It will be some time then. I only met you yesterday."

"Was it?" he asked intently. "Seems like I know you already. Seems like I've known you for a long time, Flora."

She was so enthralled with his words, and his nearness, that she never even noticed he called her by her given name. Nervously she stood, brushing her skirt, and somehow stumbled just a little.

He took her arm, presumably to steady her, but somehow she took a step, and he took a step and then they were standing close, facing each other. She stared up at him, directly into his piercing eyes, as he slowly searched her face almost hungrily. Very slowly he put his hands on her waist, and his fingers met in the tiny span. Flora felt the warmth from his hands spread through her, an oddly heavy sensation that made her catch her breath. He made a very slight move, lowering his face closer to hers, but then she saw a clear reluctance cloud his eyes and tighten his mouth. And suddenly she knew, as women sometimes did, that he was afraid to embrace her, afraid to make such advances too soon, afraid he would offend her, afraid he would frighten her away.

But Flora was not frightened, not at all; and she did not want him to be either. "May I . . . ," she said softly, almost imperceptibly moving closer to him.

"What?" he asked in a deep voice.

"May I . . . touch your beard, sir?" she

asked, smiling a little.

"Yes," he answered abruptly. His hands tightened on her waist until he almost hurt her.

Slowly she reached up and buried her fingers in his thick cinnamon-colored beard. "It's very soft," she said.

He stared at her, his eyes suddenly dark and brooding.

With one finger, she traced the outline of his beard up to the thick mustache, smoothing it a little, and then touched his lips. "So warm . . . ," she murmured.

He kissed her then. She could tell how difficult it was for him to restrain himself, because his hands on her waist were urgent, but his kiss was light, a mere brushing of his mouth against hers.

Then he lifted his head, and with an obvious effort dropped his hands and moved away from her. "I'm — I'm sorry," he said in a guttural tone.

"I'm not," Flora said lightly. To give him a few moments to recover himself, she bent to pick up the remaining flowers, still lying on the fallen log. She herself was deeply stirred and realized that already this man had a power over her that she had never imagined could exist. She took a deep, shuddering breath as she commanded her mind, her emotions, and even her body back under control. With careful movements, she rearranged the flowers back into a tight little bouquet and turned back to him.

He had recovered, all right. He was watching her, again with the joyful merriment that seemed to emanate like an aura from him. "I've never known a woman like you. I've sure never known a lady like you, Flora."

"You may call me Flora," she said primly. "But for my part, I shall still address you as Lieutenant Stuart."

"You won't know my plan until you call me Jeb, remember?" he teased, taking her arm, lightly now but with a slight air of possession.

"I may already suspect more of your plan than you realize, Lieutenant Stuart," she said airily. "But it may be that now you don't know mine."

"That's probably all too true," Jeb agreed. "What man was ever such a fool to imagine he knows what a woman's thinking? Not me."

They slowly walked back to the field, where the horses were well in sight, grazing. Flora and Jeb walked right up to Juliet, who stood obediently and let Flora take the reins.

Curiously she watched as Jeb reached in his pocket then called out in a clear ringing voice, "Ace! C'mere, boy!" He whistled, a clean, loud, boyish sound on the still hot air. Alertly the horse lifted his great head then set out at a gallop straight for Jeb, coming to a sliding stop just in front of him. Jeb chuckled and pulled a little packet tied with string out of his pocket. Quickly he untied the string and emptied the white granules into his hand. "Sugar," he told Flora. "Works every time."

"Yes, I can see that it does work very well for you, Lieutenant Stuart," she said sweetly. "Every time. We had better be getting back. In spite of what you may think, sir, I have not utterly lost my sense of propriety. We've been gone for almost two hours, and that is quite long enough, considering."

Jeb stepped up to her, again put his hands around her waist, and bodily lifted her up to set her on her saddle before she could protest. "You could never lose any sense of propriety, Miss Cooke. In fact, as far as I'm concerned, you're just about perfect. And so, since tomorrow will be our second ride, perhaps it may be for three hours?"

"You truly are very sure of yourself, aren't you?" she demanded, a little flustered.

"Am now," he said, swinging up into his saddle. "Tomorrow, then?"

"Yes — yes. Tomorrow."

# CHAPTER THREE

Flora dipped her hand into the milk-glass jar, got three full fingers of the rich cream, and started applying it to her face.

Ruby came to the dressing table, snatched up the jar, and set a corked bottle down in its place. "Here, you needs to put this on yo' face, Miss Flora."

Suspiciously Flora picked up the bottle. It was colored a dark purple, and she could barely see a thick substance coating the sides as she turned it back and forth. "It looks like bacon skimmings. What is it?"

"It's Mam Dowd's Anti-Freckle Skin Lotion. You know, Mam Dowd, down to town, that makes all the herbs and potions and cosmeticals for white ladies?"

Flora uncorked it and held it up to her nose, then yanked it away. "Good heavens, it smells like rancid bacon skimmings, too!"

Stubbornly Ruby crossed her arms. "Now you just put that on your face, Miss Flora.

You out riding in the summer sun all day ever day, with that pretty white skin. You got to cover it with some pertection."

"I'm not going to get freckles. Give me back my Essence of Gardenia cream, Ruby. It's protection enough."

"Hit says in Levitican that if youse got spots youse has to go outside the camp," Ruby said with an air of triumph. "And that was for sure talkin' about freckled white ladies."

"It's Leviticus, and it was talking about — Oh, never mind what it was talking about! Give me back my cream, Ruby. If I put that grease on me, I'll likely slide off my horse. And after one whiff of that, Jeb would turn and run away at a gallop."

With a dire frown, Ruby put the jar of cream back on the dressing table and quickly whisked the bottle into the bosom of her shirt. "Listen at you, callin' him by his give name already! And you barely knowing him a month!"

"It's been a little over a month and a half," Flora retorted.

"Mm-hmm. And you ridin' out all over the countryside with him most every day. What does that tell me, Miss Flora? You lettin' him take some liberties?"

Flora stopped rubbing the cream into her

skin, and her gaze went to a far-off distance.

Since that very first time they had ridden out together, and Flora had dared to touch Jeb and invite him as she had, they had both known the powerful attraction they had for each other — and they had both been wary ever since. For Flora, even though she had not quite realized it at the time, it had been a test for her. She already knew that she was attracted to Jeb Stuart — to his jovial personality, his humor, his ready laugh, his avid attentions to her — but she had not really understood what it was like to feel passion for a man. And in those few moments, and in that brief kiss, she had come to know passion, deep passion, and had comprehended in some way that this tremendous rush of feeling was what men found so very difficult to control. But women could. And Jeb did.

From then on they had held hands sometimes, and Jeb often took her arm. One twilit night on the veranda he had kissed her very lightly again, to say good night. But they had been very careful to keep a certain distance from each other. Flora did admit to herself that she reveled in Jeb's touch, and sometimes she deliberately took off her gloves — that perennial, eternal must for a well-brought-up young woman — just so she could feel his rough, heated hand. Jeb knew when she felt this way, she could tell, and she could just as certainly sense his reining himself in, holding himself back, only giving her as much as she asked for, as much as she was ready for.

She smiled dreamily. "Maybe I'm taking some liberties with him," she whispered to herself.

"Whut'd you say?" Ruby said suspiciously. She was behind Flora, putting a final polish on her riding boots.

"Nothing."

"Well, the scriptures say dat a woman what lets a man take liberties is gonna end up in the pit!" With righteous vigor she polished away.

Flora laughed. "I don't think so, but neither Jeb nor I are going to end up in the pit. And yes, I call him Jeb and he calls me Flora because we've given permission for each other to use our given names."

"Right out of the pit," Ruby said grimly. "With you knowin' him less'n a month."

"I believe this is what is termed 'a circular conversation.' All right, Ruby, I'm ready. Please help me with my boots."

With a final defiant rub, Ruby knelt down to help pull on Flora's boots. They were fine, black knee-high leather boots, hand-made by a boot maker in Baltimore especially for Flora, and the fit was so close that Flora could neither get them on nor pull them off by herself.

"For — such little — feet as — you got — these boots sure is — hard to git on." Ruby grunted as she pulled up on the uppers to get Flora's foot into the boot. Finally she got the right one on and went to work on the left one. "But — hit's a mighty — good thing — that you got — such little feet — 'cause white ladies — don't s'pose to have — big feet." She stood up and looked Flora up and down with satisfaction. "You is such a tiny lady, no wonder Mr. Lieutenant Jeb throws you around like a little kitten."

Ruby had caught them once, when Jeb had come to fetch her for a ride. Her father had been at headquarters, and Jeb had picked her up, swung her around, and then tossed her onto the saddle. He did this often when they were alone, but this time Ruby had seen them, and she had been holding it over Flora's head ever since. "I'm of a mind that the colonel might not like to think that Mr. Lieutenant Jeb is jugglin' his daughter around like some clown in a travelin' fair."

"You're not going to tell him, Ruby . . . ," Flora said, her cheeks reddening. "Please don't tell him."

"Well . . ."

"You can have that magenta silk petticoat you like so much, Ruby," Flora said with inspiration. "I don't like that color much for me, but it would be wonderful on you."

Ruby's eyes lit up. She had longed for the petticoat ever since Flora had received it along with some dresses she had ordered. "Well, I'm not one to be carryin' no tales; in the Proverbs it says talebearers will be backbit. So thank you for the petticoat, Miss Flora." Hurriedly she disappeared into Flora's dressing room to find the treasured article.

Flora was wearing her navy blue riding habit, trimmed in light blue. As it looked so much like the cavalry uniforms, Flora had bought a wide-brimmed felt hat and had trimmed it with some of her father's gold military braid and a tassel. Now she crammed the hat on her head, cocked it to a jaunty angle, pinned it securely, and hurried downstairs. It was almost three o'clock, and Jeb was never late.

Her father was in the parlor, gravely pacing before the empty fireplace. He looked up as she came in. She hurried to kiss him. "Hello, Papa. You were so quiet I thought you were taking your afternoon nap."

Colonel Cooke didn't smile much, but he

did when Flora kissed him. "No, actually I was waiting so that I might speak with you, Flora. I assume Lieutenant Stuart is on his way?"

"Yes, sir. He should be here at three."

"I see. That does give us a few minutes." He led her to the sofa, and they sat down. "I've had another letter from Mrs. St. George. She says that although you have delayed your visit, you've still given them no reason for the delay nor a date when they may expect you."

"Yes, I know, Father," she said quietly.

"You haven't confided in me either, Flora. But I think I understand. It's Lieutenant Stuart, isn't it?"

She looked up at him and met his gaze directly. "Yes, sir."

He studied her for long moments. "You don't want to leave because of him. Flora, you first met this man on the Fourth of July. How can you make such a momentous decision, to put off such an important event as your social debut, on the basis of such a short acquaintance?"

"I — I can hardly explain it to you, Father. But I can promise you that I know I am not making a mistake. I know what I'm doing." He looked doubtful, and she went on eagerly. "Papa, I know how very much you love the Lord, and how you've taught us to trust in Him in all things. And I do. I trust in the Lord, especially in this. I trust in the Lord, and I trust Jeb Stuart."

He listened to her closely then nodded. "Flora, ever since you were a child, you've been strong in the Lord, and you've been sure of yourself and your place in this world. You were a good child, and you've grown to be a good Christian woman. I don't know Lieutenant Stuart very well, and so I can't say that I trust him, but I do know you, and I do trust you. He does make you happy, doesn't he?"

"Oh yes, Papa! So very happy!"

"Then I'm glad for you, my dear. I hear him thundering up now. I declare that man can sound like an entire squad when he's galloping around on that great thumping stallion. Go on, Flora. After about thirty times I suppose he doesn't have to come in and make any obeisance to me anymore," he finished gruffly.

"Thank you, Papa, and I won't be too late!" She rushed out, her face glowing.

Jeb had found a way to ride down to the Missouri River. Just south of the fort the high bluffs lowered a bit, and he had found a place that was not at such a steep incline.

Ace had managed it easily. Jeb told her he had waited until he was certain of her expertise on a horse, and then he had taken her there.

Today was only the second time they had come, for it took over an hour from the fort, riding at a businesslike trot. But on this day they rode slowly, talking and enjoying the cheerful summer day, the cool breezes that found their way up the banks from the river to sweep across the deserted fields, the smell of wild honeysuckle and green grass and thick rich dirt.

When they reached the path down to the river, with a smile Jeb went in front of Flora, assuring her that if Juliet were following Ace she would be less likely to let herself get in a dangerous slide down the still-steep hill. Ace picked his way carefully, and so did Juliet. When they got to the riverbank, Jeb tied up their reins and let them loose.

"Do you have your old trick, your sugar?" Flora teased.

"Of course." He looked at her face expectantly, and in unison they said, "Works every time!"

They began to walk along, arm in arm. "You and your tricks," Flora muttered, now with ill humor. "All sugar, all the time, with the ladies especially."

"Are you jealous?" he asked slyly.

"No."

"You sure?"

"Yes, I am sure. It's just such a spectacle sometimes. Some of them, like my friend Leona Pruitt and those two blond sisters, the Aldridge girls, practically swoon every time you talk to them. For shame, Jeb Stuart. You shouldn't flirt so much."

"I can't help it," he said with an ingenuous, bemused air. "Ladies are just so pretty, so little and soft and sweet."

"You can't keep a bunch of ladies as pets, Jeb," Flora said darkly.

"You are jealous," he said with delight. "It's so cute."

"I am not cute. And I am not jealous."

He patted her arm. "You sure don't have a reason to be."

The shores of the Missouri River were sometimes thick yellow mud in the rainy season, but now, in August, they were dry and cracked. The river was still strong, its flow sure and steady, the clear water twinkling like stars in the late red sunlight.

"Did you know that the Missouri River is the longest on the continent?" Jeb asked.

"Longer than the Mississippi?" Flora asked with surprise.

"Yes ma'am." They looked up at the buff-colored bluffs high above them. "It is one of God's wonders of creation."

"I'm so very glad that you think such things," Flora said quietly. "So often you're so rollicking and rowdy that one would think you never had a serious thought in your head."

He glanced at her. "But you know different, don't you, Flora?"

"Oh yes. I may not know everything about you, Jeb, but I know you. I know you very well. I know that you are a loving, giving Christian man."

He stopped and turned her to him. "But Flora, do you really know me? Can you know my heart? I feel that you do. I've felt that ever since the first night we met."

She stared up at him; she was so tiny, and he loomed over her. But that fact had nothing to do with her sense of the power she felt from him. It was, she knew, because he had spoken the truth that night, and she had known it in her mind, in her body, and in her spirit. "You said that God made each man for a certain woman, and that that woman was made for that man," she said softly. "I remember. I'll never forget it. I can't forget it."

Suddenly he dropped to one knee, took her hand, yanked off her glove, and pressed his lips to her fingers. He looked up at her, and his blue eyes blazed as the hottest part of the fire. "Flora, you are the woman for me. I've known it all along. There's never been any other woman, and never will be, that God has made for me. Only you. Please, Flora dearest, would you do me the greatest honor, bestow upon me the greatest joy a man could ever have, and consent to be my wife?"

Breathlessly she replied, "Yes, Jeb. I was meant for you. I always was and forever will be."

He leaped to his feet and kissed her, deeply, a long kiss full of joy and passion and giving. For the first time, Flora surrendered herself. She gave in completely to all of the love and longing that she had for him and matched his desire with her own.

It was Jeb who finally pulled away from her. He swallowed hard and was breathing a little heavily. But the old Jeb could not be held down for long. He threw his hat up in the air and shouted, "Did you hear that? Miss Flora Cooke is mine! Finally! Whoo hoo!" Then he grabbed her around the waist, hoisted her up, and whirled around and around.

Flora laughed with sheer delight, throwing her head back and her arms in the air.

Jeb set her down and then, grinning like a fool, went to fetch his hat.

Flora was trying to straighten her own hat, as it had fallen to her back, held on by the gold braided straps. "I'm dizzy," she told Jeb, "and I don't think it's only from turning in circles. I can hardly believe it, even though — even though —"

"You've always known it, that you would marry me, ever since the Independence Ball," he said smugly, helping her settle her hat and pulling the bolo tie up under her chin.

"I didn't even think I'd be calling you Jeb by this time," she replied smartly. "Much less that I'd be calling you my fiancé. Oh! My fiancé!"

"Sounds good, doesn't it? But I can't wait till it's 'my husband.' That sounds even better. Can we get married now?"

"Silly bear," she said, playfully pinching him. It was like pinching a concrete pillar. "I do think we should at least have a decent engagement, considering we've hardly had what's considered a decent time for a courtship."

Impatiently Jeb took her left hand, removed her glove, and tucked it into his waistband along with the other. "You are now my fiancée, and I am going to hold your ungloved hand, no matter how scandalous it is. And what do you mean by a 'decent engagement'? There's nothing at all indecent in us, and I'll fight any man who says there is."

"I just meant that we should plan a wedding far enough in the future so that we could make arrangements for our families to be there," Flora said soothingly.

"Your family and my family are scattered all over about a dozen states," Jeb argued. "It would take too long to try to herd them all together. I want to get married now."

"Jeb, stop saying that. You know perfectly well that we can't get married now."

"I know not now, like today. But soon. It already seems like I've been waiting for you forever, Flora. I mean it."

She looked up at him and saw that he was perfectly serious. *And why not?* she thought. *By the standards of time, we haven't been together long enough to be this much in love . . . but Jeb is right. It does seem as if we've been waiting our whole lives for each other . . . and I suppose we have. We know it's the right thing in God's eyes. What do we care what men think?*

"What about November, Jeb?" she asked finally. "I would like to have a nice church wedding and for at least some of my family to be able to come. The St. Georges and the Virginia Cookes. And surely in that time your father and some of your sisters and brothers may be able to make arrangements to be here."

"Still too long," he grumbled, "but if that's what you want, my heart, then that's what we'll do. We'll marry in November." Then he added, "Do you know what day it is?"

"Thursday?" Flora guessed, mystified.

"Actually it's Wednesday, but that's not what I meant. Today is August 15th."

"Oh, August 15th," Flora repeated with wonder. "I was going to leave today."

"Oh no you weren't, not unless me and Ace hopped on that train with you. That was my plan, you see. I can tell you all about it now. I planned that you would not leave on August 15th or any other day. I planned that you'd be with me, on this day and every day from now on."

She smiled at him. "I won't pretend anymore, Jeb. I knew. Maybe not at the ball, but the very next day, I knew. And I was happy."

"Are you, Flora? Can you really be as happy with me as I am with you?" he asked, putting his arm around her and pulling her close.

"Yes, because I believe in the Lord, and I believe you are my gift from Him," Flora answered. "Even better than us, Jeb, He knew. God always knew."

Flora was happier than she had ever known, had ever known that a woman could be, as she prepared for her wedding. Her friends — and also now Jeb's friends, who included just about every man he met — teased her about moving from the grand Rookery to "one room and a kitchen." The officer's quarters were little more than that — though they did, of course, have a bedroom — but Flora and Ruby had hours of fun fixing it up.

As always, Jeb was the dashing, careless cavalryman. He would find Flora at the Rookery or at their new little house, come rushing in dusty and smelling of horses, and grab Flora to kiss her and hug her as if he hadn't seen her for months.

He teased Ruby unmercifully, and she adored him. She was fully as determined to make the house nice for "Miss Flora and Mr. Lieutenant Jeb" as Flora was, but sometimes Flora suspected she was so enamored of Jeb that she worked twice as long and twice as hard, sewing new bed linens, polishing the hardwood floors, and scrubbing the kitchen until it shone. Ruby even papered the dreary wooden walls with fine wallpaper Colonel Cooke ordered for them from New York, a small rose print that Ruby spent hours upon end matching up as she hung the thick strips. Jeb's family sent them a fine woolen carpet for the bedroom, and Ruby would barely let Flora walk on it.

In the middle of September, the 1st Cavalry was sent on a raid, a hard raid hunting wild Cheyenne, and Jeb didn't return until November 4th. Sorrowfully Flora had to break the news to him of the death of his father. Jeb couldn't possibly go to Virginia. The 1st Virginia was a brand-new regiment and leaves were hard to come by, and besides that, Jeb's father had actually died on September 20th.

And then the snows came hard in November, so Jeb and Flora had a small wedding at the Rookery, with only fifteen in attendance and Flora's father. Flora wore her white graduation dress, and she glowed.

For once Jeb Stuart was serious, his voice deep and sure as he promised to love, honor, and cherish Flora until death parted them. In her heart, Flora knew he spoke truth, and she knew that she would cherish this man for all of her life.

He kissed her, his new bride, and they

walked out of the parlor, for there was to be no reception. Jeb and Flora just wanted to go home. As they left, Jeb said, "Flora, I knew of God's goodness, but I never knew He would be so good to me. You are my life, Flora. I loved you when I met you, and I promise I will love you until the day I die."

"You are my heart and my life, Jeb," she said simply. "I can't believe God has blessed me with you."

"It was meant to be," he said, smiling. "I always knew it was meant to be."

Two weeks before, Jeb had written a cousin. In telling him of Flora, he had repeated Julius Caesar's famous quote, somewhat altered: *Veni, vidi, victus sum.*

*I came, I saw, I was conquered.*

And so, for the only time in his life, he was.

# CHAPTER FOUR

The room was cold even though the fireplace held a roaring, lusty fire. Flora huddled in one of the big overstuffed horsehair armchairs by it, covered with a woolen lap robe, reading the Bible by a kerosene lamp. The cabin was rough, but Flora and Ruby had made it, on the inside at least, into a snug little cottage, with pictures on the walls and rag rugs on the floor and nice heavy black velveteen drapes for keeping out the Kansas winter.

With affection Flora looked at the twin chair next to hers. It was Jeb's, and it had the imprint of his bulky frame in it. For many nights they had sat close together, reading or talking, holding hands, staring dreamily at the fire, contented and happy.

She looked up, and the calendar on the wall caught her eye. It was one she'd gotten with a picture of an angel watching over two children who were making their way down a dangerous pathway. *December 23, 1856. I can't believe we've been married for over a year. It seems like no time at all . . . or it seems like always.*

Ruby came in the kitchen door.

Flora could hear her stamping the snow off her boots and muttering to herself. Wrapping the robe around her, she went into the tiny kitchen. "Ruby, dear, what are you doing here this time of night?"

Ruby was still Flora's maid, but she had moved in with a man named Turley. The circumstances of their relationship were a little vague, but Flora never pressed her. Ruby was certainly not a slave; she was a paid servant, and Flora believed that Ruby's personal life was none of her business.

"Tomorrow's Christmas Eve, ain't it? And looky here, not a sign of a fire in this here stove! What you gwine to feed Mr. Jeb when he gets home, I ask you? Snow?"

"I don't think he'll be able to make it home for Christmas, Ruby," Flora said dispiritedly. "No one's heard from the 1st Cavalry in two weeks."

"He'll be here," Ruby said solidly, shedding several layers of outer clothes, scattering snow as she went. "And you with no Christmas dinner fixed for him. Good thing I brung over this here turkey to cook tonight, with Mr. Jeb comin' home with no fire in the stove and jes' icicles to eat."

"He's a soldier, Ruby. He can't always do what he wants," Flora argued.

"He said he'd be here, an' he'll be here. If 'n you don't know Jeb Stuart, I do. When dat man sets his head on something, he gets it done." Finally down to her skirt and blouse, she started tying on an apron and stared at Flora. "Am I standin' here lookin' at you with your bare feet?"

"I — I was just reading —"

"Miss Flora, you git back to that sittin' room right now and set down and wrap up, and I mean it," she scolded. "Otherwisen, your toes'll likely freeze off, and then what? Then you'll just have little hooves like a little tiny pony, and they won't be cloven hooves, neither. So that means the Bible says they'd be dirty."

"I think you mean unclean, Ruby," Flora said with amusement over her shoulder.

Ruby disappeared into the bedroom muttering, "Like I got time to go huntin' wool socks for silly white ladies dat would let their own feet freeze off and can't even cook their own supper." She fetched Flora two pairs of wool socks, still muttering. "You is a good woman, Miss Flora, but you better make sure you be a good wife to Mr. Jeb.

Freezing your feet off is one thing, but not havin' a man his dinner when he gets home is 'nother can of worms altogether."

Ruby had cheered her up; she had been depressed, missing Jeb. She always missed Jeb terribly when he was on a patrol. She felt alone, lonely, and somehow bereft, as if a part of her were missing. *And I suppose it is. I am bone of his bone and flesh of his flesh,* she reflected. She had been reading Genesis, and she turned back a few pages to read again of the union of Adam and Eve and how God had ordained this miracle for all married people.

*And in spite of what Ruby thinks, I am a good wife to Jeb. And oh, I'm so glad! I was so afraid I wouldn't be, that I wouldn't know how to be, that I wouldn't be good enough for a man like him.* But it hadn't worked out that way. She smiled, thinking about her honeymoon and how wonderful it had been. Jeb had been very gentle, and she had quickly learned to please him. A memory floated to her mind of how she had awakened the morning after her wedding and how for a moment she'd been terrified to find a man in her bed. But since then, every night she slept with him and every morning she woke up to him, she had been filled with joy. She'd learned that the intimacies of marriage were part of the wonder of being a wife, married to a man she loved passionately. She was so grateful that she and Jeb suited each other in that way.

From the kitchen, Ruby called, "I got this here fire going good now, no thanks to some folks. And I got that lazy Turley to scrounge around and get you a turkey. It's a little scrawny, but I'll roast it up good. And he got some sweet taters, too, and I knows how much Mr. Jeb loves sweet tater pie."

Suddenly Flora was hungry; she had been listless all day, missing Jeb so much that she didn't really want to eat. But she felt much better now, and so she got up, fetched her warm wool robe and slippers, and joined Ruby in the kitchen. "Where in the world did Turley get that turkey, Ruby?"

"Hit's a wild turkey, but he dressed it out so nice it almost looks like one boughten at a market. Turley, he's a right good hunter. And he does what I says, 'cause then he knows I'll be nice to him."

Flora reached out and touched the bird. "He is a good size." A thought came to her, and she glanced up at Ruby. "What do you mean 'be nice to him'?"

"Jes' whut it say."

"Why, Ruby, surely you don't mean you'd

be letting Turley take some liberties?" Flora teased.

Ruby smiled, and the new gold in one of her front teeth gleamed. She had just gotten it from the new dentist in Leavenworth, and it was her pride and joy, so she smiled most of the time. "I knows what I be doin', Miss Flora, and ain't no call for you to be tellin' me about no liberties. Me and your poor papa thought you and Mr. Jeb would scandal the place up to heaven till we got you two married. Good thing we did, too, jest in the devil's nick of time."

"Yes, thank you so much for that, Ruby. Jeb and I are grateful."

"Orter be. What are you doing in here, anyways?"

"I'm hungry."

"Oh, so now Miss Flora's hungry, is she? Droopin' too much over Mr. Jeb to even put on socks like a Christian woman, but now youse hungry?"

"Yes," Flora said meekly. "But I'll just fix myself some ham and beans real quick, and then I'll help you."

"Oh, jest sit down at the table there. I can fix them ham and beans faster'n you can find the pot to cook 'em in."

"But I want to help," Flora insisted. "Jeb should have a good Christmas dinner, and I

74

really am very grateful to you and Mr. Turley for providing us with this feast."

"Thought you said Mr. Jeb wasn't coming home for Christmas," Ruby said smartly.

"Well, perhaps he will," Flora said, with much less doubt now.

"He said he would, and he don't tell no stories, not dat man. Men like Jeb Stuart don't grow on no trees. You jest better hang onter him, Miss I'm-Too-Pouty-to-Make-Supper."

"I intend to do that, Ruby. So you just step aside and tend to that turkey. I can fix my ham and beans, and then I'll help you with those sweet potatoes for Jeb's pie."

The day dawned with a bright sun, and the snow began melting. The bitter cold of the Kansas winters had not been pleasant, but Flora was used to them. She'd gotten up early, and she and Ruby had spent all day cooking. Ruby knew how to make corn bread dressing, so the two of them had gone to the commissary and had gotten cornmeal and fresh milk so Ruby could teach her how to make it. They were busy all day, and the time went quickly. They finished cooking in the late afternoon.

As evening fell, Flora had again almost

lost hope of Jeb returning in time for Christmas.

"You might as well quit looking out dat window. He'll come when he come," Ruby said. "Now you set down here and behave. I'm gwine ter knit Mr. Jeb a pair of new wool socks. They'll be too late for Christmas, but I knows his birthday is in February. I'll be finished long afore then."

"I should learn to knit," Flora said aimlessly, her gaze wandering again toward the window. Though night was falling, she still hadn't closed the curtains. She hoped Jeb would see the welcoming light — if he came home.

"He'll be here," Ruby repeated with emphasis. "You got dat present wrapped you got for him?"

"Yes, it's under the bed."

"What about me? You gots mine wrapped?"

Flora smiled. "Yes, I have. Do you want it now?"

"No, I don't want it now. It ain't Christmas. I'll take it tomorrow 'fore we eat all dis turkey and dressing."

Ruby went to bed early that night. The small house had a room in the attic that had been fixed up by the previous tenant, and she often stayed up there when she worked late. It was actually warmer, Ruby said, than the downstairs.

Flora waited and listened to every sound. The night was quiet, and a soft gentle snow had begun to fall. She finally rose and murmured sadly to herself, "I might as well go to bed. He's not coming."

She turned to go to the bedroom, when suddenly she heard the sound of horses. She quickly ran to the door, and despite the cold she threw it open.

Bordering their tiny yard were the parade grounds, and a troop was coming in — and then she saw Jeb! He swung out of his saddle, gave some orders, tossed the reins of his horse to one of the men, then hurried toward the house. Flora could see his blue eyes sparkling yards away. He bounded to her, swept her up, and swung her around. "How's my very favorite girl? I've missed you so much! I bet you didn't think I'd make it in time."

"I wasn't sure, but Ruby was positive." She took his heavy overcoat.

Jeb kissed her lovingly and said, "I'm going to thaw out a little." He went to the fireplace, holding his hands out to warm them.

"Did you see any Indians?" she asked as she hung his coat on the back of a cane-back chair to thaw out and dry.

"Not a one. I think they're all hunkered down for the winter, which shows that they're smarter than the 1st Cav. What's been happening around here?"

"Nothing much. We're going to have a good dinner tomorrow."

"That sounds fine! I'm tired of eating stringy antelope."

Flora scrunched her nose and made a sour face, thinking about eating stringy antelope. "That man Turley, the one so sweet on Ruby, brought her a turkey, so we're going to have turkey and dressing with sweet potato pie."

"My favorite!"

As he stood there warming his hands by the stove, Flora was aware of the strange feeling she had. She called it an expansion, but that didn't adequately describe it. She just felt more alive, more energetic, so much happier with Jeb. When he came into the room or when she touched him, the love she felt for him seemed to grow larger and larger. She went to him and took his rugged hands and held them to her cheeks. "You're so cold."

"My hands are grubby and dirty. Flora, you're going to freeze yourself."

"I don't care."

"One of the men asked me what it was like to be married. One of the younger fellows. He must have marriage on his mind."

"What did you tell him, Jeb?"

"I told him it was like going to heaven here on earth."

Flora laughed and lightly pulled his beard, something she often did. "Well, your supper may not exactly be heaven on earth. Ham and beans."

"Better than antelope. Oh, I'm so glad to be home for Christmas with you, my best love! I got you a present, but you can't have it until tomorrow morning."

"I have presents for you, too, Jeb. So yes, let's wait until tomorrow."

He picked her up and squeezed her and said, "I'll go clean up, and then I'll eat. But I'll hurry, because I'm ready to go to bed," he added mischievously. "I haven't slept with you for two weeks. In fact, I may skip supper."

"You'll do no such thing! Ruby tells me that if I don't feed you a good supper when you get home, I'm headed straight for the pit. Or you are. Or someone is, anyway. No, I want you to eat, my darling. I'll wait." She smiled at him. "After all, I haven't slept with my very own stove for two weeks, either, and I want you to be nice and full and happy when we go to bed."

The next morning, Flora arose early. As she dressed, she could smell the sweet scent of burning oak. Jeb never seemed to get tired. Even after long patrols, he came back with boundless energy. Quickly she finished dressing and did her hair. She went in to find that he already had big hot fires made in the fireplace and also in the cooking stove.

"Can't have too much fire after those snowy prairies," he said. He came over and kissed her. "When do I get my present?"

"Anytime you want it."

"I want it now, then," he said boyishly.

"I want mine first," Flora said.

"All right." He walked over to where he'd thrown his camp bag. He sorted through it and pulled out two packages, one larger than the other, wrapped in brown paper. "This one first."

Flora took the larger of the two packages and tore it open. Inside she found a bolt of beautiful emerald green muslin with tiny white flowers.

"You look so pretty in that color. I know Ruby can make you a dress fine enough for a queen."

"Oh Jeb, it's perfect! Thank you so much, my darling."

"Here's the other present." He handed her a small velvet box.

She opened it and found a necklace with a gold chain and a tiny cross of emeralds that matched the fabric perfectly. "Oh my goodness, Jeb, it's absolutely beautiful! But however did you pay for this? It must have been a dear price, indeed."

"No, you are the pearl of great price," Jeb said, fastening the necklace around her neck. "And its beauty cannot compare to you, Flora, my dearest." He kissed her tenderly.

Then she said excitedly, "I have two presents for you, Jeb." She went back into the bedroom, came out with a box, and handed it to him. "I think you'll like it. She watched as he opened the box and then laughed as his blue eyes lit up. "You didn't expect that, did you?"

Jeb pulled out the golden spurs. One of the other officers had ordered them for Flora, so she had been able to keep them a secret from Jeb. "Now you can be the most dashing cavalier of all, riding around with your golden spurs. But promise when you wear them you'll always think of me."

"Flora, my girl, these are something!" Jeb

rubbed the gold admiringly and said, "No one else can beat this finery. I'll be strutting for sure." He looked up at her with his ever-present boyish grin. "And who else would I think of but you? I think of you always, my dear."

"I knew you'd like them, and they suit you, Jeb."

"Thank you, thank you, Flora. So . . . where's my other present?"

She rose and came to sit on his lap. "Well, I'm afraid that you can't actually have that one until around August."

Jeb stared at her for a moment. "What? What does that — in August? Are we going to have a baby? In August?"

"Yes, we are. Merry Christmas!" She watched him as he absorbed this, and she saw the intense pleasure come over his face. Flora had been a little worried about this, because though she and Jeb had always agreed that they wanted children, it was different when it became a reality.

But now Jeb's blue eyes positively sparked, and he hugged her, hard. "Just what I wanted! You couldn't have given me anything better! Think I'll be a good papa?"

"You'll be a wonderful father, just like you're a wonderful husband," she answered, rising to seat herself back in her own arm-chair.

Jeb, radiating energy as always, started walking the floor. He couldn't hide his excitement, nor did he want to. He wasn't a man who hid things like that. "The dragoons have a good carpenter. I'll have him make us up a cradle and a crib and . . . and . . . some little tiny chairs and a table . . ."

Flora laughed. "It might be a while before we'll be needing all that, Jeb."

Then Ruby came down the ladder that led up to the attic, yawning.

Jeb said in his booming voice, "Ruby, guess what? Me and Miss Flora are going to have a baby around August."

"Well, ain't dat fine." Ruby grinned. "You wants it to be a boy or a girl?"

"Either. Or both would be just fine with me." He winked and laughed. "I don't care as long as it's healthy and strong. You ought to get married and have a bunch of babies, Ruby."

"I ain't studyin' about any of that foolish-ness now. I'll be busy helpin' Miss Flora to take care of your baby, Mr. Jeb."

"That's real good, Ruby. Miss Flora and I need you. That reminds me. I have a present for you, Ruby," Jeb said. "It's a surprise." He went back to his bag and pulled out another package and said, "I'll bet you'll like this one."

Ruby opened the package, stared up at Jeb openmouthed, and said, "Dis is the finest bonnet I ever saw in my livin' life, Mr. Jeb." It was a black silk hat trimmed with dangling jet beads and an enormous bunch of cherries.

"I've got something for you, too, Ruby," Flora said. She went to a small table with a drawer and pulled out a package. She handed it to Ruby.

She opened it with obvious anticipation. "It's a ring! Ain't it pretty? And it's gold just like my tooth."

Jeb slid an arm around Flora's waist. "I hope you like your presents, Ruby."

"Why, a woman would have to be crazy to not like dis bonnet and dis here ring. Jest wait till Miss Alma Strong sees me. I'll put one in her eye, I will. Now you two set back and lemme get dis turkey going. We're going to have the bestest meal you ever had, Mr. Jeb Stuart, and you, too, Miss Flora, to go with the bestest Christmas I ever had."

"Me, too," Jeb said to Flora. "The best I ever had."

That winter passed happily for the Stuarts.

As Jeb had said, there were no reports of troublesome Indians at all. They had indeed gone into winter quarters.

Flora, as tiny as she was, began very soon to show. By early spring she had already gained so much baby weight she had to be very careful about doing any energetic housework or even taking long walks. She encouraged Jeb, however, to get out and ride around and visit with his men as often as possible.

He was not a homey kind of man. After he found out Flora was pregnant, he hung around the house most of the time, but Flora was reminded of a caged lion. He paced, he fidgeted, he made unneeded repairs on the cottage just so he could hammer something and make noise.

Finally she persuaded him that he needed to ride the horses to keep them in good condition, he needed exercise, and he needed to be with the new 1st Cavalry as they were still a regiment in training. With ill-disguised relief, he started riding, some for pleasure and some patrolling, scouting around the countryside, learning the ground and the territory.

And soon he was called to his grim duty again. The 1st Cavalry got news from the frontier that the Cheyenne were raiding wagon trains, and in May they rode out to hunt them down.

It was a fine spring morning, even on the dreary plains of the border of Kansas Territory. The 1st Cavalry had been following a number of Cheyenne for nine days, their scouts finding clear tracks but always days old.

Jeb rode with two of his longtime friends who had joined the 1st Cavalry, along with Jeb, back in St. Louis: Pat Stanley and Lunsford Lomax. Their commanding officer was Colonel Edmund Sumner, and the men respected him as a good soldier and officer. Still, the men were restless, for they had thought they would find the renegade Indians before now.

"We'll find 'em," Jeb said confidently.

"How do you know?" Stanley asked.

"Because if we don't chase them down, if they've got any grit at all, I'd imagine they'll find us," he answered.

Two days later his words proved prophetic. They had come into a small bowl of the prairie surrounded on three sides by small, smooth hills. That afternoon they stared into the west and saw three hundred Cheyenne warriors lined along one of them.

Colonel Sumner immediately shouted

orders for battle formation, and the straggling column quickly formed up as the Cheyenne, screaming bloodily, started riding down the little hill. Jeb fully expected Colonel Sumner to order a carbine volley — Jeb had already started pulling his rifle out of the sheath — when the commander thundered, "1st Cavalry! Draw sabers! Charge!"

The men, sabers glinting like steely death in the dying red sun, charged, screaming and yelling furiously. The line of Cheyenne riding toward them wavered, slowed . . . and then they turned and fled.

Jeb spurred Ace so furiously that he got ahead of the battle line and rushed into the scattered Indians, yelling like fury. Only a few of the officers had barely kept up with him, including Stanley and Lomax. Close by him, Stuart saw an Indian turn and point a rifle right at Lunsford Lomax, and Jeb thrust at him but landed only a thin slash on the Indian's side and rode past him, then turned back. The Indian now had his rifle pointed at Jeb.

Close by Jeb heard, "Wait, Jeb! I'll fetch him!" He saw Pat Stanley, unhorsed, kneeling and pointing a carbine at the Indian. He pulled the trigger, but the rifle misfired, and Stanley was out of ammunition. Quickly the

Cheyenne rode toward Stanley, who watched helplessly as the warrior raised his rifle to point directly at Stanley's head.

Jeb shot forward, and this time landed a killing blow to the Indian's head. But as he fell he fired, and Jeb felt the shot hit him high on the breast.

Stanley jumped up and ran to him. "Jeb, you're shot! Stay here. I'll get my horse and get you to the rear." He disappeared and soon came back riding his horse, which had managed to unseat Stanley in the middle of the fray but then had only moved a few feet off to unconcernedly graze a little.

"I don't think it's too bad," Jeb said cheerfully. "But I guess I had better go get it seen to. No sense bounding around on Ace, here, until the bullet plows around and finally blunders into my heart." Blithely he rode to the rear.

. . . I rejoice to inform you that the wound is not regarded as dangerous, though I may be confined to my bed for weeks. I am now enjoying health in every other respect . . .

Flora kept reading those two lines over and over and weeping harder each time the words burned into her heart.

Her father had been an Indian fighter for many years, and she and her sisters had always worried about him when he was on patrols. Flora had seen injured men, had even seen men killed and brought home to weeping wives and families.

She'd thought she knew and understood the dangers of a soldier's life. But this was different. This was her husband, her beloved Jeb. And though his letter was so obviously cheerful, with the energetic note of his demeanor clearly coming through, Flora sobbed helplessly with the sudden harsh reality she was now facing. Jeb was a soldier, he was in constant mortal danger, he could be injured — he could even be killed. Thinking of it, she felt as if she herself might simply pass out into a cold, lonely darkness and oblivion.

How long she remained in this desolation, she really didn't know. But finally she rose and washed her tearstained, swollen face and smoothed her hand over her swollen belly. She couldn't do this to herself. She couldn't do it to the baby. And most certainly she could not do it to Jeb. If she were a weeping, wailing wreck of a woman all the time, Jeb would go mad with grief, she knew. He was happy with her, he found joy and pleasure in his life with her, and she was determined that she would keep it that way.

She would find the strength in the Lord, to live with His comfort, to live under His care. She would learn to live her life with Jeb — no matter what the circumstances, no matter what the hardships or the grief — to the fullest, every day, to be grateful to God every day for him, and never to forget all of the countless treasured moments they had. She would be strong, and she would be full of joy, always, for Jeb.

She would do this. No matter what the cost.

The wounded of the 1st Cavalry were not able to get back to Fort Leavenworth until August 17th.

Flora saw them come into the parade grounds, and she saw Jeb's big body lying on a travois. Though she was so big now she couldn't possibly run, she hurried as fast as she could to his side. He looked up at her, and with an almost stunned relief, Flora saw that his eyes were clear and dancing as merrily as ever. She knelt by him, awkwardly.

"The baby's not here yet," Jeb murmured. "Oh, I'm glad."

"I am, too. He waited until he could see

his father."

"Flora, my best girl, you can't know how I've missed you." He joked, "I would have hurried back much sooner, but these lazy fellows wouldn't come along with me."

She ran her fingers down his face and entangled them in his soft beard. "You're pale, my darling. Your letters . . . You seem not to be hurt too badly."

"I'm not," he grunted then pulled himself up to a sitting position. "And I'm as tired of this infernal machine as a man can be. I can walk into that infirmary myself. There're no men big enough to carry an ox like me, and somehow I don't think they'd welcome Ace pulling me in."

"No Jeb, don't. You're scaring me," Flora begged even as he stubbornly pushed himself to his feet.

He took her hand, brought it to his lips, and kissed it, as he had so many times before. Flora never tired of it. "Please don't be frightened, Flora. I never want you to be frightened of anything in this world. I am fine, really. I'm so much better, thank the Lord, and I feel very well, if only a little weak."

Flora nodded. "All right, then. I do have to agree that perhaps I might walk you into the infirmary, instead of Ace." She put her arm through his.

He hesitated and said uncertainly, "Flora, I know this must be so hard for you, but you're really all right, aren't you? I mean, you grew up in a soldier's house and you married a soldier. You always knew, didn't you? You always knew what it would mean?"

She could see the fear in him, as she knew she would. And she steeled her thoughts and cried out to God and then smiled up at him. "Of course, Jeb. Just know that I love you, I will always love you, and I will always be waiting for you when you come home. Now come on, silly bear, and let the doctor see you."

*No matter the cost.*

# CHAPTER FIVE

Flora entered the room and paused abruptly at the scene that was taking place before her. Her lips curved upward in a smile, and she felt a rush of love mixed with pride.

She had been confident, almost from when she met him, that Jeb Stuart would make a good husband. He was always considerate, even gallant to her, a man who was faithful to everything that marriage stood for. But many men who had these qualities didn't necessarily take well to infants. She'd been relieved, however, as Little Flora had come through the first year and a half utterly adored by her father.

Flora remained silent, watching as Jeb, who was lying flat on his back, set Little Flora down upon his chest. She leaned forward, making little yelps of joy. Grabbing Jeb's luxurious beard, she tugged at it and yelled, "Paaah! Paaah!"

"Well, be careful there, little darling.

You're going to pull my beard out, and you would see what an ugly fellow I am. Did you know I grew this beard just to hide my ugly face?" He suddenly reached out and grabbed her and held her high in the air. She chortled with joy, and he lowered her until their noses touched.

"Jeb, what in the world are you doing? You always have to play on the floor," Flora demanded, coming to stand over them.

"I'm just too big. There's not enough room anywhere else," Jeb said, lifting Little Flora high again as she squealed.

"You're supposed to be rocking her to sleep."

"I tried to, but she talked me out of it." Jeb grinned. His eyes sparkled with merriment, and his red lips, almost hidden beneath his thick mustache, revealed a smile, exposing his excellent teeth. "I miss out on so much time with our little princess here, I have to make up for it."

"You've been playing with her for over an hour. We have to feed her and put her to bed."

Jeb got to his feet reluctantly.

Flora reached out and took their daughter.

"I'll just watch and you feed," Jeb said. "I think it'll be better that way."

Flora was still nursing Little Flora, so she

94

opened the front of her dress and the baby began to nurse noisily.

"No sweeter sight on earth than that to me," Jeb said. "Everyone I know says children take in their mother's character when they nurse, so she's going to be sweet and beautiful like you."

Flora couldn't help but smile. "You must want something, Jeb. You never say those sweet things to me unless you want something."

"You hurt my feelings, darling."

"I couldn't hurt your feelings with a sledgehammer. What is it you want?"

Jeb pulled a straight chair close beside her. A thoughtful expression replaced his wide smile. "I've been giving a lot of thinking of what I am to the Lord."

"I don't know what you mean."

"I've never been a very deep thinker. I'm a lot better at action," Jeb said, stroking his beard. "But a man has to think about his spiritual life, too, and I've been doing a lot of that."

Flora felt thrilled, for she had often wondered about the depth of Jeb's spiritual life. He had an experience with the Lord years ago, but Flora wasn't certain it was a conversion as she thought of it. She thought of being "converted" as she was. This included repenting of her sins at the preaching of a traveling Methodist evangelist, confessing Jesus and following Him in baptism, and taking the Lord's Supper. Her life had been tied up with church and such devotions, but Jeb had never seemed pressed to do such service to the Lord.

Jeb leaned back, teetering on the back legs of his chair, as he often did. He kept his hands on his heavy thighs. He was wearing only trousers and an undershirt, for May had come, bringing hot weather with it. He teetered back and forth. "I've been a believer in Jesus for a long time, Flora. You know that. There's never been a doubt in my mind that He is who He says He is and He came to do what He said He did. But since we've been married, I've been watching you, and I can't help but think that I've let the Lord down."

"And what is it you want to do, Jeb?"

Stuart spread his arms out in gesture and his eyes opened wide. He had piercing eyes that could see farther than any man in the company, and when he turned them on people, they were riveted, as they were on Flora now. "Why, Flora, I need to do what you've done. I need to join a church and start living as a Christian."

"I think that would be wonderful, Jeb.

You've always been a good man, I know."

"I try to be, but from what I read in the scripture, that's not enough. I wrote this letter to my mother. Let me read you just a bit of it." He pulled a paper from his pocket and began to read in a low, serious tone:

"I wish to devote one hundred dollars to the purchase of a comfortable log church near your place, because in all my observation I believe one is more needed in that neighborhood than any other I know of; and besides, 'charity begins at home.' Seventy-five of this one hundred dollars I have in trust for that purpose, and the remainder is my own contribution."

Flora exclaimed, "Why, Jeb, I know your mother will be so pleased. The church is so far she can't go very often."

"She mentioned that a few times to me."

Flora stroked Little Flora's silky hair. "And what church were you thinking about joining?"

Surprise washed across Jeb's face. "Why, Flora, I want to belong to the same church as you and my mother. The Episcopal church."

Joy flooded through Flora, for she'd spoken to Jeb's mother, and they had written each other, both praying that Jeb would make a step just as this. "I have to write your mother and tell her." Then she shook her head. "No, you put it in that letter that you're going to join the Episcopal church. I know she will be so glad."

"It wasn't a hard decision. You know, I promised my mother when I was very young that I'd never touch a drop of liquor, and I never have and I never will. But I think there's more to being a Christian than just not doing things that are evil. When I ride into battle, I'd like to know that if I get put down I'd be in the presence of the Lord."

Flora held out her hand, and Jeb took it. "What a wonderful surprise you've given me, Jeb." She hesitated then added, "And I have a surprise for you, too."

"You do? What is it?"

"It's about your son." Flora laughed when she saw Jeb's expression. This sentence seemed to amaze him completely.

Then he cried with delight, "You mean we're going to have another child?"

"Yes we are, and I'm praying that God gives us a little Jeb to go along with Little Flora."

Jeb came off of his chair and began pacing the floor. "Well, thank God above! Nothing could've pleased me better." He leaned over and kissed her cheek. "You're a perfect mother, and I'm working hard to be a good father."

Flora reached up and put her arm around his neck to pull him closer to her. His beard was scratchy, but she didn't care. "I'm so happy, Jeb. You're the best husband any woman could ever have. And you already are better than a good father. You're a wonderful father."

Jeb straightened up and said, "You know, it's even more important now that I try to make some extra money. I think I'm going to go to the War Department."

Jeb had been working on a simple mechanism that would allow a soldier to remove his saber from his belt instantly and replace it exactly the same way. At the present time, the removal of the saber was awkward and unwieldy.

He went on, "If I can get them to adopt this, we'll make some money off of it. It'll be good for the army, too."

"Jeb, I think that's wonderful. When will you take it to them?"

"I'm going to write up the proposal and draw diagrams. Then I'll be ready to present it to them."

"I bet they'll buy it, too. You're a resourceful man, Jeb Stuart."

■ ■ ■ ■

Summer had passed, but in October it seemed that it was almost as sweltering in Washington as it had been in August.

Jeb sat waiting in a large anteroom at the War Department. It had been with some trepidation that he'd asked the sergeant at the desk to deliver his message to General Stratton. That had been over an hour ago.

As Jeb waited, he noticed an odd escalation of activity in the War Department offices. Men hurried up and down the corridors, clutching papers, doors opened and slammed, and soldiers went into General Stratton's office and then came back out, barely glancing at the bearded young officer from the 1st U.S. Cavalry waiting in his outer room.

And then General Stratton opened his door himself. Stratton was a lean, hungry-looking individual with hawklike features. He had the red eyes of a drinker. He was known to be a good officer, however. He called to Jeb, "Lieutenant Stuart, please come in."

"Yes, General." Springing to his feet, he went into the office. It wasn't as ornate as he expected, although Jeb admitted to himself that he'd had little enough to do with generals.

Before he could say a word about his invention, Stratton said, "I've got a duty for you, Lieutenant. I know you came here of your own doing, but there's something you must do for me."

"Certainly, General, you just name it."

"I need for you to take a message personally to Robert E. Lee. You're acquainted with Colonel Lee, if I'm not mistaken?"

"Yes, sir, he was the commander at West Point when I was there."

"A very serious matter has occurred. There's been a rebellion led by a man named John Brown. Have you heard of him, Stuart?"

"Yes, sir. I even met him once. Old Osawatomie Brown. He was causing trouble in Kansas. He is always causing trouble."

"That's the man, all right. I've written this letter to order Colonel Lee to take charge of a force. Brown and his men have taken the arsenal at Harpers Ferry. They are trapped in the engine house, and they have hostages. We have sent ninety U.S. Marines ahead, because we have no army units close, only local militia. You might as well know what the orders are. Colonel Lee is to take command of all forces in Harpers Ferry and arrest John Brown and the other mutineers. The War Department has authorized him to use any means necessary to do so. Please hurry, Lieutenant."

"Yes, General, I'll leave immediately."

Lieutenant Stuart arrived at Arlington, the Lees' gracious white-columned mansion, just a few hours later. They visited only briefly, for Stuart's message, and the orders he carried, were urgent. No train was available, but the War Department sent a locomotive to take Colonel Lee to Harpers Ferry. Jeb asked to go along as his aide, and Lee agreed. Just before they left, he telegraphed ahead for all action to stop until he was there.

The two men talked of old times at West Point. Lee was interested in Jeb's career, news about the Indians, the Stuart family, every detail of Stuart's life. Stuart remembered that Commander Lee had always been this way with the cadets.

The train arrived at Harpers Ferry, and they immediately left the car. Lee was in civilian dress, a black suit, well-tailored and neatly pressed. He looked like a prosperous merchant on holiday. But he was a soldier and a leader, and he took charge immediately.

"What is the situation, Lieutenant Green?" he asked as soon as they arrived.

Lieutenant John Green, head of the militia, summed up the action briefly. He was a short young man, well built, with a thick, solid neck and a pair of steady gray eyes.

"Brown has raised a rebellion, and there are at least a dozen men dead, including the mayor of Harpers Ferry. We are pretty sure he has about thirty hostages. And sir, one of them is Colonel Lewis Washington." He was George Washington's great-grandnephew.

"Indeed?" Lee asked. "Do we know of the well-being of the hostages?"

"Sir, we don't know, but we think that none of them have been harmed. Old John Brown has been communicating, somewhat, with us. He doesn't seem to intend to harm his hostages. Not now, anyway."

"Where are the mutineers now?"

"They're in the engine house, Colonel."

"Take us there, sir."

"Yes, Colonel, this way." Green led them to a solid brick structure about thirty feet by thirty feet.

The doors were stoutly battened. Lee considered it, then asked, "How many do you think are inside now?"

"Not too many, Colonel. Half a dozen, maybe."

Lee nodded then turned away, his eyes sharp, his face intent. He looked up behind them, he looked around, and he studied the engine house itself for a long time. Then decisively he said, "Lieutenant Stuart, I want you to carry to the engine house a written demand for surrender. If the raiders refuse, a party of marines will rush the doors. We want to avoid killing them, so we'll use bayonets only."

Lee found a place where he could write and took some time to compose the message to Brown. He handed it to Stuart and said, "Can you read this, Stuart?"

The dawn was breaking, but the light was still weak. Jeb narrowed his eyes, scanned the paper, and said, "Yes, sir."

"Very well. Lieutenant Stuart, you will go to the engine house and relay the terms to John Brown. If he refuses to surrender, wave your hat. That will be the signal for attack. Lieutenant Green, please pick twelve marines to make the attack and twelve marines to be held in reserve."

The marines ran to the engine house and lined the walls in the front.

Jeb simply walked up to the door, banged on it, and called, "John Brown! Lieutenant Jeb Stuart here. Please come to the door."

It cracked slightly, and a carbine, cocked,

was shoved through and pointed right at Jeb's belly. Behind it in the half-light, Jeb saw Old Osawatomie Brown.

Unconcernedly Jeb read:

"Colonel Lee, United States Army, commanding the troops sent by the president of the United States to suppress the insurrection at this place, demands the surrender of the persons in the Armory buildings.

If they will peaceably surrender themselves and restore the pillaged property, they shall be kept in safety to await the orders of the president. Colonel Lee represents to them, in all frankness, that it is impossible for them to escape; that the armory is surrounded on all sides by troops; and that if he is compelled to take them by force, he cannot answer for their safety."

Brown was silent as Jeb read the note, but as soon as Stuart finished, he began to talk. He made demands, he argued, he wanted this, and he demanded that.

From inside someone called, "Ask for Colonel Lee to amend his terms."

And another voice shouted, "Never mind us! Fire!"

Robert E. Lee was standing at least forty feet away, by a masonry pillar, but even at that distance he recognized the voice of Colonel Lewis Washington. "The old revolutionary blood does tell," he said.

Finally Brown shouted, "Well, Lieutenant, I see we can't agree. You have the numbers on me, but you know that we soldiers aren't afraid of death. I would as leave die by bullet than on the gallows."

"Is this your final answer, Mr. Brown?"

"Yes."

Stuart stepped back and waved his hat.

The marines looked up at Colonel Lee, who raised his hand. The marines battered in the door and rushed in with Lieutenant Green.

Colonel Washington stepped up and said coolly, "Hello, Green." The two men shook hands, and Washington pulled on a pair of green gloves. The sight of such finery was in odd contrast to his disheveled appearance.

Firing began, lasting for no more than three minutes. When it ended, a marine lay at the entrance of the engine house, clutching his abdomen. Old John Brown lay on the floor, unconscious from blows from the broad side of a marine's sword.

Lieutenant Stuart went in just as the firing stopped and the raiders were captured.

He reached down and snatched Old Brown's bowie knife to keep as a souvenir.

During the night, some congressmen and several reporters had come to Harpers Ferry. The leading men of Virginia quizzed Brown, who refused to incriminate others. He was perfectly calm and made no attempt to try to defend himself.

Finally one reporter asked, "What brought you here, Brown?"

"Duty, sir."

"Is it then your idea of duty to shoot down men upon their own hearthstones for defending their rights?"

"I did my duty as I saw it."

Colonel Lee and Lieutenant Stuart, having accomplished their task, were obviously finished. They remained in the town for another day, mostly to rest from their sleepless night. The next day they took the train back to Washington as casually as if Harpers Ferry were just an interesting interlude, no more.

But Old John Brown's raid was big news, all over the North in particular. Good and responsible men cried for his release and defended his actions as that of a righteous, godly man. And when they executed John Brown, he was lionized as a saint.

His death was possibly the first small

tendril of the clouds of war that would soon gather over America.

Revolution had for years merely been a political topic. But in November 1859, when Abraham Lincoln was elected president of the United States, the rhetoric was over, at last bursting into flames. The Southern states began to secede from the United States to form their own sovereign country, the Confederate States of America.

The beginning of the war took place in a fort just off the coast of Charleston. The man who lit the first spark was white-haired Edmond Ruffin, an editor and ardent secessionist at sixty-seven years of age. At 4:30 a.m., on April 12, 1861, he pulled a lanyard, and the first shot of the Civil War drew a red parabola against the sky and burst with a glare, outlining the dark pentagon of Fort Sumter.

Fort Sumter was a United States Army post, but it had no real military value. In April Major Robert Anderson, commander of the post, had few supplies, and the Confederates had turned away his supply boat. Fort Sumter was built to accommodate a garrison of 650 men, but for years it had only had a nominal military presence. On that day in April there were 125 men there. Forty of them were workmen.

The fall of Sumter was simply a matter of time. The people of Charleston stood on the balconies and the roofs of houses to watch the blazing of the guns and the firing of the shells. Major Anderson surrendered the fort the next day.

Thus the war began. Five bloody, terrible years lay ahead for America.

If ever men found themselves in a terrible position, the soldiers of the United States Army in the spring and summer of 1861 were well and truly caught in the worst. Many of the finest soldiers and officers were Southerners. Jeb Stuart knew each man would have to make the wrenching decision of whether to remain with the Union and fight against his home state or resign from the Federal Army and take up arms with the newly formed Confederate States of America.

However, for Stuart, whose undying loyalty was to Virginia, the decision was easy. As soon as President Lincoln called for seventy-five thousand volunteers to fight the war against the South, with Virginia's quota of eight thousand men, Stuart's mind was settled. He began packing as soon as he received notice he'd been appointed a captain in the 1st United States Calvary. On May 3rd, he wrote the Adjutant General of the U.S. Army:

Colonel: for a sense of duty to my native state (Va.), I hereby resign my position as an officer of the Army of the United States.

That very same day, he sent a letter to General Samuel Cooper, Adjutant General of the Confederate Army:

General: having resigned my position (Captain 1st Cavalry) in the U.S. Army, and being now on my way to unite my destinies to Virginia, my native state, I write to apprize you of the fact in order that you may assign me such a position in the Army of the South as will accord with that lately held by me in the Federal Army.

My preference is Cavalry — light artillery — Light Infantry in the order named. My address will be: Care of Governor Letcher, Richmond.

Jeb Stuart and his family reached Richmond on May 6th and found a commission waiting for him as Lieutenant Colonel of Virginia Infantry. The city was filled with men spoiling for a fight. The Army of the

Confederate States of America was quickly coming to life.

# CHAPTER SIX

To Flora, Richmond was dirty, noisy, and crowded. Men from all over Virginia were hurrying to the capital to enlist in the hundreds of companies that were putting out the call. The streets teemed with rough men, and the shops were always crowded and couldn't keep stocked.

Flora didn't have any friends in the city. The Stuarts had been in Richmond for only three days when she fell ill.

Their son, Philip St. George Cooke Stuart, had been born the previous June and was almost a year old. Little Flora was not quite four.

Flora bent over Philip's crib, and a wave of dizziness and nausea washed over her. Black spots danced in front of her eyes. She felt her way to the sofa and fell on it. For a moment, she tried to properly sit up, but she felt so weak that she finally just lay down on it.

Philip fussed for a few minutes, but then he grew silent again and Flora was glad he had gone back to sleep. Little Flora was on her bed in the single bedroom, napping. Wearily Flora closed her eyes to rest, though she could never fall asleep during the day when she was alone with both of the children.

Ruby had refused to leave Fort Leavenworth, for she had a new man and she had sworn that they were to be married. Flora missed her terribly.

She fought the feelings of bitterness that she felt because of the war that had brought her husband to this place. She was cooped up in a tiny house in a strange city with two small children, and she had barely seen Jeb since they had arrived. Drawing a deep shaking breath, Flora thought, *And this is only the beginning. He'll leave any day, and I won't know when he'll ever come back. I won't know if he's well or if he . . .*

She left the thought unfinished. But Flora was quite sure she would feel this same dread, for the war's duration, as a burden on her heart. She knew this, but she fought hard not to dwell on it.

After a while, the dizziness subsided and Flora got up and went to Philip's crib. He was still asleep, and no sound came from

Little Flora in the bedroom. She thought of Jeb, of how God had been so good to her in her marriage. She was to this day still desperately in love with Jeb Stuart. She knew every angle and bone of his body. She knew every inflection of his voice. Her eyes knew in detail every inch of that cherished face. With the single-mindedness only found in women so desperately in love did she think of him.

As she made her slow way into the kitchen, she prayed. *Lord Jesus, I need Your strength, and I need Your help. Please send someone to help me, Lord, someone who can help me with the children . . . someone who can be my friend.*

*And Lord, watch over Jeb, always.*

Jeb dismounted and went into the house. He called out, "Flora!" and heard her answer faintly from the bedroom.

He found her lying on the bed, covered with two thick quilts in spite of the heat. She was pale and had purple shadows under her eyes.

"Flora, my darling, what's wrong?"

"I'm — I guess I'm just tired," she replied weakly.

He laid his big hand on her forehead, his touch as delicate as a woman's. "No, you're ill. You're feverish. How long have you been sick?" Jeb had been gone for a day and a night, working with his new recruits, doing the mounds of paperwork required for a unit commander, meeting with his new officers.

Flora relented and said, "I started feeling a little unwell yesterday. I got up early and took care of the children, but I thought that I would just lie down and rest for a little while."

Jeb said grimly, "This won't do, Flora. I'm going to find someone to stay with you."

"Who?" Flora asked. "And however can you find a woman, just like that? You're so busy you don't have time for such things."

Jeb was stricken. The melancholy in his wife's voice and her words wounded him as surely as if he had been stabbed. He had a tender heart as far as his wife and children were concerned. He stroked her hair and said quietly, "I'm going to leave you just for a little while. I promise you that the Lord will help me find someone to help you and take care of you."

Flora managed to smile.

Jeb leaned over and kissed her and looked over at Little Flora, who lay beside her. She was asleep sucking her thumb. "There's my princess," he whispered and touched her silky hair. He straightened up and said, "I won't be long, my dearest."

"All right, Jeb. You're right. I know that the Lord will help us."

Stuart left the house, his mind racing and sorting through ideas. The problem was even more severe and immediate than he had let on to Flora. He had just received word that it was time for his regiment to report to Harpers Ferry, where he would be second-in-command to Colonel Thomas J. Jackson, and he couldn't think of a single person who could help him. He had to leave at dawn.

Finally he headed toward the fairgrounds. Many men from Richmond had enlisted in his command, and perhaps one of them would know of a suitable woman whom Jeb could hire as a maid and companion. Riding onto the fairgrounds, crowded with tents, he went straight to his headquarters.

One of his newest officers, Lieutenant Clay Tremayne, was on his magnificent black stallion, drilling six mounted men on maneuvering commands. Jeb watched them for a while with satisfaction. Though his command was infantry, many of the men had fine horses, and it was perfectly accept-able to their commander. He would have mounted all of them if he could, for he had wanted a cavalry command above all things.

When they finished, Jeb called Tremayne to him and said, "You cut a fine figure on a horse, Lieutenant. And you've learned the orders very well. You drill them like an old hand."

"Thank you, sir," he said with pleasure. He was a fine-looking man, six feet tall with broad shoulders. His face was strong with a hard jaw and dark, intense eyes.

Jeb frowned and shifted on his feet. "By any chance, Lieutenant, do you recall that man who was talking about having such a large family? He's from here, and his family has been here for a long time."

Clay thought and finally answered, "I'm sorry, sir. I know many of the men are from Richmond, but I can't recall exactly the one you're speaking of. Colonel Stuart, is something wrong? Do you need me to find this man?"

"No, it's a personal matter, nothing to do in particular with the man I'm thinking of," he replied, worried. "It's just that my wife is ill, and we have two small children. I really need to find a woman to come in and help her. It's very important that I find one quickly, since we have to move out in the morning."

Clay gave him a crooked smile. "Sir, I just

happen to know of a woman — or a girl — who is an excellent nurse. I can personally assure you of that. And she is here."

"Here?" Jeb repeated. "What do you mean? Here, at the fairgrounds?"

"Well, yes sir, she is. She's . . . rather unorthodox. But as I said, I can personally vouch for her character. I'm sure she would be happy to help you and your wife."

"Tell me more about her," Jeb said, his eyes piercing as they drilled into Clay.

"She is with her grandfather, and they are peddlers. Their wagon is here, and they've been selling goods to the men. She's young, only seventeen. And she wears, uh, breeches."

"Breeches?" Jeb repeated blankly. "You mean men's trousers?"

"Yes, sir. She's from Louisiana, and — oh, I think you'll understand better if you meet her, sir."

"Take me to her," Jeb ordered.

Clay led him to the north side of the crowded field, where a big wagon stood. Outside it a small man sat on a camp stool by a small campfire. The figure that knelt close to him, feeding small logs onto the fire, looked like a young boy. As Clay and Stuart drew near, she looked up, and then

Jeb could clearly see the delicate features of a girl.

Clay bowed, rather formally. "Sir, I'd like for you to meet two good friends of mine. This is Jacob Steiner, and this is Miss Chantel Fortier. This is Colonel Stuart, my commanding officer."

"I'm very happy to meet you," Jacob Steiner said, bowing his head. He was a small elderly man, rather stooped.

"You've just arrived in Richmond, Mr. Steiner?"

"Yes, although we've been here several times before. I've been a peddler for many years, and I've been all over. But I am beginning to believe that in these coming perilous days, the Lord has led us here, to the South, for a purpose."

"You're a Christian man?"

Jacob Steiner smiled. "You've noticed I am Jewish, but yes, I am one of those rare converted Jews."

Clay spoke up, "I have to tell you, Colonel, that Miss Chantel saved both of us."

"Saved you in what way?" Stuart asked with interest. He studied the young woman dressed in a man's trousers and shirt, with a floppy hat that covered most of her black hair. She had the strangest violet eyes. But in her gaze Jeb found kindness.

Jacob Steiner answered, "She found me sick on the side of the road and nursed me back to health. The same thing happened with Mr. — I mean, Lieutenant Tremayne. We found him wounded. My granddaughter is such a good nurse that he recovered very quickly."

"She's the best nurse I've ever known or heard of," Clay said vehemently.

Jeb Stuart was a man who could assess a situation and make quick decisions. "Miss Chantel, I have a problem, and I need some help."

Chantel asked him, "What sort of a problem, Colonel?"

"My wife has fallen ill. We have two small children, and she's simply not able to take care of them by herself right now. I need someone to come in and help with cleaning and cooking, but mostly to take care of my wife and children. Would you be interested in helping me, ma'am?"

Chantel glanced at Jacob. "If *Grandpere* agrees, I'll be happy to do what I can."

"Why, of course, Colonel," Jacob said readily. "Chantel is a good person and has a healing touch, I believe. If you need her to stay at your home, I will go and check on her and your family each day to see to their needs."

"Thank you, sir," Jeb said with great relief. "And thank you, Miss Chantel. I will be glad to pay you a fair wage."

"I don't need money, me," she said carelessly. "Grandpere gives me all the money I need."

"I'm glad of that," Jeb said, "but still I insist on paying you. I know this is very sudden, but I'm afraid that my command is ordered to move out in the morning. Would it be possible for you to come with me now, Miss Chantel, to meet my wife?"

"I will come," she answered. "Just let me get a few things."

She turned, but Jeb said, "Ma'am?"

"Yes?" she asked, turning back to him.

"I just wanted to tell you that you're an answer to a prayer. I'm very worried about my wife, but now I feel that you're going to be a very big help to her."

Chantel said warmly, "I will help her, and I will take care of your little ones, Colonel Stuart. And may the good God bless you and your men as you go to fight." Her gaze slid to Clay Tremayne.

Jeb noted that Clay smiled at her, but she merely turned and disappeared into the wagon.

Jeb opened the door to his home and motioned for Chantel to enter, following closely on her heels.

Flora was stretched out on the couch with Philip lying beside her. Little Flora was sitting on the floor, playing with a rag doll.

Jeb hurried to kneel by the sofa. He took Flora's hand and kissed it. "Dear Flora, the Lord has blessed us. This is Miss Chantel Fortier. Miss Chantel, this is my wife, Flora."

Flora said weakly, "I'm very glad to meet you, Chantel. I'm — I'm sorry I can't get up to meet you properly."

"No," Chantel said firmly. "You're sick, Miss Flora. That's why I'm here. And for these two darlings, too."

"This is Little Flora. She's a little grubby right now, but she's my angel. And this is our son, Philip."

Chantel took off her hat, laid her pack down by the sofa, and said in a businesslike manner, "First, I give Little Flora a bath, and Philip a bath. And then I give you a bath, Miss Flora."

Jeb laughed as he stood. "The best thing in the world for them. I'm already very glad that you're here, Miss Chantel."

"Oh, I am, too," Flora agreed. "I haven't felt like bathing the children. I haven't even felt like cleaning up myself."

Expertly Chantel picked Philip up and pressed her hand to his fat bottom. "First his cloths need changing, then baths. After that, I fix you something good to eat, Miss Flora, so you can get strong again."

"That would be wonderful," Flora said. "Jeb, are you going to be here tonight?"

"I am," he said slowly. "But there's something I have to talk to you about."

Chantel held out her hand to Little Flora, who immediately grinned up at her and took it. Carrying Philip, she led the little girl into the bedroom and quietly closed the door.

Flora searched Jeb's face, and then she sighed. "You've been called out, haven't you? When must you leave?"

"At dawn."

"Then," Flora said quietly, "it is very good that the Lord has sent Chantel to us."

Jeb knelt by her again and took her hand. "The Lord is good," he said. "He will never forsake us. Not you, Flora, and not me. I know that, wherever I go now, He is with me."

"Yes, He is," Flora whispered, pressing his hand to her cheek. "And wherever you go, I will always be here, waiting for you to come home."

■ ■ ■ ■

# PART TWO:
# CHANTEL & JACOB
# 1859–1861

■ ■ ■ ■

# CHAPTER SEVEN

Chantel Fortier came out of a deep sleep as a sudden and blinding fear shot through her. Hands were touching her body. When her eyes flew open, she looked into the face of her stepfather, Rufus Bragg. Bragg had a brutal face, and he was leering at her and running his hands over her body. Chantel cried out, "You leave me alone!"

"You need a man, girl," Bragg said, grinning like a sly snake. He grabbed the top of the lightweight shirt that Chantel wore.

She had been sitting up late with her mother and was exhausted, so she had simply gotten into bed without undressing.

"I know how to make women feel good," Bragg snickered. He gripped the top of the thin shirt and tore it.

Chantel struck out with both hands, fingers extended like claws, and raked Bragg's face. He cursed and lost his grip on her. As he did, Chantel rolled to the other side of the bed and jumped up into the corner. She was trapped in the room, and Bragg was laughing at her.

"I like a woman with spirit," he growled, moving slowly around the bed.

Chantel whirled and picked up the sawed-off shotgun that was leaning on the wall beside her bed. She had put it there for just a time like this, for this wasn't the first time her stepfather had put his hands on her. She drew back the twin hammers, and the deadly metallic clicking stopped Bragg in his tracks.

He stared at her, his eyes narrowing, "You wouldn't have the nerve to shoot me, little girl."

"Get out of here or I'll give you both barrels!" She was deathly afraid but determined. "You leave me alone, or I swear I'll kill you, Bragg."

For a moment, he looked uncertain, but then he laughed in his ugly hyena bray. "You got some spit, Chantel. As soon as your ma dies, I'm gonna marry up with you."

"I would never marry you! Never!"

"You ain't but fifteen, and the law says you got to do what I say when your momma dies. Everything she has will be mine — and that means you, too. So you will marry me, too, little girl." He crossed his arms and nodded as if she had agreed with him. "I'm gonna have you, Chantel. You just make up your mind to that." With one last leer, he turned abruptly and left the room.

Chantel was so shaken she thought that her legs wouldn't support her. She sat down on the bed, trembling in every nerve. Bragg had been after her for over a year, since her mother had been sick. He found excuses to touch her, and he made crude remarks. The fear that had driven Chantel to fight him off turned into a sick emptiness deep inside her. Still she trembled, but now with a treacherous, nauseous weakness. With an effort, she leaned the shotgun back against the wall; then she fell on the bed and began to weep. Her body shook, but she muffled her sobs, for her mother was in the next room.

Finally the storm of weeping ceased. Chantel took a deep shuddering breath. She stood up and retrieved the shotgun. The weight of the gun gave her some courage.

*He'll get me . . . He'll never stop coming at me, no!*

Moving to the window, she gazed out at the bayou. The moon cast its silver image on the still dark waters, and the hoarse grunt of a bull gator broke the silence.

Chantel leaned over and put one hand

against the wall and began to pray. *I can't leave ma mere, good God. So You keep him from me, yes!*

Chantel's spirit was crying out for her mother, who was dying. She knew that her stepfather was evil and would never leave her alone. She'd never understood why her mother had married Bragg after her first husband, Chantel's father, had died. The thick hatred she bore for her stepfather was like a sickening sour taste in her mouth.

Chantel knew nothing about the law, but she suspected that Bragg might be right. *When ma mere dies, he'll take me.* The thought caused a wave of fear, as sharp as the knife she always carried. She lay on the bed, grasping her knife in its leather sheaf in one sweaty hand and holding the shotgun with the other. Chantel waited for the dawn.

At daybreak, just as the sun was coming up, Chantel heard the sound of Bragg riding away and felt a welcome relief. She rose quickly, still fully dressed, for she had been wakeful all night, expecting Bragg to come back into her bedroom at any moment. Hurriedly she went into the kitchen and fixed a broth of turtle soup for her mother.

Carefully she set a tray with the broth and some hot ginger tea. After staring at it for a

130

moment, she turned and ran outside, then returned with a piece of honeysuckle vine and laid it across the plain tray to make it look as pretty as she could. She then took the tray into her mother's room.

Even though her mother had been very ill for more than a year, still Chantel received a small shock when she saw her for the first time every day. She was so pale and thin! Her eyes were sunken, and her color was pale. Chantel forced herself to smile. "I have something good for you, Mere. You'll like it."

"I'm not very hungry, child."

"You've got to eat to keep your strength up, yes."

"Maybe just a little bit."

Chantel set the bowl down and helped her mother sit up. Her mother's bones felt as fragile as those of a bird, and there was practically no flesh on them. The doctors had said that it was "the wasting disease" and they could do nothing for her. In the last two months it had seemed that the life was draining out of her moment by moment.

Chantel fed her mother, but she could eat only a few spoonfuls of the broth. Wearily she then said, "I can't eat no more, me."

"Maybe you eat some later."

"Chantel, sit down. There is something I must say."

Chantel put the tray aside and drew a chair close to the bed. "What is it, Mere?"

Her mother reached out and took her hand. "The good God has told me that it's time for me to go."

"No, Mere, you mustn't say that!"

"It is the good God who has told me this in my spirit. You must not grieve for me. I'll be glad to go home, I'm so tired and I hurt so bad."

"Maybe you get better."

"No, Chantel, you know I won't, and I'm ready. I want you to listen carefully."

"Yes, Mere, what is it?"

"I've been praying for you to find the Lord Jesus, and you will. But when I'm gone, you must leave this place. You must go to my sister Lorraine in Mississippi."

Chantel didn't question her mother, for she knew that her mother was aware of Bragg's evil ways, and this was her attempt to protect her. "It will be safe for you there. Promise me, *cherie!*"

"I promise," Chantel said, "but my heart is breaking for you."

Her mother pressed her hand. "God has appointed us a time to go, and it will be good for me. Now I pray that God will watch over you." She bowed her head and began to pray.

As she did, Chantel felt the tears begin to run down her cheeks. She wiped her eyes on her sleeve, and after her mother ended her prayer, she said, "It will be well, ma mere. God will take good care of me."

Chantel left the room, carrying the tray, her heart as heavy as it had ever been. She knew that her mother couldn't live long. She also knew that as soon as she was gone, Bragg would be after her, and there was not a soul in the world who could help.

Chantel had helped her father make the boat called a pirogue before he died. She remembered as she pushed it out into the dark waters of the bayou how they had worked on it together. He hadn't lived long after this, but he'd taught Chantel how to get through the waters of the bayou and the swamp in the frail craft.

Taking up a pole, she pushed off from the shore, and the *pirogue* seemed to glide across the water. The smell of humus was thick in her nostrils. She glanced up as a flight of brown pelicans in a V formation made their way across the sky. The sun was as yellow as an egg yolk. Despite the heaviness of her heart, Chantel admired the beautiful wild orchids that carpeted the still waters. Then she made her way through large pools, green with lily pads that clustered along the bayou's banks. They were bursting with flowers. She quickly went into the heart of the bayou, where she watched a flight of egrets, then a blue heron lifting its spindly legs carefully, its needlelike beak darting down on a fish. He tossed the fish up in the air, caught it, and swallowed it. Chantel smiled as it went down his long thin neck. "You have a good breakfast, you," she said.

The air was moist and cool, but it wouldn't remain so long. She reached the enormous cypress, where she had tied one end of a trotline. She started to pull up the line, and she felt it trembling. "I got me a big fish," she said with satisfaction. Even as she spoke, a flash of white caught the corner of her eye. She whirled around quickly and saw a cottonmouth that was thicker than her leg. The white in the mouth was exposed, giving it the name. She smelled the stench that these snakes give off, and it made her shudder. Quickly, Chantel reached down and picked up the shotgun. In one smooth motion, she loaded it and pulled one of the triggers. It tore the monster's head off, and Chantel nodded with satisfaction. "You ain't gonna bite nobody no more, you!"

She looked around to be sure that there were no alligators. She saw none, so she began to run the trot line. She pulled up the line, and on the third baited hook, she found a large catfish that weighed over six pounds she assumed. Carefully she pulled it off, avoiding the spines, which were poison. When it was free, she kept her thumb in its mouth, holding it carefully. She picked up a pair of clippers and clipped off the spines, then tossed the fish into a sack that she had brought.

Picking up the line, she continued to check for more fish. Many of the baits had been lost, but finally the line resisted her. "I got me something down there," she said. She tugged at the main line, and finally the head of a huge snapping turtle appeared. He'd swallowed the bait and was now snapping at her and hissing. "You go on and hiss, old turtle. You're gonna make a nice soup, I tell you." She heaved the turtle into the boat, and with the hatchet she always carried, she chopped off its head. The mouth kept snapping as it lay in the boat. She picked it up with her thumb and forefinger and threw it into the swamp. "I gonna eat you tonight, me."

She continued until she'd run the trotline; then she reversed the boat and headed back. As she reached the shore, she saw Ansel Vernier, a good friend. "Ansel, I got plenty of fish. I give you some."

Ansel helped her pull the pirogue to the bank. She pulled a large catfish out and handed it to him. He spoke in French saying, "Thank you, Chantel. You have good luck today."

"See this big turtle? He'll make a good soup. Come over tomorrow. I give you some of it."

"Maybe I will."

Ansel was a small dark man with a mouth as big as the catfish he held in his hand. He now said, "How is your good mother?"

"Not good at all, Ansel, very weak."

"I will pray for her and light a candle when I go to church." He shot an unhappy glance toward the house then turned to her. "Is Rufus at home?"

"No, he's gone to get drunk in town. I wish he'd just stay there."

Ansel nodded. He knew that Bragg was an evil man, and he feared for Chantel. "What will you do when your mother goes to God?"

"I will stay here, me. This was ma pere's place."

Ansel was troubled. "Thanks for the fish. Let me know if you have trouble, little one."

Two days passed and Chantel knew that her mother couldn't live much longer. She had no family, but the Cajuns who lived close in the bayou came by. They tried to comfort her, and they brought food, which her mother was too sick to eat. Chantel was just too grieved.

Eventually Bragg came home drunk. As he entered the house, he grabbed at Chantel.

She whipped her knife out of the sheath.

"That's all right, Chantel. I'll have you soon."

"You'll never have me!"

"Yes I will. You'll see."

That night Chantel sat up with her mother, who was in a terminal sleep. Her breathing was barely discernible. She finally woke up sometime in the early hours. "I go to meet — Him. May the good God take care of you."

Her mother didn't move again, and Chantel was unable to tell the moment when she left this life. She folded her mother's hands across her breast as the hot tears rolled down her cheeks.

She was only fifteen, and she was more

alone in the world than any fifteen-year-old ever should be. She knew that she would have to leave, but she knew that no matter what Rufus Bragg did, she had to see her beloved mere buried like the Christian woman that she had been.

Chantel was surprised at how many people came to the funeral. The priest was there, and the neighbors, young and old. Most of them had known Chantel's mother for many years. They all came by, some of them embracing her, all of them expressing their grief.

Ansel came by and took her hands and kissed them. "Why you not come and stay with me and my family? You be safe there, cherie."

"I'll be all right, me," she said dully.

Chantel noticed that none of them said much to Bragg. He seemed to expect it. His eyes rested on her often. Every time she caught him looking at her, fear grasped her.

Father Billaud was one of the last to leave. "What will you do now, Chantel?"

"I will stay here. This was ma mere's house, ma pere's house."

The priest was obviously upset by this. "It may not be the best thing for you."

Chantel shrugged.

"Do you have no other relatives?"

"My mother has a sister who's in Mississippi. Maybe I go there."

"I think that would be the best. Come to me if you need help, child."

"Yes, Father."

As Billaud turned and left, Chantel followed him out. They saw Bragg outside waiting, it seemed, for Father Billaud to leave.

He was a small man, this priest, and there was a light of anger in his eyes. "I will warn you, Rufus Bragg, that if anything happens to that girl, you'll pay for it."

"You would make me pay, priest?" Bragg was laughing at him. "Nothing will happen to her. After all, I'm her family."

"You're an evil man, Bragg. You mind what I say. I will have the law on you."

"There ain't no law in the bayou. Now get off my land, priest!"

Father Billaud had no choice. He turned and walked away.

Chantel heard Bragg laughing at him as he left.

Four days after the funeral, Chantel was alone in the house. Rufus had gone out again to get drunk. She had been afraid, and she fastened her door with a bar that she used each night. She also kept her shotgun and knife beside her. She didn't see Bragg that day, but still she lay awake for a long time. Finally, she drifted off to sleep.

She awoke to the sound of a crash and saw the door, battered and hanging on its hinges. Bragg came in, his eyes red with drink and lust written on his face. "I'm gonna have you, girl, just like I said."

"You leave me alone!"

"No, I won't. Not ever." He reached out and grabbed her. Chantel ran to the door. He was drunk and clumsy, but fast for a big man. He grabbed at her gown, which tore off one shoulder. He laughed. "You ain't gonna have no place to run, you!"

Chantel dodged as he made another grab for her. She ran to the fireplace and grabbed the iron poker. Moving faster than she ever knew she could, she turned, swung with all her strength, and hit him in his head.

He staggered back and put both hands to his forehead. Then he held them up in front of his eyes, and they ran with blood. "I'll get you for this, Chantel!" he growled. He moved toward her again, reaching out to grab the poker.

But Chantel took a quick step back, then hit him again, a solid blow.

This time his eyes rolled up. He went to his knees and fell forward.

Chantel could hardly breathe. "I have killed him," she whispered. She then saw that he was breathing.

She ran back to her room and dressed quickly. Earlier that day, she'd already decided to leave, for she knew this would come sooner or later. She grabbed the sack filled with her mother's jewelry that she'd kept hidden from Bragg. She had the money from her father that they'd never told Bragg about. She left the room and went into her mother's room. She took the fine pistol that was her father's and the Bible that was her mother's. She went into the kitchen and began stuffing bacon, flour, and coffee into a bag. She then she added a frying pan, a saucepan, and a coffeepot.

She went back into the front parlor to see if Bragg was still breathing. She saw that he was, so she ran back to her room in a hurry. She grabbed two blankets and the sawed-off shotgun and went outside. She wrapped everything in two blanket rolls. She grabbed some grain for the horse, Rosie. She saddled Rosie, put the blanket rolls on, and then mounted the mare. "Go, Rosie," she said and kicked with her heels. The big horse moved ahead at a trot. She wasn't a fast horse, but she was a strong one and had stamina.

Chantel didn't look back at the house, but she stopped by the small graveyard where her father and now her mother lay. She bowed her head and tried to pray. All she could think to say was, "I'll be fine, ma mere. The good God will take care of me."

As she left their land she was thinking, *Bragg will come after me. I must leave the bayou.* With one last look behind her at the house and the dark waters just beyond, Chantel rode away from the only life she'd ever known.

# CHAPTER EIGHT

Chantel kept Rosie at a steady pace all night long, pausing only once to let her rest. Finally she stopped and wrapped herself in a blanket, and despite her fear of Rufus Bragg finding her, she fell asleep. Dreams came to her, and she woke once to find herself whimpering, drawn up in as small a space as she could.

The sun finally touched her face and awakened her. She rose quickly, her eyes going to Rosie, whom she'd tied out in a patch of grass that bordered the swamp. Rosie was still dozing.

Quickly Chantel gathered enough sticks to make a nice, hot cooking fire. She filled a pan with water, then spooned in the coffee and balanced the pot on two stones. As soon as the coffee was bubbling and wafting a delicious smell to her nostrils, she broke out the pan and fried up some bacon. When the grease had melted, she poured it out then tossed two slices of bread in to let them toast. She ate nervously, and from time to time she glanced back to the south, wondering if Rufus had gained consciousness and was already after her.

When she finished, she cleaned up the pots and utensils, packed them, and then fed Rosie some grain and watered her. After Rosie was finished, she saddled her and put the blanket rolls in place, tying them down with strips of rawhide. Mounting up, she said with a confidence she did not feel, "Come on, Rosie. We got places to go."

Rosie seemed tireless as Chantel rode all day, only pausing once to rest. She was still in bayou country. The air smelled of the soaked earth. Once, far away, she saw a blue heron rising from the reeds and knew that it must surely be the bayou's edge.

She knew roughly where her aunt Lorraine lived. She'd been there once on a visit when she was only seven years old. She had made so few trips in her life that it was burned in her memory.

She rode until sunset and slept lightly. At dawn she rose, and she and Rosie continued on their lonely journey.

Chantel slept well that night. Already the hard riding and even the solitude seemed to be making her feel more peaceful and less afraid.

The next day she came to a crossroads that she remembered. More by shrewd instinct than remembrance, she took the right-hand road, due east. There were a few travelers on the road, but they were the first people she had seen since she'd left her home days before.

Eventually around midday, she came to the small town — really just a settlement of a dozen houses, a general store, and a blacksmith's shop. She remembered it distinctly and guided Rosie to the house where her aunt Lorraine lived. She saw that the huge walnut tree was still out in the yard behind the house. She remembered her mother gathering walnuts and breaking them with a hammer.

Dismounting in front of the house, she tied Rosie to a small tree. Then she went up to the door and knocked. No one came, and she grew discouraged.

She was about to go around the house to see if perhaps they may have outbuildings when suddenly the door opened and an elderly woman stood before her. "What you do here?" she demanded.

"I'm looking for my aunt. Her name is Lorraine Calvert."

"She no live here no more." She peered suspiciously at Chantel. "This is my place now, me."

"Where did she go?"

"She find a man, and they move away. Someone say they go up north to find work. Go away now. This is my house."

A bleak depression settled over Chantel. She was barely able to mutter a slight thank-you to the lady. She went back and mounted Rosie. She turned her head almost instinctively to the west to make sure Bragg wasn't there. Not knowing what else to do, she rode east the rest of the day, keeping a steady pace.

She stopped at an inviting little clearing by the side of a small river. Chantel filled her canteen with fresh water then let Rosie drink and graze a little as Chantel rested in the cool shade. But still Chantel felt closed in, and in spite of herself, pictures rose up in her mind of Rufus Bragg coming around the bend of the road at any moment.

They rode on. It seemed like a long, dreary day.

Finally the sun dropped beneath the horizon and darkness overtook them. Along with the darkness a fear closed in on Chantel Fortier. As she made her camp and cooked her evening meal, she felt more alone than she'd ever felt in her life. In some way, she felt more desolate than she had when her mother had died. She supposed that even then some hope for her aunt Lorraine had comforted her. But now that faint shred of hope was gone.

She lay down and put her hands behind her head, remaining wakeful and worried. After a time, she began to pray aloud, for it seemed to give her some comfort. "God, do You know I got nowhere to go? I got no people and nobody to look after me except You. I've lost ma mere, and now You are all that I have. Help me to find a place, me. Please, keep me safe from all harm."

She began to think. *I better keep going northeast. I'd do better in a big town. Maybe I could find some work, me. I can cook and sew and read and write and take care of horses. I can fish and hunt. Maybe I find someone to help me . . . someone to be with, to be friends with. Maybe I'll even find a home . . .*

Chantel had thought that she was too burdened and worried to sleep, but she was very young. She pulled her blanket closer around her and fell into a deep dreamless sleep.

The sun was high in the sky. Chantel had ridden steadily northeast after rising at dawn. She began to pass more travelers and realized she was coming to a settlement. She thought about cutting across the country to bypass it, but she did need more supplies.

It was a small but busy little town, with several houses, several shacks, and even a hotel. Businesses lined the main dirt road through the settlement: a tailor's, blacksmith, livery, mercantile, and two saloons. The biggest and finest of these had a sign: LAUREL GENERAL STORE.

Nudging Rosie ahead, she dismounted and tied her to the hitching post just outside it. In front of the saloon just down the road were two rough-looking men sitting on straight-backed chairs, with an upturned crate for a table that held checkers. As she went into the store, one of them whistled at her and said, "Hey, sweetheart, get your grub; then you can have a drink with Leon and me."

Paying no attention to them, Chantel went into the store and found no customers, but a heavyset, whiskered man was there working. He had pale skin and dark eyes with a droopy mustache that hid most of his mouth. "Good day, miss. What can I get you?"

"I need coffee, bacon, and a loaf of that

sourdough bread." Chantel waited in front of the counter as the man found what she asked for.

"Thirty-three cents, ma'am," he said. As she counted out the money, he cocked his head to the side and asked, "Where's a young lady like you heading all by yourself?"

"South. To Lafayette," she answered shortly, not looking him in the eye. Quickly she grabbed the bag of her goods and hurried out of the store.

She tied her sack to the pommel. She was anxious to get out of this dirty little town, and she would sort out the supplies later.

Out of the corner of her eye, she saw the two checker-playing men sauntering toward her. One of them was tall and had a slight limp. The other was a small man, odd-looking because his hat was much too big for him. He looked like a little boy wearing his father's headgear.

"Hello there. My name's Charlie, and this is Leon. What's your name, pretty lady?" the tall one asked her.

Chantel didn't answer. She grabbed the saddle horn and started to raise her foot to the stirrup.

The smaller man — Leon — said, "Wait a minute, there. Why don't we talk for a while? Make acquaintance, like? You'd like me and Charlie. We're nice fellows."

"That's it," Charlie agreed, sucking on a shred of a toothpick. "Come on. We'll buy you a drink."

"No," Chantel said evenly.

With her left hand she reached up again for the pommel, but the one called Charlie grabbed her arm and pulled at her, muttering, "Now just wait a minute here —"

Instantly Chantel drew the knife from the sheath at her side and held it up so that the sun glinted on the sharp blade. "Let me alone, you!"

Charlie laughed and put both his hands up in a gesture of surrender. "You don't need no knife. We just gonna have a little fun."

"No, we're not gonna have fun," Chantel said between gritted teeth. "I'm not going to tell you my name, I don't care what your names are, and I don't want to drink with you. And if you don't leave me alone, I'll cut you. I swear I will, me."

"She's a little spitfire, ain't she?" Charlie said with admiration.

"Uh — yep, she is," Leon agreed, but not with quite so much admiration. He was very slowly backing away.

With one last disgusted look at them, Chantel mounted, still holding the knife in her right hand. Without another word, she turned and headed out of town. Though she wanted to look back, she made herself stare straight ahead. Though no one could have seen it, Chantel was very scared, her heart skipping along like a wary little rabbit's. She whispered, "Thank You, good God, for taking care of me."

She was at least two miles past the settlement, riding again in silence and solitude, before she could calm herself down, and then a weary sort of numbness settled on her. Blindly, not knowing what new fears may lie ahead, she rode east with the sun warm on her back, but she had a coldness in her heart.

Ten days after her encounter with the two men, Chantel was still traveling steadily northeast. She was getting low on supplies because she was avoiding towns.

She had tried to stop once more, but the same thing had happened. A group of toughs were lounging around outside the saloon, and they called out and whistled to her as she passed. One young man with a knife scar on his face ran up to Rosie and grabbed her reins, grinning and calling Chantel "a pretty piece." Chantel had kicked his face then spurred Rosie to her fastest lumbering gallop, bypassing the general store without regret.

Right then she knew that, as young as she was and with the way she looked and traveling alone, it was bound to happen no matter where she went. Once again she stiffened her resolve and decided that if she had to she'd drink water and eat fish and small game.

She had traveled far from the bayou now, but it was pretty country. There were a lot of farms with cotton fields, and the few homes she saw were usually whitewashed two-story homes with painted shutters and deep verandas. The woods were deep and secret-looking, and sometimes Chantel thought she might like to just disappear into them and live there, like a wild thing that would not be tamed. But something kept her on the road, and something kept her going northeast. She was past questioning why. She just rode.

Not far off the road, she saw a nice farmhouse. A young lady sat on the porch holding a baby. On impulse Chantel went up the path to the house. "Hello, ma'am," she said uncertainly.

The woman was in her middle twenties and pleasant-looking. "Hello. Are you traveling alone?"

"Yes, ma'am, to my family in Tennessee, ma'am," Chantel said her polite lie.

"About a mile up this road there's a fork. The left one will take you to Jackson. The right one continues northeast, just a mule track, really, and it's a long way to the next settlement that way, all the way to Baxley. Would you like some lemonade?"

"No thank you, ma'am, I'd better be going on, me." Chantel left, with the woman staring after her. She came to the crossroads and followed the right-hand fork, which led in a more northerly direction than Chantel had been riding. The woman hadn't lied, for the road was no wider than the width of a wagon. She could even see the ruts that wagon wheels made.

She traveled on in her dogged way for two days.

That morning she awoke to a dirt-gray dawn and ugly dark clouds in the east. After two hours a light rain started and then turned into a downpour. Rosie was soaked, and Chantel was soaked, but she was lucky because she had a good piece of canvas that she could arrange over the saddle to cover the saddlebags that held her supplies. Still, she made a miserable sodden camp and wished she were back in her nice house on the peaceful bayou. Without Rufus Bragg, of course.

The next day the rain kept on, and she gave up and found a deserted barn. Half the roof was falling down, but the other half seemed solid enough. She pulled Rosie in and unsaddled her. She found enough dry wood in the barn to get a fire started. She took off her clothes and wrung them out and hung them on a few sticks and branches close to the fire. She fed Rosie and rubbed her down good. The barn still had some sweet-smelling hay, and Rosie munched happily on it.

Chantel was hungry and ate four eggs, all that she had left, a big greasy chunk of fried salt pork, and her last piece of bread. She huddled by the fire, glad to be out of the rain, savoring the warmth and comfort of the fire. She had managed to keep her blanket rolls dry, and after she ate she was sleepy. That night she slept sounder than she had in days.

She slept a little later than usual because the day was still gray. Though the rain hadn't completely stopped, it wasn't the mad torrent it had been the day before. At first she was tempted to stay in the barn, but whatever it was that seemed to be driving her made her decide to ride on that day. It rained off and on, and the twilight fell early, for the sun had never come out that miserable day.

Suddenly something caught her eye up in the road, and she pulled Rosie over. "Whoa, girl," she whispered. "There's something up ahead." It was just a big shadow, looming up right in the middle of the road. Cautiously she rode closer until she could make out that it was a wagon, stopped right on the track. She stopped Rosie again to watch. For long moments she listened, but she heard no sound and saw no movement.

She pulled the shotgun from the sheath and rode slowly past the wagon, giving it a wide berth. As she passed it, she saw a horse, still in the traces, lying in the road. It was obviously dead. Again she pulled Rosie to a stop, turned her, and called out softly, "Hello, is anyone here?"

The crickets had begun singing, but just barely louder than their shrill calls she heard a voice coming from the wagon. Dismounting, Chantel tied Rosie to the seat upright, still holding the shotgun. She went to the rear of the wagon, stopping once again to listen but hearing nothing. Finally she came to the opening at the back and lifted the canvas cover. No lamp was lit inside, but she could make out the form of a man lying on the floor. "Are you sick?" she asked hesitantly.

A man's weak voice answered. "Yes, I'm afraid I am. Very sick."

Chantel stood irresolutely, afraid of being out there in the wilderness, alone, and maybe trying to help a man who was not good, a man who might be like Rufus Bragg or the men in towns who looked at her so greedily and licked their lips. She shuddered a little but then closed her eyes and took a deep breath. Chantel knew herself. She couldn't ride on and just forget. She had to help this man. Whoever or whatever he was, she would not leave him here, like her, alone and frightened in the wilderness.

# CHAPTER NINE

With determination Chantel tucked up the canvas flap and climbed up into the wagon. She drew close and looked down at the man.

He was elderly, she could tell, lying flat on his back, and as her eyes grew accustomed to the dim starlight, she could even see the lines in his face. His hair and his beard were as white as snow. He didn't speak, and she could see that his cheeks were sunken in and his eyes were dull with pain. Even as he stared at her, his eyes began to close and his head lolled to the side.

She glanced around and saw that, although the wagon was huge, most of the space was taken up with shelves filled with goods of all kind. There were canned goods, fresh vegetables and fruits, bolts of cloth, hardware, tack, tools, and many small unlabeled boxes. The man lay stretched in the space between the shelves in the middle of the wagon, and there was barely enough room for her to kneel beside him. She spotted a lantern hanging just by the canvas flap for the opening, with a box of matches on a neat little shelf just underneath it. Quickly she lit the lantern and squeezed by so that she could kneel down by the sick man.

"You are very sick," she observed. Now that she could see him more clearly, she could make out the pallor of the old man's face, the skin that looked stretched too thinly over the bones. It was a death's-head look, they called it, and she had seen it on her mother.

The old man coughed weakly. "Yes, I've been very ill indeed. How did you find me?"

"I was just traveling along the road, and I saw your wagon. Your horse is dead, no?"

"Yes, that was the problem." Another coughing fit seized him and racked his small frame. When it passed he continued in a weak whisper, "My horse died, and I tried to dig a hole to bury him. But I was so tired, and then the rain caught me. I got wet and there wasn't any way to dry off."

"You're still wet," Chantel said, feeling the dampness of his clothes. "You need to get warm and put on dry clothes."

"Yes, but first some water, please? I had my canteen here, but I drank it all." Bewildered, he looked around.

Chantel knew he had a fever. When she had been feeling his clothes, she had touched his neck, and it was hot. She jumped up. "Never mind, you. I'll get water."

Chantel hurried to get her canteen and the tin cup she used for coffee. She filled it half full and gave it to him. She had to pull him up and hold him in a half-sitting position, but he drank thirstily.

"Could I have some more?"

"Maybe you drink just a little bit at a time, yes?"

"Maybe that would be better."

Chantel nodded. "It's still wet outside, but I'll build a fire and get you dried off."

"There are two tents stored under the wagon. One of them is much too large, but the other is small, maybe small enough for you to put up. There's also a small stove stored right behind the seat. In the cold weather, I heat the tent up with the stove."

"I can do this," Chantel said sturdily. She got her blankets and hurried back up into the wagon. She put one of them over him and rolled up another to rest against his back so he could stay in a half-seated position. Once again she refilled the cup and warned, "Little sips only, yes?"

"Yes, I'll do that," he agreed.

"I'll be taking the lantern. I'll need it to find everything," she told him.

He merely nodded, obviously exhausted, and his eyes closed again.

Chantel headed for the wagon opening and for the first time saw the fold-down steps that made it so much easier to come in and out of the wagon. Without hesitation she flattened herself in the mud beside the wagon and looked at the frame underneath.

Sure enough, there was a great roll of canvas that must have been a huge tent and another much smaller roll, both tied with sturdy rope and simple knots to the under-carriage. Quickly she untied the smaller tent and pulled it out. She had never had a tent, had never even been in one. But she had seen them before, and Chantel had a quick mind, so it took her little time to figure it out. She found the stakes and tent poles and immediately could picture how to stake out the tent and then raise it. This she did, quickly and efficiently. It was a small tent, but it was high enough for one to stand upright.

Secured right behind the driver's seat was a stove, and beside it was a box that held rich pine, which would burn almost in-stantly and was the best and quickest way to start a fire. The stove was small indeed, but large enough to warm the little tent and cook a little bit on the top. She set it down near the tent opening and laid the pine knots along the bottom.

Running now, she hunted, almost despairing of finding any dry wood, but not far off the road she found an enormous oak tree with many fallen branches, some of them as thick as her arm. The thick greenery of the leaves above seemed to have sheltered them from much of the rain.

Soon the stove was throwing out a cheery heat, and Chantel was heartened. But she looked around at the muddy ground and knew that she couldn't lay the old man on the ground.

She went back into the wagon and saw that the man was still sleeping, his head fallen to the side, his mouth slightly open. His breathing had a funny, rattling, wet sound. She sighed and held the lantern high to look around.

Soon she spotted them, cleverly stored, as all the many items in this wagon seemed to be. Folding cots were attached to brackets above the shelves, and they had thin but soft canvas mattresses. On a shelf underneath the neatly piled bolts of fabric were several blankets folded into uniform squares. Chantel hurried to make him up a bed in the tent, which was now pleasantly warm.

Returning to the back of the wagon, she climbed in and said, "I have the tent up, and the stove is making it warm. If I help you, can you go there?"

"I think so." The old man struggled, and Chantel went to his side and put her arm around him to lift him up. He coughed then smiled faintly and said, "I'm sorry for being such a bother."

"No bother to me," she said awkwardly.

She helped him as he took tentative steps. He was weak indeed, and she practically had to carry him. It took them a long time to reach the tent. Immediately he collapsed onto the cot gratefully.

"Mister, you need to get outta those wet clothes."

"Yes, I'm — so — very cold."

Chantel went back to the wagon and found some dry clothes for him. She returned and saw that he had been able to sit up on the edge of the cot and remove his shirt. "Here, put this warm shirt on." She helped him put his arm through the sleeve and buttoned it up. "You lie down. I take your pants." The old man didn't argue. He lay back, and Chantel lifted his feet and legs onto the cot. She removed his sodden shoes and wet socks, and she put on a pair of thick socks she found with the rest of his clothing. He was very thin, and his skin was sodden, but he still burned with fever. She looked up and she saw that he had passed out again. It took a little struggle, but she finally was able to put the dry pants on him. She then put the blankets around him. "You be warm soon, you," she said quietly.

The old man didn't answer. By the dim lantern light she studied him. He was thin-boned, his cheekbones pronounced, his cheeks hollowed. His mouth was short and full, and he had a pronounced nose. She knew that he was old, but at fifteen years of age, she couldn't tell the difference between thirty and sixty. He seemed to be resting quietly now, so Chantel decided to take care of Rosie and investigate the wagon more. She was hungry, and she knew that when the old man woke up she should try to get him to eat.

First she went and untied Rosie and led her to the great oak tree. Although the rain had stopped, it was still the driest, most comfortable place she could think of for her sweet, hardworking horse. Chantel unsaddled her, rubbed her down, and gave her the last of the grain. There was grass growing underneath the tree, though, and soon Rosie was grazing contentedly.

For perhaps the dozenth time that night, she climbed back in the wagon. She rummaged around in the foodstuffs, and to her surprise she found something she had never seen before: chicken broth in a can. She set about trying to figure out how to open it; it seemed like it would be a dangerous business with her hunting knife. It took her a little while before she figured out the tool she needed to open it, and then triumphantly she found a can opener. She took a couple of carrots and stalks of celery and with satisfaction used her opener on the can of broth. Soon she had a thin but nourishing soup bubbling on the stove.

"It smells good."

Startled, Chantel turned to see that the old man was awake. "Hello," she said a little shyly. "You sit up and eat. It's good for you when you're sick." Again she had to help him sit up and propped him with some rolled-up blankets from the store in the wagon.

When he was comfortable, he asked, "What is your name, child?"

"Chantel Fortier," she answered, spooning up soup into the ever-useful tin cup.

"That's a French name."

"Yes, ma mere gave it to me. *Chantel* means song."

"Yes, I know. It's a very pretty name. It's very nice to meet you, Miss Fortier. My name is Jacob Steiner."

"How long since you ate, Mr. Steiner?"

"Two days, I think." He passed a trembling hand over his forehead.

Chantel said firmly, "I better feed you." She dipped the spoon in the broth, tasted it first, and then blew on it. "Ver' hot, too hot. I blow it for you, me." She blew on the spoon, tasted it again, and then fed it to him.

He opened his mouth immediately, swallowed it, and whispered, "That's very good, child."

"We feed you a little bit at a time." She fed him half the cupful of broth, but that was all he could manage. Again he asked for water, and Chantel gave him a small amount, again cautioning him to take small sips. "You're so sick, Mr. Steiner, you'll just eat a little, drink a little, then more when you're better."

He took several small sips then sighed tremulously. "I think you saved my life, Miss Fortier."

"You call me Chantel. Everybody does." She knelt down beside him and put the

165

broth down. "You want to lie down and sleep?"

"No, I want to sit for a while. The heat feels so good."

"You talk so funny — why is that?"

"Because I grew up in another country, Germany."

"Where's that?"

"Far across the sea. I've been here many years, but I know I still have an accent. You have an accent, too, Chantel."

"I talk like Cajun. That's what I am."

Steiner seemed to be revived by the warmth of the tent and by the warm food. He smiled a little, a gentle smile so genuine that Chantel could clearly see the kindness and warmth in him. The very few remaining wisps of doubt she had about him disappeared.

"Cajun," he repeated. "Creoles from the southern parts of Louisiana, I believe. Is that where your people are?"

"I have no family."

"You're all alone?"

"Yes, all alone."

"How did you end up on this abandoned road?"

She stared at him, bemused, and finally answered slowly, "I don't know. I just rode and rode and came here. It's a good thing for you I did, me."

Steiner smiled, "Yes, indeed very good. I owe you my life, child. I could feel myself getting ready to go meet God."

Chantel was silent for a moment. "My mother went to meet with the good God not long ago."

"And your father?"

"Him, too, but longer ago. And my step-father —" Abruptly she broke off.

Steiner shot a quick glance at her. "You were afraid of him?"

"He — he wasn't a good man. He wouldn't leave me alone, so I have to run away."

Jacob nodded sadly. "And so where were you running?"

"My mother had a sister. But when I got there, she'd gone, so now I have no one."

Jacob said quietly, "Well, that isn't exactly true. You have God and you have me. You've saved me, and now I'll be your friend."

Suddenly tears came to Chantel's eyes. She'd felt so alone so many nights under the canopy of stars. Even when the sun was shining and the world was bright around her, she had an emptiness in her that was almost like a physical ache. "That — that would be good, Mr. Steiner."

"Call me Jacob. Friends call each other by

their given names."

"Is Jacob a German name?"

"No, Jacob is a Bible name."

"You named from a man in the Bible?"

"Yes, in the book of Genesis."

"You're a Christian man then?"

"I'm a Jew, Chantel. Do you know what a Jew is?"

"No, I never knew any Jews."

"It would take a long time to tell you. Let me say this: I was born into a Jewish family, and we were taught that one day a Savior would come, a Messiah. All Jews are waiting for that."

"And who is he? Do you mean Jesus?"

"Yes, it is Jesus. Most Jews don't believe that. They're still waiting for a Messiah. I found Jesus as my Messiah, so now I'm a Christian Jew. That's very hard for some people to understand, but I love the Lord Jesus."

"Ma mere loved Jesus. She talked to me about Him sometimes."

"Do you have Jesus in your heart?"

"No, I'm alone, me." She hesitated then added, "I go sometimes to church, but I don't know what it means."

"Well, perhaps later we can talk about that."

She saw that his eyes were drooping, so

she said, "You sleep for a little. When you wake up, I give you more broth."

As she helped him to lie back down, he asked, "Chantel, shall I tell you something?"

"Yes, what is it?"

"I knew you were coming."

Chantel stared at him. "How did you know that?"

"When I was so very sick, it seemed as if I were awake, and I had a dream. Do you ever dream, Chantel?"

"Sometimes, but not when I'm awake."

"I still don't know if I was awake or asleep, but I dreamed that I wasn't going to die. I just knew someone was coming to help me, and so I rested better. Then I woke up and saw you, and I knew that God had sent you."

"The good God? I talk to Him sometimes, but He don't answer me. He didn't tell me to come. He doesn't know where I go."

"God knows you and has known you since before you were born. And He chose you to help a poor old man that was dying." He put out his hand.

Chantel instinctively took it. "I don't know about all that. I just know I find you."

"We'll talk later. I'm very sleepy." He lay back.

Chantel covered him with the blankets.

She checked the stove and then walked outside. She was fascinated with Jacob Steiner. She hadn't ever met anyone like him. His appearance, his speech, and everything about him was strange to her. She studied the stars for a while and then decided that she might sleep in the wagon. Making up a nice bed with one of the cot mattresses under her and a clean blanket, she thought about Jacob Steiner, about his dream, and about his insistence that God had sent her to save him. She thought that was just the old man's mind wandering in his sickness and settled down to sleep.

As she drifted off, it fleetingly occurred to her that maybe Jacob Steiner had been sent to save her.

The next day Jacob had improved considerably. Chantel fed him eggs, for he had a large supply. He ate three of them for breakfast. "You're a good cook, Chantel," he said.

"Anybody can cook eggs."

"People who can cook eggs always say that. But the people who can't cook eggs know better."

The sun had come out and the earth had warmed up. The smell of the earth and the woods was strong in Chantel's nostrils, and she sniffed appreciatively. Then she turned to him and said, "You rest some more, Jacob. I think you'll need to rest a few days. I'll cook for you, and you'll get better and stronger. Right now I'll get Rosie, me, and we'll move your poor old horse far away. Not good to be so near dead animals."

"You're a very resourceful child, Chantel," he said, settling back down on the cot.

"I don't know what that means, me," she said uncertainly.

"It means that I'm glad God sent me such a smart and strong girl to help me," he said then closed his eyes.

For three days Jacob rested. Chantel cooked for him and helped him get up and walk around for a while on the third day. Even she realized that, as sick as he had been when she found him, it was amazing that he recovered so quickly.

He talked to her, and she found it easy to converse with him. Surprising even herself, she told him all about her mother, the tragic death of her father, and her evil stepfather. She told him all about her journey, how frightened and lonely she had been. Finally she was able to admit how glad she was that she had found him.

"It was a miracle of God, my dear," he

told her over and over. "A miracle for me and a miracle for you."

He read the Bible to her, and even though she didn't understand much of it, it gave her the same warm, secure feeling that she used to have when her mother was alive. Her mere would read to her on the long, velvet nights on the bayou, her voice quiet and soothing, and Chantel felt as if the world was a good place, and her life was rich and would always be happy.

Oddly, in the hours Jacob Steiner read to her, sometimes this same peace would steal over her, an almost forgotten dream. She still thought of the good God as a very great Being, off somewhere up in the sky, who talked to a few lucky people like her mother and Jacob Steiner and Father Billaud. It was a worship of Him, of a sort, and in Chantel's childlike way, she loved Him. Considering the hardships of the past month, that in itself was a miracle.

The wagon lurched in the deeply rutted road. Chantel and Jacob were tossed from side to side. But now Jacob knew he was strong enough to ride most of a day, with two or perhaps three rests.

The wagon lurched again, sticking a little in the old timeworn tracks. But Rosie was a strong animal, so she pulled the wagon easily.

Jacob commented, "That's a good horse you have."

"She's not fast but ver' strong."

Jacob didn't say anything for a while, thinking on an idea that had been forming over the last couple of days. Finally he turned to her and said, "You're running away from this evil man, your stepfather."

"It wouldn't be good if he finds me."

Jacob nodded. "You do well to be afraid of men like that. I've been praying, and I believe that God wants us to travel together."

"Together, you and me?"

"Yes, and we'll help each other."

"How will we do that?"

"Well, you see, you, Chantel, have a horse. And here I am with a wagon."

Chantel laughed, something she had been doing more often lately. "They go together, they do."

"Yes, they do. Let me tell you what I do. I am a peddler. I buy materials and food cheaply, then I go through the country and I stop at houses. I stay in the country mostly, for people there can't get to stores as often. I sell the goods, and when I run low, I go buy more goods. I have a good business. And I would like for you to be my partner."

"A partner?"

"Yes, we'll work together. I'm getting old now. Have you wondered how old?"

"Yes, me, I am fifteen."

"And I am sixty-one, and I cannot do what I could when I was young. You're young and strong. You can do the things I can't do." He could see that she was considering it, her eyes alight. "Would you like to do that?"

"Yes, I would like to, me. I'll go with you, Jacob."

"I'm very pleased." He smiled as his eyes rested on her. "The Bible says that two are better than one."

"That is true," Chantel agreed with a deep sigh. "I've been one. I don't want to be one, me."

"You and I are partners. We will help each other. The good God will look after us."

Chantel sat back, relaxed,

Jacob watched her. He could see a peace come over her face. He recognized that much of the hurt and the fear she carried with her was in the process of healing.

*God, You must help me to be good to this young woman. Keep that evil man far away from her, and help us that together we can find a way to serve You. I pray this in the name of Jesus.* And he whispered, "Amen, and Amen."

# CHAPTER TEN

"I guess you know what you're doing, Morgan, but if I was you, then I'd let Clay simmer down in there for a week or two."

Morgan Tremayne shrugged and said, "Well, Mac, if I thought it would do Clay any good, I'd do that. But it doesn't seem to matter if he's in jail or out. Clay is just Clay."

Mac Rogers, the jailer in charge of the Richmond jail, scratched his face. His fingernails rasped across his unshaven cheek. "How many times is this you've bailed him out?"

"Too many."

"Why don't you quit doing it then?" Rogers asked. "It's just throwing money down the drain."

"He's my brother, Mac. Family, you know. You're just stuck with them."

"Well, it's your money, Morgan. I'll fetch him for you." He took the twenty dollars that Morgan handed him, jammed it into his pocket, and went through the back door leading to the cells.

Left alone in the office, Morgan stood with his feet planted firmly, staring into space. He waited without moving until the door opened again and his brother, Clay Tremayne, came in. As always, Morgan couldn't keep himself from comparing himself to his brother and feeling he came up lacking in many ways.

Morgan was six feet tall, but he was not a large man. He was slim and lithe, with smooth muscles. He took after his mother, with dark auburn hair and dark blue eyes. His face was finely modeled, with a thin nose and wide mouth.

Clay Tremayne was as tall as Morgan but was more strongly built. His hair was dark brown, almost black, and he had brown eyes with thick curly eyelashes. His face was more masculine than Morgan's fine features, with a strong jaw and high cheekbones. He was a fine-looking man, well-built and athletic. There was a rashness and devilment in his smile that seemed typical of everything that Clay Tremayne was.

"I knew you'd be here to rescue me sooner or later," Clay said with that familiar smile on his handsome face.

"Why do you have to make such a fool of yourself, Clay?" Morgan asked.

"Because everything I'm not supposed to do is what I like to do."

"Don't you ever feel bad about the way you're treating your family?"

"Once in a while" — Clay shrugged — "my conscience hurts me a little bit. Maybe I'll straighten up one of these days."

"Clay, you've been getting into these scrapes ever since we were kids. You're not happy; you know you're not. You need to let God into your life."

Clay stared at Morgan and the smile disappeared as if an unpleasant thought had come to him. "Why don't you give up on me, Morgan? God has."

"That's not true."

"It is true, and I don't blame Him. I tried God, but it never worked out."

"No, you've never tried God. You've done what you wanted to your whole life, and most of those things are not good."

"I know," Clay retorted shortly. "But they sure can be fun. In any case, I appreciate you bailing me out, Morgan. You're a good fellow."

They went outside. Morgan's horse was hitched there, and just down the street — perhaps luckily for Clay — was the Planter's

Hotel, where Clay kept a permanent apartment. Morgan mounted up then said, "Clay, I've got to warn you about something."

"What is it this time?"

"Stay away from Belle Howard. And stop your gambling."

"Why should I stay away from Belle? She's one of the best-looking women I've ever seen. And as for the gambling, I win more than I lose."

"Well, I guess maybe your gambling is your business, but with Belle you're playing with fire. Don't you realize the Howard family is as proud as Lucifer?"

"I'm not running around with Belle's family, just her."

Morgan's eyes narrowed, and then his lips grew tight. "Clay, you know her brothers are fire-eaters. They almost killed Shelby Stevens. He wasn't doing much more than looking at her."

"Ah, those fellows have an overdeveloped sense of honor." Suddenly Clay grinned. "Belle doesn't, though."

Morgan grimaced. "Why is it, Clay, that you always want what you can't have? There are plenty of loose women for you to chase after, but Belle Howard is a different story. She's from a respected family, she's supposed to be a lady, and if you mess with

179

her, it can get you killed."

"Not if they don't catch me," he said, grinning.

That same night Clay went to the Silver Slipper with only five dollars in his pocket. He boosted it up to fifty playing blackjack. He didn't like blackjack all that much, so he soon found a poker game. For over two hours he played, losing some but winning more.

His chief opponent at the table was Lester Goodnight. Clay told him carelessly as he shuffled, "You need to find another hobby besides poker, Les."

"I'm a good poker player, but somehow when you play I never win." He sat up straight on his chair. He was a thin man with stubborn features and a ready temper. "Nobody wins as much as you do on luck alone."

Clay's eyes narrowed and darkened to a smoldering black. "You want to explain what you mean by that, Goodnight?"

Goodnight had lost a great deal of money. He leaned forward, and as he did, the gun at his side was clearly visible. "I'm saying a man that wins like you do isn't a straight player."

Kyle Tolliver had been in the game, and

now he leaned forward and said, "Clay, let's get out of here." He was Clay's best friend, and he saw that Goodnight had been drinking and was known to pull a gun on other men.

Clay turned and grinned at Kyle. "My family must pay you a fee to follow me around and make sure I do the right thing."

"Let's go. You've won enough."

"He ain't leaving until he gives me a chance to win back my money," Goodnight muttered.

Clay considered him, his gaze still fiery, but then he suddenly appeared utterly bored. "How about tomorrow night, then? I'm tired. I didn't get much rest in that jail, Les."

"All right, you be here tomorrow or I'll come looking for you."

"I wouldn't do that if I were you," Clay said casually, rising and straightening his cuffs, flicking off an imaginary speck. "You don't know what kind of mood you might find me in. I'm in a pretty good mood tonight, or I might have taken offense at some of those fool things you said, Les. I'll be right here tomorrow night. You just be here and bring your money."

Kyle and Clay left the Silver Slipper and headed back toward the hotel. Kyle grumbled, "You could've been shot back there. What's even worse, I could have been shot back there."

"Oh, Goodnight ain't gonna do that. He's just sore from losing. He needs to learn how to lose gracefully, don't you think?'

"I think I don't want to go through any more duels over your dumb honor again," Kyle retorted. "Poor old Manny Clarkson bled like a slaughtered pig."

"Squealed like one, too. Aw, c'mon, I never meant to kill him. You know that, Kyle," Clay said good-humoredly. "He's just like Lester Goodnight. Needed a lesson in manners."

"Right, just like I said. I don't want you to feel like you have to teach some manners to Lester Goodnight, even if you do just shoot him in the shoulder. Maybe going to the Silver Slipper tomorrow night isn't such a good idea."

"You sound like Morgan. He gave me a sermon this morning about gambling. And about leaving Belle Howard alone."

"Morgan has sense. You should listen to him."

"I do listen to him. I've always listened to him. It's just that I don't necessarily do all that stuff he says."

Kyle insisted, "Morgan's a good man, a

smart man, Clay, and you know it. He's a man to listen to."

"All he did was tell me to leave Belle Howard alone."

"That's good advice. Those brothers of hers will kill you if they catch you fooling with her."

"Aw, everyone's getting their knickers in a twist over Belle Howard. Truth to tell, Kyle, I've no plans to see her. I haven't called on her."

"Then why are you worrying Morgan and me so much by talking about her all the time?" Kyle demanded.

Clay shrugged. "Sorry, buddy. It's just too much fun."

Belle Howard and her sister Virginia had come into town from the family plantation outside Richmond. They were doing some shopping and made plans to attend a production of *Hamlet,* which was to be performed by a traveling group of actors at the Drury Theater.

The two women were in their hotel room, and Belle was trying to pick out a dress to wear. She finally chose a pink satin with white satin braiding trimming the many ruffles, held it up to herself, and turned to her sister. "What about this one, Virginia?"

Virginia was sitting down by a side table that held a silver tea set, reading a book. She looked up to answer her sister. "It looks very well, but it's cut too low in the front."

Belle Howard smiled and came over and patted her sister on the shoulder. "We're here to have fun, remember?" Belle said. "I know, Virginia, why don't you wear my pearls tonight? They would look so well with your new dress. And my pearl comb, too."

Belle Howard was two years younger than her sister Virginia. She knew she had a spectacular figure that men often desired. Her sister was a thin woman with mousy brown hair and brown eyes that often reflected dissatisfaction with Belle. In truth, Belle knew Virginia was jealous of her, which was natural enough. She couldn't possibly voice a complaint such as Belle had been given all the good looks and she'd been given none. Virginia was in fact smarter than Belle, but of course this didn't matter to the men who were only interested in Belle's beautiful features and buxom figure.

Belle patted Virginia again and said, "We'll have a good time tonight. Don't worry." She turned to the mirror, held up the dress again, and studied herself. She liked what she saw in the mirror, which was a woman with rich dark hair and velvety blue eyes that were shadowed by thick lashes. Her complexion was perfect, and her features were bold. She had a mouth that seemed to be made for kissing. She was full-figured; her waist was not as small as she would have liked, but tied into a strong corset she had an hourglass figure. Belle sighed as she glanced back at her sister. She was well aware of Virginia's resentment, but there was nothing she could do about it.

A knock on the door sounded. Virginia rose and said, "I'll get it." She opened the door and found Amy Cousins waiting. "Come in, Amy."

Amy and Virginia were the same age and the best of friends. Amy was pretty enough but didn't possess Belle's startling beauty.

"I'm glad you were able to come," Virginia said, obviously pleased. "Are you looking forward to going to the theater?"

"*Hamlet* is such a gloomy play," Amy answered. "I don't know why we want to sit through it and see everyone die."

"Oh, don't be so grouchy," Belle said. "It'll be fun. You're looking so nice, Amy."

"Thank you, Belle. Are you wearing that pink? You'll look gorgeous in it, as you always do." She turned back to Virginia. "Anyway, Virginia, I want to ask you to stay the night with me, at our house."

"That's very nice of you, Amy, but as you see, Belle and I have this wonderful room."

"My cousin, Vincent Young, is visiting us," Amy said eagerly. "You know how fond he is of you."

Virginia paused. Belle knew her sister liked Vincent Young. He was twenty and rather bookish, studying to be a lawyer, but Belle had heard Virginia say that in the times they had met at parties and balls and dinners they had done very well together.

"I think Vincent is in love with you," Amy prodded her. "If you stay the night, you can spend some time with him."

"Papa would never agree to have Vince as a son-in-law," Belle said carelessly.

"Yes, he would. His family is doing well in their business. Vincent will be a successful lawyer one day. He is respectable enough to suit Father," Virginia retorted.

"I heard Vince tell my mama that he'd be a good match for you," Amy said.

"Did you really?"

"Yes, I did, but you've got to put your foot forward because he's shy. Won't you come stay with me? And then, of course, we would all go to the theater together."

Belle smiled, for she saw the interest that her sister had shown. "I think you should go, Virginia. I like Vince, and I think he is interested in you."

"Do you really think so, Belle?"

"I do."

"You come, too, Belle," Amy urged her. "You know we have lots of room."

"No, you two go along. I'll be all right." Secretly Belle was pleased, for she knew that as long as her sister was around her fun would be severely curtailed.

"If you think it's all right, Belle," Virginia said.

"I'll be just fine, and you two will have such fun. Now run along. I'll see you at the play."

Belle made her way to the theater, just down and across the main street of Richmond. It was scandalous, her going alone, but she knew that she was such a favorite of her father's that even if word got to him, nothing would be done about it.

She had been to the Drury Theater several times before, and she saw people of Richmond society whom she knew. She took her seat, which would be next to the Cousins family, but then changed her mind. *I'll have to stay away from Vince. I never told Virginia, but he was interested in me at one time. He may be Virginia's last chance to get married.*

She got up and moved to a seat well

toward the back of the theater. The play began, and she watched intently. Truthfully, however, she found Shakespeare hard to follow, so her mind roamed elsewhere. It was a very long play, too, and when it was over, she saw Virginia, escorted by Vincent Young, leaving the theater with the Cousins family.

Belle had no desire to see them. She found that she was tired and bored with the evening and decided just to go back to her room and make an early night of it. A couple of her gentleman acquaintances spotted her and begged her to let them escort her back to the hotel, take her to supper, come back to their homes for after-theater parties. . . . But rather shortly Belle disentangled herself from them. They were boring, actually, and represented no interesting new conquests.

When she reached the Planter's Hotel, to her surprise she saw Clay Tremayne lounging outside, smoking a cigar. When he saw her, he grinned and threw the cigar away, as men never smoked in the presence of a lady. It was just that usually ladies were not out on the street at this time of night.

"Belle! How wonderful to see you," he said, coming forward to take her hand and kiss it.

"Hello, Clay," she answered coolly. "How

are you? Did you go to see *Hamlet*?"

"No, I was in the card room, but it got so close and stuffy. And I am heartily sick of hearing talk about politics and secession. So I decided to come outside for some fresh air," he answered. "And to wait for you, of course."

"You lie, sir." Belle studied Clay carefully. She liked his manly good looks, and he was fine company. On two occasions he had halfheartedly tried to take liberties with her, but she simply laughed at him and shoved him away. It had irked her that he had given up so easily. She added, smiling invitingly at him, "You had no idea I was even in town."

"I'm caught. I certainly didn't know you were staying here at the hotel. May I invite you up to my room for an after-theater sip of brandy, perhaps?" he asked innocently.

"I'd just be another notch on your belt," she said drily. "You have enough of those already. Your belt is so notched there's barely room left on it for another."

"Either you're complimenting me, ma'am, or insulting me," Clay said mischievously. "I choose to take your consideration as a compliment. Now, please allow me to return the compliment and take you to supper."

"I don't know, Clay. I'm tired. I was just going to go to my room and go to bed early tonight," she said.

"It's just supper, Miss Belle," he said, grinning. He had a most attractive smile, full of devilment . . . and promise. "I heard a rumor that Wickham's Restaurant got in a shipment of fresh oysters today, particularly for the theater-goers. I do recall, do I not, that fresh oysters are a particular favorite of yours?" Wickham's was one of the few restaurants in Richmond that stayed open late on theater nights for the attendees to have a late supper.

Belle did love fresh oysters, and they were a rare treat. Still she hesitated. Going to the theater alone was just on the edge of respectability, but dining alone with a man in a public restaurant went over that edge. Still . . . she was suddenly hungry, and Clay did look particularly handsome that night in a black suit coat and tie and a silver satin waistcoat. "All right, Clay. You remember correctly, sir, fresh oysters are my favorite, and I suddenly find that I am overcome with hunger," she said, her smile dazzling.

Clay bribed the maître d' so that they would have a curtained booth to themselves. Clay encouraged Belle to order whatever she liked, and they frivolously ordered two dozen fresh oysters. Clay also ordered champagne.

Belle had only drunk champagne a couple of times before, but she loved it dearly. "What have you been doing with yourself, Clay, besides being in jail?" she asked playfully between oysters and continual small sips of the cool, fizzy champagne.

"You heard about that, did you?"

"Everybody's heard about it. I don't see why your family puts up with you."

"They have to. Key word is *family*, you see. They're sort of stuck with me." He quickly ate one of the oysters while staring at Belle. "And that's not necessarily a bad thing. I think, if you'd give me a chance, you might even like to get stuck with me."

"Oh? And whatever makes you think such an impertinent thing?"

"I don't know. But you really should give it a try, just to see, you know. I could start out by coming and calling on your father and sitting on your porch and courting you like the other young gentlemen do."

"I doubt you'd ever find a seat on my porch, Clay Tremayne," she said primly. "I would guess all you'd see is it flying by when my father booted you out of the house."

"He doesn't like me? That's hard to believe, isn't it?"

Belle laughed, a small ladylike tinkling laugh that she knew men liked. "I'm sure you think so. He wouldn't think about it for a minute."

They finished all of the oysters and the entire bottle of champagne. Belle hadn't noticed, but she had drunk most of it while Clay had merely sipped on two glasses. As they left, she felt light-headed, giddy — and reckless.

When they reached the hotel, Clay said, "You must let me escort you to your room, Miss Belle. A gentleman would never leave a lady on the steps of a hotel."

"That is very true," Belle agreed happily. "I am on the second floor."

"Are you? What a very great coincidence. So am I," Clay said. They reached her room, which was several doors down from Clay's apartments. "Why don't I go to my room and fetch a nice bottle of old brandy that I've been keeping for a special occasion? I can come back, and we'll have a toast. To *Hamlet* and to oysters."

A small voice in the back of Belle's mind insisted that this was a very bad idea, but she felt so happy and careless that she ignored the little nag in her head. "Oh, that sounds wonderful. Brandy is a fine spirit to top off a wonderful meal."

He bowed deeply. "I shall join you shortly then, ma'am."

Belle hurried into her room, took off her hat, gloves, and cape, and quickly patted her hair into place. She saw that the color in her cheeks was high, and her eyes were sparkling like stars. She reflected with satisfaction that she was in particularly good looks this evening. Perhaps it had something to do with the very welcome attentions of Clay Tremayne.

He returned with a bottle and two heavy crystal brandy snifters. She started to just drink from her snifter, but with a smile, Clay stopped her. "Fine brandy is much like a fine woman. You have to warm it up gently, savor its scent, breathe it in, before you finally partake of it."

Vaguely Belle knew that in another time and another place she might have taken some offense at this, but she couldn't quite work it out. Giggling, she rolled the brandy in the snifter, holding the crystal in the palm of her hand as Clay instructed, breathing in the intoxicating scent, and finally sipping the liquid.

The next drink, and the next, were not quite so polite and poetic.

She never knew afterward when it got out of hand, but she found herself falling more and more under his spell. When he put his arms around her and kissed her, she seemed unable to resist. *You don't want him to stop,* were the final whispers of that little warning voice in her mind.

Things were going exactly as Clay had hoped. He had Belle right where he wanted her and continued to press his advances.

"Clay . . . we shouldn't," she whispered weakly.

"We should," Clay answered in a deep voice, caressing her cheek and her neck. "Belle, I want you. I need you. You're so very beautiful —"

It was exactly at that point that the door burst open. Barton Howard, Belle's eldest brother, was standing there. His face was flushed with rage, and his eyes were glittering.

Before Clay could say a word, Barton drew a gun and fired. The bullet struck Clay in the side, and it turned him half around.

Even slightly drunk, Clay was quick. His own pistol was hanging from his belt, draped over the back of a satin chair by the bed. He pulled the pistol and fired in the general direction of Barton Howard, who stumbled, reeled backward, and fell face-down.

Belle stood and cried, "You've got to get out of here, Clay! They'll hang you if my other brothers don't kill you first."

Clay hesitated, staring down at Barton Howard. He was an excellent shot, and he surely never would have shot to kill Barton if he'd been sober. In fact, he had aimed just in the man's general direction, more to scare him than shoot him. But he had been drinking too much, and his shot was wild. Had he killed this man?

Belle knelt by her brother. She looked up at Clay, her eyes wide and horror-stricken, her face deadly pale. "He's still alive, Clay, but that won't matter to either of my brothers, Charlie or Ed. Don't you see? Even if you haven't killed Barton, you'll have to kill them — or let them kill you!"

Barton Howard, even now, was muttering and scrabbling vaguely at the floor.

Clay was still frozen, rooted to the floor, staring down at him.

Belle hissed, "Clay, don't be a fool. Run!"

Clay looked at her, and then his mouth tightened into a thin line. He knew she was right. He grabbed his pistol belt and his coat and shot outside her room. He could hear heavy footsteps pounding up the west stairwell and suspected that it was probably Belle's other brothers.

He hurried to his room and gathered up all his money. His side was red with blood, but he knew that the bullet barely grazed him. Cautiously opening the door, he could hear Charlie Howard's angry roar from the direction of Belle's room.

Feeling completely like a coward and a heel, Clay silently ran down the east stairwell and to the livery stables. Quickly he saddled his horse and mounted up. His one thought was to get away. He spurred Lightning into a run and headed away from the city of Richmond.

Entering his own sitting room, Dr. Ritchie said, "Barton's not going to die." The doctor was young for his profession, but he had a successful practice in Richmond. An earnest-looking man, he polished his glasses as he gave the news to Belle Howard and her other brothers. "The bullet hit him in the chest, but it bounced off a rib and missed all the vital organs. The surgery to remove it was tough, though, so he'll need to stay in bed, probably for several weeks."

Ed and Charles stood tensely by the fireplace, while Belle sat in a straight chair, bent over, her face buried in her hands. She looked up as Ed said, "Thank you, doctor." He then stared hard at her.

The doctor glanced at Belle, then at her two angry brothers, and returned to his examination room, where Barton Howard lay, still unconscious.

Ed muttered, "You've disgraced yourself, Belle."

Belle looked up at him beseechingly. It had been a horrifically long night. Her brother's surgery had taken hours. It was still an hour till dawn, one of the bleakest hours. Her eyes were so swollen from weeping that they were barely open. "I — I — I just drank too much, Ed. It got out of control."

Ed Howard shook his head, a jerky, furious movement. "You know what kind of man he is. I'm ashamed of you, Belle. Tremayne is a no-good piece of trash. What I want to know is where he was going."

"I don't know. How should I know? We — we weren't exactly discussing future plans," she said, burying her face in her hands again.

With a last disgusted look at his sister, Charlie turned to Ed. "His people live in Lexington. If he's hurt, he'll probably head there. Belle did say that Barton got off a shot. Even if it didn't knock Tremayne off his feet, Barton couldn't have missed at that range."

"He was bleeding," Belle moaned.

Neither of them seemed to pay any attention to her.

"He won't go home. He's the bad seed in the family, but he does keep them out of his affairs," Ed said reluctantly. "What about Atlanta? He's got Tremayne cousins there, I know."

"Why can't you just leave him alone?" Belle said, looking up and feeling a spark of life for the first time. Her very first inclination had been to blame everything on Clay, but Belle Howard was a strong woman, and she had her own sense of honor, in spite of the way she had behaved. "It's not like he blindfolded me and kidnapped me, you know. It's not all his fault."

Ed glared at her. "You're not going to be a tramp, Belle, if we have to keep you locked up, so you just stop that kind of talk right now. Tremayne is the one who has to pay for this. I'm not going to think any more about shooting him than I would about shooting a rabid dog."

Clay rode through the night, hard. He stopped once to check his wound. The bullet had hit him in the upper abdomen on the right side, had slid along a rib, and then had ricocheted out. He had a gash six inches long on his side, and he could see bare bone. Gritting his teeth, he poured brandy on it from a flask he always carried, thinking grimly, *And this is the last time I'm touching this stuff!* Then he tore up one of his white cotton shirts into strips and bound it up. It was extremely painful, but still he kept riding. He planned on riding straight through to Petersburg, where he could take a train to Charlotte, North Carolina. He had friends there, and some business connections. It never entered his mind to involve his family in this sordid affair.

Just before dawn, Lightning started limping, and Clay knew he had pulled a tendon. This was not too uncommon for hard-ridden horses, and not really serious, but the only way for the horse to recover was to rest. He knew of a settlement called Lucky Way about a half mile off the main road to Petersburg. After he turned off on the rough trail that led to the little town, he dismounted to walk Lightning so as not to stress his foreleg any more. "Let's just hope this really is a Lucky Way for us, boy," he managed to joke.

His plan was to stay out of sight, which he did. Ordinarily he would've gone to the saloon and gotten into a poker game, but he stayed in his own room in a dirty five-room boardinghouse. The only time he went out of his room was to stop at the general store, buy some horse liniment, and tend to Lightning.

He slipped around the town at dusk. It was a small town, which made it difficult to keep from calling attention to himself, but he spoke to no one except the stable hand and the surly woman who ran the boarding-house.

After three days, Lightning had lost all signs of soreness in his foreleg. Clay decided to ride on to Petersburg. It was a hard ride, a day and a night straight through, and Clay knew that he shouldn't put much stress on Lightning, but he realized that once they had gotten on the train, Lightning could rest up again. He left Lucky Way in a sad, blurry dawn that promised rain later.

Clay thought of little else but of what had taken place in Richmond. He cursed himself for a fool, and a stupid one at that. He knew he had acted like the worst kind of scrub with Belle. *I should've stayed away from her. She didn't deserve all this. I hope Barton doesn't die. That'll get me hanged for sure.*

Once he got on the main road, he kept Lightning at a steady fast trot that would eat up the miles. During the day, he passed several wagons and other riders, but the traffic waned as night fell. The whole day had been overcast, but it had never rained.

Now, dark ominous clouds scudded over the half-moon brooding above him.

About three hours after sunset, he heard riders behind him. Clay was not the type of man to always be looking over his shoulder with fear, so he had wasted very little time worrying about the Howards. If anything, he thought they might search Richmond for him and maybe contact Morgan in Lexington, but it simply had not occurred to him that they might hunt him down. So, since the unknown riders were moving at a fast pace behind him, and the night was so dark, he cautiously pulled Lightning over to one side to let them pass.

They drew nearer, two men, riding hard. They were still at least forty feet away from him when the black clouds cleared the moon. Even in the dimness, Clay recognized the bulk of big Ed Howard. At the same time Ed shouted, "That's him, Charlie! Standing right there! Ride!"

Clay spurred Lightning, and like his name, he bounded into a gallop so fast that the men fell farther behind. Still they rode, yelling like hounds baying.

Clay barely heard the gunshot before it seemed as if a giant had simply kicked him in the back. He flew through the air and landed in the mud. He felt himself losing consciousness, and his last thought before the blackness set in was, *I'm dead, God. You've finally killed me . . .*

The two brothers rode slowly to the side of the road and looked down at Clay Tremayne, sprawled facedown, unmoving. Ed lowered his shotgun then slowly dismounted. He kicked Clay, not very hard, in the side. "He's dead, Charlie," he muttered. "Miserable dog."

Charlie didn't speak. He dismounted his horse and stood beside Clay, then knelt down by him. He grabbed his hair and yanked up his face. Clay's eyes remained closed. Charlie took his pistol then started working on taking a diamond signet ring off Clay's finger.

"Stop it, Charlie," Ed ordered him in a harsh voice. "He's dead. We had to kill him for what he did to Belle, but we're no thieving trash. Just leave him."

Charlie grunted then stood and threw Clay's pistol down to the ground. "You're right, Ed. I'm not going to sink as low as he is. Was. Let the buzzards have him."

They mounted up and rode back north without looking back.

But each knew Clay Tremayne lay in the mud without moving.

# CHAPTER ELEVEN

"I think we need to celebrate, child."

Chantel sat loosely on the wagon seat holding the lines. Spring in the Southern states was lovelier than anything she had ever known. Sweet-scented breezes blew the trees back and forth so that they swayed like dancers. All along the back roads were foxes, rabbits, squirrels, and multitudes of butterflies. She turned to smile at Jacob, who was watching her intently. "What do we have to celebrate?"

"You don't know?"

"Well, I know things are going ver' well. We've sold lots of goods, and I think, Grandpere, that we've made a lot of money, you and me. Is that what we want to celebrate?"

"The Lord has blessed us exceedingly," Jacob agreed placidly, "and that is always something to celebrate. But what I meant was, we should celebrate the two years we've been together. If I'm not mistaken, it was as the month of March was ending, two years ago, that you saved me."

A surprised look came to Chantel's face. "Has it been that long? It has, yes? I'm seventeen now. I was fifteen, me, when I found you, Grandpere."

Jacob nodded. "Every day I thank God for bringing us together. I know I would have died if you hadn't saved me, daughter, and these last two years of life would not have been nearly so good as they have been . . . if they would have even been. I could never have continued in this work without you, Chantel. I can never thank God — or you — enough."

"Never you mind that, Grandpere," she said quickly.

Jacob still thanked her, often, and expressed his affection to her.

It embarrassed her, for though her mother and father had been loving people, they were not outwardly affectionate. "I've been so happy. My life has been so good, yes, so much better than I ever dreamed it would be." She reached over with her right hand and patted his shoulder a little awkwardly, aware of the thinness of his frame and the fragility of his bone structure. "We make a good pair, don't we, you and me?"

Indeed the two were very happy together, if they were something of an odd couple: the elderly Jew in the sunset of life and the exotic-looking young woman that Chantel had become. She had come into full bloom, and she had a dream of a figure, for she was strong and lithe and worked hard every single day. Her skin was an attractive golden hue, as Cajuns sometimes had, and her violet-blue eyes, wide-set and perfect almond shapes, were of startling beauty. She was in perfect health and always felt energetic and strong and eager for each new day.

Still, she had an abhorrence of male attention, so she stubbornly wore loose men's breeches and men's cotton shirts that were too big for her. She kept her trousers up with a wide leather belt that had her knife sheath fitted to it, for she still carried it, always. She crammed her blue-black hair up into a felt hat with a big floppy brim that half hid her face. Jacob had bought her two pairs of fine leather boots, one brown pair and one black pair, but no matter how he pleaded, Chantel would not let him buy her any women's clothes, even modest skirts and plain blouses, much less pretty dresses.

As they rode along, Chantel thought back over the last two years. They had indeed been good for her. Her fear of being caught by her stepfather had long faded, like a vague remembrance of a bad dream. They always traveled the South, crisscrossing the roads across Alabama, Georgia, the Carolinas, Tennessee, and Virginia.

"Pah," Jacob had grunted to her one time. "Business isn't nearly so good in the North. Too many cities, too many big towns, too many people all huddled together, and too many mercantile stores. Here the farmers are glad to see us because they need us. They are hospitable, and there aren't nearly as many ruffians riding the roads."

It was true. People received them everywhere they went. They were lonely on the homesteads, they were anxious to talk, and they definitely had need of Jacob's goods. Sometimes it could be three days' journey from a farm to a nearby town to get supplies.

Today it was an easy ride, for they were going north to Richmond, and it was a good road. For the last two months they had been lazily roaming around southern Virginia, cotton and cash-farming country, and business had been good. Most of the great plantations in the South were close to the big towns, like Charleston and Savannah and Atlanta and Richmond. It was the smaller farmers, farther from the cities, who welcomed the peddlers so happily.

Chantel glanced affectionately at Jacob. She had made a fine feather cushion for the wagon seat and had fashioned two pillows to fit in the corner of the seat, leaning against the back and the side upright. He had plumped them up and settled back in them, and Chantel thought he was falling asleep.

Before he dropped off, he murmured, "Virginia . . . I think it is my favorite . . . the Shenandoah Valley."

In silence she drove, enjoying the freshening day. The night before it had rained off and on, so Chantel had set up the little tent and stove for Jacob. Even in the warmth of spring he still was chilled at night. Last night Chantel had slept in the tent, but on clear nights she usually slept out under the stars, by a small, comforting campfire.

Now all traces of yesterday's lowering skies were gone. The air was fresh and smelled of wet dirt and new grass. Clouds of spring's first yellow butterflies floated in front of the wagon sometimes, and once a fat honeybee made a lazy dizzy flight alongside it for a while. Chantel watched it with amusement.

"What's this?" she asked herself. Just ahead, on the left side of the road, was a big black stallion. He was fully saddled, his reins hanging down to the ground. He seemed to be grazing, but as they drew closer, Chantel could see a lump on the ground. The horse was nuzzling it, it seemed, with some agitation.

"Grandpere," she said softly, so as not to startle him.

"Hm! Hmm?" he said, pushing his hat back and looking around sleepily.

"Just up here. Do you see him? A fine horse, he is, with no rider."

Jacob straightened up and stared. "What's that at his feet? Better stop the wagon, daughter."

By the time they drew up to the horse, they could see the man.

Chantel pulled Rosie to a stop and leaped down to the ground, her boots making a squishing sound in the deep mud as she ran. Sliding to a stop, she came to her knees right beside him. In the bright innocent sunshine, she could clearly see the matted blood in his dark hair and the dried blood on his back. One or two places were still oozing. She touched her finger to it and held it up to Jacob, who had reached her side. "Fresh," she said. "He's still alive."

Ignoring the wet ground, he creakily got to his knees beside the wounded man. "He's been shot in the back. It looks like with a shotgun."

"We'll have to get him to a doctor, Grand-pere," Chantel said in a low urgent voice.

Jacob shook his head. "It's still at least three days to Richmond. I don't know of any settlements around here, and if we start getting off the road hunting one, this man will probably die on us. We have to do what we can here, now."

Chantel bit her lower lip. "I can nurse sick people, me. But I don't know anything about gunshot wounds."

With some difficulty, Jacob got to his feet. "Neither do I, daughter. But I don't think the Lord has given us a choice about it, so that means He will guide us. You'll have to put up the tent. Thank goodness you were smart enough to start hauling stove wood in the wagon. It'll take us both to get him into the tent, but I know that we can help this man. Can you do all that, daughter?"

"Yes, I can, me. You watch what I do."

Jacob wasn't able to do much physical work. While Chantel put up the tent, he started gathering supplies he knew he would need. Before he was finished, she had put up the tent, made up the cot, and started a fire in the tent stove.

"What do I do now?" she asked breathlessly, popping up in the wagon's opening at the back.

"We'll have to get him inside. I'll help. Not much, maybe, but it will take both of us."

They went back to the man. The horse still stood close to him, though he shied a little every time Chantel and Jacob drew near.

"I'm strong, Grandpere. I can probably drag him to the tent. I'm afraid I'm going to hurt him though."

"Better hurt him than let him die."

Chantel rolled the man over and reached under his arms. He was a big man and strongly built. She began to back up to the tent that she had set up in a shady stand of three big oak trees, not far off the road. Although she was indeed a strong young woman, the man's heavy weight was hard to handle, and she had to stop twice. She was breathing hard and grunting by the time she got to the tent.

When she finally dragged him inside and up to the cot, she looked down doubtfully. "Do you think we can get him up on the cot, me and you?"

"I can do that much," Jacob said with determination. "I'll get under his legs, and you get him under his arms again. You count to three, and we'll heave him up."

"This is too much for you," Chantel fretted. "Maybe I can do it, me."

"Not this, not by yourself." Jacob leaned over and grabbed the man by the legs and nodded. "Do it, daughter."

Chantel took a deep breath, got as firm a grip on him as she could manage, and murmured, *"Un, deux, trois!"*

To Chantel's surprise, they lifted the man easily and quickly onto the cot.

Jacob said, "We have to take his clothes off and wash him up as best as we possibly can, and hurry. Then we have to turn him over so I can get those shotgun pellets out."

Chantel fetched a cracker box for Jacob to sit on, then knelt by the cot to help clean up the man.

"He has nice clothes, this poor man," Chantel said as they undressed him. Even though the garments were caked with mud and dried blood, she could tell the quality of the fabric and the tailoring.

"And nice jewelry and lots of money and a very expensive pistol, too," Jacob said speculatively. "He was grazed once, in the side, some days ago, I think. It's bandaged and healing. But whoever shot him with the shotgun and left him for dead didn't rob him, and they didn't steal his fine horse."

The big kettle of water was hot, and Jacob instructed her to pour half of it into a wash-basin and the rest of it into a big clean pot. "Let the water in the pot boil," he said, "while we wash him off. Quickly, quickly, Chantel."

They sponged him clean then turned him and carefully dabbed off the dirt and blood from his wounds. Once they got him cleaned up into a recognizable human, they could see that he was still breathing. His respiration was deep and slow.

"That's good, I think," Jacob said. "Now, you see that bag I've brought? Get all of those implements out of it and throw them into the pot. And set the big tongs in so the teeth are in the water but the handle is out of it, leaning to the side."

"This pot of boiling water?" Chantel asked hesitantly.

"Yes. While they boil, I'll finish cleaning out these wounds. You'd better go and move the wagon up here, out of the road, and unhitch Rosie. And see if you can catch this man's horse."

At that moment, they heard a soft thump, and the big black horse stuck his nose inside the tent and made a snuffling sound. In spite of the man's grave condition, Jacob and Chantel laughed softly. "I don't think

I'll have trouble catching this horse, me," Chantel said. "I'll hurry, Grandpere, so I can help you."

She moved the wagon up by the tent then unhitched Rosie. The black horse watched her solemnly, staying close to the tent. She let Rosie graze, not tethered, for Chantel had found that the gentle horse rarely wandered more than a few feet from their camp.

She walked up to the black horse. He shied just a little and tossed his head but stayed still as she reached up to pat his nose. She rubbed his neck for a while, murmuring little endearments in broken French. He seemed to be completely relaxed, so she unsaddled him and stored the fine-tooled saddle and the man's saddlebags and blanket roll in the wagon.

The stallion's skin twitched with relief, and he pawed the ground. Then he began to graze, all the while staying close to the tent.

"You're not going anywhere, are you, boy? I don't think I'll tie you up either. You stay. Rosie never had such a fine gentleman to keep her company."

She went back inside the tent. Jacob had taken all of the tools out of the water with the tongs: two sets of tweezers, one large and one small; a tiny, very sharp knife; and a small pair of pliers. Chantel watched as he took the knife and made a very small cut. Then with the tweezers, he pulled out a steel shotgun pellet and dropped it into an empty basin, where four others rolled around making a loud tinny noise.

"Most of these wounds are not very deep. He must've been some distance away from whoever shot him."

Chantel watched as he continued to pull the pellets out of the man's back.

"See if you can see any more," Jacob finally said, standing up for a few minutes to stretch. "My eyes are getting tired."

"It's getting dark. I'll light some lanterns," Chantel said. She took a lantern and carefully searched all over the man's back then looked back up at Jacob. "You got them all, I think, Grandpere. But what about his head? His hair, it's thick, yes?"

"I may have to shave it to be able to find them," he said wearily. "I can't see as well as I could when I was younger."

"No, I think he wouldn't like that," Chantel said with a vehemence that surprised her.

"Oh? Why would you think that, daughter?" Jacob asked curiously.

"He just wouldn't. He has such pretty hair, so nice and thick. He doesn't want to be bald, him," Chantel answered firmly. "But, Grandpere, I watch you. I see, I know. I'll take the little balls out of his head. You rest then maybe cook us some nice stew."

Jacob watched her with some amusement then said, "All right, daughter. You generally can do exactly what you put your mind to do. But before you touch him or the tools, you must wash your hands, wash them good, with the carbolic soap. Scrub under your fingernails with the brush."

Chantel cocked her head to the side. "How you know all this, Grandpere? I thought you didn't know gunshots."

"I don't," he admitted. "But you know I've been praying for this man ever since we found him. And the Lord keeps bringing Leviticus to my mind. It's filled with many rules for keeping clean, for cleansing, and so I felt that He was teaching me how to take care of this man."

"It's in the Bible to take care of gunshots?" Chantel repeated, astonished.

"No, no, dear daughter. I'll read some of Leviticus to you sometime and explain," he said. "But for now you go ahead and wash up in that hot water, but be careful not to burn yourself. I'll rest for a while, and then I'll get us some supper together."

It took Chantel almost three hours to

make sure she had removed all of the shotgun pellets from the man's head. The experience had felt very odd to her. She had hung two lanterns close over his head and had bent over him. Time and time again she had run her fingers through his hair to feel the small bumps where the pellets were buried. They had sponged the man's hair, but of course they had not thoroughly washed it. Still, Chantel could catch a drift of a fragrance, a very slight scent. It was not a heavy or strong smell like hair pomade, but a clean scent, something like lemons.

During the entire time she tended him, she was very aware of the peculiarity of the situation, doing something that under other circumstances would be so intimate, running her hands through his hair and caressing it. Except for when she had tended Jacob, it was the only time she could recall ever touching a man in such a manner.

Jacob fixed them a hearty stew, and they ate it slowly with soda crackers, watching the still-unconscious man.

They had left him lying on his stomach, and Chantel had fixed a small pillow to cradle his head, with his face turned to the side. "Do you think he will wake up?" she asked Jacob hesitantly. "Do you think he can?"

"He can if the Lord wills it. And I know the Lord has willed it. So we will pray that He will do the real healing for him."

"How do you know, Grandpere? Has the good God been talking to you again?"

"No, the good God didn't have to tell me that this man will live."

"He didn't? Then how can you be so sure, to know?" Chantel demanded.

"Because once, about two years ago, an angel was sent to find a dead horse and a live man," he said. "Today an angel found a live horse . . . and what we thought was a dead man. But he wasn't. If we had been sent here to give him a Christian burial, Chantel, we would have found him dead. Haven't you thought, haven't you wondered? We had passed several riders and wagons on the road today, coming and going. How was it that no one found this man, that only you found him?"

She considered this, her fine brow slightly wrinkled. "Maybe this horse, he runs away and is afraid when the people came. And then they couldn't see the man down in the ditch."

"Maybe. But this horse didn't run away when we came, did he? Not even when we stopped and walked up to the man."

Suddenly Chantel smiled, and it lit up her

face. "So, Grandpere, now the good God, He is talking to the horse?"

It gave Jacob such pleasure to see Chantel smile. Although he knew that she was happy, she rarely smiled so freely, so openly. Seeing her glowing face, he couldn't help but smile back at her. "All creatures serve God, Chantel, even that horse out there. It's by the Lord's will that we all live and breathe. I don't know this man, but I know one thing: it was not God's will for him to die. Not today."

The next day the stranger woke up.

It was early afternoon. Jacob had put a cot out under the tree, and he was napping peacefully in the kind March sun.

Chantel was in the tent, cutting strips of clean white linen to make more bandages. From time to time she glanced up at the man, who was still in the same position, lying on his stomach with his face turned toward her, eyes closed.

She was looking down, folding the strips into neat squares, when she heard a rustling sound. The man had managed to prop himself up on his elbows, and he was watching her.

Chantel flew to the cot. "You're awake! Be careful, don't move around too much.

You've been shot. In the back."

"Mm — uh," he groaned softly. "Shot . . . it hurts."

"I know," she said soothingly. "That's why you have to lie on your stomach."

His head dropped, mainly from weakness. He licked his lips. "So . . . thirsty."

"Water, I'll get it, me," she said and hurried to pour water from the canteen into a cup. She held it to his lips, and he took small sips, the only way he could manage in his awkward position. Then he allowed himself to sink back onto the cot.

"Thank — thank —"

"It's all right," Chantel said. "Just rest."

"Stay . . . ," he whispered, and then his eyes closed again.

He was much the same for two more days, only waking up for minutes at a time, sipping water, talking very little.

Chantel stayed close, for she had found that the moment his eyes opened he would immediately search for her. She washed his clothes and hung them in the sun to dry, but wryly she reflected that there was no way to mend all the little holes that the shotgun blast had made. She cleaned his boots and polished them until they shone, then stood them up in the wagon, stuffed with brown paper to keep their shape. She made him a new shirt out of the same bolt of soft linen that they were using to make the bandages.

She read her mother's Bible, and Jacob would often sit with her and read aloud. Several times a day Jacob prayed for the injured man, and Chantel was, as always, amazed at the fervency, the sense of realness, of her grandfather's prayers.

And the man got better. Early in the morning of the third day, he woke up, focused on Chantel, and then pulled himself up. "Good — morning, isn't it?"

"Yes, morning. You look better," she said, filling the water cup.

"That's good. Because I still feel like a train ran over me," he said. He drank thirstily, and this time he took the cup for himself. "I — I think I'd like to sit up. Can you please help me, ma'am?"

"I drag you in here like a dray horse," she said, her eyes alight. "I think I can help you sit up, me."

It really was hard, though, getting him turned over and turned around, and then pulling him up to sit on the edge of the cot. When they finished, he was out of breath. "I'm as — weak as a newborn little kitten," he gasped. "What — what day is it?"

"I don't know," Chantel said with endearing sincerity, "for I haven't looked at Grand-pere's calendar today. But I think you want to know this. We found you five days ago, all shot, you. We thought you were dead."

"Five days," Clay repeated with shock. "I've been out for five days?"

"Only four," Chantel said. "Today is five days, and here you are now."

He nodded. "I hate to trouble you, ma'am, but I'm not quite ready to crawl over to that canteen. May I have more water?"

As she poured his cup full, she studied him from the corner of her eyes. It was the first time she had really seen him. He was very handsome, she thought. His eyes were dark brown, wide-set, and fringed by thick, dark lashes. His nose was a straight English nose with a thin bridge, his cheekbones high and pronounced, his jawline firm. Though he was still pale, he looked tough, not pretty, very masculine.

She handed him the cup, and he drank slowly, not gulping. She sat down on the upturned cracker barrel and watched him.

"Thank you, ma'am," he finally said. "May I ask your name?"

"My name is Chantel Fortier. What is yours?"

"Clay Tremayne. I'm so happy to make your acquaintance, Miss Fortier. I have a feeling that I owe you a very great debt. I haven't been aware of too much these last days, but I do know that you have been an angel, taking care of me as you have. And — isn't there an older gentleman?"

"Oh yes, ma grandpere. He naps in the sun, like an old lizard, he says. He'll wake soon. He'll be glad to see you sitting up and talking."

"I wouldn't be if it weren't for you two, I believe," Clay said gravely. "I don't remember being shot. All I remember is lying in the mud, thinking that I was dying. I guess I would have if you hadn't found me."

"Do you know who shot you?" Chantel asked curiously.

Jacob had told her that when he woke up he might not remember much, might not even know who he was. Sometimes that happened to people who had head wounds.

"Oh yes, I remember that," Clay answered drily. "But begging your pardon, Miss Fortier, I really don't want to talk about it."

"No, no, it's not my business, me," she said hastily.

"It's not that. It's just that — let's say it's better if you and your grandfather don't get involved," Clay said quietly. "At least, no more than you already are."

Jacob came in then, blinking in the half-light of the tent. "So sir! It's a blessing to see you sitting up and looking so well. Thank God for His tender mercies." He sat down on the other cot, for Chantel had set up one so Jacob could sleep in the tent as well.

"Let me introduce you, Grandpere," Chantel said quickly. Clay's courtly manners had impressed her, and she had learned much of polite social convention from Jacob. She introduced them, merely naming Clay as "the gentleman that has been staying with us."

Jacob asked, "How are you feeling? How are your back and your head?"

"My back is sore, and it burns," Clay admitted. "And my head aches. But my mind is so much clearer. I feel as if I've been wandering in a nightmare. Except when I woke up to see Miss Fortier, here. You have done me a great service, sir. I can only say thank you right now."

"You are welcome, sir, and do not forget to thank the Lord, who showed great mercy to you by sending us along to find you. Is there anyone that we should send word to that you're all right?"

"I don't think so, Mr. Steiner."

"What about your family?"

■ ■ ■ ■

Clay swallowed hard. He faltered at Mr. Steiner's query about his family. What should he say? What could he say?

He felt that he ought to lie to these people, simply to protect them. He had been left for dead, but what if it was known that he was still alive? For all he knew, he had murdered Barton Howard, and they might very well try him and hang him for that.

But looking at Jacob Steiner's kind face and Chantel's innocent eyes, he knew he could not lie. "Sir, I have not been a good man, and it's possible that I may have committed a serious crime. To tell you the truth, until I can find out — some things — I believe it would be better for my family not to be notified of my . . . difficult circumstances."

"But surely, no matter what you have done, your family should not think that you may be dead!" Jacob exclaimed.

Clay shook his head and was shocked at the excruciating pain it caused. "N–no, sir. I have thought about it, and it's almost certain that my family thinks I have traveled to the Carolinas to visit friends."

This made perfect sense to Clay. After all,

one of the Howards had shot him in the back and left him for dead in the ditch on a lonely road.

Although in the South a man might defend his sister's honor even to the death, that was not the gentlemanly — or legal — way to do so. Clay was sure that the brothers would have told no one that they had done this. There had been such a ruckus at the hotel, Clay knew that it had caused a scandal for Belle, and it was indeed very likely that his family would think he had just left town for a few days. He had done so before.

"Very well, Mr. Tremayne, you must do as you see fit," Jacob finally agreed.

"Thank you, sir. And I would like to assure you — that is, I'm not the kind of man — I wouldn't —"

Jacob rose slowly. "I don't believe you would ever do any harm to me or to Chantel," he said evenly. "I don't know what you have done or think that you might have done. It's none of my business. That kind of thing is between a man and God. He alone has the right to judge you, Mr. Tremayne, not I. And I can already see that you are not the kind of man to steal from us," he added with some amusement. "Such a man with such a horse . . . Even though I don't know horses, I can see that one must have cost you a pretty penny."

Actually, Clay had won Lightning on a bet, but somehow he was extremely reluctant to admit this to Jacob Steiner. And he was surprised. "Lightning? I figured he was long gone, either bolted or stolen."

"No, he stays with you," Chantel said. "Always. He's the reason I found you. His name is Lightning? That a good name for that horse."

"The reason you found me?" Clay repeated. "But what — how — ?"

Jacob said firmly, "Mr. Tremayne, you may feel better, but I can assure you that you're still in a very weak condition, and you are starting to look exhausted again. Rest now. Chantel and I will be here when you wake up."

"You're right, sir," Clay murmured. "I do still feel very unwell." He struggled to lie back on the cot, and Chantel helped him. "Thank you, Miss . . ."

"Chantel," she said. "Everyone calls me Chantel."

But he was already slipping into sleep.

# Chapter Twelve

Clay opened his eyes to stare up at the top of the tent. He had come to know that stretch of canvas very well, even when it was dark. He knew every crease, every spot, every loose thread. He had been staring up at it for a week now. But even as he monotonously traced the familiar folds, he was grateful, at least, that he could lie on his back to look up at it.

He still had not remembered anything of those first four days after Chantel and Jacob had saved him, lying on his stomach, his back in shreds, his head banging as if a strongman were hammering on it. The only thing he had known in that dark time had been Chantel's lovely face, her quiet voice, her soft hands. Idly he wondered how she kept her hands so soft. She worked like a man every day.

Earlier she had had to saddle Lightning for him. He had been determined to try riding, though Chantel and Jacob had warned him that he was still weak. Stubbornly he had led Lightning out to the wagon, hauled his saddle out of it — and promptly dropped it.

Without a single word, but with a dire I-told-you-so look, Chantel had picked it up and saddled Lightning.

Clay had managed to mount by himself, but after ten minutes of riding Lightning even at a slow walk, his head was pounding so hard he could hardly see through the red veil of pain. His back felt as if it were on fire. He had given up, retreated to his cot, and collapsed.

Suddenly his mouth started watering. He remembered he had eaten nothing since breakfast, and he was ravenously hungry. It might have had something to do with the fact that a thick, rich aroma of stew floated into the tent. With an effort, he rose, steeling himself against the dizziness he still felt when he stood up quickly, and went outside.

Chantel looked up from the campfire. "Going for a ride?"

"Very funny, ma'am," Clay grumbled.

"Come over here and sit down, you."

In the past two weeks, Chantel and Jacob had made their campsite into a homey, comfortable place under the stand of the oak trees. The trees were very old, their trunks enormous, their branches spreading and joining to make a thick roof of spring-green leaves. The cot mattresses were thin enough to bend, and they made nice comfortable seats leaned up against the trees.

Chantel had cleared a space right in the middle of the three trees for a good campfire, with a place to roast eggs and potatoes in the hot ashes and a tripod over the center. Now she bent back over, stirring the big iron pot full of beef stew. Jacob had had one roast of smoked beef that was about to ruin, so she had decided not to let it go to waste.

Clay moved one of the empty cracker boxes close to the fire, where Chantel had already placed hers. He watched her. He had never known a young woman like her before. She was the most curious combination of tomboy, toughness, sweetness, and world-weary innocence. At seventeen she was still coltish, with only hints of the grace that would surely be hers in full womanhood. He reflected how tender and gentle she had been when he was helpless, but as soon as he had come to his full senses and regained some of his strength, she had immediately withdrawn from him. She had been polite, but she didn't stay in the tent when he was resting or seek out his company in any way.

She glanced at him, and he could see that his scrutiny was making her uncomfortable. "Did you tell me you just turned seventeen, Chantel?" he asked casually, dropping his gaze.

"Last month I'm seventeen years. And you, Mr. Tremayne, how many years are you?"

"It's a coincidence, I believe. My birthday is in February, too, so last month I turned twenty-five."

"And you don't have a wife," she said with elaborate casualness.

"No, no wife."

"Why not?" she asked, coming to sit by him. "Don't you like women?"

Clay laughed shortly. "Oh yes, Chantel, I like women. I like them a lot. It's just that I never found a woman who could put up with my wicked ways."

Her mouth tightened. "So. You are a wicked man?"

"Guess I am."

"Why? How are you so wicked?" she demanded.

"I don't know," he answered with a wry half smile. "Just too lazy to be good, I guess. I'm the black sheep in all of my family, so I can't blame my heritage or my upbringing. What about you, Chantel? You've never said anything about your family."

"Ma mere and ma pere are dead. Now Jacob is ma grandpere," she answered shortly then jumped up. "The stew, it is done. Are you hungry?"

"The smell of that stew has been making me hungry since I opened my eyes."

She brought him a bowl of steaming stew and a big wedge of corn bread. "I make corn bread. Grandpere loves it. Do you like it?"

"Yes, ma'am, I surely do. Thank you."

Jacob came into the little campsite. He usually took a walk at twilight to be alone and pray. "If this were a restaurant, the aroma of that stew would bring in a full house," he announced, seating himself on one of the cot mattresses against a tree.

Chantel hurried to plump the mattress behind him so he could settle in comfortably. "You're hungry, Grandpere? You want me to bring you some stew?"

"You take such wonderful care of me, daughter," he said. Jacob found another box and sat down.

Chantel brought him stew and corn bread then fixed her own bowl of soup. Clay noted that she sat down near Jacob, cross-legged on the ground, instead of returning to her seat on the cracker box by him.

Sighing, Clay got up and moved his box closer to them. He took another bite of stew then said tentatively, "Even though I've been utterly at your mercy for two weeks, I know we don't know each other very well. But may I ask you two a personal question?"

"Of course," Jacob answered.

"What — would you please explain about your family? I mean, how did a German Jew get to be the grandfather of a Louisiana Cajun?"

Jacob smiled. Chantel looked amused but didn't smile. "We are not related by blood, Mr. Tremayne," Jacob answered. "But the Lord has done a wonderful thing in uniting us in affection. And the story of how we met is going to sound oddly familiar to you."

Jacob told Clay all about how Chantel had found him, so deathly ill, and had nursed him back to health. Chantel kept her eyes downcast, steadily taking a bite of stew then a bite of corn bread. He finished by saying, "And so you see, Mr. Tremayne, she has not only been your savior; she also saved me."

"You saved Mr. Tremayne, Grandpere," Chantel said.

"No, Chantel," he said gently, "you saved

him and me. God sent you to save us. It's just that simple."

"That's an amazing story," Clay said. "We both have amazing stories, Mr. Steiner, of our guardian angel."

"I am no angel, me," Chantel said impatiently. "And I keep telling you, Grandpere, the good God never told me to go look for you or for Mr. Tremayne. He doesn't tell me things like He tells you."

"Me neither," Clay agreed.

"Pah, He talks to both of you all the time," Jacob argued. "You just don't listen. Both of you are running away from God. I don't know why. Maybe I'm too old, and I've forgotten what it's like to be so young and full of yourself that you don't have time for God. But you will. One day He will catch up with you, Chantel, and you, too, Mr. Tremayne."

Clay and Chantel exchanged glances as if to say, He's very old, after all. At least that was what Clay's meant.

Jacob noticed and first frowned darkly, but then he was amused. He was generally a very good-humored man. "Anyway, speaking of catching up to you, Mr. Tremayne, I would like to ask you a question. No, don't look so disturbed. I quite understand that you don't wish to talk about your recent

233

experience. It's just that I was curious about your future plans."

Clay looked troubled. "I don't have any. I did, but somehow, since I was . . . injured, and I've been here with you and Miss Fortier, I just haven't felt like following through with what I had originally intended to do. You've both been so good to me, and I find that I am rather reluctant to — to —"

"To leave us?" Jacob suggested. "That is good, Mr. Tremayne, because you see, that is God talking to you. I know, I know, you don't hear a great booming voice from the heavens or a whisper in your ear, but it is God leading you all the same. So please, Mr. Tremayne, we would like to invite you to stay with us for as long as you would like."

Clay's eyes rested on Chantel. She nodded, and again Clay was reminded of the contradictions in this mercurial girl. "Please stay with us, Mr. Tremayne, if you would like to."

"I would," he said with relief. "For a little while. But there is one problem."

"What is that?" Jacob asked.

"Where were you planning on going?" Clay asked. "This is the main north-south road out of Richmond. Were you traveling north or south?"

"We were on our way to Richmond," Jacob replied. Seeing Clay's face darken, he went on casually, "But there is one wonderful thing you will find about being a peddler. You can go wherever you wish whenever you wish. Perhaps we may go south instead."

"But I thought we were going to buy supplies in Richmond, Grandpere," Chantel said, mystified.

"I don't think Mr. Tremayne wishes to go to Richmond," Jacob told her gently.

"Ohh," Chantel said solemnly, studying Clay's face.

"It might be awkward for me at this time," he said reluctantly. "If possible, I would like to find out something before I return. I was thinking that perhaps I could find the last two weeks' Richmond newspapers in Petersburg. They would tell me what I need to know."

Jacob nodded. "We passed through Petersburg two days before we found you. I can stock up there just as well as I can in Richmond. With the railroad junctions there are many warehouses where I can buy supplies wholesale. We'll go to Petersburg then."

"Thank you, sir," Clay said with relief. "And thank you, Chantel, for saving my life and now for inviting me into yours."

Even by the dim light he could tell that she blushed as she dropped her gaze. "You're welcome, Mr. Tremayne."

"You've allowed me to call you Chantel," he said lightly, "and I feel that you know me well enough now. Won't you please call me Clay?"

She hesitated, then a trace of a smile moved her mobile mouth and her eyes lit up. "All right then. You're welcome — Clay."

Chantel drove the wagon very slowly, because even though they had waited for two more days, Clay couldn't ride Lightning for long periods at a time. Sometimes he would lie down in the wagon, and sometimes he would sit up in the driver's seat with her while Jacob took a turn resting in the wagon. During one of these times, out of the corner of her eye, she saw Clay running his hand over the back of his head, over and over again.

"Does it hurt, your head?" she asked.

"It's better. I get better every day. It's just that I can feel a lot of little places back there, especially when I wash my hair. They're starting to itch."

"Don't scratch them, They're where the little pellets were," Chantel warned him.

"I can't believe Jacob didn't shave my

head to get to them," he murmured. "But I'm glad he didn't. Ruining my manly beauty and all."

Chantel smiled to herself but said nothing.

They traveled until late afternoon. Clay was riding Lightning while Jacob took a turn driving, and Chantel sat beside him. Clay said, "It's getting late. We'd better start looking for a place to camp."

"I see a house up there with lights in the windows," Jacob said. "It looks very welcoming. Perhaps the Lord is giving us a sign."

"It's a little late to be calling on people, isn't it?" Clay asked.

"We're peddlers, not rich cotton planters," Jacob said complacently. "We don't have to go by such rules."

"Ah yes. I forgot," Clay said with an odd look on his face. It was, after all, the first time he'd been a peddler.

They pulled up into the yard and saw a man and a woman peering out of the curtained windows. Jacob got down while Chantel and Clay stayed near the wagon, watching.

Jacob knocked on the door and was met by a tall, lanky man with blue eyes and red hair. He looked suspicious until he saw

Chantel, the peddler's wagon, and Clay holding the horses. Then he asked in a pleasant tone, "Good evening, sir. Are you having some trouble?"

"No, no, thank you, sir. I am Jacob Steiner, a peddler. Although it is late, I saw the lights, so warm and welcoming, of your lovely home and thought perhaps you and your wife would like to see some of my goods. I have hard-to-get spices, dress goods, canned foods, tools and knives, pots and pans, kitchen utensils, and many other things you may find of interest."

"I see," he said, considering. "Well, Mr. Steiner, my name is Everett Sloane, and you are welcome in my home. And . . . ?" he made an inquiring wave to Chantel and Clay.

Jacob motioned them over and made proper introductions. "Please, come in, come in, all of you," Sloane said. As they came in, a thin woman just a little shorter than her husband entered. She had brown hair and kind brown eyes. "This is my wife. Anna, I'd like you to meet Mr. Jacob Steiner, his granddaughter, Chantel Fortier, and their good friend, Mr. Clay Tremayne."

"Please come in," Anna said. "As soon as we saw you drive up into the yard, I knew we would have good company for a pot of hot coffee, and I put the kettle right on."

"Her coffee's terrible," Sloane said, his blue eyes dancing. "But at least it'll be hot."

She was already returning to the kitchen, and she threw back over her shoulder, "You won't have to worry about it, since you won't be having any, Everett Sloane."

They settled in the Sloanes' sitting room, a comfortable room with overstuffed chairs, two rocking chairs set by a pleasant fire, a horsehair sofa, and two side tables. One held an open Bible, the other had a stack of books, including *The Farmer's Almanac, Virginia Crop Reports 1850–1855, Common Diseases of Cattle,* and surprisingly, *Great Expectations* by Charles Dickens and *Sense and Sensibility* by Jane Austen.

Jacob nodded approvingly as he took his seat on the sofa. "I see the Word is well read in your house, Mr. Sloane. That is a good thing, a blessing upon a house."

"Yes, my wife and I are Christians, Mr. Steiner. Er . . . you aren't from these parts, are you?"

"No, I am Jewish. I come from Germany originally. But God blessed me exceedingly, and I have come to know the Lord Jesus as my Savior. In my travels it is always heartening to meet others of His flock."

Anna came in with a large tray with a coffeepot, plain stoneware cups, and cream and sugar. She set it on a side table and said, "I'm not much of a one for standing on formalities. I'd feel better if you all came and fixed it the way you like it."

"Anna, Mr. Steiner here is one of God's chosen people," Sloane announced. To Jacob he said, "Pardon us, Mr. Steiner, but we've never actually met a Jew. And I wasn't aware that there were any that were Christians, too."

"They are few and far between," Jacob said.

Seating herself beside Jacob on the sofa, Anna said with interest, "A Jew? A Christian Jew? Why, that is very interesting. There are so many things I'd like to know about Jews."

"You're welcome to ask me anything you like, Mrs. Sloane," Jacob said placidly.

"Well, then, the first thing I'll ask is if you would all do us a great honor and stay the night with us," she said, beaming. "And the next thing I'd ask is — Mr. Stein, could you, as a Jew, eat ham for breakfast?"

Jacob laughed, an old man's creaking, wheezy laugh that still was delightful to hear. The rest of them grinned along with him. "Why, Mrs. Sloane, when the Lord Jesus died for me, He set me free from burdensome rites and rituals. And I have to tell you that eating a thick slab of fried ham for breakfast is one of the greatest freedoms I've known!"

Jacob told them of growing up in the synagogue, of living in a Jewish family, of the richness of his heritage, of how their lives revolved around their history and their beliefs. He brought Judaism alive to his listeners.

Even Chantel, who had often heard Jacob speak of these things, got much more of a sense of what it meant to be Jewish than she ever had before.

"Although it is true my kinsmen don't know the Lord Jesus," he finished, "we, as Jews, learn much more of the great Jehovah, or Yahweh, than is usually taught Christians."

"Do you speak Hebrew, sir?" Clay asked with curiosity.

"Oh yes, we are all taught Hebrew," Jacob answered, his eyes alight. "It is my second language. English is only my third."

Apparently he had forgotten that he had hosts, for Clay requested, "And do you have a Hebrew Bible?"

"Oh, I would love to hear the Word read in Hebrew," Anna said. "I've always been curious as to how it sounds."

"Chantel, would you fetch my Hebrew Bible?" Jacob asked.

She slipped out of the room and soon returned with a big leather-worn book. She had always been fascinated by the book, wondering at the words written in a language she did not understand.

Jacob read the first five verses of Genesis to them.

Clay murmured, "So that's what it sounds like. It's rich and very beautiful."

They were silent for long moments, the Old Testament sounds echoing in their thoughts.

Finally Everett Sloane roused and said, "And so, Mr. Steiner, I understand that you may have a few items I'm in need of out there in your wagon. I'd surely like to have a new whetstone. If Anna would be nice to me and make me some tea every once in a while, I might be persuaded to buy her some cloth for a new dress."

"We've been out of tea for months, and you know it," Anna retorted. "But I'll take the material for a new dress anyway, particularly if you have any sprigged muslin."

"Oh, we do," Chantel said, jumping to her feet. "A pretty light green with little pink flowers, it is, Mrs. Sloane, and it will look so pretty on you, yes."

Clay and Chantel went to the wagon to fetch bolts of fabric, some tools, a selection of whetstones, and some newly sharpened glittering knives, both kitchen knives and hunting knives. Jacob had taught Chantel how to sharpen knives, and she was an expert cutler.

They talked and looked at much of Jacob's goods and finery. Everett Sloane did buy a whetstone and the green sprigged muslin for Anna. As a gift, Jacob gave Anna a slim, white leather lady's New Testament, and he gave Everett a new hunting knife. "And so that peace may rest upon this house," he said solemnly, "I give you both a tin of Earl Grey tea."

Clay traveled better the next day, staying on horseback for most of the time. Still, it was early evening when they had reached the outskirts of Petersburg. They decided to camp and go into the city early in the morning.

"What do you want for supper, Grandpere?" Chantel asked as she considered the supplies they had.

"Mm . . . how about ham and eggs?" he asked mischievously.

True to her word, Anna Sloane had prepared them an enormous breakfast of smoked ham slices, fluffy scrambled eggs, griddle cakes, bacon, little boiled potatoes, biscuits, redeye gravy, white gravy, and a delicious apple conserve, her own recipe. Jacob had eaten three slices of fried ham and a big pile of eggs. Anna had sent with them an enormous smoked ham and a dozen fresh eggs.

"Again? You really do love that ham, don't you, Grandpere?" Chantel said, giggling. Clay watched her curiously, for he could honestly say that he had never seen such a light, girlish expression from Chantel.

They feasted — again — on ham and eggs and biscuits slathered with butter and Anna's apple conserve.

After they ate, Jacob said he was tired and was going to bed early, and he retired to the little tent. In the field where they had camped, the grass was so thick and deep that Chantel and Clay had simply laid down a couple of horse blankets by the campfire to sit on.

The night was cool. A thousand fireflies lit up their campsite. Their ethereal lights delighted Chantel. "I've never seen so many," she said softly. "It's like being in the stars, they twinkle and shine so."

"I haven't camped out since I was a young boy," Clay said. "I'd forgotten how very beautiful spring nights can be. So much better than smoky card rooms and stinking saloons. You always feel kind of . . . soiled, I guess you'd say, afterward. This is clean and fresh and makes you feel healthy and strong. No wonder I've recovered so quickly."

He watched Chantel. She was sitting gracefully, her face upturned, her legs tucked trimly under her. Her face was dimly lit, and her profile was stunning, with her wide dark eyes and straight nose and generous mouth.

She turned to him, her expression curious but with a trace of pity there that pierced Clay's heart. "Is that your life, Clay? Is that what it's been, gambling and saloons?"

He dropped his eyes. "Guess so. Told you I was wicked." He was uncomfortable, so he asked quickly, "So what about your life, Chantel, before you saved Jacob and he became your grandpere?"

She picked at her breeches. "When I was little, life was good, with ma mere and ma pere. But then he died, and ma mere" — she swallowed hard — "she married a man. A very bad man."

"Your stepfather," Clay murmured. "So he was not good to you."

"Not good at all, him," she said vehemently, and then she drooped a little and said so quietly that Clay could barely hear her, "And then ma mere died. And I had to run away."

"Oh Chantel," Clay sighed. "No one should have to go through what you've been through. Especially a wonderful, lovely, giving woman like you."

"Do — do you really think I am lovely?" she asked shyly. "I think I look like an ugly boy, me."

"No, no," he said. On impulse he put his arm around her, and she moved closer to him. "You try to look like an ugly boy, Chantel, and now I think I understand why. But you aren't, and you never could be. I think that you may be one of the most beautiful women I've ever known. Inside and outside."

She listened to him, so closely, her eyes burning on his face, so eager she was to hear this reassurance. A slight breeze stirred her heavy, glossy hair, and Clay smoothed it back then caressed her cheek. Her skin was soft and warm. He leaned closer, and then his lips were on hers. The kiss was soft, not at all demanding. He merely touched his mouth to hers gently, as if he were tasting her.

Chantel closed her eyes and breathed deeply, and she touched his face. Before he even realized what he was doing, he pulled her to him and kissed her again, with more urgency. For long moments she surrendered to him, her body soft and pliant beneath his hands.

But suddenly she stiffened, her eyelids flew open, and she pushed him away. "What — what are you doing, Clay?" she said with abrupt shock. "Stop it!"

"Chantel, please," he said gutturally, trying to pull her close again, so deeply was he filled with her sweet scent, the warmth and softness of her lips, the passion but yet the innocence of her kiss.

She slapped at his hands, her distressed expression turning to one of outrage. "Get your hands off me!"

He jerked back, suddenly appalled at what he had done. "No — Chantel, I'm sorry —"

"No, you're not," she said, grimacing. She jumped to her feet and gave him a last glance, one of disgust. "You warned me, you. You told me you were a wicked man. And you are."

She ran and jumped into the wagon and yanked the canvas flap closed behind her.

Clay pressed one hand to his now-aching head. *She's right. I am a wicked man. What's happened to me? How did I turn into this — this — worthless weasel, to treat women like this? With Belle, at least she did know what she was getting into, even if she was drunk. But Chantel? A pure, innocent girl like that, and she saved my life, and this is how I repay her? By pawing her like some sweaty, greasy piece of trash?*

Clay had never felt so badly in his life, even after the sordid situation with Belle. He thought that he should saddle Lightning and just disappear. But then he realized how cowardly that would be. He owed Chantel more than an apology. He had to face her and confess to her and beg her forgiveness. And he had to face Jacob Steiner, too, and ask his forgiveness as well, for betraying his trust.

He stayed up most of the night, feeding the fire, berating himself and rehearsing the speeches he would give Chantel and Jacob in the morning. Several times he tried to lie down, but he was so miserable he knew he couldn't sleep. The self-recriminations going around and around in his head seemed so loud that his head ached almost as badly as when he had first been injured. So he jumped up and paced more. Finally he fell into an uneasy doze just before dawn and slept for about an hour, stretched out on the horse blanket with no pillow and no blanket. When the first cheerful rays of the rising sun caught his face, he woke up with a groan.

He would have made coffee and breakfast for Chantel and Jacob, but all of the supplies were in the wagon. They had camped just beside a small stream, so he went and hurriedly bathed in the cold water. After he dressed, he began saddling Lightning.

Chantel came out of the wagon and warily looked around for him. A question came into her eyes as she saw that he was already saddling up, but she merely said, "I'll fix breakfast, me. Jacob will be up soon."

"I'll help you," Clay said. "Since you've taught me how to cook so well."

"No," she said curtly. "I'll do it myself."

She had just gotten the pans and utensils and food out of the wagon when Jacob came out of the tent, blinking and yawning. He observed Clay saddling up Lightning and arranging his packed saddlebags and bedroll. He saw Chantel's grim face and the shadows under her eyes. "It's a beautiful morning for such mournful faces," he observed, taking a seat on one of the cracker boxes Chantel had brought out of the wagon.

With the air of a man going to a flogging, Clay came to stand by him and Chantel, who was sitting by the fire, heating up the frying pan. "Chantel, I cannot express to you how very sorry I am for my behavior last night. You have been nothing but polite and kind to me, and I was very wrong in what I thought and what I did last night. All I can do is ask you to forgive me. Can you do that, Chantel?"

She had slowly risen as he spoke, watching him warily. For long moments, her face was hard and suspicious. Then the darkness in her eyes faded, though she still looked distant. "Ma grandpere has taught me this, that we can't carry around bad things in our hearts, like being angry and upset at people for the things they do," she said evenly. "I forgive you."

"Th–thank you, Chantel," he said awkwardly. He had been ready for her to berate him, to accuse him, to shout how terrible he had been to her. With a grieved sigh, he turned to Jacob. "I have betrayed your trust, Mr. Steiner," he said simply. "And this is so much worse, so much more treacherous of me, because you and Chantel literally saved my life. Please forgive me."

"I forgive you, my son," he said gently. "It takes a very good man, a very strong man, to face the wrongs he has done and to honestly express his sorrow for them. It would be a sin indeed not to forgive you."

A humorless grin twitched Clay's mouth. "I'm the only sinner here," he muttered.

"No," Jacob said firmly. "We are all sinners. Our sins differ, that is all." His eyes went to Chantel, who at first looked defiant but then dropped her eyes. His eyes went to Lightning, who stood saddled and already tossing his head, ready to go.

Clay saw his gaze and said, "I'll be leaving you now."

"Where are you going?" Chantel asked abruptly.

"I — I don't know," Clay said wearily. "I just think it's for the best."

"Why would you think that is best?" Jacob asked. "You have made a mistake, you have admitted it and asked forgiveness and received it. Whatever it is, it is over and forgotten. Stay with us, Mr. Tremayne, for I believe the Lord will tell you where you need to go and what you need to do. Don't you think that's right, Chantel?" he asked her gently.

"Yes, Mr. Tremayne, if Grandpere feels it is right, it is right," she said quietly. "It would be fine with me if you will stay."

He studied her, and she met his inquiring gaze directly. He saw cool courtesy, a distant gaze, with no hint of either welcome or censure. He noted, of course, the formal use of Mr. Tremayne. Resignedly he said, "Thank you, Miss Chantel, Mr. Steiner. That is more than I expected and certainly much better than I deserve. I would be glad to stay with you, at least until I find out what my situation is in Richmond."

Chantel fixed breakfast while Clay and Jacob sat talking, mostly about the town of Petersburg. It was a central terminus for the railroads, and though it was not a large city, it was always busy. They ate, and Clay felt the awkward silence between him and Chantel so acutely that it was a relief to him when they finally were packed up and pulling back out onto the busy road. Clay rode ahead a bit, attempting to put some space between him and these people he had treated so badly. These people whose treatment of him left him wondering about many, many things.

Jacob and Chantel rode in silence for a while. Chantel was driving, and she stared straight ahead, her eyes searching the far distance. Finally Jacob said, "He's just human, you know. He's just like all of us. He needs the Lord in his heart and spirit so that he can learn to be a better man."

"I didn't say he was a bad man," Chantel said tightly. "I've known much worse, me. I don't hate him, but I'm still angry at him. I know, I know, Grandpere. I will try to stop the anger in me. But one thing won't change. I'll never trust him."

"I understand, daughter," Jacob said sadly. "That is the thing about sin. It is a betrayal of God and a betrayal of others. Sometimes even of those we love most."

Chantel shot him a strange look but said nothing more. She stayed silent until they reached the city.

# CHAPTER THIRTEEN

As soon as they started down the main road of Petersburg, they knew something momentous had happened. Men rushed up and down the street, clutching newspapers, calling out to acquaintances. Boys ran, too, from sheer excitement, ducking among the crowds, yelling. Prosperous-looking men smoking fat cigars stood in groups of three or four, talking animatedly. Southern gentlewomen were never known to stand out on the street for any reason, but here and there were groups of them, dressed in their graceful wide skirts, poring over newspapers and talking among themselves with animation. Riders galloped recklessly up and down; the road was choked with wagons and buggies.

"I wanted to go to the newspaper office first thing," Clay told Jacob and Chantel.

Jacob nodded. "We'll drive on up to the edge of town and wait. Will you come and let us know what's going on?"

"Yes, sir, I'll find you," Clay replied. Dismounting, he tied Lightning to a hitching post and began to thread his way through the throngs.

He found the newspaper office, but there was such a crowd that he couldn't even get outside the building.

A tall rawboned man who was dressed in a farmer's rough clothing was standing beside him.

Clay said, "Good day, sir. Would you mind telling me what's going on?"

"Waiting for the next edition," he answered succinctly.

"But — you mean the paper is putting out more editions than just the morning one?"

"Oh yes, as soon as they get more information by the telegraph they print it up," he answered then looked at Clay curiously. "Haven't you heard the news?"

"I guess not, sir. I've been — er — in the country for three weeks. We didn't hear much news."

The man's pale blue eyes lit up. "U.S. Army tried to resupply Fort Sumter in South Carolina. Confederate forces fired on the supply ship, turned them away. Virginia seceded from the Union, and now the Confederacy is gearing up. There's going to be a war, all right."

Clay was shocked. Of course he had been aware of the political tensions ever since Abraham Lincoln had been elected, and seven Southern states had seceded in January and February. But other Southern states were hesitant, distancing themselves somewhat from the most voluble "fire-eating" states like South Carolina and Mississippi.

Though he had not closely followed all of the political maneuverings, Clay had thought, somewhat vaguely, that a compromise would be found. In particular, he had believed that Virginia, with her close ties to Washington just across the Potomac River, would not make such a momentous decision, even though she definitely depended on the cotton economy and had many slaves.

As he stood there brooding, a man came out with his arms stacked with newspapers up to his chin. The crowd started shouting and waving coins in the air. Clay pushed forward, paid his nickel, and grabbed the paper. Two-inch-high headlines read: LOYAL SONS OF VIRGINIA! ANSWER THE CALL! There were two small articles about some appointments to the Confederate States of America War Department, but most of the two pages were covered with advertisements of different units forming as volunteer companies, with prominent Petersburg men organizing them.

After the crowd had dispersed, Clay went into the busy office. A small, bespectacled man looked up from a littered desk and asked, "May I help you, sir?"

"I hope so," Clay answered. "By any chance do you carry copies of any Richmond newspapers?"

"Oh yes, sir, we do. But they've been as hard to keep on hand as our own *Petersburg Sentinel* has been. Were you looking for any specific date, sir?"

"I'm not exactly sure. Do you have editions for the last two weeks?"

The man shook his head. "Oh no, I'm afraid those would be long gone. Or — perhaps we might have one or two, in the storeroom."

"Would you mind just checking, sir?" Clay asked courteously. "It would be a very great help to me."

"I don't mind," the man said. "Wait here just a moment and I'll see what I can find." He went to the back of the offices and through a door.

In only a few minutes, he returned. "As I said, it's not as if there are stacks to go through. We've had a difficult time keeping any editions on hand. I'm afraid all I could find were two editions of the *Richmond Dispatch,* from just two and three days ago."

"Thank you, sir, you've been most helpful," Clay said. After paying him for the newspapers, he left. But he was so anxious to see if he could find some news about Barton Howard that he stopped on the plank sidewalk just outside the newspaper office and started to search through them. A small whisper went through his mind, *Not an obituary, please, God, no notice of a funeral . . .*

But on the second page of the newspaper from three days ago, he found what he was looking for. A sizable advertisement read:

MOUNTED RIFLES — The undersigned are engaged in raising a company of Mounted Rifles, the services of which to be offered to the State as soon as the organization is effected. Such persons in the country who are used to the rifle who wish to join will apply to us, at the office of the Virginia Life Insurance Company. Uniforms free.

Barton C. Howard
Charles Howard
Edward Howard

Clay threw his head back and closed his

eyes with relief. "He's alive," he murmured to himself. "Alive."

Passersby stared at him curiously, but he stood unmoving, muttering to himself for a few moments. Then he tucked the newspapers under his arm and walked slowly down the street to where he had hitched Lightning. As he walked, he collected himself, and his mind began to churn.

He patted the horse's silky black nose then opened the newspaper again. Notices such as the one the Howards had placed were numerous. Also, there were a lot of articles about the organizations of the hospitals and the ladies of Richmond meeting to assemble small sewing kits for the men, to roll bandages, and to collect funds to buy pencils and paper for each soldier.

But two of the notices in particular caught Clay's attention.

VOLUNTEER COMPANIES, now in Richmond, or men who intend to volunteer, will proceed at once to the Camp of Instruction, at the Hermitage Fair Grounds. All Captains and volunteers will report in person to Lieut. Cunningham, Acting Assistant Adjutant General.

And:

RESIGNATION OF A U.S. ARMY OFFI-
CER — Capt. J. E. B. Stuart, late of the
U.S. Cavalry, has resigned his commission, rather than head the minions of
Lincoln in their piratical quest after
"booty and beauty" in the South. The
officer in question arrived yesterday, and
tendered his services to Virginia.

Clay had read of Captain — then Lieutenant — J. E. B. Stuart and Colonel Robert E.
Lee in their involvement with John Brown
at Harpers Ferry. The newspapers had been
fulsome in praise of Lieutenant Stuart and
Colonel Lee's decisive and quick action in
apprehending the raiders. For days they had
written articles about John Brown, of
course, but usually they included more
praise of the two officers, and there had
been much about Lieutenant Stuart's ex-
ploits in the West, fighting Indians.

Staring at Lightning thoughtfully, he said,
"Well, old boy, I think we're bound for the
cavalry. Captain J. E. B. Stuart sounds like
the kind of man I'd like to serve with. And
I'll bet you can beat his horse."

Mounting up, he made his slow way
through the crowded streets until he reached
the warehouse district north of town, close
to the railroad junction.

Jacob and Chantel waited for him there, under some shade trees by a tin dispatcher's shack.

"I brought some newspapers," Clay said. "The South is going to war."

Jacob nodded sadly. "Those dark clouds have been gathering for some time now."

"And I found out what I needed to know," Clay said, dismounting and coming to stand by the wagon. They were sitting in the back. He hesitated for long moments, slowly tying Lightning to the wagon, his head down. "I thought I might have killed a man. But I didn't."

Jacob and Chantel glanced at each other. "Why did you try to kill this man?" Chantel asked.

Clay stared off into the distance. "It's a long story, and it's not a story that I want to tell anyone if I don't have to. He did take a shot at me first. But in a way he had good reason to."

Jacob said, "Clay, Chantel and I already know you are a sinner. We know this because all men are sinners. We have no right to judge you and no right to demand that you confess to us. Leave your sin behind, and ask forgiveness from God, and He will save you from all of your sins. Simple."

Clay smiled, a twisting of his mouth with

no humor in it. "It's not always that simple, Mr. Steiner. Not for a man like me anyway."

Jacob started to reply, but then he stopped and grew silent. As a wise man, he knew that arguing with men in Clay's position did little good.

Chantel stared gravely at Clay, her violet eyes wide and dark. Her face was unreadable. All that Clay saw was disgust and dislike when she looked at him, but his perception was colored by guilt.

He dropped his eyes.

Finally she asked quietly, "So, what will you do, Mr. Tremayne?"

Again it pained Clay that all warm familiarity was gone from her voice, and they were back to the formalities of relative strangers. "I'm going to join the army, of course, Miss Chantel."

"But why?" Chantel asked with a quickness that surprised him.

For the first time that day he was able to look her squarely in the eye and speak pure truth. "Virginia is my home. I may be a wastrel, but I love my home. If Virginia fights, then I fight."

"One thing I have learned, in all my time in the South," Jacob said, "is that these people love this country. And, in some ways, they already consider themselves set apart from the North. Many men will fight, Chantel. It will be a terrible war."

Clay asked curiously, "And what will you do, Mr. Steiner? Where will you go?"

"I've been praying for God to give me some direction," he answered, frowning. "But sometimes He demands that we walk in faith, without clearly seeing the path laid out for us. I do feel, though, that I will stay here, in Virginia. If, of course, my granddaughter will stay with me," he said, patting her shoulder affectionately.

"I will stay with you always, Grandpere," Chantel said in a low voice. "You're my family, you."

Jacob smiled at her then turned to Clay. "And so, Clay, you are going to join the army. Do you go to Richmond then?"

"Yes, sir."

"All right. Would you be so kind to escort two peddlers there?"

Sheriff Asa Butler appeared shocked to see Clay walk into his office. He was leaning back in a wooden chair on wheels but shot bolt upright when he saw him. "Clay Tremayne! I figured you were halfway to Atlanta by now."

"No, Sheriff. I've been — in Petersburg," Clay said. "I came back to town to join the army. But first I wanted to come here to see if I have any charges against me."

He leaned back again, the chair creaking noisily with his considerable bulk. "No, as a matter of fact, you don't. And that would be because of Miss Belle Howard. Those brothers of hers tried to send her back home before I could talk to her, but she just came sashaying in here by herself and told me what happened. Or most of it anyway. Enough for me to know that Barton Howard came busting in on you two, guns blazing. Miss Howard said that you weren't even really trying to shoot him. You were just returning fire, and then you took off."

Clay said, "It's true I didn't shoot first, Sheriff."

Butler nodded; then his eyes narrowed as he looked Clay up and down. "So where'd you go, Clay? Ed and Charles disappeared for a couple of days after all the ruckus. Thought maybe they might have gone looking for you."

"Yes, they did."

"Did they find you?" Butler asked alertly. "You're looking kind of whipped, Clay. You're skinnier and pale."

Clay shifted on his feet uncomfortably. "They found me, all right. But Sheriff, I want to forget all that now. If I'm not going to jail, I'm going to war. Somehow that makes all this seem kind of . . . unimportant, if you understand me."

"No, I don't think I do," Butler said grimly. "If there's a crime committed in my territory, I need to know it, and I need to do something about it."

"I've committed a crime. I shot a man, and even if it was self-defense, in other days you would have arrested me and made me stand trial for it. But those old days are gone now, aren't they? We're getting ready to go to war, and the Howard brothers and I are on the same side, fighting for Virginia. I want stupid arguments like the one we had to be forgotten. There are much more important things at stake now."

Butler continued to stare hard at Clay. "If I know those boys — and I do — I think they might have been so red-eyed mad about Belle that they might've chased you down. I think they might've chased you down like a stray dog. And when they found you, they might not have worried about who shot first or any niceties like self-defense."

Clay was surprised at how close Butler had come to the truth. But it was true — the Howard brothers were all notorious for their tempers. Butler had dealt with them before. Clay merely shrugged and said,

265

"Like I said, Sheriff, I want to forget all that now. So, unless you need me for anything more, I'm headed over to the fairgrounds."

The sheriff finally nodded. "All right, Clay. Maybe you're right. It's time to fight some Yankees instead of each other. Me and my boy are joining up, too. I expect you'll run into the Howards. If you have any more trouble with them, you just let me know. War or no war, I'll slap them behind bars so fast their eyes will cross."

"Thank you, Sheriff. But I don't think I'll have any more trouble with them."

"Better not," he said.

The Hermitage Fair Grounds, a wide field just northwest of the city, had in October of 1860 been renamed "Camp Lee," after Colonel Henry Lee, or as he was better known, "Light-Horse Harry Lee," the best cavalryman in the Revolutionary War and a proud son of Virginia. Even before Lincoln's election, soldiers — in particular, cavalrymen, for Virginia men loved their horses — had gathered as volunteer companies in Richmond. By November, sixteen companies, about eight hundred men, were camped there and gave weekly parades and reviews. An article in the *Richmond Dispatch* praising the encampment said, "The land is now overshadowed with ominous clouds, and none of us can tell how soon the services of the troops may be needed."

Now that the time had come, the fair-grounds — as people continued to call it — was a mass of men, with hundreds of tents large and small.

As Clay rode onto the grounds, he saw that there were probably as many horses as there were men. Even poor men in Virginia usually had at least one fine saddle horse.

There was much shouting:

"Here! Henrico Light Dragoons here!"

"Hey you, Private What's-your-name! What do you think you're doing, riding a mule? Get down off that horse!"

"Officers of Company B Chesterfield! Meeting at two o'clock this afternoon!"

Such was the confusion that Clay had no idea where to go to enlist. A big two-story home was on a small rise overlooking the fairgrounds, and he guessed that would be the headquarters, so he carefully moved Lightning along in that general direction.

He paused before a large tent, obviously a field headquarters. Two men on powerful horses were standing at the ready behind a line drawn in the dirt. Ahead of them a path had been cleared to the far side of the grounds. Obviously a race was in the making, and Clay stopped to watch. The signal was given, and the snorting horses thundered off. Men lining the path cheered and whistled and yelled catcalls. When the race ended, the smaller horse, a graceful bay, had won over a much larger and more powerful gray. The two men turned and trotted back, grinning.

Someone slapped Lightning on the neck, and Clay looked down. A man stood there, broad-shouldered and barrel-chested, wearing a wide-brimmed U.S. Cavalry hat. He was wearing a U.S. Army frock coat, but the insignia had been removed. As he looked up, eyes narrowing in the bright sunlight, Clay saw that he had blue eyes so bright they looked as if they projected their own light. His cinammon-colored mustache and beard were thick and bushy.

"Hello, sir," he said, "that is a fine-looking mount you have there."

"Thank you, sir," Clay said, dismounting to shake the man's hand. "I'm Clay Tremayne, from Lexington."

"I'm Jeb Stuart," he said, "of the great state of Virginia. I've just been commissioned as a Lieutenant Colonel of Virginia infantry. Are you here to enlist, Mr. Tremayne?"

"Yes, sir, I am," Clay replied. "I was just

on my way up to headquarters to see the adjutant."

Stuart stroked Lightning's neck then in the expert manner of a true horseman, ran his hands down his chest and forelegs. "Very fine animal." Standing upright again, he looked at Clay, and again Clay was impressed by his piercing blue eyes. Just now they were dancing with joviality. "I'd like to invite you to join me, Mr. Tremayne. I've already assembled a very fine group of men, and I think you'd be a valuable addition."

"Me or my horse, sir?" Clay asked, stolid.

Stuart laughed, a rolling, booming laugh from deep in his chest. The men surrounding him couldn't help but grin, including Clay.

"Both," Stuart said. "In fact, if you think you might want to join up with some other outfit, I may ask your horse to volunteer."

"But sir, didn't I understand that you're a colonel commanding infantry?" Clay asked in confusion.

"So they tell me," Stuart said with some regret. "But somehow, it seems, most of the men who have volunteered for my command have very fine horses. It looks like we may be mounted infantry. Until we're cavalry, that is," he finished with a devilish grin.

Clay thrust out his hand. "Sir, my horse's name is Lightning, and he wishes to volunteer. And sometimes I think this horse is smarter than I am, so I generally do whatever he wants to do."

Jeb Stuart said, "My kind of man."

It was nine o'clock before Clay returned to Jacob's wagon.

He and Chantel had stopped under a stand of trees just north of the fairgrounds, and they had been doing a brisk business all day. Although the government was provisioning the soldiers effectively, their numbers had grown to around eight thousand men in the city of Richmond, and so the food was spare and plain. Men flocked to the peddler's wagon, buying candy and dried beef and canned foods.

Even at nine o'clock at night, there were still a bunch of them there, gathered around Jacob's campfire, laughing and talking and trying to flirt with Chantel. Clay noticed that she smiled at them and was polite to them, but she took no part in any private conversation with any of them.

After a while they drifted away, and Clay rode in.

Jacob called, "Clay! Come in, come in. Share our fire. And I think that we have something left for supper, though I must say that we've almost been cleaned out of foodstuffs. I'll have to get busy tomorrow and go to the warehouse district. I know I'll be able to find wholesalers there. Anyway, we want to hear about your day."

Clay dismounted and hurried to help Chantel, who was setting up a tripod over the fire. Soon they had it done, and she brought out a big iron pot. "I've been soaking these potatoes and carrots in beef broth all day, me," she told Clay. "I put back one big slab of beef. I had to hide it or Grandpere would have sold it." She gave him a very small smile.

Chantel had laid out the cot mattresses under the trees, and they went to sit by Jacob. Clay told them about Jeb Stuart. "And so Lightning volunteered to fight for the Glorious Cause, and Colonel Stuart is allowing me to come along with him. I hope you get to meet Colonel Stuart. He's a very interesting man."

Jacob looked out over the field, a sea of tents lit by hundreds of lanterns. "So many men," he murmured. "And they've come so quickly to go to war."

"All over the South there are camps like this," Clay said. "And we're spoiling for a fight. In fact, Colonel Stuart already has his orders. In a few days, we're going to Harpers Ferry. The commanding officer there is a Colonel Thomas Jackson. He's already invaded," he told them, grinning. "Colonel Stuart told me he crossed the Potomac and seized Maryland Heights. Sounds like a good start to me."

"It sounds as if you and your colonel spent some time talking," Jacob observed. "That's unusual, isn't it?"

"Yes, but then he's not like any officer I ever heard of," Clay answered. "He's not at all standoffish. We started out talking about horseflesh and went to see some of the horses that his men have. Then we just started talking about the forces and some of the plans the War Department has already formed. And then he did something else I've never heard of."

"What's that?" Chantel asked curiously.

"He gave me a note to take to the adjutant when I enlisted," he said. "I thought it was something to do with the regiment. But when I went in to enroll, the clerk looked up at me and asked, 'Have you attended West Point, sir?' Of course I said that I hadn't, and then he told me that Colonel Stuart had recommended me as an officer. Second Lieutenant," he finished with pride.

"Is — is that a good thing?" Chantel asked

uncertainly.

"Sure is. I mean, this is a whole new way of forming an army, so a lot of the companies that form elect their officers. It's not as if you have to have a commission from the War Department, unless it's a promotion to a colonel or above. But still, I can't imagine why Colonel Stuart just decided like that to make me one of his second lieutenants. Maybe it was because it's so obvious that Lightning is a gentleman of quality."

"Maybe," Jacob said lightly. "But then again, maybe he saw the same thing in you."

"Doubt that," Clay said, smiling a little at Chantel. She didn't return it, but he thought that maybe her expression was not quite as remote as it had been.

"I wonder," Jacob went on, "just how many men will join this new army in the South. It will take many, many men to form an army that could defeat the United States Army in the North."

Carelessly Clay said, "Who are they, anyway? They're businessmen and merchants and farmers. In the South we grow up with rifles in our hands from the time we can walk. I believe with leaders like Colonel Stuart we will outfight them every time."

"Maybe," Jacob said softly. "I only pray

God will shorten the time, and it will be over quickly."

"It will be," Clay said confidently. "I think that we'll whip them, Jacob. And I think that they'll turn and run right back across that river and leave us alone."

Jacob nodded, but his thoughts were nowhere in agreement with Clay's. He had lived in the North, traveled around it for years. He had seen the enormous bustling cities and gotten a sense of the hundreds of thousands of men who were of age to be in an army. He had seen the great factories, the commerce, the prosperity of the northern parts of America.

All of these were in stark contrast to the South. It was sparsely populated, its economy was based on cotton, and almost all of the industries that existed were based on cotton, too. There were no great munitions factories in the South, and as far as he knew, it had not developed an import-export trade to the extent that they could easily import arms.

But he said nothing of this to Clay, who was so obviously excited. Since he had known him, Clay had seemed to be a beaten man, aimless, unhappy. At least now he had a sense of purpose.

Chantel was saying, "But you said you'll be leaving in a few days?"

"Yes, ma'am, that's the word."

"You mean, you're going to go, and there will be fighting?"

"The war has started," Clay said. "Not here in Richmond. But yes, Miss Chantel, I am going to leave, and I am going to war."

She started to say something and then seemed to change her mind. Finally she said, "May the good God watch over you always, Clay."

■ ■ ■ ■

# PART THREE:
# CLAY & THE
# GENERAL
# 1861–1862

■ ■ ■ ■

# CHAPTER FOURTEEN

"Go to sleep, little baby.
Go to sleep, little baby.
Four angels around your bed.
To calm your sleepy little head."

Chantel was singing softly to Little Flora, or *La Petite,* as Jeb and Flora had begun to call her sometimes, who had gone to sleep on her lap. Looking across the room, she saw that Flora was watching her with a smile on her lips.

Flora was holding Philip, and they were playing with some wooden blocks.

"Why are you laughing at me, Miss Flora?" Chantel asked.

Flora said, "I was just thinking what a good mother you would make."

"Me? I don't have a man. I don't have any plans to get one, me."

"You'll get a man. I'm sure of that, and a good one, too."

Chantel continued to rock, studying the face of the child in her lap. "She is such a pretty girl," she whispered softly.

"We think she's going to look like her father. She has his eyes."

"I think no. I think she's going to be pretty like you. It's hard to tell what your husband looks like with that bushy beard. Why don't you make him shave?"

"I gave up on that a long time ago," Flora smiled. "He's proud of his beard. Besides, he says it hides his ugly face, but I don't think he's ugly. I think he just hates to shave."

From the open window, the sounds of birds singing drifted in. Chantel listened, and memories came to her of the different birds she had known in the bayou. She missed the large herons and the brown pelicans and the other birds that she knew so well.

The door opened, and Jeb stepped inside. He always looked as if he was in a hurry, and he never seemed to be tired, which always amazed Chantel. "Don't be so loud. You'll wake La Petite," Chantel warned.

"She'll be glad to see me." Jeb smiled. He kissed Flora and Philip, then came over, put his hand on Little Flora's head, and stroked the soft hair. "Well, you won't have to be taking care of us any longer, Chantel."

Chantel stood up. "You found someone?"

"Yes. She's a widow woman about thirty-five, I guess. Her husband was one of my men killed at Harpers Ferry. I had to go tell her of her husband's death and found her all alone. She truly needs the money. I think she'll do well."

Chantel felt a sudden pang and said, "I will miss your family. I will even miss you, too, sir. I will. Even if you are a general."

Suddenly Jeb laughed. His laugh, like the man, was big and rollicking and seemed too large for the room. La Petite stirred and opened her eyes. Jeb picked her up and swung her around, as he still did Flora sometimes. She squealed with delight.

His command had indeed been changed to the cavalry, and he had received promotion first to full colonel and then to brigadier general. Now he was commanding the 1st Virginia Cavalry. Ever since this had happened, Jeb had been happier and jollier than ever before.

"Jeb, you are going to make that child dizzy and give her a sick stomach," Flora said with mock sternness. "Just because you're the best officer in the Confederate Army doesn't mean you can mistreat the children."

Jeb walked over and put his hands on Flora's shoulders. "You always think I'm the best soldier in the world."

"Because you are," Flora said firmly. "Everyone knows it."

"All of this 'everyone' you're talking about doesn't include my men. They think I'm a slave driver."

"I think you are the best cavalryman and the best officer, Jeb," Flora said. "You never get tired. You're so strong and active. Most men wear out at the pace you drive yourself."

"Well, when they decided to join the cavalry, that's what they signed on for." He moved toward Chantel, fishing in his pocket. "Miss Chantel, I don't know what we would have done without you." He pulled an envelope from his pocket and held it out to her. "Here. I added a little extra to your wages."

"You don't have to do that, General Stuart," Chantel said. "I like your family, and Miss Flora has been a good friend to me."

"You're worth every penny of it. Now, you be sure and come back and see us all. Especially the children. They've grown very attached to you."

"Please do visit me, Chantel," Flora said

sincerely. "You've been a good friend to me, too."

"I will do that," Chantel promised. She had only stayed with the Stuarts that first week, while Flora recovered from her illness. After that she had come every other day, bringing supplies and food, cooking staples, taking care of the children, and giving Flora a rest. She had no belongings at the Stuart home, so she said her good-byes and left.

She reached the main street of Richmond, which was, as usual, swarming with all sorts of activity. The streets were clogged with wagons being brought in and others that were outward bound, filled with supplies to be carried to various points of the Confederacy. The air echoed with the noise of people shouting and talking, and even the curses of the mule skinners came to her loud and clear. She had often wondered why mule skinners spoke in such rough language but had given up trying to figure it out.

Suddenly a man stepped in front of her and stopped her. "Well, I know who you are. You're the woman that took up with Clay Tremayne."

"Let me pass."

"Just a minute, missy. You're a right pretty girl. You may have been Tremayne's woman, but you need a real man like me. I'm Ed Howard."

Suddenly things came together. "You are one of the men who shot Clay."

"Sure am. I'll do it again, too, if I get a chance. Come along. You and me will go have something to drink."

"Leave me alone!" Chantel tried to pull her arm out of Ed Howard's grasp, but he held it tightly and laughed at her efforts. She slapped at him, and her hand made a red outline on Howard's face.

"Why, you little cat!" he snarled and started to shake her.

But then his wrist was grasped so tightly he grunted involuntarily. He turned and saw that Morgan Tremayne was holding him. Morgan was not a big man, but he had a wiry strength, and his mild blue eyes were now hot with anger.

"Let go of me, Tremayne," Ed said, grunting, writhing a little in the awkward position. "What do you care about this little bit of sauce?"

"Apologize to the lady," Morgan said, and twitched his hand just a bit.

Ed Howard cried out as the pressure on his hand grew intense. "Leave it, Morgan. You're breaking my fingers."

"You need to learn some manners," Morgan said. "I said, apologize."

Charles Howard came up behind Morgan. He had a cane in his hand, and Chantel saw him swing it and cried, "Look out!" But it was too late. The cane struck Morgan in the back of the neck, and he fell forward.

Both men laughed, and Charles said, "So, this is Clay's little piece. That's right, little lady, I want to have a word with you, too." Both brothers started toward her.

From down the street, Sheriff Asa Butler had seen Charles knock Morgan down, and he had hurried to stand in front of the brothers like a big wall. He put his hands — they were wide and powerful — on both brothers' chests and shoved them so hard they staggered. "Back off, you two."

They both started yelling at Butler, but he made a quick cutting motion with his hand, and they shut up. "So, lemme get this straight. Morgan hurt your dainty little hand, Ed. And you, Charles, you're kinda getting in the habit of sneaking up on people and hitting them from behind, aren't you?"

Charles's face turned a deep crimson, but then he said rather sulkily, "C'mon, Ed. Waste of our time anyway." They went strutting down the street.

Chantel said, "Thank you, Sheriff."

"You be careful, Miss Chantel. If these two bother you anymore, you just let me know. You look kind of shook up, Morgan. You all right?"

Morgan had gotten to his feet during this exchange. He rubbed the back of his neck where Charles Howard's cane had hit him with the force of a hammer. "Aw, guess I'm all right, Sheriff. Probably have a good headache tonight though."

Butler considered him. "You know, Morgan, I could arrest Charles Howard for assault. If you want to press charges."

"I think our two families have tangled enough," Morgan said drily. "Thanks, though, Sheriff."

The two men shook hands, and the sheriff walked back down the street.

Chantel said to Morgan, "You tried to help me. Thank you very much."

"I wasn't enough help," Morgan said. "I sure am sorry that I couldn't keep those swine from insulting you."

"Well, you tried, and that's what counts. You're a much better man than them, you," she said disdainfully.

Morgan made a little bow. "I'm Morgan Tremayne, ma'am."

"Yes, I heard the sheriff. You're Clay's brother?"

"I am. He's told you about me?"

"Not really," Chantel said. "Mr. Tremayne, he doesn't talk much about his family or his past."

"But he's told me about you," Morgan said. "When I was walking by, I heard what Ed Howard said. I knew you must be Chantel, the angel that saved my brother's life."

Chantel shrugged. "I must go back to camp now. Ma grandpere will be waiting for me."

"There's going to be a celebration at the fairgrounds tonight. There'll be some food and music and fireworks and speeches. I don't like the speeches much, but the food will probably be pretty good. Would you go with me?"

Chantel considered it then said carelessly. "Yes, I'll go with you, Mr. Tremayne. But only if ma grandpere comes with me."

Morgan grinned. "Your grandfather is welcome to come, too, Miss Fortier."

"Our wagon is at the camp. You'll ask for me there. Any of the soldiers will know."

"I'll come about five o'clock. That'll give us plenty of time to get there for the food."

"All right, Mr. Tremayne." She was interested in Morgan Tremayne. He didn't look like Clay, except maybe in their stances and the way they walked. But she had been

287

impressed by the way he had so quickly defended her from Ed Howard's unwelcome attentions.

Making her way back to the wagon, Chantel found Jacob sitting on a box staring out into space. "Hello, daughter. How were Miss Flora and the children today?"

"Ver' well. Colonel Stuart came home. He found a woman to help take care of his wife and baby, a live-in. What are you doing, Grandpere? You look funny when I come up, like you're wondering about something."

Jacob shook his head and chewed his lower lip. "I can't figure God out."

Chantel laughed. "I don't think anyone can figure God out. If you could figure Him out, He wouldn't be God. No?"

"No, He would not be," Jacob agreed, "but it doesn't stop silly men like me from trying to figure Him out. Anyway, what would you like for supper? What about we go see if the butcher on Front Street has barbecue today?"

"We don't have to. There'll be a lot of barbecue at the celebration, I think."

"What celebration?"

"The celebration at the fairgrounds tonight. I met Clay Tremayne's brother. Morgan is his name. He asked me to come, and I told him I would only come with him if I could bring you. Will you come, Grandpere? Because I won't go if you won't. And there will be fireworks," Chantel said, her eyes sparkling. She had never seen fireworks until they had come to Richmond.

"Fireworks," Jacob considered, "and barbecue. Of course I will come."

"Good. So, Grandpere, what is it you are worried about? About the great God?"

Jacob frowned. "You know, Chantel, in the Bible there are so many cases of men, and women, too, that God told exactly what to do. You take Moses, when he saw that burning bush. God said, 'Moses, you go to Egypt. You're going to deliver My people.' No question about it. Moses argued a little bit, but he knew what God wanted."

"You still worried about what we're going to do?"

"Well, I'm too old to fight. I'm no good with mechanical things. I couldn't work in a factory; I'm too old for that even. But you know, Chantel, I'm still certain that God has brought us here. You and me."

Chantel said sturdily, "Then we wait. That Scripture you read to me from the book of Revelation last night . . . it was what God said to one of the churches there. He said, 'I have set before you an open door and no man can close it.' When God opens a door, we will go through it. Yes?"

"You have turned into a very smart and sensible young woman," Jacob said. "Yes, indeed, we will wait, and a door will open. I'm so glad you're with me, daughter. You're such a blessing to me."

"Thank you, Grandpere," Chantel said, a little embarrassed, as she always was with any expression of affection. But she knew, deep in her heart, that she loved Jacob Steiner as much as any granddaughter ever loved her grandfather.

"Hello, Clay," Morgan said, coming up to pat Lightning's nose.

Clay looked up from his grooming. "Well, hello, Morgan. What are you doing here?"

"I wanted to come and talk to you. I've been worried about you, Clay."

Clay put down the currying brush and gave Lightning one last rub. "I've got some coffee over here."

The two men went over to the stove inside the stables. Clay picked up a battered coffeepot, found two mugs, and filled both of them up. "So what is it that's worrying you now, Morgan?"

"Clay, you know I don't like to interfere in your personal life, right?"

Clay simply nodded in response.

With some hesitation, Morgan finally said, "I just met Miss Chantel Fortier."

"Did you? And what did you think?"

"Well, she looks strange in that men's garb, but she seems like a lady anyway, and a nice one."

"So how did you meet Chantel?"

Morgan told him about the run-in he'd had with the two Howard brothers. "I didn't even see Charles until he knocked me down with his cane. I think they might've commenced with a beating, but Sheriff Butler showed up just in time."

Clay grimaced. "I guess I'll have the Howard brothers on my back for the rest of my life. Sorry, Morgan."

Morgan shrugged. "I didn't do it for you, Clay. I did it for Chantel. And by the way, I asked her to go to the celebration with me tonight."

"And she agreed?" Clay said with surprise.

"Yes, she did. Why are you so shocked? Some people think I'm the brother with the looks in the family," Morgan said, punching his shoulder.

"Not at you, you handsome devil," Clay said, grinning. "At her. I didn't think Chantel was much for letting men escort her around."

"Well, she did say she wouldn't come unless her grandfather did," Morgan admitted. "So I kinda doubt she's smitten with me."

Clay shook his head. "I kinda doubt she's smitten with men much at all. And maybe especially Tremayne men."

Morgan gave him a sharp look. "Is there some reason for that, Clay? Something I should know about?"

"No, Morgan," Clay said with a hint of sadness. "It's over and forgotten."

Morgan showed up at exactly five o'clock, and Chantel introduced him to Jacob.

"I'm glad to know you, young man," Jacob said and put out his hand. "It's nice to meet Clay's family."

Morgan shook his hand. "I'm happy to know you, sir."

Jacob looked mischievous as he said, "Thank you for inviting me to go with you two young people. I wouldn't go, but Chantel promised me that there would be barbecue."

"Oh yes, sir, I'm sure there will. There always is at a Southern feast," Morgan said. "Lots of eating and drinking and making merry."

"And fireworks, yes," Chantel said happily.

Traveling through the growing throngs of people in wagons and on horses, Chantel, Morgan, and Jacob soon arrived at the fairgrounds. As Morgan escorted her toward the attractions, Chantel quickly became aware of people staring at her, as they always did. It was beginning to make her uncomfortable, and she began to think that perhaps her breeches and men's shirts were reflecting on her much more scandalously than simple skirts and blouses might. After all, her hunting and fishing days in the bayou were long gone — as were the days when breeches could hide her figure.

But soon she forgot her worries. There were lanterns strung all along the fairgrounds, and many torches on long poles stuck into the ground. And indeed the fireworks were splendid. The cadets from the Virginia Military Institute, who were there training the volunteer companies as they formed, fired off their cannons. The artillery show made a delightful rolling roar, with spectacular flames spitting from the cannon mouths.

Also, there were not one, but three barbecues — a steer, a pig, and a goat. Jacob gleefully ate some of all three, along with tastes of many of the side dishes supplied by the merchants of Richmond. "If only they could find a way to put this potato salad in a can," he mourned. "I could sell hundreds of cans of this."

A band played marching music, and patriotic songs were sung, and there were speeches from various politicians. President Jefferson Davis was there, and Chantel was fascinated by him. He was the most dignified man she had ever seen. His face was hawklike, his cheeks sunken in, and one of his eyes seemed to have a film over it. He was not an inspiring speaker, but people listened respectfully and cheered loudly when he finished.

Finally the speeches were over, and the band started playing dance music. Morgan asked her to dance.

"No, thank you," she said firmly. "I don't dance."

"But why not?" he asked.

"I never learned those fancy dances, me. All I know is a *zydeco*."

"What's a zydeco?"

"A Cajun dance."

"Well, we don't have to dance. We can listen to the music."

Jacob said, "Now that I've eaten, I think I'm going to go on back to the wagon and get a good night's sleep. You'll bring my granddaughter home, Mr. Tremayne?"

"Yes, sir, I will. I will see she gets home safely."

As soon as Jacob left, Morgan said, "He seems like a fine man. Strange, isn't it? I mean, your grandfather being a Jew and a Christian."

"Ma grandpere, he is wonderful," Chantel said softly. "I don't care if he is Jewish and Christian."

A group of cavalrymen walked by, splendid in their new Hussar jackets and cavalry sabers. All of them wore brogues, with their pants tucked into their socks, except for one — Clay Tremayne. He grinned when he caught sight of them and came over. "Hello, Morgan, Chantel," he said. "You're staring at my boots." Clay had new cavalry boots, thigh-high, polished to a sheen.

"Trust you to turn out like a dandy, even in uniform," Morgan said.

"I think they look nice, me," Chantel said. "General Stuart wears these boots."

"Chantel to my rescue again," Clay said. "Are you having a good time, Chantel?"

"Oh yes, I love fireworks. And Grandpere ate so much barbecue and potato salad it made him sleepy."

"For such a small man, he sure can put away the food," Clay said. "It's a good thing you're such a fine cook, Chantel. Morgan,

I've been thinking. Since Mother and Father are here in town, don't you think they'd like to meet Chantel and Mr. Steiner?"

"I think that's a very good idea, Clay," Morgan agreed. He turned to Chantel. "Clay's told the family — finally — about what happened with the Howards and how you and Mr. Steiner saved his life. How about having supper with our family tomorrow night?"

"I was asking her, Morgan," Clay objected.

"What difference does it make?" Morgan argued. "Either one of us —"

"Never mind, you," Chantel said, amused. "If ma grandpere will come, I will come."

"He'll come," Clay said firmly. "I'll tell him that we're having supper at Wickham's."

Clay had not told the whole story to his family until they had come to Richmond, as almost all of the prominent citizens of Virginia had, to find out about the organization and plans for the coming war. Although he had not mentioned names — out of consideration for Belle — of course his parents had already heard of the scandal. Clay had told them of how sorry he was that he had behaved so badly and had even excused the Howard brothers. "You know, once I thought about it, I'd probably do the

296

same thing if some lousy dog had treated the Bluebells that way."

Clay took after his father — muscular, with thick brown hair and intense brown eyes. Morgan took after his mother — slim and tall, with auburn hair and dark blue eyes. And then, of course, were the Tremaynes' surprises — late-in-life twins, Belinda and Brenda, now seven years old. They were like foundlings, with strawberry-blond hair, angelic little heart-shaped faces, and big, round sky-blue eyes. There was such a difference in the ages between the twins and the brothers that usually Clay and Morgan just called them the Bluebells.

Clay had reserved a small private dining room at Wickham's, and the Tremaynes, Chantel, and Jacob Steiner all settled in.

"I recommend the fresh oysters," Morgan announced.

Clay looked pained, while Chantel made a horrible face. "I don't like raw oysters, me. They're cold. Food should be hot and drink should be cold."

"Very well, then, no oysters," Caleb Tremayne said. "Clay tells us you are such a good cook, Miss Fortier, that even Wickham's can't outdo your meals. Does anything sound good to you?"

"Everyone calls me Chantel, me," she said

rather shyly. "I like steak, Mr. Tremayne."

"As do I," Jacob said. "One grows weary of preserved meat. As peddlers, so often that is all we have."

They all settled on steaks, even Belinda and Brenda. As they were eating the first remove, lettuce and tomato with mayonnaise, they kept glancing out of the corner of their eyes at Chantel. Clay had warned them about Chantel's masculine clothing, and his mother had impressed upon them how rude it would be to mention it.

Still, Chantel could see the little girls' wide-eyed amazement, and she asked kindly, "Have you ever seen a girl wear men's breeches?"

"Oh no, Chantel," Belinda answered.

"Mother said we were not to say anything. It would not be polite," Brenda said.

"But you didn't say anything, did you? I did. You see, back in Louisiana I live in the swamp, me. I go fishing there for fish and for turtles and alligators, and a dress is no good for fishing."

"Alligators?" Belinda and Belle repeated in unison. They did this often.

"Did you ever catch one?" Belinda asked.

"Oh, all the time. Once I got one on as tall as you. Big enough to bite my head off."

"How did you catch him?"

"Well, ma pere did most of it," Chantel admitted. "But I helped ma mere cook him, me. He was good eating, that fat alligator."

Caleb and Bethany Tremayne looked vastly amused, and Bethany said, "I've never had alligator. I doubt anyone in Virginia would know how to cook one."

Chantel ducked her head. "No, I don't fish and hunt much now, me. But these breeches, I wear them since I was a little girl. It's all I have."

Clay watched her with some surprise. He had not been aware that Chantel had become embarrassed about her clothing until now.

"Well, skirts and blouses are easy to make," Bethany said lightly. "Clay tells me that, along with cooking, you are an excellent seamstress, Chantel. You know, there is a dressmaker here in Richmond that has nice working clothes for sale at a very reasonable price. If you required alterations, we could make them together, for I love to sew."

"No, I — that would cost so much money, wouldn't it?" Chantel asked.

"Not too much for my granddaughter," Jacob said firmly. "Mrs. Tremayne, if you would be so kind as to tell us about this dressmaker, I will certainly see to it that

Chantel gets some clothes."

"I would like to visit her myself," Bethany said. "I'm going to order new dresses for me and the girls, in Confederate gray with gold trim. It's going to be all the rage now, you know. I would be happy if Chantel would accompany us."

"That would be nice," Chantel said awkwardly. "Thank you, Mrs. Tremayne."

Chantel was fascinated by Clay's family. Instinctively she had realized that Clay, in spite of his rakishness, was a quality Southern gentleman. But she had never met any of the Virginia aristocracy, the old moneyed families. She had a feeling that perhaps the Tremaynes gave her and Jacob a much better reception than others of their class would. But then she recalled how kind and uncritical Jeb and Flora Stuart had been, and they were of very good family, too, Clay had told her. She wondered that people so far above her station would be so kind to her.

Caleb turned to Jacob and said, "Clay's told us about how you two saved his life. I'd like to hear your story, Mr. Steiner."

Jacob smiled. "Let me tell you, sir. I became a Christian many years ago. Very hard for a Jewish man. The synagogues will not have you because you are not holding up the traditions of Judaism, and some Christians are suspicious of you. But I did the best I could to study the Bible and find out how to follow the Lord Jesus."

"I think that's very admirable, sir," Caleb said. "How did you meet Miss Fortier? Chantel, I mean," he added with a courtly bow in her direction.

"Almost the same way your son met her. I grew sick. I was all alone. I could hardly move. As a matter of fact, I was dying, and this young woman" — he turned to her and smiled beatifically — "she nursed me back to health. And she decided to stay with me. We were coming here, to Richmond, and on the way we found your son badly hurt, and it was Chantel who nursed him back to health. She makes a fine nurse."

Chantel thoroughly enjoyed the meal and visiting with Clay's family. She hated to see the evening coming to an end. Before leaving, she and Bethany confirmed plans to visit the dressmaker's the very next day.

Clay and Morgan walked Chantel and Jacob out to the carriage they had hired to bring their guests to the restaurant. Jacob began questioning Morgan about the best warehouses in Richmond for foodstuffs.

Clay took the opportunity to lead Chantel

a few feet away for a bit of privacy. "My family is very grateful to you."

Chantel replied earnestly, "You have a good family, Clay. You are a lucky man, you."

"I am, though I sure don't deserve it."

Chantel sighed. "I'm jealous. All I have is Grandpere." She looked toward Jacob with love in her eyes. "He's wonderful, but it's good to have a big family."

"Well, I think my family would take you in a moment. They've asked me a thousand questions about you, and I can tell even the Bluebells love you. They pester you with questions, but that shows they like you."

"I like them, too."

Clay sighed. "I've been a bad son, Chantel. Very bad."

Chantel stared at him. "Why have you been a bad son, Clay? Nobody makes you do these bad things." As Clay lifted his eyes, Chantel saw they were filled with misery.

"I don't know. Everybody seems to know where they are going except me. I was raised in a Christian family, as you can see. They make it seem so easy to live for God and do what is right."

"That's what Grandpere always says, that it is easy."

Clay looked at her. "What about you,

Chantel? Are you a Christian?"

"Well, no. I'm not like Grandpere or your family," she said with some difficulty. "The good God doesn't talk to me. I don't understand Him."

"Not as easy as they make it out to be, is it?" Clay said wryly. "In any case, it's been a good visit. Maybe you and Jacob could go back to the valley with my parents. He's told me how much you like the Shenandoah Valley. You know, Chantel, the war is going to be here, in Virginia, especially around Richmond since it's the capital. You and Jacob would do better to be out of it."

"No, I don't think Grandpere is going to leave," she said thoughtfully. "He hasn't told me anything, me. But I know him. The good God is telling him something, and I think it will be here for us."

Clay frowned. "Well, at least the city should be safe. For a time, anyway."

Jacob and Morgan joined them at that moment. After thanking them again, Jacob climbed into the carriage.

"Good-bye, Chantel, Jacob," Morgan said.

Clay added, "I expect I'll be seeing you soon."

"Good-bye, Clay, Morgan," Chantel said. She joined Jacob in the carriage then turned to see the Tremaynes all had come out. They were calling their farewells and waving, all of them smiling. She smiled back at them and waved. "They are good people, Grandpere."

"Yes. Very fine. Even Clay, for all his faults."

"I wish he were different."

"I think he wishes that, too," Jacob said, "and we'll pray that he will find Jesus."

# CHAPTER FIFTEEN

With a sigh of relief, Clay sat down at the base of a huge chestnut tree. The patrol had been out for four days now, riding hard and far, and although the men were mostly drained of energy, General Jeb Stuart never slowed down. Clay closed his eyes wearily and leaned back against the tree.

*The man's unbelievable. Never tires, rides into enemy fire like a fiend, comes back laughing, then comes back to camp to have music and dancing.*

They had eaten a good meal, for somehow Major Dabney Ball, the chaplain of the regiment, had rounded up some chickens. Clay had gotten his share and finished up one last fat chicken leg as the sun slid ponderously down behind the rim of a ridge to the west. He heard a nightjar whining, and over to his left a nightingale began its sweet song.

He opened his eyes in slits and watched for a time as the dark purpling into the night went on, and slowly the dying light fell across the grove of trees where they had camped. Each tree in the woods stood out singly and purely against the sky and then turned green-gold by some magic mixture of the disappearing sun and the drifting clouds far overhead. July had brought blistering heat, but with evening came a blessed coolness. Clay simply let the weariness drain from his body as the night came on.

The campfires were burning, and as usual, the music had started up. A slight smile creased Clay's broad lips as he thought of the strange incongruity of Stuart, the fierce fighting general and Stuart the music lover.

Stuart must have music! He had practically kidnapped Sam Sweeney, a tall, good-looking fellow in his early thirties who was a magician, of sorts, on a banjo. He was the younger brother of Joe Sweeney, who was probably the most famous of the traveling minstrels and was said by some to be the inventor of the banjo. He had once played for Queen Victoria. But Joe had died, and now it was his younger brother, Sam Sweeney, who carried on the tradition in Brigadier General Jeb Stuart's camp.

Clay had noticed that as soon as music of any kind would start, Stuart's feet would begin to tap and shuffle, and it was not unusual to see him dancing around to the music when they played rousing fast songs. "He sure does love music," Clay murmured. He opened his eyes more fully and watched the men who had gathered, Sweeney on the banjo, Mulatto Bob on the bones, two fiddlers, and the Negro singers and dancers. They were singing "Her Bright Smile Haunts Me Still," a plaintive sad song, but then they played the "Corn Top's Ripe," and finally one that seemed to have been written especially for General Jeb Stuart: "Jine the Cavalry."

A movement caught his eye, and Clay looked up to see Major Dabney Ball leaving the campfire. The chaplain came over, plopped himself down beside Clay, and exhaled his breath. "That's good music, Lieutenant."

"Yes, it is, Major. Of course, General Stuart would get rid of them if they weren't good musicians, and go 'volunteer' some more," he told the parson.

Dabney Ball was a tall, lanky man with long arms and legs. Even his feet were long, and his face, also. He was unlike any chaplain Clay had ever seen or heard of. Ball was called the "foraging parson," for he was a self-appointed commissary officer. No chicken was safe in a territory covered by Preacher Ball. No, nor pigs or even yearling calves. He not only foraged meat, but occasionally he would set up bakeries for the unit. He was one of Stuart's myriad kinfolk, a thirty-nine-year-old minister who had left a Washington pastorate after eighteen years in the pulpit and now served as the most colorful chaplain in the Confederate Army.

Clay said, "I heard you had a little trouble with a Yankee, Chaplain, as you were helping these chickens contribute to the Glorious Cause."

"Oh, that didn't amount to a thing. I met a Yankee plunderer on the highway. He had got a bunch of chickens, hams, and ducks that were obviously Southern property. So I shot him and took his feet out of the stirrups and dropped him on the ground. And then his horse volunteered for the Confederacy."

"You think that was the Christian thing to do?" Clay asked, his dark eyes alight. The men often teased the chaplain about his warlike attitude.

"We're in a holy war, Lieutenant Tremayne," Ball said. "We've got to wipe the Yankees out so that God can rule over this land."

"Amen," Clay said but could not cover his

grin. "That was a fine prayer you prayed at our service last Sabbath day, Chaplain. Usually I have a tendency to doze in services, but I remember that fine prayer."

Ball turned and said, "Are you a believer in the Lord God Jehovah, Lieutenant?"

Clay answered with surprise, "Well, of course I believe in God, sir. Only a fool wouldn't."

"It's not enough just to believe," Ball said. He leaned closer to Clay and looked deep into his eyes. "The Bible says you must be born again. Have you ever been born again, sir?"

"No, I haven't, I'm sorry to say."

"Sorry to say!" Ball snorted. "What a feeble excuse of a reason for not trusting in God. You're sorry to say. Do you have any plans for letting God have your life as He demands, Lieutenant Tremayne?"

Clay was accustomed to Major Ball's outspoken evangelism, but somehow it still intimidated him. "I don't have any plans right now, Major Ball," he said in a low voice. "Except to live out the night."

"God's going to catch up with you, Clay Tremayne," Ball said, echoing Jacob Steiner's words. "One of these days you'll be just like the apostle Paul. He was just on the road, commencing to his sin, and God simply knocked him out of the saddle."

"If that happened to me, God would sure get my attention," Clay said lamely.

"Don't wait for it! Don't wait for it! You've got to find God, boy. You're here tonight in good health. As you said, tomorrow you may be facing God in judgment."

"I sure hope not, sir."

Ball leaned over and put his bony hand on Clay's shoulder and squeezed it hard. "I don't want that to happen to you, my boy. Jesus died for you. He loves you. Keep that on your mind. It's not enough to be afraid of hell as you ought to be, but you need to find the Friend of all friends. When your father and mother forsake you, when your friends betray you, Jesus will still be your friend. You think about that, Lieutenant."

Using Clay as a fulcrum, Ball shoved himself up. "I'm going to talk to Private Finch. He's right close to the kingdom. I'm hoping he'll come in tonight."

As Ball walked off into the growing darkness, Clay shook his head. *He's a funny fellow,* he observed to himself. *Shoot a Yankee down and then come back to camp and preach to all of us lost men. The next day he goes out and steals a bunch of chickens for all of us. I guess he fits in real well with Jeb Stuart's cavalry.*

■ ■ ■ ■

Chantel had been into town, and when she returned, she saw that Jacob was excited.

His dark eyes were flashing, and he was pacing back and forth. It was most unlike him.

"What's the matter, Grandpere?" Chantel demanded. "Is something wrong?"

"Wrong? Oh, no, no, no. As a matter of fact, daughter, I'm telling you that the greatest thing has happened."

"What is it? Tell me, tell me!"

"All right, I will. Come here and sit down, daughter. This will take some telling." Jacob led her to the two camp chairs he had set up.

Since they had been camped in Richmond for three months, Jacob had finally bought six fine wooden straight-back chairs, and Chantel had fixed racks on the outside of the wagons so they could be conveniently hung there.

Chantel sat down, and at once Jacob said, "You know, daughter, for months now we have been praying that God would give us an answer. Isn't that right?"

"Yes, Grandpere."

"Well, I'm here to tell you" — Jacob

grinned broadly — "I have had a revelation."

"And so the good God has been talking to you again?"

"No, not His voice, of course, Chantel. I've tried to explain that to you, but it's difficult. I was just sitting here peeling an apple and watching that big squirrel that comes every day for a bite to eat. I hope no hungry private shoots him. He's gotten quite fat and sassy since I've been feeding him. Anyway, I wasn't even praying or anything like that, and all of a sudden something began to make itself known. I don't know how to say it any different."

Chantel nodded, though she, of course, didn't and couldn't understand.

Jacob continued, "We've been wondering how we could best serve God, and I had never thought of such a thing before, but this is what God told me we would be doing. We're going to serve the Lord by serving our men. These fine fellows in uniform."

"Serve them?" Chantel asked in surprise. "But how? We're peddlers. We travel. We sell our goods."

"Oh, we will still travel, yes. We are going to be sutlers, and we are going to serve the officers and soldiers of the Confederate

Army. And you are going to have a new title."

"What is this, a title?" Chantel asked, mystified.

"Here, look at this. It was in a newspaper from New York, and I clipped it out. I had read about a woman serving, but it was with the U.S. Army. She had a special uniform. I'd seen it in a paper and clipped it out."

Jacob handed her the clipping. It was faded and not very clear, but Chantel could make it out clearly enough. The woman was young, apparently, and facing the camera. She wore clothes with a distinct military style. It was a dark skirt, a white blouse with a string tie, and a short black jacket, with the conspicuous Hussar stripes that many military units sported, including the Confederate cavalry. On her head she wore a campaign cap, and around her shoulder was a strap that suspended what appeared to be a canteen.

"Read what it says, daughter."

"All right:

"Mary Tippee is one of those ladies who is serving as a sutler, or as the French have it, a *vivandiere*. Miss Tippee serves in the one hundred and fourteenth Pennsylvania regiment otherwise known

313

as Collis's Zouaves. Miss Tippee follows the troops as they cover the ground headed toward a battle and passes out tracts and small copies of the Gospel. She also carries canteens and a supply of water so that she can supply the troops when they are thirsty."

"There . . . you see?" Jacob cried. "That's what you are. I'm a sutler, and you are a vivandiere."

"Pretty French word," Chantel said. "I like her clothes. Much more than these boring skirts and blouses I've been wearing." True to her word, Bethany Tremayne had taken her to a dressmaker's, and Jacob had encouraged her to buy five skirts and five blouses. Chantel had chosen two black skirts and three gray skirts, and plain white blouses. She still wanted to stay in the background, not to be noticed, but she was young, and she secretly yearned for pretty clothes sometimes.

"We will go to the dressmaker's," Jacob decided. "You will have bonnie blue skirts, a shiny white blouse, and a red sash around your waist. And your jackets, we will tell her to make them of Confederate gray, with the black stripes for facings, like General Stuart's men wear. And I know that Clay

314

Tremayne will help us find you a campaign cap. You will look lovely, dear daughter, and when the men see you they will know you are their vivandiere."

"But, Grandpere, there are hardly any sutlers in the South. They know they can't run the blockades to get supplies. We can't get them here — that is what I was going to tell you. Everything that comes in goes to the army. Even the merchants aren't getting their regular shipments," Chantel said worriedly. "How will we get supplies? How will we have anything to sell to the men?"

"God will provide, oh yes, Chantel," Jacob said happily. "Now that He has finally let me know what I am to do, He has also shown me how to do it. And you and I, we will carry the Gospel to these young men before they go out to risk their lives in battle. And when they return, we will give them comfort and hope in the Lord Jesus."

The excitement of a battle to come was in the air. As Chantel and Jacob made their way to General Thomas Jackson's headquarters, many of the men, on catching sight of Chantel, stopped and stared blatantly. She was self-conscious in her new demi-uniform, her vivandiere clothes. But, she told herself sturdily, it was no worse than when she was wearing her trousers or even her modest skirts and blouses. Chantel was the type of woman whom men stared at. She looked straight ahead.

Jacob stopped a short rotund lieutenant with rosy cheeks and mild blue eyes. "Lieutenant, could you direct me to the tent of General Jackson, the commanding officer?"

"I certainly can, sir. You head on right as you are going, and within a hundred yards you will see a tent with a flag in front of it. That will be General Jackson's. Shall I take you there?"

"No, that won't be necessary, Lieutenant. We can find our way. Thank you very much."

Jacob moved steadily, and Chantel followed him.

Some of the men were singing, and others were cleaning their equipment. None of them seemed at all concerned that very soon they might very well be lying dead on a battlefield.

"Why aren't they afraid, Grandpere?"

"They've never seen a battle. They have ideas about what war is like, glorious and noble. I'm afraid they'll soon find out that it's nothing like that."

General Jackson's tent was indeed marked by a flag. A tall, skinny corporal stood outside at attention. He studied Jacob and Chantel and then asked evenly, "Can I help you?"

"We would like to see General Jackson, if that's possible, young man," Jacob said pleasantly.

"Sir, General Jackson is very busy at the moment with military matters. I'm sure you understand."

"Please, sir. Could you at least ask him? It's very important to us." Jacob's sincerity was so obvious, the corporal relented.

"All right, sir. I'll ask if he might have a moment." The soldier turned and went into the tent. He was so tall he had to duck his head. Almost at once he returned and said with some surprise, "Come in, sir, ma'am. The general will see you."

Chantel stepped inside followed by Jacob.

From behind a camp desk a tall soldier with a full dark beard stood to his feet at once. He was not a handsome man, but he had penetrating light blue eyes. He was dressed in a shabby old army coat with major's stripes, faded and peeling, still visible on the collar. He bowed slightly to his visitors saying, "I'm General Thomas Jackson, at your service."

"My name is Jacob Steiner, General, and this is my granddaughter, Chantel Fortier.

317

We thank you for seeing us."

"How can I help you, Mr. Steiner?" He was not rude, but he was businesslike.

"We want a permit to follow the troops. I am a sutler, sir, but I have no permit. I've been told that's necessary. Miss Fortier is a vivandiere."

"I don't believe I know that term."

"It really means a female sutler, General. We'll be taking our wares to the troops so that they can buy foodstuffs and supplies of all kinds, except alcohol."

"You don't serve alcohol, Mr. Steiner? I would have thought that sutlers would, in an army camp."

"No sir, I do not. I have seen too many lives wrecked and ruined by alcohol to have any part in that vicious trade."

"I congratulate you." Jackson's eyes then lit up warmly, and he smiled, giving his stern face a more welcome look. He waved to two backless canvas stools in front of his desk. "Please, sit down, Mr. Steiner, Miss Fortier."

Jacob continued, "We also intend to pass out Gospel tracts and small pamphlets containing the Gospel of John. I'm hopeful that we will be able to witness to the men about the Lord Jesus Christ."

Jackson looked curiously at Jacob. "I see,

sir. So you are a Christian?"

Chantel saw that Jacob was smiling. "Ah, you see that I am Jewish, General Jackson. But I am a born-again believer. I like to call myself a completed Jew. I'm an old man now and can do little for the war effort, but I can bear witness to the glory of God in the Gospel of Jesus Christ."

"Excellent! Excellent!" Jackson said. "I am happy to hear it. I wish we had five hundred more just like you, Mr. Steiner. But I am afraid sutlers in the South are going to be few and far between."

"You will give us the permit then, sir?"

"Certainly I will. Here. I will make it out now." Jackson moved around to his desk, sat down, took a sheet of paper, scribbled on it, and then said, "You will be given a formal permit, a printed one, but this will do if anyone challenges you." He turned to Chantel. "Miss Fortier, I would hope that most of the Southern men in the army are gentlemen. Sadly, that is not always true. It is possible that you might hear things that would offend you."

Chantel smiled. "General Jackson, these men don't bother me, no. I am happy to be with ma grandpere and to help in this way."

"Well, if any of them become troublesome, you come to me, and I will see that they are taught better manners," he said, and there was no doubt that this intense man meant exactly what he said. "I'm glad that you will be here for my men, Mr. Steiner, Miss Fortier. Men always need God, but in war, they need Him more than ever, for His strength, His courage, and His comfort."

"So true, General," Jacob said, folding the paper up and sticking it in his inner pocket. "And the Lord has shown me that that is exactly why Chantel and I have been called to serve Him in this way. To minister to your men."

"Good. If I may be of any help to you, let me know."

Jacob bowed slightly and said, "Thank you, sir,"

As they left and walked back toward their wagon, Chantel said, "He is a stern man, him. But not so much when he talks about the good God."

"I had heard that Thomas Jackson was a Christian man," Jacob said. "And he will need God for the heavy burdens he must bear."

The morning air was clear, and the men were fresh, as were their mounts as they galloped along the road. Jeb led them, and Clay rode alongside him. He saw that Jeb's face was aglow, and he called out, "Sir, you don't expect we're going to have any action, do you?" It was just a routine patrol, three days north of Richmond. They had heard that the Yankees sometimes sent small troops, just probing really, to test the lines on the south side of the Potomac.

"You never can tell, Lieutenant," Jeb said airily. "We might get lucky."

No sooner had Jeb spoken than he stood up in his stirrups and said, "Speak of the devil; there's some bluebellies."

Clay looked down the road and saw a troop of Union soldiers. They had come to a halt, having spotted the cavalry.

"Let's get 'em, boys!" Jeb yelled. "Draw sabers! Charge!"

Following orders, Clay drew his saber and spurred Lightning.

The entire troop rode their horses at full speed in a charge, yelling like wild men.

Clay saw at once that the Federals had no hope. They were unseasoned troops, and the sight of the cavalry rushing with sabers flashing was too much for them. Most of them threw their weapons down and ran. Clay thought that they would pursue them and take prisoners, but Stuart ordered, "Don't let them escape! Cut them down!"

They rode, hard and fast, catching up

quickly with the fleeing soldiers, and Clay saw the men in blue cut down easily, too easily. He took no pleasure in the action, for it was a slaughter.

The entire action took less than five minutes. The bodies were scattered about half a mile along the small back road, mostly men in Union blue. But Clay saw also that three of their own troops were lying on the ground.

He quickly guided Lightning to them and saw that two of them were obviously dead, but one man was alive. He stepped out of the saddle quickly and knelt beside the soldier who was on his face. When he rolled him over, he saw that it was Sam Benton, a young man in his company who always had a ready smile, an expert fisherman who often caught fish for his company when they were out in the deep woods. He could coax fish out of the smallest and most unlikely stream, and he always shared with as many men as his catch allowed. Now Clay saw that there was a terrible wound in Sam's chest, and there was no hope for him.

As he knelt over the dying soldier, Clay remembered how Sam had told them a couple of nights ago that he was engaged to marry a girl named Johanna Redmond. The young man had been very excited and was hoping that he could persuade her to marry him soon, before the army had to move out, as they surely would. Now the blood bubbled up from his lips, and he whispered something. Clay put his ear down close to his face.

"Guess . . . they got me good, Lieutenant Tremayne." He shuddered for breath and said, "Sir, when you get back to Richmond, would you . . . go to Johanna?"

"I remember Miss Johanna Redmond," Clay said, picking up his hand and squeezing it. It was already dead-cold. "I'll find her."

"Tell . . . Johanna not to grieve long. Tell her I want her to find a good man, have his children — be — be — happy. You tell her that, sir, and that I loved . . . her . . . dearly."

Those were his last words. A compassion that he had not known he was capable of suddenly welled up inside Clay, and he felt as if his heart was bruised. In Sam Benton's death something precious was lost, and he knew that this was a symbol of the thousands of young men who would redden the soil with their blood before the war was over.

Chantel stepped out of the wagon, blinking in the early morning sunlight. She and Jacob had been taking inventory, listing all of the supplies — and there were many — that they needed to restock. She was carrying a big box of buttons. The box was cleverly slotted for each type of button to be sorted — black, blue, and white bone, brass and copper — but somehow they had gotten all mixed up, and she was going to sit down, have a second cup of coffee, and sort them again.

To her surprise, she saw Clay riding slowly across the fairgrounds toward the wagon. His uniform was soiled, and his back was bent wearily. He dismounted and said, "Hello, Chantel. It's been a while, hasn't it?"

"Hello, Clay. Yes, I believe it's been nine or ten days since we've seen you. You don't look well, you."

He nodded grimly. "I've been better." Rousing a little, he asked, "What's that uniform? You look very pretty."

"We're sutlers. We're staying with the army," she said proudly. "And this" — she held out her skirt — "is my uniform. I'm a vivandiere now, me."

Clay frowned darkly. "So Mr. Steiner has decided to stay? Here, with the South?"

"Yes, the good God has told him this. What's wrong, Clay?"

He pulled off his hat, pulled two chairs off

of the rack on the wagon, and courteously held one for Chantel before seating himself. Leaning forward, he rested his elbows on his knees, clasped his hands, and stared off into the distance. "Don't stay here, Chantel. You and Mr. Steiner should leave. You should go far away from here, someplace safe."

Chantel shook her head stubbornly. "The good God doesn't talk to me like he does Grandpere. He doesn't tell me this, to stay here with the army. But He told Grandpere, and so we will stay. I'm not afraid, me."

"No, you wouldn't be, would you?" Clay said, turning back to her. "You have great courage, Chantel. I know you're not afraid. It's just that it's war. It's not just the danger. It's the horrible things you see, the terrible things that men do to each other, the great sorrow of it."

"What's happened?" Chantel asked softly.

Clay sighed, a deep, grieved sound. "We've just had an action where some of our fellows didn't make it. One of them has a sweetheart here. Her name is Johanna Redmond. He died with her name on his lips, and he asked me to go to her and tell her. The bad thing about it is I didn't really know him that well. That's what's so bad about it, in a way. That he died with only me there to comfort him. But I promised, and I must find her and tell her."

"Yes, if you promised, then you must do it," Chantel said. "But you see, Clay, that when the time comes for some of these soldiers, we will be there. Grandpere and I will be there, and Grandpere will tell them of the Lord Jesus, and He will comfort them."

"I wish you and Mr. Steiner had been there to be with Sam. I know he was a Christian, but I — I didn't know what to say to him. And I don't know how I'm going to comfort his sweetheart, either."

An impulse came to Chantel, and she said, "I will go with you, Clay. I will help you."

Clay said with surprise, "You will? You would do that for me?"

"I will do it for the dead soldier and for his lady," Chantel answered. Seeing Clay's crestfallen look, she softly added, "And to help you, Clay. Wait just a moment; I will tell Grandpere."

She went to the wagon, where Jacob was still listing supplies, and spoke to him.

She returned to Clay, who was tying Lightning to the wagon. "The Redmond house is just off the town square. We can walk."

They began walking. She waited for him

to tell about the action, but he said nothing. Finally she asked, "Were there many men killed?"

"Only three of ours, but quite a few of theirs. I really don't want to talk about it, if you'll pardon me." Bitterness tinged his tone, and his head was bowed as they walked along the street.

One of the other young men in Clay's company knew Sam Benton and the Redmond family, and he had told Clay where the Redmonds' home was.

The two of them mounted the steps and knocked on the door, and after a few moments a young woman timidly cracked the door.

"Miss Johanna Redmond?" Clay asked, quickly removing his hat. "I'm Lieutenant Clay Tremayne, of the Richmond 2nd Horse. This is my good friend, Miss Chantel Fortier."

Her eyes searched his face and saw the sorrow there. With some sort of a plea, she looked at Chantel and saw the compassion there, on the face of a stranger. She closed her eyes for a moment then opened the door wider.

"Please, come in." She led them into a small parlor and sat down on the sofa. "It's Sam, isn't it?" she said, the fear making her voice hoarse.

"I'm afraid so, Miss Redmond," Clay said with difficulty. "There was an action, two days ago, and — and —"

"Is he going to be all right?" The tone was hopeful, but the look on Johanna Redmond's face was already knowing and agonized. "He's all right, isn't he? He's in the hospital?"

Clay tried to speak, but he simply could not find the words. He looked down and fiddled with his hat.

Chantel sat down by the woman and took her hand. "I'm so sorry, Miss Redmond. Your fiancé was shot, and he died. Lieutenant Tremayne was with him."

Johanna Redmond stood for a moment, and her face slowly dissolved into a rictus of grief. She turned away from them, went to a wall, and leaned against it, racked with great sobs. "Oh, Sam! My Sam!" she cried out.

Clay stood helplessly, his head down.

Chantel went over and put an arm around the woman and comforted her in a low voice. Finally Johanna allowed Chantel to lead her back to the sofa, and she sat down, her head buried in her hands.

Clay swallowed hard and said, "Miss Redmond? I was there, with Sam, when he — I was there, and he asked me to give you a message. I think I know it word for word. He said, 'Tell Johanna not to grieve long. Tell her I want her to find a good man, have his children, and be happy. Tell her that I loved her dearly.' He died with your name on his lips, and he was a good man. A fine soldier." Clay could not think of another word to say.

Chantel asked, "Do you have anyone here with you, Miss Redmond?"

"My mother — she is upstairs napping. I'll go up to her. . . ."

Chantel looked at Clay, and he nodded. "May the good God be with you, Miss Redmond," she said, rising.

Clay said, "General Stuart sends his regrets and asked me to tell you that you have his prayers."

When they got outside in the clear sunlight, Clay murmured sadly, "He was a good man, Chantel. He had a whole wonderful life ahead of him, with her. And now he's dead."

Chantel had had trouble forgetting her resentment toward Clay ever since he had attempted to kiss her back in those first days, but now she saw something else in him. He had a bad reputation and he had done evil things, but she saw now that he was a man of great compassion, and this counted for much.

She entwined her arm with his, the first time she had touched him with any familiar gesture since that night. "Come with me, Clay. We will go talk to Grandpere. He will comfort us. He and the good God will comfort us."

# CHAPTER SIXTEEN

Abraham Lincoln sat in his office in Washington, and Jefferson Davis, one hundred miles away, occupied the office of the presidency of the Confederate States of America. The two men were in precarious positions politically, for both the South and the North were clamoring for battle to settle the question of slavery. Both the North and the South had visions that the war would be short. The South expected that the North would be beaten decisively and would allow them to go their own way, with the Confederacy a permanent political entity. The North, on the other hand, was equally convinced that they must crush the Confederacy and maintain the Union.

Abraham Lincoln had been chosen to lead the people of the North, but he was by no means a unanimous choice. Now as he sat in his office and looked around his cabinet, he saw doubt and even disdain on the faces of some of the men he had chosen to help him lead the Union in the battle that was to come. His face was drawn, already lined, even though his presidency was in its infancy. He listened quietly to these men who were entrusted with the union of the United States of America.

Lincoln kept his eye on the ranking general of the North, the hero of the Mexican War, General Winfield Scott. Scott was old and overweight and exhausted from a lifetime of serving his country, but Lincoln could see that he was stirred and determined. Scott had already proposed his plan of crushing the Southern forces. It was called the Anaconda Plan, and it was simple. Winfield said it would be necessary to throw a ring around the Confederacy and crush it slowly, as a boa constrictor crushes its prey.

Lincoln's glance went around the room, and he listened as man after man insisted that Scott's plan was too slow. Most of them saw Scott as being outdated and not a fit man to lead the nation in this tremendous endeavor. They were all in favor of immediate action and continued arguing with the old general.

Finally, Secretary of State William Seward, who felt himself more able to govern than Lincoln, said, "Mr. President, we must take the quick road. We have a fine army, and we must use it at once. Our armies are more numerous, our equipment is better, and they have nothing but a group of individuals."

"They have Robert E. Lee," General Scott said loudly. "He is the South's greatest military asset, and he can out-general any man we put against him."

Immediately the rest of the cabinet took exception to Scott's statement, and finally Lincoln, sensing which way the wind was blowing, broke in saying, "Gentlemen, I see great value in General Scott's plan, and I feel we must pursue it . . . in the long run. In the meanwhile, the people are protesting that we are doing nothing. They forget that our army is composed mostly of volunteers for the term of three months. That is not time to train an army, as we all well know."

"The very reason why we shouldn't fight right now," Scott spoke up.

"I wish that it were possible to wait, General. I know you are right and our men are green, but the men of the South are fighting forces that are green, also. I've made the decision that we will throw the Army of the Potomac into action against the South."

"Who will be the commander?" Seward

demanded at once.

Lincoln knew that everyone in the room expected him to name George McClellan, who had experienced some success in minor actions. Lincoln, however, felt differently. He said plainly, "I am appointing Irvin McDowell as the commander of the Union armies." He saw the arguments rising and cut them off short. "General McDowell will be the commanding officer. My mind is made up. I will instruct him to attack the Southern forces at once."

Doubt was as thick as a night fog in the room, but there was no arguing with Abraham Lincoln when he spoke this firmly. So the cabinet began to make plans for an immediate attack on the South.

General Irvin McDowell was a large man, six feet tall and heavyset, with dark brown hair and a grizzled beard. His manner was modest, and only from time to time was he dogmatic in his conversations. He had a strong will along certain lines, for instance, in his belief that alcohol was an evil. Once he had suffered an accident in a fall from a horse that had rendered him unconscious. The surgeon who tried to administer some brandy found General McDowell's teeth so tightly clenched together that he could not

administer it. McDowell was determined —
apparently even when unconscious — not
to take liquor.

Now he was prodded into motion by a
civilian president who could only identify
the seriousness of the battle to come by saying that both armies were equally green and
untrained. McDowell saw clearly that Lincoln did not take into consideration that the
Northern army would be on the attack
while the Southerners would defend. Mc-
Dowell was not a military genius, but he
knew that defense was simpler than attack.

But orders were orders, and he set out at
once to put the army into motion. He re-
issued ammunition and saw to it that food
for the entire campaign was ordered and
would be in place when the men needed it
and made certain that his supply line was
well established. Then he gave orders for
the army to move toward Virginia. He knew
that the South was already thrown into a
battle line around a small town called Manassas. A creek called Bull Run flowed by
that town, and it was there McDowell knew
that the action would take place.

Lincoln's counterpart, Jefferson Davis, had
been chosen over fire-eaters in the South
with the hope that he might be able to

obtain a peaceful solution. Davis had been a military hero during the Mexican War and a powerful member of Congress for years. The Southern people were charmed by the music of his oratory, the handsomeness of his clear-cut features, and the dignity of his manner.

As he sat in his office preparing for the battle that he was being forced to order, Davis was troubled by the superior forces that the North would assuredly throw against the Confederacy. Davis had taken what steps he could to provide for defense.

The main line of advance from Washington was blocked at Manassas Junction, and Davis had chosen General P. G. T. Beauregard, the hero of Fort Sumter, with twenty-two thousand men and a smaller army of twelve thousand men under General Joe Johnston, to meet McDowell. Davis was well aware of the greenness of the Confederate troops, and he was also aware that the men of the South would be outnumbered by the Northern troops. He had done all he humanly could, and then he prayed.

This was the setting for the first battle of the war, called Bull Run by the South and Manassas by the North. It was fought on Sunday, July 21, 1861. As that day approached, the two armies left their homes and prepared for the largest battle thus far in the Civil War.

"This is not what I thought war would be like, no," Chantel said as she and Jacob made their way down the crowded streets of town. They were following all of the companies stationed in Richmond as they marched to Manassas. Townspeople crowded the streets, tossing flowers to them and cheering them.

Jacob glanced around and shook his head. "It won't be like this after the battle."

"What do you mean, Grandpere?"

"You see these men? These soldiers that are laughing now, and drinking and singing? Many of them will be dead. Others will have lost arms or legs or been wounded terribly. But they haven't seen war yet. They don't realize. God give them strength, for they will."

Indeed, there was a carnival-like atmosphere throughout the South. The saying had become commonplace: one Confederate could beat three Union soldiers. Sometimes that was even amended to say that one Confederate could beat ten Union soldiers. No one knew exactly why or how this equation had been decided, but the men of the South believed it firmly.

Chantel heard her name called and turned to see Armand-Pierre Latane shouldering his way through the crowd, smiling as he approached. A captain in Major Roberdeau Wheat's Louisiana Tigers, he had come to Jacob's wagon one day to purchase some new handkerchiefs, for he was something of a dandy, from New Orleans. He had been delighted to find Chantel, a beautiful young Cajun girl, in the camp. He stopped by the wagon often, ostensibly to buy buttons or tinned oysters or bootblack, but mostly to talk to Chantel.

He came to walk beside them. He looked trim and neat in his dress uniform, a gray frock coat with gold trim, light blue breeches with the navy blue infantry stripe down the side, and a long, gold-handled sword in a silver sheath. "Good day, Mr. Steiner. Hello, cherie," he said. "So you've come to join the fun."

Chantel said, "I didn't think it would be like this, Armand. You're going to fight in a battle, not on your way to a party. Aren't you afraid, you?"

"Afraid? No, not me. Somebody else may get shot but not Armand Latane."

Jacob saw that the man was being deliberately obtuse and asked gently, "I trust your heart is right with God, Captain. You should know that there is a chance that you may be wounded or even die."

Armand's face grew more serious, but he shrugged carelessly. He was a handsome man with well-shaped features and jet-black hair. "Even if we were afraid, no man would show it. We each try to outdo the other in audacity, you may say."

"Where are we going, exactly?" Chantel asked. "And when will the battle start?"

"It's not far to Bull Run. We have word that troops have already left Washington and are headed this way. Our men are ready for them. Perhaps tomorrow, perhaps the day after, we will fight."

The soldiers were not keeping very good parade line; they mingled with the crowds, stopped for drinks at the saloons, wandered here and there to say good-bye to friends. Now a company of cavalry, trotting in close order, shouldered the crowds aside. Chantel saw that Clay was leading the column. He looked toward the wagon, obviously seeing if it was Jacob's, then pulled Lightning out of the formation with a muttered order to the corporal riding beside him.

He saluted Latane smartly, and Armand gave him a crisp salute back. "Lieutenant Tremayne, you and your men look like you're ready for a fight."

Clay smiled briefly. "General Stuart's always ready for a fight. And I know that Major Wheat and you Tigers will give a good account of yourselves, too, Armand."

"*C'est ca,*" Armand said, shrugging carelessly. "The Tigers will taste blood tonight, Clay."

Clay said, "Good morning, Chantel, Mr. Steiner. So, you're following us to Bull Run?"

"Oh yes," Jacob said eagerly. "I've never been so sure of God's will for me. And I am blessed to have Chantel with me. She is so courageous and strong, she follows this hard path with me."

"Yes," Clay agreed, smiling at Chantel, "we are all blessed to have you both. Chantel, soon you won't just be my angel and your grandfather's angel. I know you'll be an angel of the battlefield."

Chantel blushed a little then asked, "Can you ride with us, Clay?"

"I'm afraid I can't. But you have a true gentlemanly escort here in Captain Latane. I have to go. I'm on an errand for Colonel Stuart. Look after them, Armand," he finished.

"It will be my honor," Armand said formally.

Clay spurred Lightning, and he trotted

ahead, but after a few steps, he turned and looked at Jacob, his eyes dark and brooding. "Pray for me," he said, then turned and galloped away.

General Irvin McDowell was unhappy. His blunt features twisted into a scowl as he said to Colonel James South, "Look at them, South. They act like they're going to a picnic."

South turned his gaze upon the marching columns of soldiers, and indeed they were in a strange mood. Many of them had plucked flowers and had shoved them down in their muskets. Even as he watched, a group left the line of march and went over to pick berries beside the road.

"Look at them picking berries! How are we supposed to win a battle with berry pickers, South?"

"They'll be all right once the firing starts."

"I'm not sure at all about that. In any case, do the best you can to sober them up. They won't be thinking about picking berries tomorrow. Many of them won't be thinking anything, for they'll be dead."

South said steadily, "I think we have a sound battle plan for whipping the Rebels, sir."

"I think we'd better have. We'll be fighting

on their grounds. So we'll hit them in the middle, South, as we decided. Then you will take your troops around to our right and close in on their left flank. They won't be expecting that."

"No, and we'll succeed, General. You'll see."

Senator Monroe Collins and his wife left Washington in a buggy. The senator told his wife, "We'll enjoy watching the Rebels take a pounding."

"But won't it be dangerous?" Minnie Collins asked. She was a rather shy woman, and the very thought of getting close to a battle frightened her.

"It'll be all right, Minnie. Our boys will run over them. They'll be running like rabbits!"

"How can you be sure, Monroe?"

"Why, our army is the best. The Rebels are just a bunch of ragtag farmers and lazy slave owners. Our men are real soldiers. We'll get to see the Rebels turn and run. It'll be something to tell our grandchildren about."

Judith Henry lay dying in her bed. She was an eighty-year-old woman who had been sick for a considerable time. Her daughter hovered over her asking, "How do you feel, Mother?"

"Not well, daughter."

"You'll be better soon. We've sent for the doctor."

Judith Henry listened then asked weakly, "What is the noise?"

"Oh, there are some soldiers, but they won't come near us."

The Henry house was not important in itself. It was a small whitewashed house not far from Young's Branch, a small creek only a few miles away from the Centerville Turnpike. It had been a peaceful valley, but on this day an air of doom hung over it.

The dying woman lay as still as if she had already passed, but she still breathed. Suddenly a terrific explosion struck the house, and a shell killed Judith Henry. A moment later her body was riddled with bullets as the house burst into flames.

Henry Settle was proud of his new uniform. He was a young farmer from Pennsylvania who had enlisted for three months against the advice and begging of his mother. Now he was a part of the Union Army that advanced toward Bull Run Creek.

Suddenly ahead there was a tremendous explosion as a cannon went off and muskets began to crackle like firecrackers. Settle looked around and saw that he was not the only one in shock. Many of his friends in the company had slowed down; some had stopped, staring ahead blankly. They had sung songs all the way, marching to Manassas, and had laughed about how they would throw the Rebels back and take over Richmond. Then the war would be over.

On both sides of Settle, men began to drop, and there were cries of agony and screams of fear as the officers pressed the men forward. For the first time, Henry Settle knew that he was in a deadly position. He tried to swallow, but his throat was dry. Just ahead of him he saw his best friend, Arnie Hunter, shot to bits by musket fire and fall facedown into the new spring grass.

"I can't get killed," Settle whispered. "I've got to go back and take care of Ma." But even as he uttered this, a cannonball hit him and killed him instantly. He fell, and no one even stopped.

Across Bull Run Creek, the Confederates were holding fast, but there were many casualties. Major Roberdeau Wheat, the tough commander of the Louisiana Tigers, had been shot down. He was carried to a field hospital, and the doctor had said, "I'm sorry, Major Wheat. You have been shot through both lungs. There's no way you can live."

Wheat grunted, "I don't feel like dying yet."

"No one's ever lived shot like this."

"Then I will be the first," Wheat said. And so it was. Roberdeau Wheat lived. Even as he argued with the doctor, he saw Jeb Stuart's cavalry riding through the field hospital. Finally, General Beauregard had called them in to hit wherever the firing was hottest.

Clay had gotten into the habit of bringing his company up as close behind Colonel Stuart as he could. He had ridden until he was beside Stuart and his aides as they advanced toward the battle.

Jeb was riding an enormous black gelding, thick in girth but fast. At full gallop they topped a little rise and faced an infantry regiment, scarlet-uniformed Zouaves.

"They may be some of the Louisiana Tigers, sir," Clay said. "Many of them wear those baggy breeches."

Jeb spurred forward almost into the midst of them, followed closely by Clay. Stuart shouted, "Don't run, boys. We're here."

At that moment a flag in the midst of the regiment unfurled and snapped in the hot breeze. It was the Stars and Stripes.

Jeb's eyes widened, but in a flash he drew his sword and yelled, "Charge!"

Clay drew his saber and slashed at the white turbans of the men in blue and scarlet.

The Yankees, a New York Zouave regiment, panicked and scattered in confusion, yelling as they ran, "The Black Horse!" Their cries echoed over the field. They left eleven guns unsupported, and a Virginia infantry regiment hurried forward to turn them back toward the Union lines.

Jeb and his men rode on, shouting madly, into the thick of battle.

The Federals watched as, time after time, the Rebel line had formed, hardened, and had run through the Union lines, capturing artillery and overrunning and capturing their supply wagons. Thomas Jackson had stood like a "stone wall," and they had smashed themselves against his infantry time and time again. The Black Horse, with the larger-than-life Jeb Stuart at the head of the column, slashed through the blue lines, here and there, wherever it seemed the Yankees stood firm.

"Where are our reserves?" the men demanded. They were wearied by thirteen hours of marching on the road, they were angry and disheartened, and finally men began to cry, "We've been sold out!" The rumor spread, and the Union troops faltered and then panicked. They turned and fled past officers on horseback, who were flailing with their sabers, urging them to stand. But the men were now afraid, and fear spread like a plague among them. They ran.

Senator Monroe Collins and his wife suddenly were surrounded by crowds of frightened men who had thrown their weapons down. "The Rebels are coming!" was the cry. "The Black Horse, they'll run us over! Save yourselves!"

Collins managed to get his buggy turned around, but on the bridge across Bull Run, it suddenly broke down and blocked the fleeing pack of soldiers. Men splashed through the creek. Behind them Rebel officers shouted orders: "Chase 'em, boys! Run 'em down!"

Jefferson Davis came to the battlefield and met General Thomas Jackson, who after this day was called "Stonewall." Jackson was covered with dust, but his blue eyes flashed like summer lightning. "Sir, give me ten thousand men, and I can be in Washington tomorrow."

Davis was ready, but his commanding officers disagreed. One said, "Sir, our men are weary. The Yankees will have a guard around Washington. We can't march that far and then fight our way through."

And so the battle ended as Jefferson Davis said, "We've come as far as we can. We've won the battle. The Yankees are whipped."

But even as he spoke, he doubted. And again he prayed.

# CHAPTER SEVENTEEN

Winter had come, and the armies went into winter quarters. Both North and South planned campaigns for the spring, but during the bitter cold months, they mostly just brooded at each other across the Potomac River.

The 1st Virginia Cavalry was quartered just south of Manassas. Sitting at a desk inside the farmhouse that he had rented for himself and his family, Jeb Stuart looked out the window. The sun falling on the white blanket caused the snow to glitter like tiny diamonds, and for a while he sat, enjoying the sight, but then he sighed and turned back to the figures on a paper he had before him. He continually pestered the commissary in Richmond for more supplies and equipment for his men.

But the Confederacy was poor. Stuart also felt the pinch of inflation, for the Northern blockade of the Southern states in the East was working all too well. The salary of a brigadier was very modest, and Jeb worried, because even the necessaries of life — food, clothing, and medicine — were getting harder and harder to come by. He was pleased that his brother, William Alexander Stuart, owner of the White Sulphur and the Salt Works, among other enterprises, had voluntarily ensured Stuart's life, making Flora the beneficiary.

He heard Flora singing softly, and he left his office and went to the bedroom. He found Flora bending over Little Flora, who was lying in their bed, pale and thin. "Is she any better, my dearest?"

Flora turned to him, fear in her eyes. "No, she isn't. As a matter of fact, Jeb, I think she may be worse."

"I'll have the doctor come by and look at her again."

"I wish you would. Still, it seems that the doctors can't help her."

Moving over to Flora, Jeb put his arm around her then reached down with his free hand and touched the child's brow. "She's burning up with fever," he murmured. Although Jeb Stuart feared nothing on the field of battle, this was a fear that gnawed at him constantly.

They stood together looking down at the

child who meant so much to them, and then Flora said, "I hope Jimmy won't catch anything like this."

When their son had been born, Jeb and Flora had been glad to name him after her father, Phillip St. George Cooke Stuart. But after the Confederacy had formed and Colonel Cooke had stayed with the Union, Jeb had staunchly refused to have his son bear Cooke's name. They had changed it to James Ewell Brown Stuart Jr., and they called him Jimmy.

"We'll pray, Flora. God's will be done," Jeb said, but his usually booming, jovial voice was quiet and sad.

The entire South had been jubilant over the victory at Bull Run, and the people were still living on that excitement. They had won the battle, but the cost had been high. The hospitals in Richmond were filled, and many wounded soldiers had been taken into private homes.

Jacob told Chantel, "I've been thinking, daughter, that it's time for us to do something for God."

"What is that, Grandpere? I thought we were doing something for God," Chantel replied.

"We are, and I'm very proud of you. But I

think we should start making regular visits at the hospital. I can get together some things to give the poor wounded men, perhaps, and you could help me give them out and talk to them."

"They love candy, they do," Chantel said. Sweets were hard to come by these lean days.

"We'll take all we have, and this afternoon you and I will make our visits. Perhaps we could lead one of the wounded men to the Lord. Wouldn't that be wonderful?"

"Yes, it would, Grandpere."

The field hospitals, during the summer, had been mostly a series of large tents pitched just outside of Richmond. But when the winter had come, and the hospitals were full, one of the large warehouses had been taken and converted into a field hospital. Cots were lined against the walls, and every bed was filled. A large woodstove was burning, throwing off a great heat, but it reached only within a few feet of the great barn-like structure with the soaring roof. It was not enough to heat the whole building, and most of the wounded were under all the blankets that could be found for them.

"Why don't you start over there with that row of men. I'll take this one," Jacob said.

He smiled. "I know they'd rather see a pretty young woman than me, but tomorrow I will see them, and you can take this side. Try to encourage them all you can, child."

Chantel, wearing her vivandiere uniform, was a little apprehensive, but her heart went out to the lines of men, many of them terribly wounded. She stopped at the first bed.

A young man looked up and asked, "Are you a soldier, miss?"

"Oh no, I'm a female sutler, a vivandiere. This is my uniform, though, for ma grandpere and I serve the army. Do you like candy?"

"Yes ma'am, I purely do."

"Good. I like candy, too, me." She reached into the paper sack, brought out a peppermint candy, and handed it to him.

Hungrily he popped it into his mouth. He was pale and obviously had taken a severe wound in the shoulder. He sucked on the sweet and said, "I always loved sweets. Reminds me of home. My mama used to make taffy for me. Sure wish I had some taffy," he said wistfully.

"Where is your home, soldier?"

"I come from Bald Knob, Arkansas."

"That's a funny name."

"Yes. Everybody laughs at that, but that's

where I'm from." He sucked on the candy thoughtfully. "Don't guess I'll ever see it again."

"Perhaps you will," Chantel said. "The good God may bless you and heal you."

"Are you a Christian, ma'am?"

At that instant Chantel fervently wished she was a believer, but she knew she had to be honest. "No — no. I don't understand this, me. I'm not like Grandpere and other people who know the Lord, so well, so easy."

"Oh," the young man murmured, obviously disheartened. "I don't understand it too good, either."

"Ma grandpere is a Christian, and I know he would like to talk to you. Would you let me get him?"

His white face and dull eyes brightened a little. "That would be good, miss. I'd like to talk to him."

Chantel turned and walked across the aisle between the two rows of beds. "Grandpere," she said, "the young man over there wants to know about the Lord. Will you come and talk to him?"

"Why, certainly I will. That's why I'm here." Jacob turned, and Chantel walked with him. "What's your name, young man?" he asked.

"Clyde Simmons, sir. I come from Arkansas. Caught this" — he grimaced and motioned to the stained bandage across his abdomen — "in a skirmish just off the river last week. It's not getting any better, and the doctors don't say much. Kinda makes me think I may not make it."

"None of us knows about that. I may go before you," Jacob said gently. "But the important thing is to be ready to go."

"I know, sir. I've heard preachers, but it never took, it seemed like. Somehow just never seemed like the time." He sighed deeply. "Seemed like I always thought there'd be more time."

"One thing about God, though, son," Jacob said firmly, "is that He always has time. It's never too late to come to Him."

Chantel brought a straight chair. "Sit down beside him, Grandpere. You'll get tired. I'll go visit some others, me, while you talk."

She continued her progress, stopping at each bedside and handing out sweets, but she kept looking back, and once she saw that her grandfather's face was lit up as he talked, he was so happy.

She turned another time and saw that her grandfather was motioning for her. She went to him, and he said, "Good news, daughter! Clyde here has confessed his sins, and he has asked Jesus to come into his heart. He's a saved man now. I'm going to give him one of the gospels of John that we brought." He took the small booklet out and handed it to Clyde Simmons, who took it and then said sadly, "I can't read, sir."

"Well, my granddaughter here will read to you, won't you, Chantel?"

"Yes. I'd be glad to, Grandpere."

"Good," Jacob said with satisfaction. "I'll go visit a few of the other men before we go."

Chantel sat down and opened the Gospel of John. She began to read. " 'In the beginning was the Word, and the Word was with God, and the Word was God. . . .' "

As Chantel left the hospital with Jacob, she said, "I'm so tired. Why am I so tired, me? I haven't done any real work."

"It is a strain, daughter," Jacob admitted. "We see all these poor boys, some of them have little hope of living, and it not only tires our spirits, it drains us physically. But God's going to bless us. Three of the young men asked Jesus into their hearts today. We'll go get a good rest, and then tomorrow we'll bring something else to them."

"You know, we have the supplies, Grandpere. I can make gingerbread."

"Yes, we have plenty of supplies," he agreed. "Tomorrow you take enough to make gingerbread for all of them, Chantel. The hospital cooks will help you."

Chantel nodded. "I would like to see Mr. Simmons again. A friend of his said he'd read to him. That's good. He looks so ill, Grandpere. Do you think he'll live?"

"I'm not sure, but I know if he dies, he'll be in the arms of Jesus. Isn't that wonderful?"

Chantel felt only sadness at the possibility of the death of the sweet young man. Again she thought, *I don't understand Grandpere, the joy he has with all this death and blood and sorrow. Sometimes it seems like the good God lets ver' bad things happen to people. But then, I'm just an ignorant girl. . . .*

The next day Chantel took the supplies for gingerbread to the hospital kitchen: flour, sugar, eggs, cinnamon, ginger, and cloves.

A very large black woman was the head cook, and she asked, "Where you come up wid all dis, little girl? I didn't think there was a speck of cinnamon to be had in the South!"

"Ma grandpere, he has it," she answered. "For him, the good God provides."

They baked great trays of the soft, mouth-watering, sweet bread, filling the whole hospital with the spicy aroma.

By early afternoon, when Jacob arrived and Chantel and the cooks brought the trays into the hospital, the men were jolly and called out to her, "Our vivandiere! Hello, Miss Chantel. We knew it was you, bringing us gingerbread."

Chantel blushed and helped hand out gingerbread to all the men. Then she went to Clyde Simmons's bedside and said, "Hello, Mr. Simmons. I thought you might like for me to read to you a little today."

"Sure would. My friend Gabe here, he read some to me. But I know we'd all like to hear you read again, Miss Chantel."

Chantel looked at his friend, a short, solid young man with an open friendly face, who was missing a leg and was on crutches. "That was good of you to read to your friend," she told him.

Someone brought her a chair, and she sat down and began to read. A small crowd of the walking wounded gathered, and other men sat on the beds close around her.

Chantel was reading Psalm 119. From time to time she looked up, and her heart felt a deep and profound sadness. They were mostly young faces, most of them filled with apprehension and fear. She well knew that the reputation of military hospitals was terrible. More men died of septic infection, or diseases that the wounded passed around, than on the field of battle. She let none of the grief show in her face, however, and she continued reading.

There was a commotion at the door, and they all looked up. A group of officers came in. The contrast they made with the sick and injured bedridden men was startling — they all seemed tall and strong, bringing in the stringent smell of the winter outdoors, shaking the snow from their coats and stamping their boots to clear the mud from them. The doctors came to speak to them, standing in a group just inside the door.

Chantel saw Clay Tremayne and Armand Latane among them.

The group broke up, and the officers began to roam among the beds, looking for their men.

Clay came to Clyde Simmons's bedside, greeted the men around her, and then said, "Hello, Chantel. I had heard that you were a hospital angel now."

"Hello, Clay," she said, a little embarrassed but pleased. "Grandpere and me, we visit the men, bring them things. I've been reading to them, me."

"She brought us a bunch of gingerbread,

Lieutenant," the man in the bed next to Simmons said. His eyes were bandaged, and his body was thin, but he was animated, which pleased Chantel.

"You come to visit one of your men, Clay?" Chantel asked.

"Yes, I'm here to see Private Mitch Kearny. He's in my company."

"Oh yes, I've met Mr. Kearny, me. He's just down the row here. I'll take you to him."

She handed the Bible to one of the men and said, "Can you read, soldier?"

"Yes ma'am, I can. Real good."

"Well, you take up where I left off while we go see the lieutenant's friend." The two moved down the aisle, and three beds from the end Chantel stopped. "You have a visitor, Mr. Kearny."

The wounded man was middle-aged and looked like he had been a farmer. He had lost an arm, which was a worry, as so many amputees died after the surgery.

"You're looking good, Mitch," Clay said. "Did you get some of that gingerbread?"

"Sure did. It was good, too. Thank you again, Miss Chantel."

Clay told him some of the news of what the unit was doing and told him of some of Jeb Stuart's patrols.

Chantel saw that Kearny seemed to be

cheered, sitting up straighter in the bed, his eyes brighter than before. She looked around and observed that all of the men that the officers were visiting seemed heartened.

Armand Latane came over to them, and Clay introduced him to Mitch Kearny. Kearny saluted with his left hand. "Heard about you Louisiana Tigers, Captain. Heard Major Roberdeau Wheat walked away from getting shot in the chest. Story goes that he was hit in both lungs, but he argued with the doc and was so ornery that he lived through it."

Armand laughed, his white teeth flashing. "Us Cajuns, we're too mean to die. Except for Miss Chantel, here. She's too sweet to die."

"You're a Cajun, Miss Chantel?" Kearny asked. "I wondered, with the way you talk and all. It's pretty, I mean."

"Ah yes, we're all pretty, too, Cajuns," Armand said airily. He turned to Chantel. "I find myself in dire need of some new gold buttons, ma'am. Would a vivandiere have anything like that in her sutler's wagon?"

"Of course, Armand," she said, rolling her eyes. "Only you still have money to buy gold buttons, you."

"Then with your permission, I'll stop by

later and collect." Armand then added mischievously, "You can show me how to sew them on, Chantel, cherie?"

"You know I'll sew them on for you," Chantel said dismissively. "Now get along with you, and go speak to Grandpere."

With a courtly bow, he went down the line of beds to where Jacob sat talking with a man with his arm in a sling and his head bandaged.

Chantel turned back to Clay, who was watching Latane with smoldering dark eyes. "What is it, Clay? You and Armand, you don't have a falling-out, do you?"

"No," he muttered. "Not yet." He said his good-byes to Mitch Kearny, then asked Chantel in a low voice, "Would you walk me out?"

"Of course," Chantel said, and she took his arm as they walked slowly to the door.

"I thought you might want to know," he said with some difficulty, "General Stuart's La Petite is very sick."

"Oh no," Chantel said, distressed. "What is it she has, poor baby?"

"The doctors say it's typhoid."

Chantel pressed her eyes shut for a moment. "Typhoid," she repeated softly with dread. "Such a terrible sickness, yes. Is she — ?"

Clay finished her unspoken question. "They don't think she's going to make it. You know, Chantel, you really helped Miss Flora when she was ill. I think you were a real comfort to her. Maybe you could stop by and talk to her. She's glad to be with General Stuart, of course, but she doesn't have any real close friends in Richmond. I think she'd be glad to see you."

"I will see her," Chantel said. "Maybe I can help with La Petite." She sighed. "I don't know about losing a child, me. But I know about losing ma mere. Sometimes friends can help when no doctors can."

Chantel went to the Stuart house, unhitching faithful Rosie and riding her the two miles to the little farmhouse. She passed through the hastily erected log huts that Stuart's men had built for the winter, and many of them called out to her as she passed. They never called out rude or suggestive things anymore. They had all come to know their vivandiere and were as proud of her as if she were a star on the stage. Sutlers, particularly beautiful vivandieres, were very scarce in the blockaded Southern army.

She reached the house, and after she knocked on the door, it was a long time before it opened.

She saw that Flora had dark shadows under eyes, and her hair had not been carefully done as it usually was. Her blue eyes were shadowed with weariness and sadness. But at the sight of Chantel, they brightened a little. "Chantel, how wonderful it is to see you. I've been thinking about you. Please come in."

Flora led her into the sitting room, seated herself on the sofa, and patted the seat next to her for Chantel to sit by her. "I've been thinking about you, because you're such a wonderful nurse. When I first came to Richmond, I was so ill. I don't know what we would have done without you, Chantel. And now . . . our La Petite is ill."

"Yes, Miss Flora, Lieutenant Tremayne tells me this. I came to see you and to see La Petite, sweet baby. How is she doing?"

Flora sighed and dropped her gaze. "She's not well at all, Chantel. She is very sick."

Jeb came in and kissed Flora then smiled rather weakly at Chantel. "How are you, Miss Chantel? It's so kind of you to come by and see my Flora. She gets lonely here in camp sometimes."

"I brought some chamomile, for tea," Chantel said. "And honey, too. Maybe La Petite, she can drink some tea. Even when you're very sick, it makes you feel better."

She and Flora made tea; then Flora took her in to see La Petite. She slept, her body wasted away to that of an infant. The little girl's eyes fluttered open once, and she smiled a little at Chantel. Chantel took her fevered hand and murmured little endearments to her. But Little Flora never stayed awake for long, and in a few minutes she had passed out again.

Chantel could see very clearly that the little girl could not live long. She offered to help Flora in any way she could and asked if there was anything that she and her grandfather could bring them.

In a distant voice, Flora answered, "Thank you, Chantel, but there's nothing in this world that you could bring to help La Petite now. But you come back, please. She was glad to see you, I think."

She left, deeply saddened. It was things like this that confused Chantel about the Lord. How could He take a sweet, innocent little child like La Petite? How could He do such a terrible thing to good Christian people like Miss Flora and Jeb Stuart? Chantel didn't know. She thought that she would never know.

Two days later little Flora Stuart died. The

doctors did all they could, but typhoid was a devastating disease with a high mortality rate, especially among children.

Chantel and Jacob called on the Stuarts.

Flora was so devastated she could hardly speak, holding herself stiffly erect on the sofa in the sitting room, her eyes haunted and filled with sorrow.

Jeb stood by her, his hand on her shoulder. "God has taken our little girl, Mr. Steiner. But Flora and I know that she is with Him, and she suffers no more. And one blessed day we'll see her again in heaven."

"It is a good thing to know the Lord Jesus in these terrible times," Jacob said, his eyes glinting with unshed tears. "He alone can comfort us in this dark night of the soul. She rejoices, General Stuart, and those who are left behind must know that and rest in Him. May the peace and blessings of God be on this house, and on you both, now and forever."

When they left, Chantel found that she was almost angry. "I'll never understand God, Grandpere," she said in a low, tense voice. "It seems that if ever He would bless someone, He would bless Miss Flora and General Stuart."

"And He has blessed them," Jacob said gently. "The Bible tells us that when someone dies, we must rejoice. I know that we cannot be happy and carefree on the outside. But when we know the Lord Jesus, our hearts have joy and peace always. Even when a child dies. Because we know that this earth, this old terrible world, is not our home. Our home is in heaven, a glorious place, where there are no more sorrows, no more tears. General Stuart and Miss Flora may be here, yes, and they will grieve. But their hearts are already at home with Little Flora and with the Lord Jesus. There they will always be, forever, and they will be at peace."

# CHAPTER EIGHTEEN

The burden of office lay heavily on Abraham Lincoln, and not the least of his problems was General George McClellan. McClellan was a small man and was already called Little Napoleon by some of his admirers.

In all truth, he had more confidence in himself than any man ought to have. It was revealed in a letter to his wife in which he wrote: "The people think me all powerful, but I am becoming daily more disgusted with this administration. It is sickening in this extreme and makes me feel heavy at heart when I see the weakness and unfitness of those in charge of our military."

The president often discussed military strategy and tactics with McClellan, but he saw quickly that McClellan had little confidence in anyone's opinion except his own.

Once a secretary, who had overheard McClellan speaking arrogantly to Lincoln, said angrily, "The man is insolent! You need to get rid of him, Mr. President."

Lincoln had said merely, "I will hold McClellan's horse if he will only bring us success."

A year had passed since Bull Run, and there had been minor battles, but only one major battle in the western theater, the Battle of Shiloh. It had been bloody, and as usual the Confederates had been outnumbered, but they had driven the Yankees back, licking their wounds.

Lincoln was anxious to move on, and he had pressed his views upon McClellan, telling him, "General, you need to follow through on the same plan we had for the first attack. We could still go right through Bull Run, and we have a powerful enough army now to overcome any resistance."

McClellan flatly refused to admit that this plan had any virtues. He stubbornly insisted that Lincoln was not a military man, and he must leave the disposition of great armies, and the military plans, to the generals. In particular, to him.

For their part, the South had been lulled into a sense of false security by their victory at Bull Run, although strategically they had accomplished little. The only grand strategy that was working at this time was the

North's blockade.

The Southern economy went downhill quickly. Meat was fifty cents a pound, butter seventy-five cents, coffee a dollar fifty cents, and tea ten dollars. All in contrast to cotton, which had fallen to five cents.

The South was hemmed in, and the blockade was working all too well. Their only hope was to be recognized by England or a foreign power that would encourage the peace party in the North to declare the war over.

Jeb was sitting on the floor playing with little Jimmy. He doted on the boy, who at the age of two was definitely showing a precocious side. He was an attractive child, resembling his father in being sturdy and having the same russet-colored hair. Jeb was throwing the boy up in the air and catching him, and little Jimmy was laughing and gasping for breath.

"Jeb, you stop that! You're going to hurt that baby," Flora said sternly.

"No. He likes it, don't you, Jimmy?"

"Yes!" he said. At the age of two, he had learned a few words, and now he said, "Throw! Throw!" which was his signal for his father to toss him up into the air.

Flora came over, took little Jimmy away,

and said, "You get up off the floor now, General. Dinner is on the table."

"All right, sweetheart." Jeb came to his feet in one swift motion and followed her into the dining room. He sat down at the table and said, "Mashed potatoes and fried chicken. What could be better?"

Flora put Jimmy in the improvised high chair then sat down.

Jeb at once bowed his head and prayed. "Lord, we thank Thee for this food and for every blessing. Bless us and our Glorious Cause, and we ask that You give us victory. In the name of Jesus, we ask this. Amen." Immediately he dumped a huge dollop of mashed potatoes on his plate and picked up both wings. "My favorite part. You can have the white meat, Flora."

Flora fixed a plate for little Jimmy and let him dabble in his mashed potatoes, trying to keep the mess to a minimum. Flora fixed her own plate and began to eat, but she looked up to say, "Jeb, I'm so happy that you haven't been in any more big battles."

"Well, I expected there to be more, but since Bull Run, all has been quiet, here at least. There have been some actions over to the west, but out there they taught the Yankees a lesson, too."

"I hope they never come."

Jeb's mouth was stuffed full, and he talked around it. "Oh, they're coming, Flora. McClellan's built up an enormous army, well equipped. Our spies have kept tabs on him, and the latest word is that they are already beginning to move. We know they're on their way. We just don't know exactly where they're going to cross into Virginia. Yet."

Flora took a small bite from the breast, chewed it thoughtfully, and then asked, "Jeb, do you think General Johnston is the right man to lead the army?"

President Davis had appointed General Joe Johnston as commander of the Southern army. He was a slow-thinking, slow-moving, cautious man. For a moment, Jeb hesitated, and she could see that he was troubled. "Sometimes I think he's timid, Flora, and that's not what we need. We need men like Stonewall Jackson. I wish we had a dozen like him! Look what he's done in the valley."

Indeed, Stonewall Jackson's Valley Campaign had been the only bright spot in the Confederate military picture. With one small army, Jackson had moved from place to place, traveling hundreds of miles on foot so that his men were called "Jackson's Foot Cavalry." He had singly defeated two

Union armies.

Jeb went on, "General Jackson is the most popular man in the Confederate Army right now. Jackson scared Lincoln so bad that he pulled back two different armies so we won't have to fight them." When he finished, Jeb got to his feet and said, "I've got to go, sweetheart. I don't know what will happen, but you'll be all right here. We'll never let them get to Richmond." He leaned over, kissed her, and then picked up Jimmy and held him. "You be a good boy, Jimmy. Be good like your mother. Not like your wicked old father." He kissed the boy, handed him to Flora, and then left.

"The Yankees are coming!"

The spies had brought word that McClellan's huge force was headed up the peninsula, and Jeb and his cavalry were in the thick of the fighting. As usual, Clay's 2nd Richmond Company stayed close behind their general.

The action was bloody and was called by some the Battle at Fair Oaks and by others Seven Pines. Both sides lost many men — dead, wounded, and captured.

But the most significant event was that General Joseph Johnston was severely wounded. Jefferson Davis, without hesitation, made the wisest move he had made since his inauguration as president. He appointed Robert E. Lee to head the Southern forces. Lee at once took charge and renamed the army the Army of Northern Virginia.

"General Stuart, I have a task for you."

Jeb had been called to General Lee's headquarters, which was nothing more than a simple soldier's tent. The two men had been good friends when Stuart studied at West Point. Jeb's eyes were fiery blue as he said, "I'm anxious for action, General Lee. Just tell me what to do."

Lee studied Jeb Stuart carefully. "I want you to make a movement in the enemy rear. Inspect their communications, take cattle and grain, burn any Federal wagon trains that you find."

"Yes, sir."

"General, the utmost vigilance on your part will be necessary. The greatest caution must be practiced to keep you from falling into the enemy hands. And let me remind you that the chief object of your expedition is to gain intelligence for the guidance of future movements. Should you find that the enemy is moving to his right or is so strongly posted as to make your expedition inopportune, you will return at once."

Jeb Stuart could not conceal his joy. He was like a small boy as he slapped his gloves against one hand and said, "General, if I find a way open, I'll ride all the way around him. My father-in-law is in charge of their cavalry, you know. I've never forgiven him for going with the North, so I'm going to show him up."

Stuart left and handpicked twelve hundred men, including Robert E. Lee's son, nicknamed Rooney. He rode at once to share the news with his men, and he made a gallant figure. His gray coat was buttoned to the chin, he carried a saber and a pistol in a black holder, and he wore his polished thigh-high cavalry boots with the golden spurs. As always, a black ostrich plume was stuck in his hat, floating above the bearded features. His eyes were brilliant, and he made the perfect picture of a dashing cavalier.

As the troop left, one officer called out, "When will you be back, Stuart?"

"It may for years. It may be forever." Stuart laughed and spurred his horse forward. The troop thundered around McClellan's men. Several times Federal horsemen appeared and tried to make a fight of it, but Stuart's yelling riders simply swallowed them up.

■ ■ ■ ■

Clay was watering Lightning when they had stopped to rest their horses. He watched Stuart, who was contemplating the country ahead of him. "What next, General?"

"Well, we've already come eighteen miles southeast of Hanover Courthouse. The enemy is going to expect me to go back to camp, I know. I've already learned what General Lee sent me to learn. The right flank of McClellan is in the air, and there are no trenches on the ridges on the west. The enemy could be struck in the flank by an infantry assault."

Clay did not speak; he merely watched and listened. Finally he saw Jeb Stuart straighten up and order, "Move the column ahead at a trot."

"Yes, sir." The pace picked up and they soon became a group of cheerful horsemen. From time to time they had to spur their horses when pickets appeared and took after them, and they had a couple of skirmishes.

But in the end, Jeb Stuart completely encircled McClellan's enormous army, something that had never even been thought of, much less accomplished, before.

When Jeb Stuart rode in with his men, he

gave his report in such colorful phrases and in rhetoric that was almost epic in praise of his officers. "Their brave men behaved with coolness and intrepidity in danger, unswerving resolution before difficulties. . . . They are horsemen and troopers beyond praise."

General Lee's order in reply reflected the pride of the command in Stuart's feat. "The general commanding announces with great satisfaction to the army the brilliant exploit of Brigadier General J. E. B. Stuart . . . in passing around the rear of the whole Federal army, taking a number of prisoners, and destroying and capturing stores to a large amount. . . . The general commanding takes great pleasure in expressing his admiration of the courage and skill so conspicuously exhibited throughout by the general and the officers and men under his command."

Word spread like wildfire across the entire Confederacy, and everywhere was heard the name of Jeb Stuart. He was a hero, and the newspapers could not find language elevated enough.

"You're going to get bigheaded, I'm afraid," Clay said, grinning at Jeb as the two of them were riding to check on the men.

"Aw, if I do, Flora will take me down a peg or two. We showed those Yankees though, didn't we, Tremayne?"

"Yes you did, sir. What do you think will happen now?"

Jeb stared to the north, where the vast Federal armies were waiting. Clay saw that he was more serious than he had ever seen him. "We're going to be hit with an army of a hundred and sixty thousand men, Lieutenant. We're outnumbered, clearly five to one. It's as I said all along, we can't match the Yankees man for man. But we will always best them in daring and courage."

At that moment, Clay Tremayne saw what it was in Jeb Stuart that made men follow him right into the mouth of guns, straight toward almost certain death. There was that quality in him that few men had. Confidence, courage, audacity — it was a mixture of all of these, plus a joy in battle that few men ever experienced.

Clay observed, "That lesson you taught them, General Stuart. You've embarrassed and humiliated McClellan, and he'll throw everything he's got at us."

"And we will stop them, Lieutenant. God will surely lead us to victory."

Historians writing about what came to be called the Seven Days Battle have great difficulty. They were days of confusion, of missed or misunderstood orders, of men wandering, lost in the unmarked countryside.

McClellan's army got caught on the wrong side of the river so that he was never able to bring his full force together at once to hit the Confederates — or so he maintained afterward.

The Confederates, on the other hand, were not accustomed to the tactics, and the sometimes vague orders, of Robert E. Lee. From the first battle to the very last, some colonel or general got confused, and men who should have led failed miserably. Even the great Stonewall Jackson faltered.

In battle after battle, no one was the victor except death and the grave.

Finally the long terrible days wore both armies down. McClellan had had all he could take, and again he ordered a retreat.

Strangely enough, McClellan could have won the battle, and the Civil War could have ended at the Seven Days Battle. But McClellan, for all of his organizational ability and all of his dynamic talk, could not do one thing that a successful military commander must do: he could not send men forward into the fires of battle. This was McClellan's tragic flaw, and Lincoln had seen it before.

Time after time during this Seven Days

campaign, McClellan might have defeated the South, but time after time he failed to throw enough forces in to win. He would send men in piecemeal, and they would be cut to pieces, and then he would send in another, equally small part of his army. Never once did he throw the full weight of the Army of the Potomac against the greatly outnumbered Confederates.

So, although no one could have been said to have won the battle, the war was lost for a time to the North and won for a time to the South.

McClellan was pulling his forces out, and they had gathered together on what was called Malvern Hill. Lee and the army were hot on their trail. When they came to the sight of Malvern Hill, Lee looked up and studied the ground. It was not the best place for an attack, but Lee was hungry to destroy it. He turned and said, "Gentlemen, we will attack."

General Longstreet said, "That's a bad hill. The Yankees are well entrenched. There's no cover."

Lee had unlimited confidence in the Army of Northern Virginia, and now he made one of the two sad mistakes in his military career. "Charge the hill," he said.

There was no choice but to obey. Clay looked up at the hill and said to his corporal, "Some of our boys aren't going to come back from this ride."

"No. You're right. I don't understand General Lee."

"He's too audacious, I think. People don't know that, but he's like a Mississippi riverboat gambler."

The bugle sounded, and Clay spurred his horse. He was in the first line of attack. The guns began to boom from the Federal emplacements. Musket balls were whistling by, and men were falling. Clay rode hard ahead, following Jeb Stuart, ignoring the sights and sounds of sure death all around him, until the retreat sounded.

He was about to turn when a terrible blow struck him in his right arm. He looked down and saw that his sleeve was already covered with blood from shoulder to cuff, and he knew that the arm was shattered. In spite of the pain that almost blinded him, he wheeled Lightning around and rode back by himself.

Thirty minutes later he was in a field hospital, his uniform stripped off his upper body. The doctor was looking down at the arm, and Clay saw his face grow stern. "That arm's got to come off, Lieutenant."

"No, it doesn't."

"You'll get gangrene in it and lose it anyway. Let me do it now."

"No!" In spite of his treacherous weakness, he almost shouted at the doctor.

Then General Stuart loomed over him. "How are you, Lieutenant?" he asked.

"Don't let them take my arm, General," Clay said harshly. "Tell him. I say no."

"A man can soldier with one arm, Tremayne," Stuart said staunchly. "You'd better let him do it."

"No! I'd rather die. . . ." That was his last word, for he began drifting away into unconsciousness.

Before the blackness closed about him, as if from faraway, he heard the doctor say, "General, we'd better take it while he's out."

"No," Stuart said with sudden decision. "It's his arm, and it's his decision. He may die, but I don't know but that I'd do the same."

All Clay knew then was the darkness.

■ ■ ■ ■

# PART FOUR:
# CHANTEL & CLAY
# 1862–1865

■ ■ ■ ■

# CHAPTER NINETEEN

Sometime during the night, Clay struggled out of the black pit of unconsciousness that held him prisoner. There was a window across from him that revealed the moon and stars as they shone brightly, peacefully in the night sky, and he stared at it blankly for a while. His mind slowly and reluctantly swam to the surface.

The room was quiet save for the moanings and mutterings of his fellow patients. He glanced to his right, and there, far down the room, a medic sat at a desk reading a book by the pale yellow light of a lantern.

As he lay there, his mind in that place where it was not yet awake and yet not fully asleep, Clay became slowly aware that something was growing in his mind. It was like a tiny light from somewhere far down a dark road, so dim that it could barely be seen. It grew larger and brighter, and it was not, Clay knew, a physical light, not a real light at all, only something deep within him. But his spirit seemed to glow — there was no other way he could think of it.

As the sensation grew, he relaxed and let his body grow limp. He had kept himself so tense waiting for the next jolt of pain in his arm that every muscle in his body ached sharply. But now a sense of quietness, almost of ease, came to him. His eyelids became heavy, so heavy he could not keep them open, and he slept again.

When he stirred again, and his mind once more started its torturous way to full consciousness, he saw through the window that the dim gray light of morning shone through. With a start, he awakened fully and looked down at his side. His right arm was still there; the doctors had obeyed Jeb Stuart's order. He lay back on his pillow with weak relief.

"How do you feel, Clay?"

Chantel was sitting by his bed. He wondered if she had been sitting there long.

"Hello, Chantel," he murmured. "I — I got shot."

"Yes, I know. Are you thirsty?"

Clay felt a raging thirst. He licked his dry lips and nodded, and she picked up a pitcher on the table beside his bed, half-filled a tumbler, then reached under his head and held it up. The water was sweeter than any drink that Clay had ever had, and when he had drained the glass, she put his head back on the pillow, and he said, "That was good. Thank you, Chantel."

Chantel replaced the glass and turned to look at him, her face grim. "Clay, I've got to talk to you, and you must listen to me."

"What is it?"

"The doctors say that your arm has to be taken. There's no other way."

"No." The word leaped to Clay's lips even before she had finished talking.

"But Clay, they say you may die if you don't. They think they see the gangrene started."

"I'd rather die than be a cripple. I know that's foolish, Chantel, but it's the way I feel."

He saw that her face was fixed in an expression of sadness, and he said, "Don't worry about me. I'm not going to die, Chantel. But even if I do, I'm going to die a whole man."

"But you may die, Clay," she pleaded. "You will leave behind so much — your family, your friends. You will leave Grandpere — and . . . you will leave me."

He stared at her, for Chantel had never expressed any endearments to him, had never shown him anything but common courtesy and politeness. His affection for her had grown much, though he worked hard to deny it, for he had always thought it was hopeless, that he had ruined any chance he might have had with her that night he had so clumsily tried to kiss her. Now she was watching him, her eyes great and dark, and suddenly he could see that she had feelings for him. But his face closed, and he said, "Chantel, I won't let them cut off my arm. You have to understand. I don't want to live like that. I won't live like that."

Chantel pleaded with him. "Many men have lost an arm, a leg, their sight, and they are still good men and happy men. That is not something an arm or an eye makes, Clay. You are a strong, handsome man, and you can be happy, even with one arm."

But Clay merely lay there, his lips drawn tightly together, until she finished. "I don't want to talk about this anymore." He closed his eyes and drifted back into sleep.

Chantel continued her silent vigil, now with a sense of hopelessness. For she had seen that Clay Tremayne would never change his mind.

She went back to the wagon and asked Jacob to talk to Clay, and Jacob agreed at once. She went to the hospital with him but left the two men alone. She talked to others down the line but kept her eye on Clay and Jacob.

She got to one young man, and he said, "You want to get this letter off for me, Miss Chantel?"

"Of course I will, Leonard."

He handed her the envelope and then said, "Maybe you better look over it to see if I spelled everything right." She read the letter quickly and was amused, for it said:

Alf sed he heard that you and hardy was a running together all the time and he thot he wod just quit having anything more to doo with you for he thot it was no more yuse. I think you made a bad chois to turn off as nise a feler as alf dyer and let that orney, theivin, drunkard, cardplaying hardy swayne come to see you. He ain't nothing but a thef and a lopeared pigen toed hellion. He is too ornery for the devil. I will shute him as shore as I see him.

"Are you sure you want to say this?"

"I purely do. I hate that Hardy Swayne. He's a dead man if he don't leave my sister alone."

Chantel struggled to find something to

say. Finally she offered, "Maybe your sister loves him."

"Ain't no sister of mine going to marry up with a no-account skunk like him. She can just find some other man to love."

"But Leonard, a woman can't just switch off love," she said with a passion that surprised her.

"Why can't she?"

"Well, when we love somebody, we can't just stop loving him even if he's not what he should be. What if our mothers, our fathers, stopped loving us when we do wicked things? What if God stopped loving us then?"

Leonard shook his head and said firmly, "God never told nobody to be stupid! Ain't any woman who marries up with Hardy Swayne gonna have a good life. He'll drink and steal and lie and beat her, and she'll have to raise her kids by herself. It's only a stupid woman would ask for that kind of life. Now, ain't that so, Miss Chantel?"

Painfully Chantel thought of her step-father and wondered for the thousandth time how her mother ever could have married such a man. Resignedly she finally answered, "I — I can't answer that, me. But if you're sure, I'll mail the letter."

"Thank you kindly, Miss Chantel."

Leaving Leonard's bed, Chantel went to visit another young man. She had become very fond of him. His name was Tommy Grangerford, and he was the same age that she was, eighteen years old. He was terribly wounded, a chest wound that very few ever survived. She forced herself to smile brightly. "Hello, Tommy. How are you feeling?"

"Oh, I can't complain."

"You never do."

"Do you have time to sit down and talk to me, Miss Chantel?" he asked hopefully. "I know you're real busy and all, but I've been kind of lonesome."

"I always have time for you, Tommy," she said kindly.

She sat down and for twenty minutes talked to him. From time to time, the terrible pain that racked him would twist him almost into impossible positions, and she would dab the clammy perspiration from his face. Finally, in desperation she went to the medic and asked for more laudanum for him.

"Might not be a good thing, Miss Chantel," the medic said reluctantly. "He's had a lot of it already, and if you give a man too much, he can die."

"He's going to die anyway, he is," Chantel

said sadly.

The orderly gave in. "All right, ma'am. Here it is."

She went back and gave Tommy a large dose of the strong drug, and soon he lay his head back on the pillow. His eyes fluttered, and he said softly, "I won't be here long, Miss Chantel. But I'm tired, and I'm ready to go home. You know, in the Bible it says that man will go to his long home. That sounds so good, so restful. My long home . . ."

She waited until his breathing grew deep and even. From his bedside, she could see Clay's bed and her grandfather talking earnestly to him.

After a while, she saw Jacob rise, motioning to her. She came down the ward and glanced at Clay, who was asleep. They left quietly.

When they got outside, Chantel asked anxiously, "What did he say, Grandpere?"

"The same thing he said to you, I'm afraid, daughter. He's got his mind made up that he will not lose that arm. I talked to him, because I know the doctors say he's going to die if they don't amputate, and asked him if he didn't know he must come to the Lord and ask Him for salvation. But," he continued with a sigh, "Clay Tremayne is a stubborn man. He says it would be a cowardly thing to come to God now that he's helpless. I can't make him realize that we're all helpless."

Chantel dropped her head wearily. "Then he is lost."

Jacob patted her arm. "We don't know that, daughter. The good God has His own plan for Clay Tremayne, just as He does for me and for you. We will wait upon God, and we will pray, and we will see."

Two days later, Chantel sat with Tommy Grangerford, for she knew he was dying. It was late, and there was no one with him but Chantel. All of the other patients slept.

They had been talking quietly, and sometimes Tommy drifted off. But once he roused, and his voice, which had been thin and weak and thready, grew stronger. "I never told you how I got saved, did I, Miss Chantel?"

"No, you never have, Tommy."

"Well, I heard a sermon, and it scared me. I was scared to death to face God with all my sins. The next day I was out in the field chopping cotton, and my ma and pa, they were down the row from me. My brothers and sisters were there, and I was doing my best just to think about chopping cotton.

But somehow that didn't happen. I knew all of a sudden that God was telling me something, and I couldn't shut it out. I never heard any words, but God told me, *'Tommy, this is your last chance. I died for you because I love you. You let Me come into your heart.'*"

Tommy shook his head and smiled. "I just couldn't stand it, Miss Chantel. I knelt down right there in the dirt in the cotton field, and I cried out, 'Oh God, I'm a sinner, but I know Jesus died for me. Forgive my sins, please, and come into my heart.'"

"And what happened, Tommy?"

"Well, my ma and pa, and my brothers and my sisters, came rushing to me, but even before they got there I knew something had happened to me. I had been carrying a heavy load, and everything was so dark and miserable. But even as I knelt there in the dirt, I knew that something had happened. That I had something new. I didn't hear voices or see visions. It was all inside me, Miss Chantel. My parents were crying and holding to me, and I was crying. My poor ma and pa had been praying for me all my life."

"And what happened then?"

"Well, I was afraid I'd lose that peace that came to me in that cotton field. But I never did. I went to the Baptist church the next

Sunday morning, and I told the preacher I wanted to be baptized, and I was baptized that very day. I started reading the Bible, and people helped me learn how to serve God. We all need someone to help us learn about Him, don't we?"

"Yes, we do," Chantel said thoughtfully.

"Miss Chantel, I think God has put Jacob Steiner in your life to help you find your way to Jesus." His voice grew softer and weaker, and he said, "Listen to your grandfather, Miss Chantel. Don't miss out on Jesus. I want to see you in heaven."

Tommy died an hour later while Chantel was still holding his hand. He had not spoken again, but his last words she knew she would never forget, his urging her to meet him in heaven.

Chantel was broken as she never had been. She held Tommy's still hand and wept, torn by sobs. She began to pray then, and suddenly, in the gloom of that hospital ward, she was aware of what Tommy had said. That God had told him that it was his last chance. A cold fear washed over her. *Maybe this is my last chance.* She tried to pray but could not frame the words.

After a long struggle, suddenly she whispered, "I can't even pray, Lord!" And then it came to her. She thought about her

stepfather and how she had hated him —
and still did. And then she suddenly knew
why she couldn't pray. She remembered a
part of the Bible that Jacob had read to her.
The Scripture was, "If you forgive men their
trespasses, your Heavenly Father will also
forgive you: but if you forgive not men their
trespasses, neither will your Father forgive
ye your trespasses."

The verse went like a sharp knife into
Chantel's spirit, and she knew that she
could not hang on to that hatred and come
into the kingdom of God. She finally bowed
her head and whispered, "I've hated my
stepfather, Lord, and You say I must forgive
him. So the best I can, I forgive him."

It took some time. Chantel struggled,
hard, for she had years of bitterness in her
spirit. Finally, blessedly, she was able to let
go of all the hatred and resentment, and
then she called on Jesus, and Jesus came
into her heart. She knew it as well as she
knew her own name. The hot tears of grief
streaming down her face changed to tears
of joy, and she began to thank God. Chantel knew that nothing for her could ever be
the same again.

Chantel saw Jacob's eyes open, and then he
reached out and held her, hugging her with

all his feeble strength. She had just awakened him and told him how she had found Jesus.

"Thank God," he kept saying. "Thank the good God."

She said, "I'm going to have to have some help."

"God will send people to help you. Me for one, and if necessary, why, the good Lord will send a mighty angel out of heaven to take care of you, for you are His daughter now and nothing will ever change that."

Chantel was still crying. "I've become a crybaby, me."

"Those are tears of joy, my sweet girl, and there will be many more of them. I thank God that He has reached down and lifted your soul out of sin and put your name in the Book of Life, and He says He will never blot it out, no never, not throughout all eternity."

Chantel listened, and the words soaked into her spirit like balm.

She hardly slept, but at dawn she didn't feel tired. She hurried to the hospital, anxious to tell Clay about her night. As soon as she came through the door she saw one of the doctors, an elderly man named Hardin, motioning to her. She went down the aisle, smiling and greeting Clay and the men, but not stopping to talk.

Dr. Hardin said, "Miss Chantel, I know that Lieutenant Tremayne is your special friend."

"Yes," Chantel said. "We've known each other a long time, you may say."

"I've talked to his family, and they've begged him. And if you're his friend, maybe you can talk some sense into him."

"I doubt it," Chantel said under her breath, but the doctor was still talking, glowering like an angry bulldog.

"The fool just will not let us take that arm off! He acts like he's the only man who ever lost a limb. I know that gangrene is setting in — by now I can tell it a mile away. What I think is we ought to dope him up, and then when he's unconscious, take the arm. He'll be angry when he wakes up, but he'll live. If we don't, then we're going to lose him."

"You can't do that," Chantel said dully. "He may be a fool, but he is a man, and he has made this decision. But I'll try, Doctor. I'll try to talk to him again, me."

Chantel went to Clay then, and he was already angry and upset.

"I saw you talking to Dr. Hardin, and I know what he said. He's already been here nagging me. Once and for all, I say no. I won't do it. Don't talk about it anymore, Chantel."

Chantel had left the hospital soon after talking to Clay, for Jacob was moving the wagon to be closer to General Stuart's headquarters, at his invitation. Chantel helped him lash down all the supplies and pack up their camp.

When they reached their new campsite, as always, Chantel unpacked the big sutler's tent and began to put it up. But by now all of the men knew her and Jacob, and she wasn't allowed to lift a finger. The soldiers put up the tent and helped Chantel and Jacob stock it.

Most of them, by now, had no money at all, but Jacob still gave them things — buttons, needles and thread, wool socks, shoes, warm undershirts. He gave away so much that for the dozenth time Chantel wondered how they ever kept a stock at all.

Then she stayed in camp, talking for hours with the soldiers and to Jacob, who was still rejoicing with her. It was late in the evening when she returned to the hospital.

The slow hours passed, and Chantel knew that it was past midnight. How far past she didn't know. She had prayed until her mind was numb. Clay had fallen into a restless sleep, and she had watched him for a couple of hours, moving restlessly and muttering, his forehead wet with perspiration. Over and over she sponged him with a cool damp cloth, but it seemed that nothing could soothe him.

Finally she leaned forward, folded her hands on his bed, and laid her head down. Her fingers barely touched his side. She began to pray aloud, though in the quietness of the ward she kept her voice to a soft whisper. She whispered, "Oh God, I ask You to help Clay." She waited, for her mind felt strangely blank. She found that it was much harder to pray aloud than in the privacy of one's own heart.

But then thoughts, and the words, came to her. "I was unfair to him. He would never have hurt me, not intentionally. I just had so much anger inside me, Lord, and I couldn't let go of it, and I blamed him for something that maybe, deep down, I wanted him to do. Because I know now that I love him, Lord. Maybe I always have. But now, here we are, we two! Finally I let You save me, and he can't find his way to You. And now he may die. Please, please, have mercy on him, Lord Jesus. Don't make this his last chance."

For a while she was quiet, merely resting,

her fingers lightly touching him, and she remembered how she had touched his face that time he had kissed her. She had loved his touch then, even though she had so cruelly pushed him away and made him feel guilty. She sat up then lightly laid her hand on his arm. It felt hot and was stiff with the thick bandages.

Bowing her head, she whispered, "Lord, I don't know much about You, but I know Jacob has read to me that You will heal people. I know there's no hope for Clay in doctors and medicine. But Jacob says nothing is impossible with You, so I'm asking You to heal Clay's arm."

She went on praying for a long time, until she grew so weary she could hardly stay awake. She finally left, still not knowing any answer from God. She felt sadness, but as Jacob had always said, still she knew joy deep in her heart.

Clay had not been asleep the entire time Chantel had been there. He wandered in a dim haze, his mind coming up to half consciousness at times. He had heard some of Chantel's prayers, and they had moved him. Dimly he thought, *Lord, I don't know what to say to You. I don't know You. I don't understand anything about You. But I'm glad*

*Chantel has found You. And about this heal-ing business, You know I couldn't ask You for that. I've no right. But I'm so grateful that she did.*

He knew he had fever, and he was having trouble thinking clearly. *Chantel loves me,* he thought with wonder. *Or was I just dreaming? That is a wonderful, blissful dream . . . but no, I heard her. I know I did.* And he knew at that moment, as hurt as he was, and as hopeless as life seemed to be, he loved her. *And like Chantel told You, Lord . . . I think I always have.*

Clay woke up, and the first thing that he was aware of was that the excruciating pain in his arm had subsided. Then he knew that his fever had passed, for he came instantly, fully awake.

One of the medics had come to change the bandage on his arm. He was a tall, thin man with a good bushy growth of whiskers. His name was Grady Wynn, and he was one of those men who had a great compassion for sick and injured men, a naturally good caregiver.

"Good morning, Lieutenant," Wynn said. "Sorry to wake you up, but it's time to change this bandage. How about, while I'm at it, we get the doctor and let him take this thing off?" he finished brightly.

"No," Clay said automatically, watching him with a newfound alertness.

"Thought not, but it never hurts to — what? What's this?" Wynn said in a shocked voice.

Clay looked at his arm curiously, but Wynn laid the last layer of bandage back on it and said, "Don't move, and for once do what I say, Lieutenant Tremayne. I'll be back."

Wynn moved quickly, and in only a few moments came hurrying back with Dr. Hardin. "Look at that arm, Dr. Hardin," Wynn said. "Just look at it."

The doctor stared at Wynn then stepped forward and lifted the bandages. Clay was watching his face, and he saw the doctor's eyes fly open wide with astonishment.

"Will someone tell me what's going on?" Clay demanded.

"Your arm. It's healing," Dr. Hardin said in a mystified voice.

"Huh?" Clay said, lifting his head up with some effort to look at his arm.

Wynn said, "But I thought gangrene wouldn't heal."

"No. It usually doesn't." Dr. Hardin poked at Clay's forearm then pinched it hard. "You feel that?"

"Yes, it hurts."

Dr. Hardin stared at him. "I pinched you yesterday, and you didn't feel anything."

Hope began to rise in Clay Tremayne. "What are you saying, Doctor?"

Dr. Hardin was a tough man. He had to be. He dealt with death and terrible wounds constantly, every day since the war had begun. His face was a study, and finally he said, "I have no explanation for this, but your arm is healing. Unless I'm mistaken — and I don't think I am — you should be all right, Lieutenant Tremayne."

Clay felt numb, in an odd sort of way. There was a seed of hope and of joy deep inside him, but for a long time he couldn't think, couldn't speak. All he could think of was the prayer that Chantel had prayed for him.

All day he lay there, feeling alternately stunned and deliriously glad. Dr. Hardin came back by several times to lift the now-loose bandage and peer at Clay's arm. He went away shaking his head.

The men heard of it, and they talked among themselves, but they didn't bother Clay. He just stared into space, sometimes smiling, rarely speaking to the doctors and medics. Sometimes he lifted the bandages himself and stared at his arm in disbelief.

Late that afternoon Chantel came. Even before they had said hello, Clay asked, "Have you talked to Dr. Hardin?"

"Yes," she said, and her eyes were glowing. "He says your arm is healed."

"He says he doesn't know how it happened, but I know, Chantel. I was awake, sometimes, when you prayed for me last night. I know this is God's answer to your prayer."

"He really is the good God, Clay." She reached out to take his hand — his right hand, now cool and not at all swollen — and tears showed in her eyes. "I'm so happy for you."

Lifting her hand, he kissed it and said, "Thank you, Chantel, for not giving up on me."

"I wouldn't give up on you, Clay. I never could." She bowed her head slightly and asked so softly that Clay could barely hear her, "And did you hear all my prayers, so?"

"Most of them," he answered. "I think, Chantel, that you are a very wise woman. I think you know that I care for you, that I've cared for you ever since I first saw your face, my angel in that dark time. And I would beg you to have me, right now . . . but I know this — I know that now you'll only have a man of God. And I'm not a man of

God. So I won't try to push you, Chantel, as I did once before. I'll never make that mistake again."

Chantel looked up, smiled, and gently smoothed his hair back from his forehead. "God has healed you. You may not know it now, but you already belong to Him. You owe Him a great debt, Clay Tremayne, and once you told me that you are a man that always pays his debts. Oh yes, you owe God now. And one day, like me, you will learn to love Him."

# CHAPTER TWENTY

Flora watched her husband and son as they played. Long ago she had given up trying to tell Jeb not to toss the child around as if he were a kitten. As she thought this, she was reminded of those long-ago days, when Ruby had said exactly the same thing to her. For Jeb was like a very large friendly dog, and he played rough. But little Jimmy was like his father. He dearly loved to play "throw."

Jeb was lying flat on his back. Little Jimmy was on his stomach, and as his father held him high, he would laugh and swing his arms as if he were trying to fly. Even though Jimmy had grown, Jeb still tossed him up in the air, over and over again.

Sitting in the rocking chair, Flora watched them, a smile on her face. But then, though she tried to fight it, a nagging worry came to her, as it so often did. She thought about the vulnerability of Jeb on the battlefield.

She had heard his men talk about his absolute disregard for danger. It was even in the newspapers that they reveled in stories of General Stuart's fearlessness. He seemed to court it, his horsemen said, riding to the sounds of the guns, waving his saber and laughing as if he were going to a party.

Flora's worry was as unfriendly and persistent as a wound, and there was nothing, it seemed, that she could do to stop it. She had learned to live with it, as women had, both North and South. They sat at home, waiting, hoping for the war to end and their men to return for good — and dreading and fearing the message that they were dead or wounded.

She had been the daughter of an army officer for her first twenty years, but only a few scattered battle actions against the hostile Indians had broken the peace. They had not been serious, and her father had never been wounded. Though of course she had worried about her father, it was nothing like the painful constant thoughts that she could be a widow.

Shaking off her fears, Flora said, "You know, Jeb, I was thinking of taking a walk and going over to see Mr. Steiner and Chantel. I've been hungry for a chocolate cake, and I don't think there's one bit of chocolate in any store in Richmond. But if there is any in this city, Jacob Steiner will have it."

"Throw," Jimmy sternly ordered, and Jeb tossed him high, then caught him and set him on his feet.

"We better escort your pretty mama to the sutler's, or some soldier's likely to snatch her up and keep her," he said, rising quickly. For such a bulky man, he moved swiftly and surely.

"That would never happen, Jeb," Flora said, secretly pleased.

He came to her, grabbed her around the waist, and swung her around, grinning as she protested.

"You put me down right now, Jeb."

"No, I won't do it. I guess I'm just too much in love with you to keep my hands off of you."

In spite of herself, she laughed, and she was almost dizzy when he finally put her down.

Swooping little Jimmy up, he took her arm. "I'd like to see Mr. Steiner, too, and thank him. He's been so good to my men. I don't know how he ever makes a cent. He gives away more than he ever sells, I think."

They went out into the August evening. It was still hot and sultry, but Flora found the evening air pleasant. The light scent of jasmine was carried on a light evening breeze. "I can't imagine where he's getting his supplies, either," she said. "He never seems to run out of anything. Somehow I can't imagine Mr. Steiner as a daring blockade runner."

Jeb laughed, a rich joyous sound that Flora never tired of hearing. "I think he's like Elijah, and that sutler's wagon is his cruse of oil. I think every night God just restocks it for him."

They walked through the forest of tents, the camp of Jeb's 1st Virginia Cavalry. The men stood stiffly and saluted him, and usually Jeb returned it with a joke or a question about them, their supplies, their sweethearts, their ailments.

Jeb put little Jimmy down and let him run around, for he was a favorite among the soldiers. Flora and Jeb walked slowly to let the men see their son, ruffle his thick hair, pick him up and hold him, and tease him about riding out with them on patrol.

Flora's eyes shadowed a little. "Your men — they're such good men. They'd follow you anywhere, Jeb, even to the death."

"I know," he said quietly. "They've done it, time and time again. I'm grateful to God to have such men, to have the honor of fighting alongside them." He glanced at Flora then added awkwardly, "Please don't trouble yourself too much, Flora. You know that all we can do is ask God to give us strength and courage. We're all in God's hands."

She sighed heavily. "I know, Jeb, and I do try. But I can't help worrying about you."

Flora realized Stuart was well aware of her concerns for him, he knew her as she knew him, but like other soldiers, he avoided making any promises he might not be able to keep. Despite what people said about her husband's eagerness for battle and the strange moods that seemed to strike him when the guns sounded and the bugles rang out the charge, she knew he was not unaware of the dangers. He had said once, "All I ask of life is that if I have to die, I do it in a cavalry charge." He was a simple man, no deep thinker, but an excellent officer and leader of men. And a wonderful husband and father.

Now he laughed, as he often did when trying to allay her fears. "I'm too tough to kill, Flora. And even if they did kill me, they couldn't kill me but once. Don't worry. Put it all out of your head."

She knew that her fears were a burden to her husband, and she had to be strong and not add to his cares. She managed to smile up at him. "I can do that, husband, for you. Now, you'd better go get Jimmy. I declare, I think that boy is actually going to set him up on that enormous horse."

Jeb went over to the group of men standing around a big chestnut gelding. Flora watched, and even though she knew what was going to happen, she still rolled her eyes when Jeb swung Jimmy up high and set him on the horse. All the men laughed, and the young man who had been holding Jimmy yelled, "Charge!"

When they reached the sutler's tent, a gentle twilight was cooling down the air.

Jacob and Chantel sat around a small campfire. One of the men had made Jacob a little table out of some spare lumber, and a bright lantern sat on it, bright enough so that he could read.

They greeted the Stuarts happily, and Chantel immediately scooped up little Jimmy. "You've grown, you! Soon you'll pick me up, no?"

He giggled and said, "Throw!"

"I think I'll leave that to your father," Chantel said.

Jacob asked them to stay for a while, but Jeb said, "No, thank you, sir, we won't be staying. We just came out for a short walk.

My wife is on a search for chocolate, and since she mentioned it, my mouth's been watering for one of her chocolate cakes. Would you have any such thing in that tent?"

"Oh yes, I believe we do," Jacob said. "Chantel, you know where everything is. Won't you take Miss Flora and give her all the chocolate she needs?"

Chantel and Flora went into the big tent, where goods were stacked all over four long tables that Jacob had bought when they made their semi-permanent camp. "Here's the chocolate, Miss Flora. Powdered or bars."

She still held little Jimmy, whose eyes lit up when he saw some hard candy wrapped in shiny red paper. "Mine," he said, pointing a stubby little finger.

"Jimmy, no, not yours," Flora said firmly.

"Oh, can't he have just one piece, Miss Flora?" Chantel pleaded. "If it's all right with you, of course."

"Well, just one," Flora relented. "And you must add it to the bill. I'll have the bar chocolate, please, and a sack of sugar. What a pleasure, to just walk in and be able to buy them. Jeb and I were saying how hard it is to find even meat and bread these days, much less such luxuries as chocolate and sugar."

"Ma grandpere, he's a good scrounger, the soldiers say," Chantel said proudly.

Flora smiled. "Jeb says he's like Elijah. We think God just restocks your wagon every night."

"I don't know Elijah yet, me," Chantel said, her brow furrowing. "It's going to take a long time to learn all the Bible."

"I don't know of anyone that knows all of it," Flora said lightly, "except for maybe your grandfather. Other than that, how is your new life, Chantel?"

"Good, ver' good," she answered with satisfaction. "I feel so much better now in the hospital with the soldiers. I can talk to them about the Lord, instead of running like a little rabbit for Grandpere."

"It is so good, what you're doing for the men. Those poor wounded boys in the hospital, they're terribly lonesome."

"Yes, and they're afraid," Chantel said a little sadly. "They don't say so, but I can see it in their eyes. They want their mothers or their sisters."

"Yes, but from what I hear, they're always so glad to see their vivandiere. And what about that young captain who was courting you. Have you been able to see him much lately?"

"Captain Latane? Yes, he comes to visit sometimes. He's a Cajun, like me, so we have fun together."

Flora nodded. "Jeb told me about Lieutenant Tremayne, about how his arm was miraculously healed. You know, that happens sometimes. It's always a mystery, but who can know the mind of God? But I know what good friends you are, and I know you're so happy for him. Jeb was very glad to have him back."

"Yes, it was a miracle, thank the good God. I — I see him, too, sometimes. But General Stuart has kept him busy, I think," she said hesitantly.

Seeing her reluctance, Flora merely smiled and said, "Well, I think this is all we need for now, Chantel. Now, how much do we owe you?"

Chantel shook her head as they left the tent. "Grandpere, he decides about the money. You'll have to ask him, Miss Flora."

Jacob staunchly refused to let Jeb pay him. "It's a gift, General Stuart, for your wife and your fine boy. All I ask is that you send me a piece of your chocolate cake, Miss Flora."

They gathered up little Jimmy, who was sucking on a second piece of candy that Chantel had sneaked him. Jacob and Chan-

tel watched them walk slowly away in the
evening shadows, arm in arm.

"He's a fine man, General Stuart," Jacob
said. "Rarely does one see such a warrior
with such a heart for God."

"She worries for him," Chantel said in a
low voice. "It must be hard for your man to
be a soldier."

Jacob glanced at her then patted her
shoulder. "It's always hard for the ones left
behind, daughter. So we must pray that
much more."

Stepping out of the wagon the next morning, she found Armand waiting for her with
a smile. "Good morning, cherie."

"Hello, Armand. What are you doing this
fine morning?"

"I came for some of that special tea you
sold me last time."

"You must have really liked it."

"Well, I did. But it's actually for my
sergeant. He absolutely loved it and says he
won't fight a war without it, him."

Chantel walked toward the tent, which
was closed up. Jacob was still asleep in the
wagon. Since they kept it cleared out now,
he and Chantel had plenty of room to set
up their cots. Armand helped her fold up
the tent flaps. She asked, "So. You and your

416

sergeant, are you moving out soon?"

Armand followed her closely as she moved down the tables looking for the tea. "You know, cherie, I think maybe you are a Yankee spy out to get military secrets from me. If you don't let me have my way with you, I'll turn you over to the guard."

He had put his hand on her shoulder and tried to look fierce, but Chantel laughed and pushed him away. "I wouldn't waste my time on a captain if I were a spy. I'd find me a general. You don't know enough about what's going on, you."

"Oh, you hurt my heart," he said, placing his hand on his chest theatrically. "And you're wrong, my cruelest love. I know everything about what's going on."

"Then tell me," Chantel demanded.

"Well, I may not know everything," Armand said, putting two chairs out for them to sit down. "But everybody knows we're going to invade the North. General Lee will hit them hard. We're tired of them coming into our country. It's time to go up there and put a stop to it."

Chantel was concerned, for she really liked Armand. "You be careful, you. Don't you get yourself hurt."

"Would you miss me?"

"Oh yes, Captain. You're the only Cajun I

know in this place."

He made a face and said, "I must settle for that, although —"

"I know. It hurts your heart," Chantel finished for him.

On September 13, 1862, three soldiers were crossing an open field that had been a recent Confederate campsite. They stopped long enough to take a break, and one of them noticed a long, thick envelope lying on the ground. He picked it up and found three cigars inside wrapped in a sheet of official-looking paper. One of the soldiers, a man named Mitchell, examined the documents. "Headquarters, Army of Northern Virginia, special orders 191." The three men took it at once to the company commander, who took them to regimental headquarters. Eventually they were standing in front of the commanding general, General McClellan. He studied the paper and saw that this was Robert E. Lee's complete battle plan for the invasion of Maryland. McClellan said with excitement, "Here is a paper with which if I cannot whip Bobby Lee, I will be willing to go home!"

Indeed it seemed that McClellan had the men, the ordnance, and now the secret plans that should have enabled him to destroy the Confederates. But when the two armies lined up facing each other across Antietam Creek, a fast-running small river that ran close to the town of Sharpsburg, it seemed that none of these great advantages did him any good.

In essence, the Union general began sending his men across the bridges that spanned Antietam Creek. From the very first, his method was wrong. Again, instead of sending a huge overwhelming force, he sent his men in piecemeal. They fought bravely, but there were not enough of them in any one charge, and the Confederates entrenched across the creek shot them down by the hundreds with musket fire and artillery.

Three times McClellan renewed the strategy, and each time he again failed to send the complete force he had. If in any of these three attempts he had sent his entire command across, the Army of Northern Virginia would indeed have been destroyed. Lee and Jackson were engaged in shifting the few men they had from one spot to the next location that was attacked. In each of the three charges, the Confederates barely survived. But they did, and three times they beat the Union forces back. It was a case of nerves, and McClellan had no taste nor stomach for this kind of fighting.

It was the bloodiest day in American history; more men were killed on that day than any single day. Lee waited for McClellan to come across the creek in force, certain that he would. He knew that he had far too few men left to defend another attack. But to his amazement, the attack did not come.

Lee gathered his wounded, bloodied army and made his way back toward Richmond. Once again he had survived along with the army, as tattered and beaten as it was. Thousands were dead, and more thousands were wounded.

Abraham Lincoln was exceedingly angry when he heard how McClellan had, once again, let the Confederate Army slip out of his grasp. He did not say so then, but he had, no doubt, made the resolution McClellan would never command the army again.

When discussing the fighting later, Jeb Stuart said sadly to Clay, "The troops we lost today were the best that General Lee had, the best that he could ever hope to have."

"What does it mean, General?"

Stuart had lost many of his own men and could barely speak, for he loved his soldiers. Finally he answered, "We will keep on fighting. God in His mercy will help us."

# CHAPTER TWENTY-ONE

Chantel noticed as she moved among the throngs on the Richmond streets how threadbare and worn some of the clothing of the citizens was. In truth, the blockade had been more successful than the North had even expected. Occasionally a ship would slip through and disembark its cargo, and in every case hundreds of people would be standing there waiting to pay almost any price to get precious goods that were unobtainable anywhere in the Confederacy.

Chantel, on her way to the Stuarts', smiled to herself, for she was carrying a quarter of fresh beef. She thought that some of these genteel ladies coming empty-handed out of the shops, had they known it, might have knocked her down and stolen it.

Jacob had finally told Chantel the mystery of how he obtained his continual store of supplies. "Gold," he had said the night before as they sat by their campfire. "Pure gold. These poor people with their Confederate money, pah! A pile of it won't buy a loaf of bread. But the love of money — real money — runs strong in a man." He told her how he went to the storehouses that still received supplies and they would always sell any goods to him first because he paid them in gold. "I have a big pile of it, hidden in the floor of the wagon. I will show you where it is, Chantel, should the Lord call me home."

"But, Grandpere," she said, shocked, "you take Confederate money for the goods when you sell them at all. How can you be making any money doing that?"

"I have lots of gold, and more where that came from," he said gleefully. "God has shown me what to do with it, and God is not interested in making money. He's only interested in us being obedient to Him when we have it."

Arriving at the house the Stuarts rented, Chantel knocked on the door.

Almost at once it was opened, and Flora stood there holding little Jimmy.

"Hello, Miss Flora," Chantel said. "Ma grandpere, he sends you some beef."

"Oh, that is so wonderful! It's been so long since we had anything but dried jerky.

Oh, please come in, Chantel." Flora's eyes lit up, and as she turned, little Jimmy made a grab at Chantel's sleeve and caught it. "He likes you, Chantel," Flora said as she led her to the kitchen.

"Well, I like him, too. Let me hold him." Flora put him down, and Chantel held out her arms.

The child came to her at once. He was learning to talk now and called her, "Cante," which was as close as he could come to her real name. "Cante! Cante!" he yelled.

Chantel reached into her bag, which was slung across her chest. "Here. You can have one piece. I don't want to spoil your supper." She laughed as Jimmy grabbed the morsel of candy and popped it into his mouth then looked up at her with a satisfied expression. "You're much easier to please than most men."

Flora laughed. "Yes, he is. Here, let me put that meat up."

After putting the meat under a cloth to keep the flies away, she and Chantel sat down at the sturdy oak worktable. Chantel sat with Jimmy on her lap. To amuse him, she pulled off her bag and set it on the table, and he immediately began to reach into it and pull out the contents. Chantel kept all kinds of things in her bag: paper, pencil, buttons, candy, a spoon, a small New Testament, headache powders. With delight Jimmy pulled out a sheaf of paper and a pencil and started drawing.

"I've got enough for one cup of coffee apiece," Flora said. "After that's gone, we'll be drinking acorn water."

"Acorn water? What's that?"

"Oh, people take acorns and bake them and crush them up."

"It sounds awful. What does it taste like?"

"Like burned acorns." Flora shrugged.

Chantel made a face. "I'll bring you some real coffee, me. Grandpere wouldn't like it if he knew General Stuart was drinking from acorns."

"I wasn't trying to hint, Chantel," Flora said, but she was smiling. "But I should have known. If your grandfather has it, he will share. He's worth his weight in gold."

"More than you know, Miss Flora," Chantel said, amused. "Now, tell me all about Jimmy and about General Stuart. Soldiers talk, they do, but they never know anything."

"Jeb doesn't tell me much," Flora said quietly. "I worry about him, you know. I try not to let him know it, but of course he does. I pray, all the time, that I'll just enjoy the time we have with him and not fear the future."

"Sometimes that's hard, not to be afraid, when men go to war," Chantel said, her eyes gazing into the distance. "Even for Christians, I know now, me."

Flora eyed her knowingly. "And who do you fear for, Chantel?" she asked gently.

Chantel dropped her eyes and ran her hand over Jimmy's hair. It was thick and looked wiry, but actually it was very soft. "He — he's just a friend," she said rather lamely. "But I've known him for three years now, me. So I worry about him, Lieutenant Tremayne."

"I see," Flora said. "Jeb says he is a fine man and one of his best soldiers. He's told me that even when he sets the formations for the column, he looks up and Lieutenant Tremayne is there, always close to him."

Chantel nodded. "He's loyal to General Stuart, he is. He said he wouldn't want to serve anywhere else, with any other man."

"He's not a Christian, is he?" Flora wisely guessed.

"No ma'am, he isn't. He just can't seem to find his way to the good God," Chantel answered. "And so, we both know . . . Anyway, I don't see him much, since he got out of the hospital."

Flora reached over and patted her hand. "One thing I know about being a Christian," she said, "it means that God has a wonderful plan for our lives if we'll just let Him lead us. He is faithful and true, and He will give us joy, always, no matter what happens."

Chantel said unhappily, "Grandpere has told me this. But it's hard sometimes. Especially when we want things the Lord doesn't want us to have."

"He will give you the desires of your heart," Flora said simply. "Trust Him."

In the three years Abraham Lincoln had held the office of the president, he looked as if he had aged thirty years. The war had worn him down, and now once again, he had to choose a commander for the Army of the Potomac.

He had chosen wrongly several times. McClellan was the wrong choice. He simply did not have the nerve of a fighter. Pope had been another failure, and Burnside a complete disaster when he was commanding at Fredericksburg. Finally, in desperation, Lincoln decided, "It will have to be Joe Hooker. They say he can fight. I hope he's able to get an army ready."

Indeed, General Joseph Hooker was probably the best Union general in seeing that his men were well cared for. He was able to wrangle new uniforms and new equipment for them in record time.

Hooker himself was a handsome man. He had a complexion as delicate as a woman's, fine blond hair, and the erect bearing and demeanor of a soldier. But he was a drinking man, and a womanizer as well, so naturally he did not have the mentality about his soldier's morals as much as others did.

He was called Fighting Joe Hooker, but no one knew exactly why, for he had not been the brightest star in the army, although he had won several minor engagements. He had more confidence than was merited, and the phrases, "When I get to Richmond," or, "After we have taken Richmond," cropped up frequently in his talk. And now he had his chance to take Richmond and stop the Confederacy, for Fighting Joe Hooker was appointed as commander-in-chief of the Army of the Potomac.

# CHAPTER TWENTY-TWO

"I want you to bring the children and come out to the camp, Flora."

Flora looked up from Jimmy, who was sitting in a dishpan enjoying his bath as usual. He was splashing and chortling, and his eyes gleamed. "What for, dear?"

"Oh, several things. First of all, there's going to be a good meal. And there's going to be good music and good preaching. You know our chaplain?"

"You mean Major Ball?"

"Yes, Major Ball, our champion scrounger."

"What's he done now, Jeb?"

"He's gone out and liberated the awfulest bunch of food you ever saw. I don't know where he gets it. People here in Richmond are going hungry, almost, and he comes into camp with the carcasses of four of the fattest pigs you ever saw and two young steers. The men have made a big barbecue pit, and he's barbecuing them."

"But where does he get these things? Does he buy them?"

Jeb's eyes sparkled. "Buy them? Not the foraging parson! He goes out and takes them from the Yankees, somehow or other. We just hear rumors of him suddenly appearing on one of the Yankees' outlying pickets and holding 'em at gunpoint and liberating their supplies. He says the Lord provides and blames all the stuff he brings in on the Lord's doing. Maybe he's right. In any case, it's going to be a great meal."

"Why yes. Of course Jimmy and I would love to be there."

"While we're eating, I'll have all my minstrel men do some singing and dancing. We might do a little dancing ourselves." Jeb came over, put his arm around Flora, hugged her and kissed her soundly, then reached over and poked little Jimmy's fat stomach with his finger. "You want something to eat, Jimmy?"

"Eat!" he cried. "Eat, Papa!"

"You're my son, all right," Jeb said.

"He looks just like you, Jeb. Or just like I think you must have looked when you were his age."

"Not likely." Jeb grinned. "Remember, they didn't call me Beauty at the Point because I was so pretty. It was because I was so homely."

"You're not homely, as I've said a thousand times. And every woman in the South, it seems to me, thinks you're just as handsome as I do. It's a good thing I trust you, Jeb. Because I would be one miserable wife if I didn't, the way women chase after you."

"I think it's my hat," he said, his blue eyes dancing. "That fancy plume gets 'em every time."

Flora laughed. "Silly old bear."

"Anyway, after the feast, Stonewall Jackson has organized a religious service. He's the finest Christian man I ever knew and the best soldier. I've never known any man like him. Guess there aren't any men like him."

"We're all very proud of the general," Flora said. "Not just for his military successes, but for being the kind of man he is."

"Did I tell you, Flora? The other day he asked for a glass of water, and someone gave it to him. I noticed he didn't drink it right off. He just sat there, holding it for a minute. I asked him, 'General, are you going to drink that water?' He looked at me with those eyes of his that look right through a man. Then he said, 'Yes, General Stuart, I am, but I always give thanks for everything.

Even a glass of water. I made it a habit to give thanks for the little things as well as the big things.' "

"It must be good to be that close to the Lord," Flora said. "Most of us aren't. We're not strong enough."

"He's a strong man, not just in the Lord but in war. If we had about five more Stonewall Jacksons, we'd run the Yankees back all the way to Washington screaming for help."

"Every Christian in the South prays for him every day. And for you, my love, and General Lee and all of our men."

"You keep it up, sweetheart. I'll be back later to fetch you and Jimmy." He gave her another kiss and leaned over to kiss little Jimmy's soapy face.

The child happily grabbed his beard.

"You're like your mama. She likes my beard, too." He laughed, and then he left.


"Look, Clay, there's Miss Flora with Jimmy." Chantel pointed and said, "Let's go speak to her. I want to see little Jimmy, too."

"He's a pistol," Clay said, "just like his papa."

The men had set up a bandstand, a platform of rough-hewn logs covered with strips of canvas, contributed by Jacob Steiner. Out in front of it they had gathered up every bench, every camp chair, and every cot they could find so that everyone could have a seat.

General Stuart and Flora were seated in the front row, as were such dignitaries as General Stonewall Jackson, Major Roberdeau Wheat, General P. G. T. Beauregard, and most all of the other officers of the Army of Northern Virginia. Even the august commander General Lee was in attendance. He was a handsome man, with his neatly trimmed beard and thick silver hair. He was always immaculate — his uniforms pressed to crisp perfection, his boots shined, his white gauntlets spotless.

Clay and Chantel made their way over, and Flora greeted them with a smile. "Hello, Chantel. Lieutenant Tremayne, you look splendid. And you look well. I'm so glad you have so miraculously recovered from your grievous wound."

"I am well, very well, thank you, ma'am," Clay replied. "It's so good to see you, Mrs. Stuart. And who's this young man? He looks like a certain general I know."

Chantel added, "It's like the general was shrunk and his beard plucked off. A tiny little General Stuart."

"Watch him," Flora said, setting him

down. Promptly he took off. "He even walks like Jeb."

"Really?" Chantel asked. "I hadn't noticed."

"As a matter of fact, Jeb has a strange walk. He's like a centaur in the saddle, with never a false move, but his walk is not graceful in the least. His upper body seems to get ahead of his feet, and he rolls along, bent somewhat from the waist."

Little Jimmy was too small to walk like anything but a toddler, but still Chantel and Clay laughed at Flora's remarks.

"I'll go get him, me," Chantel said. "He looks like he's marching to Washington."

She ran to catch him, and she swooped him up into her arms so fast he whooped with surprise. Then he turned to see who had latched onto him and said with delight, "Cante! Eat, eat, Cante!"

"As you can see, he takes after Jeb in other ways, too," Flora said as Chantel rejoined them, the wiggling little Jimmy held tightly in her arms.

"I agree with Jimmy," Clay said. "Let's eat. Shall we, ladies?"

He led the two women, Chantel still holding Jimmy, over to a long table, two of them put together and covered, somewhat oddly in the rustic setting, with two fine white linen tablecloths. Four soldiers stood carving the pork and the beef from still-steaming big cuts.

"Mrs. Stuart, we're so glad you came to be with us," the private said, a young man who had joined Jeb Stuart as soon as the 1st Cavalry was formed. "May I have the pleasure of serving you some of this fine beef?"

"That would be nice, sir," Flora said kindly. "Thank you so much."

They moved down the table. At the other end were piled mounds of fresh-baked bread and many hundreds of roasted potatoes. All they had had in camp, in quantities enough for the crowd of men, was the chaplain's kidnapped meat and flour for bread, and that was all they had planned on serving. But early the previous morning, Jacob had disappeared with the wagon, and when he returned, he had twenty cases of roasting potatoes. Chantel had teased him. "I guess you spent more of our gold on all that, hmm, partner?"

The three got their plates filled, and Clay carried his and Chantel's back to the front row of benches, for Chantel still carried little Jimmy. They got seated, and Flora handed him an enormous beef rib, which he gnawed happily on, smearing his entire face with grease.

"Like a little hungry puppy, you," Chantel said affectionately.

Major Ball came to them and bowed. "Good day, Mrs. Stuart, Miss Chantel. Hello, Lieutenant Tremayne. Mrs. Stuart, I'm so happy you and Jimmy could come be with us today and share in this feast that the gracious Lord has provided. Will you be staying for the service?"

"Of course I will, Major Ball. I'm looking forward to it," Flora replied.

"What about you, Lieutenant?" he asked, turning to Clay. "Are you ready for a good dose of Gospel preaching?"

"Looks like I'll have to be, won't I?" Clay said grinning.

He liked the chaplain a great deal. He had been shocked at their first patrol, when Major Dabney Ball had ridden to the front right alongside of Jeb. When they had met the enemy, he fought just as fiercely as all of Stuart's men did. After the battles, Clay had watched as he walked around among the wounded, even in the midst of action, as if he were in a park on a summer day.

He had asked Ball later, "Weren't you afraid you'd get hit, Major?"

"No sir, I am not afraid. The Lord is going to take care of me. Besides, when the

Lord means for me to go, then I'll go."

Major Ball saw the men taking the stage, and he said, "Well, it looks like your husband's minstrel show is about to start. General Stuart does dearly love his music."

Clay had seen and heard the musicians many times. They began to play, and Stuart joined them. Often he sang along, and the whole crowd joined in. They sang, "Her Bright Smile Haunts Me Still," "The Corn Top's Ripe," "Lorena," and finally the one that they always sang, that Jeb Stuart loved the best: "Jine the Cavalry." Even Stonewall Jackson and the grave Robert E. Lee sang.

As the music was going on, Chantel leaned over and said to Clay, "I've never seen an officer like General Stuart. He jokes and talks with the soldiers just like he was one of them."

"That's right," Clay said heartily. "That's the kind of man he is. He's the only general I've ever seen that could make a common soldier feel absolutely at ease."

"He's gotten to be such a hero, so famous," Chantel said. "It's hard to believe that he would have any humility at all."

"You know, I asked the general once," Clay said very quietly so that Flora could not hear him, "why he put himself in the front. He's so recognizable, any Yankee would give his boots to shoot him. I told him he was going to get himself killed if he didn't use a little caution."

"What did he say, Clay?"

"He said, 'Oh, I reckon not. If I am, they'll easily find someone to fill my place.' "

Suddenly a laugh went up, for the general had gotten up. Jeb Stuart, the terror of the Yankees, the master of the Black Horse, began dancing around, a great bearded warrior with his plumed hat and his golden spurs clanking at his heels. He began dancing around with one of the black men, and then the others joined in a mad frolic.

Flora sat shaking her head.

But Stonewall Jackson and even General Lee laughed.

After a while, the musicians left the platform, and Major Ball stepped up. "All right. We're going to have a service right here. We've had our party, and now we're going to hear a word from God."

Major Ball was a tall, thick-set man with a shock of black hair and a pair of strangely colored eyes, penetrating hazel eyes. His voice normally was quiet and even, but when he stood up to preach, it was like the sound of a trumpet. "I'm going to preach a very simple sermon to you today. My text is one that you all know — one that has often been called 'the Gospel in a nutshell.' I refer to John 3:16. You know the verse. It says, 'For God so loved the world, that he gave his only begotten Son, that whosoever believeth in him should not perish, but have everlasting life.' "

Chantel was fascinated as the chaplain began to speak. He had a compassion for lost men that showed clearly on his face. He spoke of how God loved the world that did not love him. "We're all of the world, and we're all sinners. It is one of the great mysteries of the Bible and of life to understand why a just and holy and perfect God could love miserable sinners such as we all are. But the Bible says He loved the world, and He gave His Son. We're going to speak now of that gift that God gave for our salvation."

As the sermon went on, Chantel had her eyes fixed on a young man who was across the way from her. It had grown dark, but there were lanterns stationed so that she could see his face clearly. She saw that he was very young and that he was somehow afraid. She could not take her eyes off of him, and she whispered to Clay, "Do you see that young man over there? The private with the yellow hair?"

Clay looked over and nodded. "I can't recall his name just now. He's in the Stonewall Brigade."

"He's so young," Chantel said. "And he looks so afraid."

Clay studied the man and nodded. "I guess he is. Most of us are, I guess. I envy men like General Jackson and the major who don't have to worry about what'll happen if they get killed."

Major Ball was saying, "There you have it, dear friends! That's who God is, a compassionate loving Father, but He still gave His only Son, His beloved Son, Jesus, and He condemned His own Son to death, so that He paid for our sins. How can we turn away from our Father God? How can we ever say to Him, 'No, I don't need Your love'? We can't. Once we realize, deep in our hearts, what He has done for us, the great and eternal and kind love that He has for us, we cannot help but ask Him humbly to take us in and to be our most beloved Father."

The silence was profound, and Chantel saw that some men wept openly. She glanced at Clay and was shocked to see his dark eyes glint with unshed tears.

The chaplain finished, now speaking quietly in the reverent silence, "I know you men. You're like all men. You've dabbled in the defilements of the world, you've shamed yourselves, perhaps you've shamed your families. Maybe you've given up and you think, 'God can't care for me. I'm not worth caring for.' But this Scripture says that He does. If you'll just come to Jesus tonight, you'll find out that He will open His arms and welcome you with a love that is everlasting."

The chaplain began to urge the men to come forward who wanted to be prayed for, and many came. It was just a few at first, but then more and more men, hats in hand, went to the chaplain and stood silently, heads bowed, as he prayed with them.

Chantel turned to Clay and saw that his face was working; he was struggling. Even as she watched, he bowed his head and closed his eyes.

Chantel knew that God was dealing with him. She slid her hand into his, and he grasped it as hard as if it were his only tenuous hold on life. Chantel bowed her head and prayed.

Finally she sensed Clay relax, and his painful grip on her hand loosened, though he still held it. She looked up at him. His face was rather pale, but he looked back at her and smiled.

She asked, "Did you ask the good God to save you, Clay?"

"I did," Clay answered steadily. "And just like you and your grandfather have told me, I feel different now. I know that He is in my heart. For the first time since this war started, I know I'm safe."

"Even unto death," she said quietly, "we know we live. Forever and ever."

Clay and his corporal, a sturdy man of about forty-five named Gabriel Tyron, were riding side by side slightly behind General Stuart. Clay was aware of the jingling of the horses' harness, some of the men laughing and talking, the ever-present sounds of the night in the South. A thousand crickets called, in the distance bullfrogs sang out their throaty single notes, the nightingale trilled her lonely sonnet. This was all a familiar scene to him, and now that he had become a Christian, he was not at the mercy of his fear. He felt alive and alert and strong.

"I think this battle is going to be bad, Lieutenant," Corporal Tyron said.

"Why do you say that, Corporal?" Clay asked curiously. The man was a career soldier, and he, like Clay, had already been through terrible battles. It was unlike him to say such a thing.

Tyron shrugged. "I got me a bad feeling."

"That's just superstition, Tyron," Clay said firmly. "We're heading for a fight, for sure. But no matter what happens, it can't be much worse than what we've already seen."

"No, this is different. My mother, she had what they call second sight."

"What does that mean?"

"It means that she saw things that couldn't be."

"What kind of things, Corporal?"

Tyron frowned. "My mother saw her brother after he was killed."

"What do you mean? At his funeral?"

"No, sir," he said, shaking his head. "Her brother, my uncle, was killed in a mining accident out west. One day, Mama, she looked up and saw my uncle standing in the door. She was surprised, and she asked him when he had come back from the West. He just smiled and said nothing, and then in a minute he was gone."

"I don't understand," Clay said with some impatience.

"My uncle, he had been killed the day before. It was a full week before Mama got the letter. But she saw him that day."

"I don't believe that's true," Clay said in a more kindly manner. "Not that I doubt your mother, but she must have been mistaken."

"You think what you like, Lieutenant, sir. But I think that God speaks to us in different ways, and I think He spoke to my mother in that kind of way."

The cavalry rode on, and late that night they made camp. They had been there for a couple of hours, and Clay was seeing to the well-being of his men, going around to ensure they had something to eat, talking to them, encouraging them.

He was at the edge of their camp, and he looked into a clearing a little ways away from them where there was a small fire. With a shock, he realized that General Lee was there. He was sitting on a cracker box, and across from him, not five feet away, was General Stonewall Jackson. General Stuart was with them, and General Lee was speaking to him in a low voice.

Stuart nodded then turned and walked fast, back toward his tent. As he passed Clay, he said, "Saddle up again, Lieutenant. We've got to ride."

They rode west, and Clay, as always, stayed close behind General Stuart. Sometimes, in the night, they heard talking and laughing just on their left, and Clay realized they were riding very close to Union pickets.

Every once in a while, Jeb would throw up a hand for the column to stop, and then he would listen, his head cocked as if he were waiting for something. Then he would nod with satisfaction and move quietly on.

They were in a wilderness, with rough tracks for roads that seemed to begin out of nowhere and then end abruptly. Finally Stuart called for the column to halt, though he didn't dismount, so neither did Clay. Stuart took a map out of his jacket and called for a lantern. An aide brought him one, and Stuart studied the map, his right leg thrown over the saddle horn in a negligent gesture, one that Clay had seen many times.

"I think that Reverend Lacy lives around here somewhere," Jeb said quietly to Clay, who had lingered close to him. "If we can find him, I'll send word with him back to General Jackson and General Lee."

Finally they found the Reverend B. T. Lacy's small cabin. He was Stonewall Jackson's chief chaplain. Jeb roused him and said, "Go back to camp, just east of here, close to the old Wellford railroad yard. Tell General Lee that I have found the end of their line, in a clearing about eight miles from them, and it looks to me like they're up in the air."

In Stuart's absence, the two generals had made a momentous decision, and some audacious plans.

■ ■ ■ ■

It was indeed a daring move, one that could have been an utter catastrophe. Robert E. Lee had asked Jackson to find a way to get at Hooker's army, and he had decided, when he got word from General Stuart, to try and flank them at the weakness in the line that Stuart had found. Stonewall had asked Lee if he could take his whole corps, leaving only two stripped-down divisions with Lee. Robert E. Lee had about 14,000 men left with him as Jackson made his flank sweep. Joe Hooker had about 100,000 men. All Hooker had to do was to drive straight at him, hard and fast, and the Army of Northern Virginia would be destroyed, and the Civil War would be over.

It never happened.

Fighting Joe Hooker talked a good game. Once he called the Army of the Potomac "the finest army on the planet." Before the battle had even begun, in his headquarters he boasted, "Robert E. Lee and the Confederate Army are now the legitimate property of the United States."

At the beginning of the battle, he was cocksure, filled with confidence, but he had never tackled the likes of Robert E. Lee and

Stonewall Jackson. As events unfolded, he grew unsure, indecisive. Instead of rushing his men into the fray and taking Lee head-on and running over the inferior force, which he easily could have done, he lingered, he made excuses, he stalled.

Then Stonewall Jackson and his corps appeared, apparently out of nowhere, shielded by Jeb Stuart's fearless cavalry, and struck his flank. Hooker completely lost himself and ended up helplessly frittering away every chance he had to effectively fight back. He never had control of the battle, and finally, in the end, he met the fate of others who had run up against Robert E. Lee and Stonewall Jackson.

Jackson's corps had, in effect, cowed Joe Hooker, and as a result, the Army of the Potomac was like a loaded cannon, but one that no one would aim and shoot. Still, Stonewall Jackson was never a man to be satisfied. Even as the darkness fell, he was leading some of his officers, looking for a way to strike Hooker another blow.

They were in the deep woods, with the lines so close and entangled that from one foot to the next they couldn't tell if they were closer to Federal troops or to Confederates. An overeager, keyed-up North Carolina infantry regiment fired a volley that knocked Jackson out of the saddle, wounded in the left shoulder, the left arm, and his palm. Jackson was carried away from the battlefield. His war was finally over.

"General Stuart," the messenger said, "I have terrible news."

"What is it, Lieutenant?"

"General Jackson has been shot. He's not expected to live. General Lee orders you to take command of the army."

What could have been the proudest moment of Jeb Stuart's life turned out to be one of the most bitter. He had admired Jackson all of his military career; in fact, the two men, polar opposites though they were, had made fast friends. It was said that Jeb Stuart was the only man in the world who could make Stonewall Jackson laugh out loud.

Now his great head dropped, and he said, "I will assume command."

Jeb Stuart was a cavalryman. But he took command of an entire army, infantry, artillery, and all, and he did a fine job. He managed to send Hooker back to Washington in disgrace. But there was no joy in Stuart's heart nor in the heart of any Southerner. In losing Jackson, they had lost so much, and they had loved him well. General Lee, when he heard that Jackson's left arm was shattered, had sent word, "You're losing your left arm, but I am losing my right arm." A pall fell over the Confederacy. It seemed that the army would never be the same again.

# CHAPTER TWENTY-THREE

If Jeb Stuart had expected to be promoted after serving so well and salvaging the Battle at Chancellorsville, he soon found out that this was not to be. There were mentions of his bravery, the excellence of his command during this battle, but he remained in charge of the cavalry. No doubt both General Lee and President Davis were convinced that this was his most valuable contribution. And though Stuart might have felt some twinges of regret at being passed over, in his heart he likely agreed with them. He loved the cavalry above all.

In midsummer he arranged for a review of the cavalry at Brandy Station. There had been little action, so the troops were all available, and by the time the review was set in motion, ten thousand cavalrymen sat their horses in lines almost two miles long, and Stuart galloped onto the field.

One of his gunners, George Neese, said

of Stuart:

He was superbly mounted, and his side-
arms gleamed in the morning sun like
burnished silver. A long black ostrich
plume waved gracefully from a black
slouch hat cocked up on one side, held
with a golden clasp. . . . He is the prettiest and most graceful rider I ever saw. I
could not help but notice with what
natural ease and comely elegance he sat
his steed as it bounded over the field . . .
he and his horse appeared to be one and
the same machine.

In those few golden days of summer, it
seemed as if the enemy was a world away.

Stuart's officers were gathered together, and
he explained that there was a drive to invade
the North. "Our job," he said, addressing
his men, "is to cover the Union Army, to
find out their dispositions, to see if we can
find a weakness in their flank. They are just
over that ridge." He pointed east, to the
Blue Ridge Mountains. "That will be an
easy enough task. We'll have no trouble."

Afterward Clay was talking with several of
the other officers. Clay had noticed some
difference in General Stuart's manner, and

he was worried. "He doesn't seem to be as alert or as focused as he usually is."

"General Stuart knows what he's doing," a major scoffed. "He's never let the army down."

Clay could argue no more against his superior officers, and so he kept his mouth shut and followed Jeb Stuart, as always. But Clay had been right. Instead of watching the Union Army and sending reports to Lee on the western side of the Blue Ridge, Stuart led his army on side trails and in ineffective and meaningless skirmishes. Once they captured a huge wagon train.

Clay was worried, and Corporal Tyron could see it clearly. "Lieutenant, won't this train slow us down?"

Clay shrugged. "General Stuart says he's ordered to interfere with their supply lines. This is interfering."

On the other side of the mountains, Robert E. Lee worried as the Union forces began to move against him. Without Stuart's intelligence, he was blind.

And Jeb Stuart's mistakes were going to haunt him.

"General . . . General Longstreet, please wake up!"

Longstreet came awake instantly and sat

up on his bed. He pulled his fingers down through his thick beard and said, "What is it, Lieutenant?"

"Harrison's back, sir."

"The spy?"

"Yes, sir. He says he's got information and you have to hear it."

"I doubt it." Nevertheless, he got up and said, "Have him come in."

The officer departed, and Longstreet sat down at a chair behind the field desk and waited. He did not care for spies as a whole, but this one seemed to be better than most. As soon as the man entered, he pulled off his hat and said, "Hello, General. I'm back."

"What have you got, Harrison?"

Harrison grinned and said, "I came right through your lines. It's a good thing I wasn't a Union Army."

"What have you got?" Longstreet repeated.

Harrison was a slight man with a foxy face, innocent-looking enough. He was able to pass for a farmer or a workman of any kind. For this reason, he was able to move anywhere unobtrusively and get information that others could not. "I got the position of the Union Army."

Longstreet grunted. "Where are they?"

"It wasn't easy."

"I've no doubt, Harrison, and I admit you've always done us a good job. So where is the army?"

"Less than a day's ride away from this here spot."

Instantly Longstreet straightened up. "Can't be," he muttered.

Harrison was offended. "I'm telling you, General, they're less than a day's ride away, and they're going to get you if you don't do something."

"Show me." Longstreet pulled out a map, and Harrison began pointing out different locations, telling him of their dispositions. Then he added, "Oh, and I forgot to tell you. They got 'em a new general."

"Who is that? What happened to Hooker?"

"Lincoln got tired of him, I reckon, after that last dust-up at Chancellorsville. Now he's got George Meade. That's what the papers say."

Longstreet knew that a catastrophe had suddenly reared up ahead of him. He got up and said, "We'll have to tell General Lee."

The two left Longstreet's tent and made their way to Lee's tent. They found Lee seated at his desk. "Harrison here says that the Federal Army is not a day's ride away, sir."

Lee stared at the scout. "I've forgotten your name."

"Harrison, sir."

"Well, Harrison, you saw this for yourself?"

"Plain as day. I saw General Buford leading his corps." He began to name off other units, and Lee and Longstreet were both silent.

Finally Lee said, "We are in your debt, sir."

Harrison knew this was his dismissal. "I'm glad to be of service, General." He turned and left the tent.

"This changes things," Lee said. "I had no idea the Union forces were so close."

"It's Stuart's fault. You haven't heard from him, have you?"

"No, I haven't. It's the first time he ever let me down, General Longstreet."

"He ought to be broken for this." Longstreet was a slow-moving man, the exact opposite of General Jeb Stuart. He liked to think things over and come to decisions slowly, whereas Stuart would throw himself in and worry later about the results.

"Never mind that now, General. We must make some decisions."

Lee walked over to a map, looked at it for a moment, and said, "We'll keep going here.

We'll come out of the mountains close to this little town."

"What town is that, General?"

Lee peered at it. "Gettysburg," he said.

The Battle of Gettysburg should never have been fought. Lee was not himself and made his worst decisions, which he himself admitted. He had a terrible case of dysentery, and the heart disease that would later kill him was giving him severe problems. He was without Stonewall Jackson, and in his place he had a man he did not fully trust.

Lieutenant General Richard Ewell was a good soldier, but he had lost a leg and apparently had lost some confidence along with it. Even before the first gray lines took the field, the Union forces had entrenched on the high ground, and the plains below were nothing but a killing field.

The battle started on July 3, 1863, and both sides incurred disastrous losses. On the second day, the next step was made by General Lee. He sent men around to his right to a place called Little Roundtop. The Confederates were unable to take it, and the following day General Lee ordered a full assault on the center of the Union line.

General Longstreet argued vehemently against the attack. He came as close to insubordination as he ever had with General Lee, for the Union army was entrenched on a ridge. They had the high ground, with full range to sweep the valley below with murderous fire. Lee listened to him, but finally he pointed at the ridge and said, "The enemy is there, and I'm going to strike him."

The Confederate division that led the strike was under the command of General Pickett. He led his men across an open field into the mouths of the artillery and muskets of a huge army. They were shot to pieces, and only a few pitiful remnants were able to stagger back to the safety of the lines.

Jeb Stuart finally rode in and went to General Lee, but Lee was angry with him and showed it. Stuart had ridden up and dismounted, and Lee had reddened at the sight of him and raised his arm as if he would strike him. "General Stuart, where have you been?"

Stuart was shocked. "I have been carrying out my assignment, sir."

"I have not heard a word from you in days, and you are the eyes and ears of my army!"

Stuart had swallowed hard and then said, "I brought you a hundred and twenty-five wagons and their teams, General."

"Yes, General Stuart, and they are an

impediment to me now!"

Stuart was dismissed, and he did well for the rest of the battle, but there was no hope for the Confederate Army. At Gettysburg, Robert E. Lee, for the first time, suffered a crushing, brutal defeat.

Chantel was horrified, as was everyone who had gathered to watch the Army of Northern Virginia come back from the battle. Endless lines of wagons were full of wounded men. Blood was dripping out of the wagons, and some were crying to be killed. "Shoot me! Shoot me!" she heard one voice pleading. "Oh, my wife! My poor babies! What will happen to them after I'm dead?" Other cries like this broke her heart. She hurried to the hospital.

Hours later she looked up and saw Clay, and she ran to him. "Are you all right, Clay?"

"I'm fine, just — tired," he said dispiritedly. Then he laid his hands on her arms and said evenly, "Chantel, Armand was hit."

Instantly she cried, "Is he dead?"

"No. I just stopped to see him for a minute. He's — there are still a lot of men out there. At the fairgrounds. I came to the hospital to see if there were any doctors." He looked around, anguished at the men lying on the beds and even on thin blankets on the floor. "But I can see that they have everything they can do right here."

"I must go to him, Clay."

"Yes, go," he said. "I'm going to see to my men that are here, and then I'll follow you."

She ran to the fairgrounds. The big field was full of wounded men just lying on the ground. Finally she found Armand and knelt over him. He was feverish and thirsty. As always after a battle, she had replaced her bag with a canteen around her neck. Now she lifted his head and gave him a drink.

"Ah, that was good," he whispered. His face was pale, and his side was bloody. "Oh, it was so bad, cherie. So very bad."

"I know, I know, Armand," she said soothingly. "Here, let me see." She gently pulled open Armand's bloody tunic. She saw that his wound, though painful, was not likely to be serious. "You're going to be all right, Armand," she said with relief. "I'm going to clean this out a little and bandage it." She poured some of the cool water in her canteen over his side, and he shivered. Pulling up her skirt, she ripped her petticoat to make a bandage.

Even wounded, Armand could not resist. "I never thought I'd see your petticoat, cherie," he joked weakly. "Especially not this way."

When she finished this rough field dressing, he drank again, still shivering, and Chantel wished desperately for a blanket. "You're going to be all right, Armand. I know it hurts, but please believe me — you're going to be fine."

He nodded weakly then murmured, "It was a terrible thing. We had no chance at all, Chantel."

"So many wounded," she said sadly.

"And more dead. We had no chance," he repeated. "We could not believe that General Lee could make such terrible decisions! Men heard, when Pickett came back from that last charge, General Lee met him. He kept saying, 'It was all my fault. It's all my fault.' He was a broken man."

Chantel stayed with him and tried to decide whether to return to the hospital and see if there was some way she could get some supplies to these many wounded men. But soon Jacob arrived with the wagon filled with supplies and medicine, and three medics were with him. She and Jacob stayed at the fairgrounds and worked all day until late into the darkness by lantern light. The wounded were still coming in, and many women from Richmond and from the country around came to the hospitals and out to the surrounding fields, the last places they had to put so many wounded. Many men died that night.

Chantel kept doggedly working, giving the wounded men water, sometimes dressing their wounds, comforting them. The medics had brought many tents, and they were organizing the wounded men and getting them all under shelter. Chantel had made sure Armand was taken care of and then had gone back to work.

She felt a soft touch on her hair as she knelt over a man who was unconscious, tucking a blanket around him. The medics had not gotten to this part of the field yet, but Chantel was bringing armloads of blankets to cover them and canteens to give them water. She looked up, and Clay was there.

He lifted her to her feet and took her arm. "I tried to get here sooner, but many of my men were taken down to the south field by the ironworks. I've been there all day. You look exhausted, Chantel. Come over to the wagon and sit down for a minute."

She allowed him to lead her to Jacob's wagon, and she sat on the back, as she had done so many times before.

Clay settled in beside her. "Did you find

Armand?"

"Yes, and the medics said that he wasn't badly wounded. I thought that, me, but I was glad to hear them say it."

"I am, too," Clay said. "I count him as a friend."

Chantel sighed. "It was terrible, wasn't it, Clay?"

"The worst I've ever seen. It was General Lee's worst day. He was ill. He had no business trying to lead an army. But it really doesn't matter who is leading you or who you are. War is a cruel, senseless business."

She took his hand and held it in hers. "I'm glad you're back. I prayed for you so hard."

Clay turned to her. "When the bullets were flying and the shells were bursting, I thought of you."

He watched her hungrily, and with a little smile, Chantel put her hands on his face. "This time I really want you to kiss me, Clay."

He kissed her then, softly and gently. "You know how much I love you, Chantel. I don't have the words to tell you."

"I know. I feel the same way. I do love you, Clay. I have, ever since I first saw you, so terribly hurt. I was so young. Maybe I don't know exactly what love is then. But I do now, me."

He swallowed, hard. In a distant voice, he said, "If we weren't in this terrible war, you know what I would ask you, Chantel. But right now I can't even think of it. I don't want to say it, not right now, in this terrible time."

Chantel, as always, was a very practical girl. "We are going to marry, you and me," she said firmly. She reached up again, pulled his head down, and kissed him solidly. Then she put her head on his shoulder. "We are going to trust God to bring us out of this terrible war, and then we will be together, and we will be happy, Clay. I know this, because it is the desire of my heart."

# CHAPTER TWENTY-FOUR

It is difficult to put a finger on the exact moment that a war makes a final turning. Most wars are either brief affairs wherein a huge force overruns a small one, or they are long tedious affairs that go on for years. In these long wars, much is done, but very few turning points in which the whole direction of a war is changed can be specifically cited.

The Civil War, however, presented a clear-cut and definite turning point. The South won many battles during the early part of the war, and this drove Abraham Lincoln and, indeed, all the Northern leaders, nearly to distraction. The source of the strength of the Confederacy was in General Robert E. Lee. He was the South's greatest military asset, and beside him was Stonewall Jackson, perhaps the second most potent force that kept the Confederacy alive and fighting ferociously.

Lincoln tried general after general, all of

them failing to defeat Lee and Jackson. At Bull Run, Lincoln sent General McDowell, which proved to be a sad mistake, for McDowell was sadly defeated. In the Seven Days Battle, which was a short but very bloody affair, General McClellan, who was the idol of the North and one of the neatest men who ever wore the uniform, proved that he was unable to stand against these two soldiers. In the Battle of Second Manassas in August of 1862, General Pope was Lincoln's choice. He failed miserably, as had his predecessors. At Antietam, the bloodiest day of the war, Lincoln tried McClellan again. McClellan had the battle in his grasp. All he had to do was make one great charge, but he was psychologically and emotionally unable to send men to their deaths. In the Battle of Fredericksburg, Ambrose Burnside threw himself against Lee and Jackson and introduced the Army of the Potomac to a slaughter from which Burnside and the army had to turn and run. Hooker spoke well and was a fine-looking general, but in the Battle of Chancelorsville, he lost his courage.

The South won that battle, but they lost Stonewall Jackson, which was a grievous loss indeed. No one can know if Gettysburg would have been any different, if this giant among men had been there, standing sure and true "like a stone wall." He was not there, and Robert E. Lee was defeated, though the Army of Northern Virginia was not decimated. Still they fought on.

But then came the turn of the tide, a point in time that fated the South to a full and final defeat. Abraham Lincoln chose Ulysses S. Grant to be commander-in-chief of all the Union armies. This sealed the fate of the Confederate States of America. Unlike most of the commanding generals before him, Grant was very unimpressive to look at and was not much of a one for talking, nor parades. His uniform was usually scruffy, and at times he even wore the uniform of a private, with the general's stars, denoting his rank, only showing on his collar.

His choice to succeed him as commanding officer of the Military Division of Mississippi, which was the command of all the troops in the Western Theater, was a general named William Tecumseh Sherman. These two men spelled the death of the Confederacy. Grant told Lincoln, "I'm going to go for Lee, and Sherman is going to go for Joe Johnston. That's the plan."

The first battle Grant engaged in with Lee was a bloody affair called the Battle of the

Wilderness. As usual, the Northern troops suffered great losses.

Always before when this had happened, the Northern generals had retreated to Washington and built up their forces again. But Grant was different. He and Sherman both were men who believed in total war, with no mercy shown, to bring a quick end to a foe. Grant was determined to wear down the South, and if he had to lose three men for every death the Southern army incurred, so be it. Behind him lay the immense numbers in the North, while the South was already sending sixteen-year-olds and fifty-year-olds into battle. Sherman was a cold-eyed realist, and his most famous statement was, "War is hell." And he set about to make it so. He set out for Georgia, and the South has never forgotten the cold-blooded and terrible devastation that followed in the wake of Sherman and his men.

With the appointment by Lincoln of Grant and Sherman, it was as if a steel door had suddenly slammed on the South and their army. For after this there really was little hope.

It was October 9, 1863, and Jeb Stuart stood beside the bed where his wife, Flora, lay. He was holding the newest Stuart, a daughter. He looked down at Flora, reached over, and put his hand on her hair. "You choose a name, dear, and I'll choose one."

Flora was exhausted from the struggles to bring the child into the world, but she answered, "I've always wanted a daughter named Virginia."

"Excellent! That's who she'll be."

"And what name will you choose?" Flora managed a weak smile.

"Of all the men I've known, my gunner Pelham was the most noble. He was indeed the gallant Pelham as everyone called him, and to this day I miss him terribly. I'd like to call this child Virginia Pelham Stuart."

"A fine name, Jeb."

Jeb walked the floor, looking into the face of his new daughter, smiling, taking her tiny hand in his strong one. Finally he gave the child back to Flora and then sat down beside her in a worn walnut rocking chair. As he rocked, he grew strangely quiet.

Flora saw that he was grieved. "What's the matter, Jeb? You look troubled."

"I guess I am, my dear Flora."

"Can you tell me what it is?"

"It's hard to say. I feel, Flora, that I let General Lee down at Gettysburg. All the papers say so, and some of my best friends in the army accused me of not being a good soldier."

Flora shook her head and extended her hand, which he took. She squeezed it and said, "You mustn't grieve, dear. You did what you thought was best. If you made a mistake, others have made theirs."

"I've told myself that many times," Jeb said in a subdued tone. "I don't know what made me act as I did. At the time it seemed as if I was following orders, doing exactly what General Lee had asked me to do. But now, looking back, I can see that I made a terrible mistake and should have come back to him days earlier."

"Jeb, you are a man of God, and you put your trust in Him," Flora said steadily. "Don't look back with useless regrets. As you said, you were doing your best, your utmost to perform your duty. That is all a man can do, even the great General Jeb Stuart. Now, let's talk about something else, something cheerful. What are we going to do when this awful war is finally over, do you think?"

Stuart looked up at her with surprise. It was as if he had never given a thought to that time. "Why, I suppose I'll stay in the army. Get a nice, comfortable command. I can sit behind a desk, and then every night I will come home to you and the children.

Maybe we can have two or three more."

Flora smiled and said, "Right now I just want to hold Virginia Pelham Stuart. She is precious."

"Yes, she is. I think she's going to look like you, Flora, and I hope she does. And I hope she is loving and kind like you. You've been the best wife a man ever had."

Tears came to Flora's eyes, for Jeb was often jocular and paid her many light, sometimes silly compliments, but this, she knew, came from his heart. "Thank you, Jeb. You can't know how much that means to me."

"It's true, Flora. I thank God for you every day. With His help and your love, I know I can fight on."

Clay and Corporal Tyron dismounted, took off their hats and gauntlets, and wearily threw themselves down to lean against a big spreading oak tree. The tree was on a small rise, and because of its deep shade, it had minimal undergrowth. It stood like a sentinel, its branches sketching a graceful silhouette against a shroud-gray sky. The two men were silent for a while, taking sips from their canteens, savoring even the tepid, gritty water.

Idly Clay said, "You know, Corporal, I had

some funny ideas about battle before I saw one."

"And what is that, sir?"

"Well, I'd seen pictures in books, you know, of armies out on open fields all neatly lined up with their rifles all held in the same position. Not a man was out of step, and they squared off facing each other, and then they marched right toward each other." He rubbed his eyes. "It's not like that. It's nothing like that."

Corporal Tyron said, "That may have happened in Europe, but when those lobsters came over here fighting for old King George, they found out that that nonsense won't do over here. We're not strutting fools. We're soldiers, and we fight hard. We fight any way we can, anyplace we can."

"It's especially true here in the South," Clay observed. "Too many trees, too many forests, too many rivers. It's hard to find a place to have a review, much less to put two huge armies together." He looked out over the desolate landscape.

The sky was a death-gray caul, and a layer of stinking gray smoke hovered over the ground. They had just fought for two days in what was to be called simply the Battle of the Wilderness.

Ulysses Grant had begun his relentless

push toward Richmond as soon as he had taken command of the Army of the Potomac. He came straight on, 122,000 strong, crossing the Rapidan and heading due south.

Lee, with his army of 66,000, chose to meet him in the middle of nowhere, miles of empty fields and dense woods just south of Fredericksburg. He counted on the bewildering trackless forest of stunted pine, scrub oak, and sweet gum, with their impenetrable thickets of wild honeysuckle vines and briars, to keep the Yankees from bringing artillery to bear. It worked.

But still the woods caught fire from the hot shot of thousands of muskets.

Tyron said, "I have to say, Lieutenant, that I have seen some bloody Indian massacres, but this was much, much worse. No such thing as a battle line. It was just men by themselves hiding behind trees and under rocks, and the bluebellies were the same. And then" — he sighed — "the woods caught fire."

Looking out over the scorched earth, Clay remembered horrific scenes from the last two days. "Men just burned to death," he murmured painfully. "They were wounded and too weak to crawl away."

Clay and certainly Max Tyron were, by

now, battle-hardened veterans. But on this dark day they were both literally exhausted. Their uniforms were filthy, as were their faces and indeed their entire bodies.

The battle had been a nightmare. After the first volley, the black powder had thrown a cloud of smoke over the thick woods, and a man could not see five feet away. He did not know at times whether he was firing at his fellow soldiers or an enemy.

Jeb's cavalry had tried to front the infantry, but scouting was impossible. In the woods, even when they could find a trail, it was merely a path, with undergrowth so thick on either side a whole division of Yankees could have been five feet away and they never would have seen them. Finally they had dismounted and joined in the killing field.

Clay started out in good formation with his company, but in the massive tangle of men in the wilderness, he and Tyron had gotten completely separated from any recognizable command, and that morning they had found themselves alone, so they had ridden to the live oak for some welcome shelter.

Clay had thought that he might never sleep again; the scenes in his mind were so fresh and vivid that he hated to close his eyes. But then he woke up with a start and realized that both he and Tyron had fallen asleep sitting straight up. "Corporal," he said, shaking Tyron's shoulder. "Wake up."

Tyron's eyes flew open, and he was alert immediately. "I hear it."

They listened, and Clay nodded grimly. "That's 1st Cav's bugle call," he said. "Just over to our left. Not too far either."

They struggled to their feet. Lightning and Tyron's horse had remained standing under the tree, not even grazing. As they mounted up, Tyron said, "Hope there's something left of us."

"And I hope," Clay said grimly, "that we're going to ride out of this wilderness and never come back."

The two armies regrouped, leaving twenty-five thousand casualties in the Wilderness. The Federals lost almost eighteen thousand men, killed, wounded, and missing. Always before, such losses sent the Union generals scuttling back to Washington. But Grant pressed on mercilessly, and Lee had to use all of his considerable military genius to move about his numerically inferior forces to counter him. Of course, Jeb's riders were all over the country, scouting out the lines and dispositions.

On May 11, Jeb was in the saddle early, and the weary 1st Virginia Cavalry rode out, heading south. As usual, Clay managed to work himself around until he was riding with Stuart. As always, Stuart was jovial, laughing, his manner as carefree as if they were going to a ball.

They had had several run-ins with Federal cavalry, which seemed to be crawling all over the countryside. Clay remarked, "I think this is the most fighting we've done one-on-one with bluebelly cavalry."

"Grant took the leash off Phil Sheridan," Jeb told him. "No Union general has ever used the cavalry like they should. They keep nibbling away at the commands, using them to guard supply trains, escorting prisoners, and standing pickets. General Sheridan is a little bitty spitfire, 'bout as tall as an upright musket, with a temper like a mad dog. But he's a smart man and a good officer. That's why all of a sudden they're everywhere we look. They're out ahead of the main body of the army, but not just to scout. They send out enough to form a fighting force."

"Guess we'll fight them then," Clay said.

"That's what you joined the cavalry for, Tremayne," Jeb said cheerfully.

They passed a pleasant oak arbor with a fresh spring bubbling up and running downhill in a fast-running, cold stream. Jeb called a brief halt for the men to refill their canteens and water the horses. As usual, he stayed in the saddle, right leg thrown over it, studying a map. Clay stayed mounted and idled near him. "Right here," Jeb said, mostly to himself. Then he looked up at Clay and said, "A little nothing place named Yellow Tavern should be right ahead of us. I figure that's where we'll find some Yanks to shoot."

"We're ready, sir," Clay said confidently.

Jeb took off his hat, smoothed his hair back, then settled it back on his head. The long ostrich plume waved airily in a light dusty breeze. "You know, Lieutenant, we're only about six miles north of Richmond."

"Yes, sir, I know," Clay said.

Jeb's blue eyes clouded, and he grew unusually grave. "I never expected to live through this war. But if we are conquered, I don't want to live anyway."

Clay stared at him. It was so unlike Stuart, and Clay had never suspected that his general felt that deeply about the war. Before he could think of a suitable reply, Jeb suddenly grinned and yelled at the men to hurry up. It was time to get moving again.

Yellow Tavern was named after an ancient inn that was painted a sickly yellow, and what town there was didn't look much better than the inn. It was a shabby, mean little bunch of old houses and storefronts all huddled together. To the north were thick woods, clearing nearer the tavern. Fenced-in fields almost surrounded the small settlement.

They reached it about 10:00 a.m., and there was not one blue coat in sight. Stuart made dispositions of his men; because the cavalry corps had been split up to counter Sheridan's numerous units, he had only about eleven hundred men with him. Basically they just took what scant cover they could find and then waited.

At about noon they saw the first Yankees, and by about two o'clock they knew they were badly outnumbered. Stuart had sent to Richmond for reinforcements and expected them at any time. The first attack came before any reinforcements reached them.

In the blue ranks of the 5th Michigan, a trooper named John A. Huff rode along, one in a sea of blue coats. He was forty-two years old and in 1861 had joined the 2nd U.S. Sharpshooters, a crack regiment that had become famous as Berdan's Sharpshooters. He had won a prize as the regiment's best shot, an expert among hundreds of crack marksmen.

Huff had been wounded and had gone home but had returned later and reenlisted in the Michigan cavalry. He was a good soldier, though he was not spectacular. He was married and had been a carpenter before the war. Huff had mild blue eyes, brown hair, and a light complexion, and stood only five feet eight inches tall. Late in the morning of May 11, he was moving toward a battle, but he, no more than the rest of his fellows, knew whom they were to fight.

Jeb Stuart's cavalry, along with the rest of the Confederate Army, were accustomed to being outnumbered. But by four o'clock, they had taken some heavy losses, and though the Yankees had, too, it seemed the distant woods never stopped crawling with more oncoming men. Every squad, every company, had wounded men.

Blithely Jeb Stuart rode here and there, whistling a tune, encouraging them. "Stay steady, boys," he shouted. "Give it to 'em! Shoot them! Shoot them!"

Clay stubbornly followed him everywhere, and he grew more and more nervous. The fire was heavy, and he said, "General, there are men behind stumps and fences being killed, and here you are out in the open."

Stuart turned, and there was laughter in his light blue eyes. "I don't reckon there's any danger, Lieutenant," he said.

He turned and in a canter rode to a placed cannon on the near side of the road from the town. Every trooper manning it had been injured. On his big gray horse Stuart called out to them, "Steady, men! Line it up and give it to them!"

Suddenly a group of Federal cavalry that had gotten through the line of battle filed along to the left of the fence on the far side of the dusty road. They were passing within ten or fifteen feet of General Stuart. One blue-coated horseman who had been dismounted in a charge trotted along with them. Clay saw him pull his pistol, take what looked to be a casual aim on the run, and fire. The man was John Huff.

Just in front of him, Stuart reeled in his saddle.

"General, are you hit?" Clay asked.

"Yes."

"You wounded bad?"

"I'm afraid I am. But don't worry, boys. Fitz will do as well for you as I have."

Clay and several other troopers surrounded Stuart. One of them, Captain

Dorsey, rode very close and steadied the general so he could stay in his saddle. They rode toward the rear.

Jeb said, "No, I don't want to leave the field!"

Captain Dorsey said gently, "We're taking you back a little, General, so as not to leave you to the enemy."

Stuart relented and said, "Take the papers from my inside pocket. Keep them from the Yankees."

Two troopers dashed off to get an ambulance and to find General Fitzhugh Lee, Robert E. Lee's nephew, who served as divisional commander of the 1st Virginia under Stuart. Under fire, Clay, Captain Dorsey, and the other men surrounding Stuart had to keep falling back. Stuart said, "You officers need to leave me and go back and drive them."

Clay said, "No sir, just a little farther in the rear now, and we'll wait for the ambulance."

"I'm afraid they've killed me, Lieutenant. I'll be of no use. You go back and fight."

"I can't obey that order," Clay said. "I'd rather they get me, too, than leave you for them. We'll have you out of here."

Very soon the ambulance, General Fitz Lee, and Jeb's doctor, John Fontaine, arrived. As soon as Lee arrived, Stuart said, "Go ahead, Fitz, old fellow. I know you'll do what's right."

They loaded him into the ambulance, and not a single word, not a groan, crossed his lips. But just before the ambulance pulled out, he raised himself up and called out in his booming voice, "Go back! Go back! Do your duty as I've done mine. I would rather die than be whipped!"

Troopers were all around them, falling back from the still-oncoming Yankees.

Clay's mouth pressed together in a tight line. Wheeling Lightning, he turned and galloped back toward Yellow Tavern, shouting to the faltering men as he went. Stuart's words had cut into his very soul, and he knew he must obey his order and return to the battle still raging behind them.

He was afraid it would be the last order he ever received from Jeb Stuart.

Although they were only six miles outside of Richmond, fighting raged all along the Brooks Turnpike, the main road into the city. The ambulance was forced to take back roads. They reached a quiet little bridge on a deserted road, and Dr. Fontaine called for a halt so he could examine Stuart.

With his final order to his men, they had

returned to the fray, so with Stuart now were Lieutenant Walter Hullihen and Major Charles Venable from his staff, Dr. Fontaine, two couriers, and three men of the general's escort.

Dr. Fontaine unhooked Stuart's double-breasted jacket and unwound his gold satin sash, now crimson with blood. His face grew grave.

Stuart turned to Hullihen, one of his favorites, whom he always called "Honey-bun." With weak cheer he asked, "Honey-bun, how do I look in the face?"

"You're looking all right, General. You'll be all right."

"Well, I don't know how it will turn out, but if it's God's will that I shall die, I am ready."

Dr. Fontaine had observed that the bullet was very close to Stuart's liver and might kill him at any time. He poured out some whiskey into a cup. "Try some of this. It will help you," he said.

"No," Stuart said at once. "I've never tasted it in my life. I promised my mother that when I was just a baby."

They urged him to drink, and finally he relented and held up his hands. "Lift me." He took a drink of the whiskey and settled back, seeming somewhat eased.

For long hours they made their torturous, circuitous way toward Richmond. They went through small towns and passed many soldiers, and the word spread that General Stuart had been wounded.

Despairing of reaching Richmond, Dr. Fontaine finally ordered the couriers to ride ahead to Mechanicsville, a small outlying district of Richmond just to the northwest. He told them to go to the home of Dr. Charles Brewer and tell them to prepare a bed for the general.

Dr. Brewer was Jeb's brother-in-law; he was married to Flora's sister, Maria. It was very late before they reached the Brewer home. At midnight a dismal thunderstorm broke, and it began to rain.

In the city the bad news spread quickly. Even before dawn crowds lined the streets and gathered outside of the Brewer home. In the throngs, women wept.

Flora Stuart was in the country, at the home of Colonel Edmund Fontaine. He was the president of the Virginia Railroad, and his gracious plantation house was about a mile and a half from the major junction at Beaver Dam. She received the telegram with the news early the next morning.

Beaver Dam was about thirty-five miles

from Mechanicsville, and in peaceful times she could have reached Jeb's side in less than a day. But war was the ruler of this land, and along with bloodshed it brought all the follies and vagaries: railroad tracks were torn up, side roads were blocked by fiery skirmishes, bridges were burned. The raging storm continued on, turning even good roads into impossible quagmires. Flora did not reach her sister's home until eleven o'clock that night. She was three hours late.

Throughout the day, Stuart's condition grew steadily worse. Like Stonewall Jackson had, almost a year ago to the day, Jeb Stuart returned again and again to the battlefield, muttering orders to his men. Once he rose up and shouted, "Make haste!"

In one of his peaceful times, when he was calm and quiet and free from the terrible pain, he gave instructions about his personal effects. He gave away his two horses to two of his men; he instructed that his gold spurs be sent to his longtime friend, Lily Lee of Shepherdstown; he said that his official papers must be disposed of. "And," he said quietly, "give my sword to my son."

President Jefferson Davis had hurried to Jeb's side. He asked, "General, how do you feel?"

"Easy, but willing to die if God and my country think I have fulfilled my destiny and done my duty."

After the president left, Reverend Joshua Peterkin of Saint James Episcopal Church came and prayed with Stuart. After the prayer, Jeb said slowly, "Sing. Let's sing 'Rock of Ages.'" The men gathered in the room sang the old stately hymn, and Stuart joined in, singing in a low voice. After the hymn was over, he was visibly weaker.

Later on in the afternoon, Stuart asked, "How long can I live, Charles? Can I last through the night?"

His brother-in-law shook his head. "I'm afraid the end is near."

Stuart nodded. "I am resigned, if it be God's will. I would like to see my wife. But God's will be done."

The day wore on, endlessly, it seemed, to Jeb's attendants. That night Dr. Brewer was standing over him, and Jeb said, "I'm going fast now. God's will be done." And then he was gone. The pulse was still. It was twenty-two minutes before eight on the evening of May 12, 1864.

As soon as Flora arrived, she knew by the gravity of the men standing aimlessly about on the veranda and in the entryway exactly what had happened. She went in to him, to be alone with him in the candlelight. Slowly grief overwhelmed her. But it did not seem strange. In her deepest heart, she had always known this would happen.

And so passed the Knight of the Golden Spurs from this world. He had gone to his long home.

Weeping, Flora's sister, Maria, snipped off a lock of Jeb's red-gold hair, tied it with a ribbon, and thrust it into an envelope. Then she slowly assembled the few things in his pockets:

An embroidered pincushion, worked on one side in gold thread: Gen. J. E. B. Stuart. On the other side was a Confederate flag bearing the legend: GLORY TO OUR IMMORTAL CAVALRY!

A copy of an order to Stuart's troops, written with his customary dash and flair:

We now, as in all battles, mourn the loss of many brave and valued comrades. Let us avenge our fallen heroes; and at the word, move upon the enemy with the determined assurance that in victory alone is honor and safety.

A letter to Flora, telling her of his plans to

485

bring her to his headquarters.

An original general order of congratulations to the victorious infantry he had led at Chancellorsville.

A letter from his brother, W. A. Stuart.

A letter asking Jeb to find a government job for a friend.

A poem on the death of a child, clipped from a newspaper.

A New Testament.

A handkerchief.

A lock of Little Flora's hair.

# Chapter Twenty-Five

The funeral was held on May 13th at Saint James Church, with the Reverend Peterkin officiating. There was no music in the Richmond streets, no military escort. The city was so nearly under siege that customary honors could not be performed, even for this most well-beloved son of Virginia.

President Davis was at the funeral, and all of the officers that could be spared from active duty, but none of Jeb's men were there. In the church, Flora's helpless sobs were drowned out by the cannon fire on the heights just above the city.

The coffin went into the waiting hearse. Four white horses drew it, and their head-dresses were made of black feathers, so suggestive of the fancy ostrich plumes that Jeb had worn in his wide-brimmed hat. At Hollywood Cemetery the Reverend Charles Minnegerode spoke very briefly in his thick German accent. They placed the coffin in a vault, and the carriages moved away. Just as the funeral party left the cemetery, the rain began once more.

North of Richmond, in a vicious skirmish on Drewry's Bluff, Clay paused for a moment as he realized that Jeb Stuart was being buried in the city below. He felt as if his heart would break, for he, and all of Jeb's men, did not think of Stuart merely as their general. He was noble and fearless and valiant, he was their leader, and they loved him.

Clay thought, *His time was so short, Lord, too short! He and Miss Flora were so happy, and even in her grief I know that she doesn't regret a single minute. I'm a fool. I've been a fool. I need to beg Chantel to marry me, right now, war or not. Even if she were my wife for only a day and I died the next, it would be worth it!*

Then, recalling his general's last command, he turned, drew his saber, yelled, "Charge!" and galloped toward the enemy.

Again, in spite of overwhelming odds against them, the Confederates beat back the Union forces from their attempt to send gunboats up the James River to Richmond. After the battle, Clay and his company were ordered to return to the front lines, about eight miles north. The night was wild, with violent thunderstorms sweeping them with walls of rain. No lantern could shine in such a maelstrom, and so the horsemen began carefully picking their way along the road north, lit only by constant stabs of lightning.

Clay lingered behind, glancing back toward Richmond. He looked up; the troop was some distance in front of them. Suddenly he wheeled Lightning and turned back south at a breathtaking gallop.

After the Battle of the Wilderness, Jacob had contributed his enormous sutler's tent to the Glorious Cause. The wounded streamed in again by the hundreds. The hospitals, the warehouses, the barns, and the private homes that could accommodate patients were already overflowing. Surrounding Richmond, in every clearing, were field hospitals. Jacob's tent had made a good surgeon's operating room.

Jacob had rented a tidy little cottage just on the northern outskirts of town, close to the fairgrounds, where hundreds of two-man pup tents still sheltered wounded men. Chantel and Jacob traveled around to the different field hospitals every day in the wagon, which had become a medical transport and which now held bandages, liniment, rubbing alcohol, and medicines instead of sutler's goods.

It was almost three o'clock in the morning when he reached the little cottage, but Clay was beyond caring. He banged on the door and called out desperately, "Chantel! Chantel, please!"

After only a few moments, she opened the door, pulling on a dressing gown. Her long black hair was down, and her eyes were huge and luminous. "Clay —" she began, but he stepped forward and swept her into his arms, holding her so tightly she could barely breathe. He kissed her with desperation. She clung to him tightly. Behind her Clay could see Jacob peek down the hallway from his bedroom, but then he quickly disappeared and closed the door.

Clay fell to his knees as if he were praying and clutched both of her hands. "Chantel, my most precious love, I had to come. I had to come *now*. I — I don't want to be alone anymore. I want you to be my wife, because then even when I'm not here with you, I won't be alone. You'll be a part of me, and I'll be a part of you. Will you please, please marry me?"

She, too, fell to her knees and took his face in her hands. "Don't you know, Clay? Don't you know me? You'll never have to beg me for anything, ever. Especially not this. I will marry you. I would marry you right now if we could."

"Oh Chantel," he said, clutching her to him. "How I wish we could, right now! But soon, soon! As soon as I can arrange it. I don't know how I will, but I know this. You're the only woman for me. God sent you to me that awful day. Just to me, because we are supposed to be together. I know this is His will."

"I know this, too," Chantel said. "I would never love anyone but you, Clay Tremayne."

Slowly he rose and helped her up. He searched her face. "I can't stay."

"I know," she said quietly. "But you send me word, Clay. I'll be right here waiting."

On May 29, Chantel and Jacob sat in the sitting room, a homey small corner of the house with two comfortable rocking chairs, a sofa, and two armchairs.

Gathered around was Clay's family. Chantel and Clay's mother, Bethany, sat on the sofa, the twins squeezed between them, quietly sewing. Chantel was making a gold satin sash for Clay, and Bethany was embroidering the distinctive Hussar's facings on a new short jacket. Although the day was warm, a fitful rain dampened the air and a small but merry fire snapped in the fire-place. Morgan and Caleb Tremayne stood by it, sipping coffee and talking quietly to Jacob, who sat close in one of the rocking chairs.

"I don't understand how he's going to get leave to come," Morgan said. He spoke in a low tone, thinking Chantel would not hear.

She didn't look up from her sewing. "He'll come," she said firmly. "He'll be here."

Grant had continued in his unyielding march toward Richmond. Lee had moved the Army of Northern Virginia to Cold Harbor and planted them squarely between Grant and the city. They were arrayed in a battle formation that was seven miles long, and they were digging in. No soldier could hope for a leave. Grant and his tens of thousands were too close.

But three nights previously, a scared little boy of only thirteen, a courier, had brought the message from Clay. *In three days, dear Chantel, you and I will be married. God bless you, my darling.*

It was noon, and they had a light dinner. Afternoon brought more rain. Bethany began to teach Chantel to knit. Chantel said very little, but she looked happy and expectant, never doubtful.

The twins grew impatient. Belinda said,

"Maybe Clay can't come. Maybe it's raining too much."

"Raining too much," Brenda echoed.

Chantel smiled. "You should know Lightning would bring Clay even in the rain. Clay promised, he did. He won't break his promise. He'll be here anytime now."

And at about three o'clock, he came riding up, Lightning snorting and stamping, and he had another cavalryman with him. Chantel had barely opened the door when they came in, snatching off their dripping hats and frock coats. Clay kissed her soundly and said, "Did you think I wouldn't make it?"

"No, I didn't think that, me," she said, blushing a little. "You promised."

Morgan was helping him out of his coat. "Well, I want to know how you wrangled a leave. There hasn't been a soldier inside the city for weeks."

"I asked politely the first time," Clay answered, "but that didn't work too well. So I told Captain Dorsey that I was going to desert. And the captain said that he couldn't hear me too well, and he turned his back and stalked off. And then I deserted. And this is my friend, Private Elijah Young. He's a preacher."

Young, a slight man of thirty with fine blond hair, wide blue eyes, and thin features, said mournfully, "Lieutenant Tremayne made me desert, too."

"Too bad," Clay grunted. "I needed you. I want to get married. Right now."

"What, like this?" Young blurted out. Both of them were dusty and damp and smelled like horses. Their boots and scabbards were splashed with red mud. Clay had a long streak of black powder on his cheek.

Nonchalantly, Chantel licked her fingers and reached up to scrub it off. "Right now, just like this, Pastor Young," she said. "I want to get married now, too, me."

And so Young fished a slim book from the pocket of his frock coat — *Rites and Ceremonies of the Christian Church* — and went to stand in front of the fireplace. Clay took his place in front of him. Jacob came to Chantel, entwined her arm in his, and escorted her to Clay's side.

"Who giveth this woman in marriage?" Pastor Young asked.

"I'm her grandfather," Jacob said quietly, "and gladly I give her to join in marriage with this man." He took his seat in the rocking chair.

Clay took Chantel's hand and turned her so that they were facing each other. When they repeated the timeworn, solemn vows, they spoke only to each other.

"And now, Lieutenant Tremayne, you may kiss your bride," Young said, grinning boyishly.

They had not kissed many times, because both of them had been so careful to preserve the purity of their relationship. This kiss, Chantel thought, was like a vow and a promise in itself, that she and her husband gave to each other.

The men all congratulated Clay, and Bethany and the twins hugged Chantel. But only minutes after he had finished the ceremony, Private Young said, "Lieutenant, you may have ordered me to desert, and I did. But now I'm heading back, before the provosts come looking for us. Please don't order me to stay deserted."

"Go on, and if you meet those provosts on their way here," Clay said grandly, "you tell them I said they can arrest me tomorrow. Because tonight is my honeymoon, and if I have to fight off a battalion to have it, I will!"

The Tremayne family was staying in town with friends, and they had invited Jacob to come stay with them so that Clay and Chantel could have their one night together in her little house. They didn't linger long, and soon Clay and Chantel were alone.

He kissed her again, softly and sweetly.

Then he lifted his head and stared down at her, slight worry furrowing his brow. "I'm so sorry it had to be like this," he said. "I would have liked for us to have had a big wedding and at least a weeklong honeymoon."

"I would like that, too," Chantel said, "but I would rather be married to you now, like this, instead of waiting for that big wedding. But I — I —" She blushed and finished shyly, "I wish we had a longer honeymoon, too. Still, one night now is better than a week when this war is over. I just — I'm not — I don't know —"

He pulled her close and ran his hands over her thick glossy black hair. "I have another promise to make to you," he said in a deep voice "I promise that on this night, we'll learn what real love, God's pure and abiding love that He gives to a man and wife, really is. Both of us will learn."

The 1st Virginia Cavalry, under the command of Fitzhugh Lee, fought on as valiantly as they ever had under Jeb Stuart, although without the same fierce joy. Clay fought the Battle of Cold Harbor in June, and then the Army of Northern Virginia wheeled around to Petersburg. Grant had circled them and invested the old city to approach Richmond from the south, and once again Lee positioned his men between him and the capital of the Confederacy. The siege of Petersburg lasted from June 1864 through March 1865.

During the winter, when both of the armies listlessly huddled in their winter quarters, Clay managed to get leave several times to ride back to Richmond and see Chantel. But that first year of their marriage, they were together few enough times that Chantel could count them on her fingers. Though she worried, she refused to lose hope. In her heart she believed that Clay had been so grievously wounded and had been healed, and that had been God's plan to bring them together. All during that endless year, even as the Confederacy slowly disintegrated into a smoking ruin, she was certain that she and Clay would live out their days, together, in peace.

By the end of March 1865, General Lee knew that the end was near, and he could no longer guard Richmond. The army moved west to join other forces in the Shenandoah Valley. Clay sent Chantel and Jacob to his parents' home in Lexington. Grant, with nothing to stop him now, occupied Richmond and dogged Lee. The forlorn retreat of the Army of Northern Virginia lasted only a week. It ended at Appomattox Court House.

General Grant rode up to Wilmer McLean's fine two-story home. He was shabby and dusty. He had on a single-breasted blouse made of dark blue flannel, unbuttoned in front, showing a waistcoat underneath. His trousers were tucked into muddy boots. He had no spurs, and he wore no sword. The only designation of his rank was a pair of faded shoulder straps with four dimmed stars.

The aides he had sent ahead were waiting for him, and a group of Confederates, dressed in rather worn full-dress uniforms stood around the home.

Grant dismounted. "He's already here?" he asked an aide.

"Yes, sir."

Grant nodded and hurried into the house.

Clay had found the remnants of the Louisiana Tigers, and Armand Latane was there, in his full-dress uniform. It was clean, but it was faded and patched, as was Clay's uniform. They watched as Grant and General Phil Sheridan went inside with several other officers.

"And so it's over," Armand murmured.

"At last. I joined, I fought, I thought that we would win. Until the winter, in Petersburg."

Clay said quietly, "You know, when I joined, I just knew the South would win. I kept thinking that, even after Grant came after us and kept pushing us back, throwing more and more men at us. But on the day Jeb Stuart was shot, I began to think that we were going to lose. It's as if all my hopes were in him. That was wrong. No one man can win a war. But I couldn't help it. Not one day since that day did I ever think again that we would be able to beat them." The two could say nothing more.

Finally the door opened, and the two generals came out. Clay sighed deeply when he saw Robert E. Lee. He was dressed in a new uniform, spotless and crisp. A great heavy sword, the hilt bejeweled, was at his side. He stood erect, his bearing as always dignified and grave, but deep sadness was written on his face. His eyes went out over the fields and valley below, where his army waited for him to speak to them for the last time. He mounted Traveler, his beautiful, graceful gray horse, and settled his hat on his head. As he rode through the silent gray ranks, he said, "Go to your homes and resume your occupations. Obey the laws and become as good citizens as you were soldiers."

Clay stacked his musket, setting it upright alongside Armand's. "I hope I never have to raise my hand to another man again," he said wearily. "All I want is a quiet life, a simple life, with Chantel."

Armand laid his hand on Clay's shoulder. "My friend, your life might be simple, yes. But with Chantel I doubt it will be quiet. You got the prize, my friend. Never forget that."

"Never," Clay repeated firmly. "I never will."

He could see his house, up on a rise, with a small green valley below it. It was almost a mile off the main road. He rode slowly, for Lightning was weary. Clay himself had grown thin and was a much weaker man than he had been before wintering in Petersburg. But as he drew nearer to his house, he suddenly felt a surge of energy that somehow translated itself to Lightning. The horse raised his lowered head as in the old days when he had caught the scent of battle, and with the slightest touch of Clay's heels, he began to canter and then to gallop.

Chantel was sitting on the veranda, sipping tea and knitting. At the first distant sounds of hoofbeats, she looked up alertly. Then she jumped to her feet, lifted her skirts, and took off down the road at a dead run.

Clay slid off Lightning even before he stopped. Chantel threw herself into his arms. For a long time they stood there, clasped in each other's arms, saying nothing. Finally Clay put one finger under her chin, lifted her face, and kissed her. The kiss, too, lasted for a long time.

Lightning stopped for a moment, but as they stayed clasped in their embrace, he unconcernedly trotted past them and went to the shade trees on the side of the yard, where there was a watering trough.

Arm in arm Clay and Chantel walked toward the house. "It's over," Clay said, marveling. "It's over, and I'm home. And the biggest miracle is that you're here. My wife. I love you dearly, my wife."

"I love you dearly, too, me," Chantel said, laughing. "It's good that you're home. You're too skinny, you. Maybe I catch an alligator and cook it, fatten you up."

"Even alligator sounds good right now," Clay sighed. "It's been a long time since I've eaten a good, solid meal."

They went up onto the veranda, and Clay started to go in, but Chantel pulled at his arm and said, "Sit down here for a minute with me. I should get to see my husband alone for a little while when he comes home from this war."

They sat down in two rockers, Clay pulling his so close to Chantel's that she couldn't rock. But she obviously didn't care. They held hands and looked out over the peaceful valley.

Clay said, "On the way home, I thought a lot about what I would like to do, Chantel."

"And what is that?"

"Well, first I want to be the best husband who ever lived," he said lightly. Then he sobered a little and continued, "I'm sick of fighting. I'm sick of killing and hurting men. I want to do something good, something to help people instead of hurting them. I think I'd like to be a doctor."

With delight Chantel clapped her hands. "Oh Clay, you would be such a good, such a fine doctor! And you can get rich and buy me lots of pretty dresses!"

"I surely will," he said, grinning. "All you want."

"But that's not the only reason I would be glad you'll be a doctor," she said firmly. "There is another reason. You must hurry, Clay, and start studying right now."

"What? Why?" he asked, bewildered.

"Because," she said slowly, "around about September I'm going to need a doctor."

He stared at her wide-eyed. Then his gaze fell to the knitting on the little low table by Chantel's chair. Slowly he reached down, lifted it up, and saw with shock that Chantel was knitting a pair of baby's booties.

"This — we're going to have a baby?" he breathed.

"Yes."

"In — in September?"

"Yes."

Clay jumped up, Chantel jumped up, and he put his hands on her waist and held her high in the air and whooped like a madman.

They were just like a young couple who had lived in Fort Leavenworth, Kansas, in 1855.

They could have been Flora and Jeb Stuart.

# ABOUT THE AUTHOR

Award-winning, bestselling author **Gilbert Morris** is well known for penning numerous Christian novels for adults and children since 1984 with 6.5 million books in print. He is probably best known for the forty-book House of Winslow series, and his *Edge of Honor* was a 2001 Christy Award winner. He lives with his wife in Gulf Shores, Alabama.